'Murder, makeovers, snappy dialogue (with a generous sprinkling of filth), and characters I did not want to leave on the last page. So much fun and so much heart' Kate Mildenhall

'Heartwarming, clever, funny and wise ... Tippy is the ultimate modern Nancy Drew, and her uncles the perfect loving, charming, wisecracking sidekicks' Amy Suiter Clarke

'Delightful and exuberant ... an enthralling mystery via bewitchingly chaotic events and characters who are a riot' *New Zealand Listener*

'A giddy, entertaining romp' *New Zealand Herald*

'I don't know if I've grinned as much reading a crime novel for a long time ... a real delight, packed with lovably unruly characters and chaotic events and perfectly seasoned with humour and heart' *Good Reading*

'An ingenious hybrid of Nancy Drew homage and social comedy for grown-ups ... R.W.R. McDonald has produced something all too rare in contemporary fiction: a book that is not afraid to have fun' *North & South*

'Quirky and funny: a murder mystery with a bizarre twist and an adventure tale with a modern spin' *Sunday Star-Times*

THE NANCYS

ABOUT THE AUTHOR

R.W.R. McDonald (Rob) is an award-winning author, a Kiwi and Queer dad living in Melbourne with his two daughters and one HarryCat. His debut novel, *The Nancys*, won Best First Novel in the 2020 Ngaio Marsh Awards, as well as being a finalist in the Best Novel category. It was shortlisted for Best First Novel in the 2020 Ned Kelly Awards, and Highly Commended for an Unpublished Manuscript in the 2017 Victorian Premier's Literary Awards. His second novel, *Nancy Business*, was a finalist for Best Novel in 2022 Ngaio Marsh Awards.

Follow Rob on Instagram @rwrmcdonald and visit his website: rwrmcdonald.com.

THE
NANCYS

AND THE CASE OF
THE MISSING NECKLACE

R.W.R. McDonald

ORENDA
BOOKS

Orenda Books
16 Carson Road
West Dulwich
London SE21 8HU
www.orendabooks.co.uk

First published in Australia and New Zealand as *The Nancys*
by Allen & Unwin, 2019
This amended edition first published in the United Kingdom by Orenda Books
2025
Copyright © R.W.R. McDonald 2025

A catalogue record for this book is available from the British Library.

ISBN 978-1-916788-90-9
eISBN 978-1-916788-91-6

Typeset in Garamond by typesetter.org.uk
Printed and bound by Clays Ltd, Elcograf S.p.A

For sales and distribution, please contact info@orendabooks or visit
www.orendabooks.co.uk.

To Ali and Grier – without you there is no colour

And Grace, the fourth Nancy

PROLOGUE

When the light turns red you have to hide. That's the rule. Green, you can do what you want. Play by the river – Mum says don't play by the river, but if the light's green you can do what you want. Climb the weepy tree, hunt animals in the long grass with Lion.

But as soon as the light ticks and changes, you better hide.

The sound of a car. Tick.

RED.

Run. Hide. My best hiding place, around the trunk of the weepy tree.

I peek.

A reindeer gets out. Why are they driving a car?

They stand still. I breathe quietly out my mouth.

Their head-sticks turn to me. I duck and squeeze my eyes shut.

The reindeer grunts, then something thuds on the grass close by.

I count, but not very far because I get mixed up after seven.

I peek again. My eyes are scratchy, so I rub them. In the tall grass is someone's arm. Someone's leg. They're lying there, maybe looking at the clouds, like me and Lion do.

Hide.

A car door opens. From the weepy tree, I look again. The reindeer's holding two black rubbish bags.

Maybe this is what they do before Christmas. Maybe it's how the toys are made.

Still red.

Hide.

A splashing, rustling sound nearby. A bad smell like the inside of one of the rusty trucks when a sheep dies in it. The reindeer laughs. I want to see but I don't peek.

The door shuts and the car drives away.

Tick.

Green.

I peer out. The grass is red. So much red. I creep closer, pulling my jersey up over my nose to keep the bad smell away. There's too much red, and something's wrong with this person.

I can't see their head.

CHAPTER ONE
Santa Comes Home

Uncle Pike's plane was late, and my hair was a sweaty mess, thanks to the crimson anti-kidnapping jacket and hateful Santa hat Mum had made me wear. She thought the hat was hilarious. So far I'd been lucky not to run into anyone from my school, but Dunedin Airport was massive, with heaps of people – way bigger than the new supermarket at Riverstone, and that was huge. I felt the opposite of undercover; Nancy Drew would have ditched me in the carpark.

My phone buzzed and I flipped it open. Todd had sent me and Sam a text: *Tits 4 real!!!!* The screen of the old phone froze, which meant a pic was on its way. I'd tried saving for a smartphone once and I wished I had one now. Mum worried I'd get groomed online, but I really wanted one for Christmas.

On my screen a tiny square appeared with a pair of boobs inside. I checked if anyone had seen, then texted back: *Prebert.* I hit send and snapped the phone shut. Pretty sure my friends were sexist.

The phone buzzed again. Todd had sent emojis, but on my phone they came up as three blank rectangles. No doubt he'd sent squirty water, eggplant and cherries.

I was about to text back when Mum rang.

'Fuck you!' she said, car horns blasting in the background. 'Sorry, honey, not you, the taxi behind me. Is he here yet?'

For the twelve-hundredth time I checked the arrival screen for the Sydney flight. *Finally.*

'Just landed.' I reached for my hat, searching for the nearest bin.

'Don't take off the hat.' She hung up.

I pulled it off. I'd put it back on when I got to the car. Or not. I scanned the crowd, not sure about taking off the anti-kidnapping jacket. I hopped from one foot to the other, waiting. After forever the first arrivals came through the automatic doors from customs.

Across from me, a little girl in pigtails suddenly put her hands to her mouth and started jumping up and down. 'Santa!' She tugged on the sleeve of an old woman who looked like she had just licked a lemon. 'Granny, it's Santa.'

Towering above the other passengers was Uncle Pike with his shaggy, snowy hair and bushy beard. He wore a black singlet and shorts, with a bag slung across his big, muscled shoulders. One hand held duty-free bags, while the other towed a huge, red plastic suitcase. He hadn't changed a bit since the funeral.

The little girl stood on her tiptoes. 'Santa, over here!' She waved, and her whole body moved like an overexcited dog wagging its tail.

My uncle spotted her and smiled. 'Ho, ho, ho!'

She froze like a rabbit. 'How come Santa's got so many tattoos?'

Uncle Pike walked over and crouched down to her eye level. 'What a good question. That's because the elves normally photoshop them out.'

She nodded. 'Like Mummy does with Daddy.'

'Exactly. Daddy's been naughty, hasn't he?'

The woman glared at him and pulled the girl away.

'Bye, Santa!' she called out.

'Merry Christmas,' he said, in his best North Pole voice.

I waved to him and he gave me a huge grin. He pushed himself back up and came over. His eyes looked red from the flight.

'Tippy Chan!' he said, startling the arrival-hall crowd. He swallowed me up in a huge bear hug and swung me around. 'How's my most favourite niece in the world?'

'I'm your only niece,' I said, muffled in his stinky singlet.

'Lucky you're his favourite then,' said a man beside us, smiling. He looked a lot like Action Man but in Barbie's clothes. His thick black hair was cut short at the sides and he had bluey-green eyes. He seemed to sparkle.

'Tippy Chan, please meet Devon.'

My uncle's boyfriend held out a big hand, which I shook. His tight camo T-shirt had *Beef Cake* scrawled across it in gold glitter, and his black pant things were like a dress. They didn't go all the way to his feet.

'Great to meet you, Tippy. Your uncle's told me a lot about you.'

'You too,' I lied. We'd only found out yesterday he was coming. Mum had said it must be serious as Uncle Pike had never brought a boyfriend home before, plus three months was a long time in gay years. Mum and I had googled Devon. He came up in 'Watch list: Australia's hot designers under thirty' and we'd seen one of his collections, with models in large square dresses made of bright-white knotted and slashed fabric. Mum hated it but I kind of liked it.

Later I had sneaked onto Mum's Facebook and seen pictures of Uncle Pike, Devon and their friends dancing – all with their shirts off, beaming. In one photo my uncle had such a big smile I could even see his chewing gum in the back of his mouth; his hair was half wet with sweat and sticking out like a mad professor's. Sam had said big pupils meant someone was on drugs; his mum was a doctor so he should know. Uncle Pike's blue eyes had been completely black.

'Where is that dreadful woman?' he said.

'She's double-parked out the front.'

'And left you here alone?' Devon asked.

I shrugged. 'I'm wearing the jacket.'

'My sister's so cheap. I blame Tippy's grandparents.'

Devon looked confused.

'Our parents said if you wore bright red you'd be repellent to strangers.'

I nodded and held out my arms, showing off my jacket. Devon was frowning.

'Come on,' my uncle said. 'Let's go see if she's been in a punch-up.'

The airport doors opened to car horns blasting from all directions. Mum had parked diagonally in a taxi drop-off zone. She yelled out of her window at the taxis wanting to pull over in her spot. Another one behind her was trying to leave but seemed wedged in by our car.

'Good to see your mother has her road rage under control,' Uncle Pike said.

Mum did get cranky with other drivers. Anything to do with cars, really. I guessed that was why Dad used to do a lot of the driving. Well, that, and he'd been much better at it.

Uncle Pike threw himself on the windscreen. 'Home *sweet as* home.'

Mum was glaring at him. 'About bloody time.'

He gave the window a massive raspberry then lifted up his singlet and rubbed it around on his chest.

'Yuck!' Mum blared the horn and popped the boot. We threw Devon's three bags in, and Uncle Pike somehow managed to shove the massive red suitcase in as well.

'Welcome to New Zealand.' He grabbed Devon and gave him a big kiss on the lips, before squashing into the front seat and smooching Mum, who laughed and pushed him away.

Devon clambered into the back seat with me and leaned over to Mum. 'Hi, I'm Devon. Thanks for picking us up. So sorry to hear about—'

'Helen Chan.' Mum smacked the horn again, wrenched the wheel and sped off, leaving the yelling and tooting behind us. 'Do you have a last name, Devon?'

'Just Devon.'

'Like Madonna or Cher,' Uncle Pike said. 'Or Kylie.'

'Who?' I said.

'Oh my God, Lennie, what've you been doing to this child?' Lennie was my uncle's nickname for Mum; when she was born he was little and couldn't say Helen. He craned his neck around to look at me. 'Whitney? Mariah?'

I shrugged. I'd heard of them.

'Don't worry, Tippy,' he said. 'We have two weeks to make a gay man out of you.'

Mum wound down her window and stuck out her head. 'Jesus, Pike, you smell like Tippy's birthday present. Seriously, how many bourbons have you had?'

'On the plane? Or in the past twenty-four hours? And I put a lot of effort into choosing the perfect single malt for Tippy, thank you very much.' He turned back around. 'Did you enjoy it?'

I nodded. In my birthday card he had written 'To the best-looking kid in that fucking dump' then had scribbled out 'that fucking dump' and put in 'town' but you could still see it. Mum had taken the card and Dad had drunk the whisky.

'Of course she did,' Mum said. 'It's what every eleven-year-old girl dreams of, a bottle of Glenlivet.'

'Good, I'm glad,' my uncle said, smiling at me.

Mum left the airport and turned onto the main road. I felt myself being pressed into the back of the seat as she floored it.

'Great to see your driving's improved,' Uncle Pike said.

Devon's eyes widened and he gripped the armrest. He turned to his window, where farmland whipped past. Herds of black-and-white cows, and some brown ones, hung out together on the flat paddocks of the Taieri Plains. 'It's very green. I feel like I'm looking through a filter.'

'Not his favourite colour,' Uncle Pike said. 'In fact, you told me you hate it.'

'You hate New Zealand?' Mum asked.

'No, no!' Devon looked alarmed.

'I'm pretty sure that's what you're implying,' she said.

'Not at all. I haven't been here before. It looks lovely.'

'Very sensitive to colour.' Uncle Pike reached back and patted Devon's leg. 'A colour savant.'

'Don't you have green in Sydney?' I said.

Mum winked at me in the rear-view mirror.

I wondered how Devon would get on in South Otago. People said it reminded them of England's countryside with its rolling green hills and hedgerows. I wouldn't know. I'd never travelled any

further than Dunedin. Flat dairy farms around us began to change
to paddocks of sheep as we headed further south.

Mum's knuckles turned white as she gripped the steering wheel
tighter. 'I think I should stay. Going away for two weeks – what
was I thinking?'

Uncle Pike snorted. 'Rubbish!'

'I'll be fine, Mum.'

'And I promise to take good care of them,' Devon said.

'Who are you again?' Mum said.

'Loosen up, Lennie. It's Christmas!'

'That's the problem with you, Pike. It's always Christmas.'

It was still light when we reached Riverstone. From the top of the
hill you could see across the valley to the faraway ridges, which
turned purple just before sunset. The town flowed down to the
banks of the Clutha River, which ran slow and deep, then on the
other side it spread outwards over the flat and up a hill. Connecting
it was Riverstone Bridge, made up of six massive concrete arches
and taking nine breath-holding seconds to cross in a car. Just off
the bridge on Main Street and around a tight corner was the town
hall and its founding tree, a giant bushy macrocarpa. It was planted
in 1854 when Riverstone was first settled, which was weird since
Māori were already living here. Every December the tree was
decorated with huge, shiny red balls on its branches and a large
gold star at the very top. Past the town hall and tree, Main Street
continued with a pub, the medical centre where Mum worked, and
shops for a couple of blocks, then houses as the road headed uphill,
snaking past the old hospital on the other side of the valley. I loved
how the evening sun made the coiling green river sparkle. Dad had
loved it too.

Devon leaned forward in his seat. 'So this is where the magic
happens?'

'Welcome to Riverstone,' Mum said as we passed the town sign.
'Population 3,687.'

'Eighty-nine now,' I said.

Uncle Pike peered out his window. 'This is it.'

'This is where your boyfriend spent the seventies and eighties,' she said.

'Until I escaped,' he said. 'Lennie spent most of the eighties on her back.'

I tried to picture Mum as a teenager lying on the grass reading or watching clouds drift across a big blue sky. All I could manage was her yelling about clean clothes and washing.

We turned left just before the bridge and drove alongside the willow-lined riverbank, passing Duncan Nunn's billboard. He was Riverstone's number-one real-estate salesman – according to his sign, his poster in the supermarket and his ad in the local paper.

Devon craned his neck out the window. 'Is that his real hair?'

'I think so,' I said.

'Speaking of,' Uncle Pike said. 'Lennie, I'm fixing that grey mess on your head before you leave, unless you plan on wearing your nurse's cap on the boat?' He wound down his window.

'Thanks.' She put on the indicator. 'Hey, aren't hairdressers supposed to have cool hair?'

We turned left again, just before a blind corner, and drove up towards the golf course. Our street was a cul-de-sac on the top of 'Snob's Hill' – well, that's the name people across the river called it. We had views across the whole town. Our white wooden house had a red corrugated-iron roof and grey garage roller door. The garage was big enough to fit the car, but once inside you couldn't fully open the doors to get out.

Mum pulled into our driveway and yanked on the handbrake. Devon bolted out of the car before the engine stopped.

'What's his hurry?' Mum said to Uncle Pike.

'Be nice,' he said as we all got out.

Devon stretched his arms above his head like a cat. 'Is this where you grew up?'

Mum nodded.

My uncle shuddered. 'A period of my life I choose not to re-enact.'

'I love it. Your garden is beautiful, so organic.' Devon crouched and then sprang up in the air. 'I need to do five of these.'

Mum raised her eyebrows. 'Thanks ... I think. We share the garden with the Browns. Saves paying for a fence.'

Roses and Dad's dahlias the colours of jellybeans competed for space among the Browns' creeping bushes.

Uncle Pike grabbed his red suitcase out of the boot.

'You know they're dying to see you,' Mum said.

'Literally,' he replied.

'Who?' Devon asked.

A loud screeching came from next door.

With a groan, Uncle Pike rubbed his face. 'Oh my God.'

'Is that a bird?' Devon said.

'More like an old bat.' My uncle opened a bottle of duty-free bourbon and took a large swig. 'I'm surprised it's taken her this long.'

Mrs Brown opened her living-room window and frantically flapped a tea towel at us.

I waved. 'Hi, Mrs Brown.'

She kept shouting something, and it sounded like she was laughing as well.

'She's pretty yelly,' Devon said.

'That old bastard must have his hearing aid out,' Uncle Pike said. 'Or he's dead.'

'Pike!' Mum said.

'What?' he said. 'She's ruining my fantasy.'

'What fantasy is that?' Mum asked.

'That I'm currently somewhere else.'

'We couldn't have that.'

The Browns' house was like a brown-brick shoebox with brown aluminium windows. Everything about them was brown: their furniture was dark wood and brown fabric; they even had oatmeal carpet and brown velvet curtains. I tried not to giggle as I pictured my uncle's horror when he saw inside.

Devon clapped. 'I can't wait to meet your childhood neighbours.'

'Is Mr Brown homophobic or does he just hate everyone?' Uncle Pike said.

'Next you'll be talking about feelings,' Mum said.

'God forbid.'

'Maybe he hates Father Christmas,' I blurted out, then froze.

Uncle Pike gave a great big belly laugh and I smiled.

'Touché, Tippy Chan. Touché.'

After dinner Uncle Pike plugged in his music player. The first track was one of my favourite dance songs. 'I love this,' I said, clearing the table.

'Excellent taste, Tippy.' He turned it up.

Mum rolled her eyes. 'Great.'

I started washing the dishes while my uncle grabbed some shot glasses and a bottle of tequila from his duty-free bag. 'I feel a quick session of ganbei-masters is in order.'

Mum groaned.

He set them up on the bench that separated the living room and dining table from the kitchen.

'What's ganbei-masters?' I said.

'A game your dad and uncle made up,' Mum tells me. 'Ganbei in Mandarin means "dry cup". You make a toast, then everyone has to drink.'

It actually made sense – Dad and Uncle Pike had drunk-dialled each other a lot.

'How do you win?' I said.

'Everyone's a winner, baby.' My uncle opened the tequila and threw the cap over his shoulder. He poured three shots and passed one to Mum.

She tipped hers back and put it down. She grimaced and showed me her empty glass. 'See? Dry cup.'

He sculled and repoured. 'Where's my boyfriend?'

Mum sniggered. '*There's* a word I never thought you'd say. Ever.'

'Really?' Devon appeared. He'd changed his top and was wearing a gold pirate shirt.

'Perfect, honey. Just in time for ganbei-masters.' My uncle poured him a shot.

'Where'd you park your pirate ship?' Mum said.

'I think it's "dock" your ship, Lennie.' My uncle put his arm around Devon. 'Don't worry, it means she likes you,' he said, shaking his head.

He raised his glass, and Mum and Devon did the same. 'Here's to dry docking,' he said.

Devon sprayed his drink all over the bench and kitchen wall as Mum and my uncle sculled theirs.

'What the hell?' she said.

'Sorry, it was just the docking thing.' Devon glanced over at me. 'Never mind.'

I grabbed a cloth and wiped up his mess; he'd even got some on the Riverstone Pharmacy wall calendar. December's picture was of a black-and-white sheep dog and a brown calf sniffing each other. I wasn't sure what that had to do with Christmas or summer.

'Thanks, Tippy.' Devon came into the kitchen and grabbed a glass of water. 'Tell me about your neighbours, sweetie.'

'Well...'

Uncle Pike was pouring another round of shots. 'Seriously, do those dreadful lizard people know I'm gay?'

Devon grabbed the tea towel off me and started drying the last of the dishes.

'Are you asking if I outed you?' Mum lifted her glass. 'Here's to finding out.' She threw back the shot and screwed up her face.

Mrs Brown answered the door wearing a tight brown dress that showed off her cleavage. 'Hi, Tippy. You keep growing and growing, don't you!'

Every time we went through this. 'Yes, I'm eleven now.'

'Eleven? Really? I thought you were nine.'

At least she didn't call me 'China doll' this time. I wasn't sure if that was racist or not, as Dad was Chinese.

She smiled and moved past me, holding out her arms. 'Pike – my, haven't you grown!'

'Like a balloon,' Mum said.

Uncle Pike winced a smile, giving Mum the rude finger as Mrs Brown hugged him.

'Hello, hello,' Mrs Brown said to the rest of us. 'Please come in.'

'This is Devon,' Uncle Pike said.

Devon flashed his white teeth and gave a large wave.

'Ahoy, Devon.' Mrs Brown accidentally elbowed me and Mum out of the way to shake his hand. 'Please call me Phyllis.'

'The pleasure, Phyllis...' he gave her air kisses on each cheek '...is all mine.'

Uncle Pike rolled his eyes and asked for a sick bag.

'Use that.' Mum pointed to their cat, Bunny Whiskers, on the hall table licking her 'whistle'. She froze, staring at us mid-lick.

'And who is this beauty?' Devon said.

Bunny Whiskers didn't look impressed and tried to saunter away from his outstretched hand, slipping off the table.

'She's the clumsiest cat I've ever met.' Mrs Brown linked her arm with Devon's.

'Isn't she?' He patted Uncle Pike on the head, and Mrs Brown giggled. Mum burst out laughing as my uncle growled beside me.

Mrs Brown shooed us towards the living room, which was separated from the kitchen/dining room by a light-tan vinyl curtain that reminded me of a piano accordion. Mr Brown sat near it in his caramel La-Z-Boy chair. He watched greyhounds run on a large TV while a race caller yelled. Sometimes Dad had hung out with Mr Brown, watching the races. I never got why – they were so boring, and Mr Brown always seemed to be in a bad mood.

'Look, dear, we have visitors,' Mrs Brown said to him. 'It's our neighbours.'

He kept watching the TV and ignored us walking past.

'Hi, Ron,' Mum said.

He waved a hand in her direction. Devon looked confused.

Uncle Pike's face went red. He seemed to want to say something as his mouth opened and closed like a fish's.

With a smile, Mrs Brown pushed open the rattly curtain. 'Come on. Let's go through here.'

I handed her our bottle of wine, chips and crackers.

'Thank you,' she said. 'Aren't you the most responsible girl in the world? Let me go find some bowls.'

The Browns' living room always amazed me with its huge number of breakable ornaments: china deer and rearing horses and ladies in bonnets feeding geese. I had no idea where the Browns bought them; I never saw china deer in the shops. Bunny Whiskers rubbed past my legs and I wondered how many she had broken.

From the couch Melanie Brown scowled at us. She reminded me of a black scribble. Her small green eyes were ringed with brown eyeliner and coated in black mascara clumps. She must have cut her blonde hair with the lawnmower. Short tufts were dyed a patchy blue-black. Todd and I had voted her most likely to survive a zombie apocalypse, arguing with Sam, who had chosen his parents. Melanie scared me; she didn't seem to be afraid of anything or anyone.

Slowly, Devon sat beside her like he was trying not to scare a wildcat. She sighed and shuffled over.

Uncle Pike glided in and stopped short. 'What the Fuji is that?' He moved his hand in a circle in front of Melanie.

Her scowl deepened as she bristled.

'That's Melanie,' I whispered, avoiding her glare in case she spoke to me.

'Indeed,' Devon said.

'Quite!' Uncle Pike crept closer to her like a cat to a bee.

I headed for a chair on the other side of the coffee table.

Mum sat beside me. 'Hi, Melanie.'

Rolling her eyes, Melanie lifted her phone up to her face. Uncle Pike wedged himself between her and Devon. She was half his size and almost disappeared down the side of the couch. I tried not to laugh at the alarm on her face.

Mrs Brown came in with a tray of snacks that were actually just the chips and crackers we'd brought over. 'I see you've met my granddaughter.'

'Step-granddaughter.' Melanie flicked her gaze to Mrs Brown then back to her phone.

'Well, I love you just the same.' She placed the tray on the coffee table. 'Helen, how lucky are you, winning a cruise? Can I hide in your suitcase?'

'I'll help stuff you in it,' Uncle Pike said, and Melanie smirked.

Mrs Brown chuckled, slapping his arm. 'Silly.'

'Ow!' He rubbed it.

'Serves you right.' She turned to Mum. 'I think it's wonderful, especially after the year you've had.'

Mum poured herself a large glass of wine. 'The year we've all had.'

Melanie hid behind her phone, scrolling with her finger.

'She works far too hard, your mum,' Mrs Brown said to me.

I nodded and put a chip in my mouth. Mum did work more hours than anyone else's parents, except maybe Sam's mum, Dr Lisa.

Mrs Brown perched beside Devon on the sofa arm. 'Pike, why do you want to have all those tattoos covering you?' She tutted. 'Melanie, don't you get any ideas.'

Uncle Pike smiled down at Melanie, who ignored everyone.

'Are you going to see your old high-school friend while you're home?' Mrs Brown asked him.

'Pike's never bothered seeing anyone before,' Mum said.

Mrs Brown leaned forward as if she was going to tell a secret. 'I saw him this afternoon – so much better-looking in real life.'

Uncle Pike reached for the chips. 'I don't know who you're talking about.'

'*You* know,' she said. 'What's his name?'

'Who's this?' Devon asked my uncle, who shrugged and moved his leg, kicking the coffee table.

Mrs Brown turned to Devon. 'Thick as thieves, they were. I'd always see them mucking around at the bottom of the garden.' She cackled.

Melanie put down her phone.

Devon flicked at his glass. 'Really?'

'Yes, it was a little bit naughty,' Mrs Brown said.

Mum laughed. 'You were rooting in the garden?'

'Who?' Devon said.

Uncle Pike's face had turned red, and he spluttered out his drink, some of it landing on Melanie.

'Gross.' She snatched a Christmas paper serviette and wiped it off.

'Sorry,' he said. 'I don't think this is appropriate for kids.'

I filled my glass with more lemonade.

Mrs Brown was tapping her forehead. 'His name will come back to me.' She poured herself some more wine and settled back beside Devon. 'You know our mayor's a lesbian?' she said in a loud whisper. 'She's lovely but her wife's not much to look at. I don't know why she picked her. Love is blind, as they say.'

Mr Brown yelled out something from the other room, drowned out by the blaring television.

'Is he going to join us, ladies?' Devon said.

Melanie snickered and Uncle Pike shifted in his seat.

'You'll have to excuse him. He loves his races,' Mrs Brown said. 'Give him a track and he's happy.' She was right – the only time I'd ever heard Mr Brown say anything positive was when he'd given Dad racing tips.

I shifted back on my chair, banging into the china cabinet behind me, which rattled.

'Keep it down!' Mr Brown shouted through the vinyl curtain.

Mrs Brown clicked her fingers. 'Michael Horn-blower. You know he's on the telly sometimes.'

Muttering something, my uncle refilled his glass and avoided Devon's raised eyebrows.

'Ah.' Mum nodded, missing Uncle Pike shaking his head at her. She reached for a chip. 'Hang on, in the garden? You guys were such rabbits.'

Mrs Brown chuckled. 'Literally.'

Mum laugh-screamed and threw a chip at my uncle.

'Bloody keep it down,' Mr Brown roared, which sent Mum and Uncle Pike into more hysterics. I smiled; I hadn't seen Mum this happy in forever.

Uncle Pike and Devon weren't up when I left for school. My uncle had explained jet lag to me last night and how it could last for several days. Mum had overheard and called him a twat.

My school was across the river, on the flat near the base of the hill, not far from where Sam and Todd lived. During lunch we heard Todd hadn't shown up for class and I asked Sam what the boobs picture was all about.

He kicked his apple core at the library window. 'Lucky he isn't here. Lollipop got my phone grounded.'

'What? How?'

'That boob pic. My parents were right there when it popped up,' Sam said. 'They lost it. Took my phone and went through everything and wiped it. All my pics and videos. I can't believe it.'

'Whoa,' I said. 'I'd hate Mum to go through mine.'

'It's ratshit. I'm only allowed to use it at home now when one of them's in the room. It's so stupid. It wasn't even my fault. I hate him, bloody Lollipop.'

The afternoon dragged until the home bell rang. Sam's dad was late for pick-up so we played outside while we waited. Finally, I got home and raced inside. Mum and Uncle Pike were sitting at the dining table having a cup of tea. Mum's hair was honey blonde, no grey hairs in sight.

'Look, the cat's running away from my singing,' my uncle said, as Bunny Whiskers leaped off the balcony and into the garden, narrowly missing a rosebush. 'It's because it's so beautiful.'

'Too beautiful for humans.' Mum got up and kissed the top of my head.

'Your hair looks pretty,' I said.

'Thank you. Your uncle's good for something. Entertain him, please? His boyfriend's run off, as Mrs Brown would say, "literally", and I need to finish packing.'

Uncle Pike gave Mum a big fake smile. 'Don't miss your plane.'

'Shut it in your pee hole,' she said, and left the room.

'Don't you mean pie hole?' he called out.

'No!'

I grabbed a glass of milk and sat across from him. Bunny Whiskers was back on the balcony licking herself.

'How was school today? Learn anything interesting?'

'Emily Watson showed us her delicate flower.'

'She showed you her *what*?'

'Her delicate flower. At show-and-tell.'

'Was your teacher there?'

'Ms Everson? Yes. It was pretty boring. Emily showed us how to make it out of paper.'

Uncle Pike slapped the table, roaring with laughter.

I laughed too. 'It was pretty weird.'

'I bet,' my uncle said, wiping the tears from his eyes.

I showed him the red origami flower I'd made.

Devon came in sweating and panting. He gave us a wave and rested his hands on his knees.

'Hi, Devon,' I said.

'Hey.' He picked up my origami. 'This is very good. Did you make this lily?'

I nodded.

'How'd you know it's a lily?' Uncle Pike said.

'We had to make them once for a design project.'

'Devon graduated from fashion school,' my uncle said.

'Cool,' I said, pretending I hadn't already stalked him with Mum. 'I've never met a fashion designer before.'

Devon beamed at me. 'You have now.'

'Tippy's been telling me about her class,' Uncle Pike said. 'Do you have a school photo? I want to see Emily Watson and your creepy teacher.'

I grabbed the photo from my bedroom, and they sat beside me on the couch.

'Look at you, Tippy,' my uncle said. 'You're beautiful.'

I thought I looked strange, like someone else's smile had been photoshopped onto me.

'Definitely the prettiest in this group,' Devon said. 'Not that looks are everything.'

'But they are,' Uncle Pike said. 'Remember that.'

I nodded and pointed out Sam at the end of the second row. Todd had just flicked a rubber band at his face when the picture was taken.

'That's Sam Campbell. He's my best friend.' Sam wasn't even facing the camera; instead, he was bent over with his hand covering his eye.

'Was he stung by a bee?' Uncle Pike said.

I grinned. 'No. Todd Landers, my other friend, pinged him. His class was waiting to go next. Sam's mum was so angry, but it was pretty funny.'

'I can imagine.'

'We all hang out at Sam's house,' I said. 'Todd's on the same street. He's a year older and can be pretty annoying, always doing stunts and pranks.' I flipped open my phone and found a selfie Todd had taken.

'Big mop on him,' Uncle Pike said.

'Yeah, we call him Lollipop.'

'Because of his massive hair?' Devon said.

I nodded.

'That's genius,' Uncle Pike said.

Laughing, I cleaned the screen with my thumb.

'Is Todd your boyfriend?' Devon said.

'Eeew, no! That's what the other kids say too. He's not my boyfriend.'

'The lady doth protest too much, methinks,' Uncle Pike said.

'Mm-hmm,' Devon said.

'What?' I said.

My uncle gave me a nudge. 'They look like good guys.'

'Thanks.' Sam and Todd were the only ones who hadn't gone weird on me after Dad died. Todd had also been the only one to speak up for Sam at the start of the year when everyone thought he was a thief. I flipped my phone shut and went through the rest of my classmates in the photo.

'Do we hate her?' Devon said. 'She looks like a drainer.'

'That's a boy,' I said.

'They look kind of catty.'

'Show me Emily Watson,' Uncle Pike said.

I pointed to Emily, who was smiling but had been crying. Mum had only forced me on one play date with her before giving up; something about boundary issues.

'Cute,' Devon said.

'What about the other girls?' Uncle Pike said. 'You friends with them?'

'They're okay.' I went through each of the four girls but didn't tell my uncle and Devon about Todd calling them 'arse-clowns', or how he'd told them to fuck off when they had been pulling faces at me. 'Arse-clowns' was one of Todd's favourite new insults, and the girls hated it. They pretty much left me alone now, except when they called me Mrs Todd.

Uncle Pike pointed. 'Who's the angry gymnast holding the class sign?'

'That's Ms Everson.' She did seem to be glaring at the photographer. Her brown hair was pulled back into her usual migraine-ponytail. That day she'd worn her red tracksuit.

They were quiet. When I looked up, Devon was mouthing something.

'What?' I asked.

'He was saying "yuck",' my uncle said.

'Bad energy.' Devon made a crucifix with his fingers and held it over her staring black eyes. 'She's scary.'

She was. I was impressed he could tell that just from a photo.

'Do you think she's possessed?' he said. 'Like, seriously?'

I giggled and held the photo to my chest. 'Maybe.' Me, Sam and Todd had talked about it before, but more whether she was a secret hell demon. We'd even come up with a test to check; so far, though, none of us had got hold of any holy water.

Bunny Whiskers sauntered in, plopped down in front of me and began licking her tummy.

'What's going on down there?' Devon said.

'The cat's whistle?' I asked.

He laughed. 'No.' He pointed out of the window across the river to the showgrounds on the flat. In winter they played rugby on the paddock beside the floodbanks. Behind the grandstand tiny trucks were pulled up, and tents and fairground equipment were being assembled. One truck had a long trailer with the Ferris wheel bits on it.

'Getting ready for the A&P Show,' I said. 'It's awesome. They have it once a year. There's a public holiday...'

'A&P Show?'

'Agricultural and Pastoral Show,' my uncle said. 'It's like the Easter Show in Sydney. There's animals and hay bales and carnies and fairy floss...'

'Candy floss,' I said.

Devon looked confused. 'Flower shows?' He shot up. 'OMG, is that a Ferris wheel?'

'Tippy!' Mum yelled.

'Better go.' I gulped down my milk.

The trip to the airport was quick; Mum's speeding helped. We arrived just as check-in was closing. She got her boarding pass, and we headed up to the departure gates.

'I was telling Tippy that you and I used to come here as kids,' Mum said.

'That's right ... I'd forgotten about that,' Uncle Pike said. 'We'd never actually go anywhere on a plane.'

'No.' She was holding my hand. 'Just have lunch and watch the planes and people.'

'Is that normal?' Devon said.

Mum stepped off the escalator. 'Probably not these days.'

'I used to love it, though,' my uncle said.

Devon hung back. 'I'll let you guys have some family time. Have an awesome trip, Helen.'

'Come here.' She gave him a hug. 'Good luck looking after these two.'

He smiled and waved as the three of us walked towards customs.

Mum hugged me, smelling of washing powder and shampoo. 'Remember everything I told you.'

I nodded.

She hugged Uncle Pike too. 'Please don't do anything to fuck up my kid.'

'What could possibly happen?' he said.

'Pike!' She punched him on the arm. 'Don't say that.'

'Relax, sis, seriously. We're going to be fine – aren't we, Tippy?'

'Sure,' I said.

'I'm leaving you in charge. I want the house looking the way I left it.'

'Of course,' he said.

'I was talking to Tippy. You are a walking disaster.'

'Three words,' he counted them off on his fingers. 'Cleaning, control, freak.'

She frowned. 'Be good.' She kissed me on the head. 'I love you.'

'Love you more. Have fun, Mum. We'll be fine.'

We hugged again, then she headed to airport security. At customs she turned around. 'Don't listen to anything your uncle says, he's full of...'

Uncle Pike covered my ears.

'I promise,' I said. 'Love you, Mum.'

'And no funny business in front of Tippy!'

The security woman frowned and glanced over at us.

Uncle Pike blew her a kiss. 'Make sure you open the gates to Mordor,' he yelled, as an elderly couple walked past.

The security woman shook her head.

'Is *The Lord of the Rings* on her boat?' I asked. Maybe Mum would finally watch the films. She'd refused to before, saying she hated Hobbiton with its dirty holes.

'Here's hoping,' he said out of the corner of his mouth. 'Keep waving and smiling.'

We stood there until she had disappeared.

'Right, are you ready to party?' Uncle Pike put his arm around me and we walked back to Devon.

It hit me. This was going to be my longest time away from Mum. Ever.

'You okay?' Devon said.

I felt like I was going to cry. Uncle Pike and Devon looked at each other.

'Hey.' Devon kneeled to my eye level. 'Your mum's going on an amazing holiday. That's pretty awesome, right?'

I nodded.

'And do you know what?'

'What?' My voice sounded small.

'So are we! And it starts now. Would you like some ice cream?'

It was really late at night, but that sounded good to me. 'Sure.'

We walked around; all the food shops were closed.

'Well, that's fucked,' Uncle Pike said.

'Don't you worry,' Devon said. 'We'll find some, somewhere.'

He held out his hand, then my uncle stuck his out too. I gazed up at them and put my hands in theirs – big and warm. They started swinging my arms, making me smile.

'Let's hit the road,' my uncle said.

CHAPTER TWO
Falling Down

Next morning the house was quiet as I crept around getting ready for school. I tried hard not to wake my uncle and Devon, but as I made my toast Devon came in yawning and blinking.

'Good morning, beautiful,' he said. I said good morning back and grabbed my plate. 'You sleep well?'

I nodded and sat at the dining table.

He filled the jug. 'I had a dream I was flying a plane, except my hands were really dirty, and then I used some wipes and they disappeared.'

'That's nice.' I unplugged my phone from charging and switched it on. It vibrated with three new messages from Sam and four missed calls. I hoped I hadn't forgotten some homework project for Ms Everson.

Devon switched on the jug and started opening cupboards. 'Love your retro phone. It's so cute.'

'It's not smart. I can't even see emojis.' I got up and showed him where the mugs and plates were.

He leaned against the bench. 'I've been meaning to ask, do you have a photo of your dad? I'd love to see him, if that's okay?'

'Sure,' I lied, handing him a mug. I'd learned over the past nine months if I just kept quiet, or agreed, people would usually stop asking me about Dad. Besides, we had a motto: 'Family business is nobody's business.' Devon didn't need to know what Mum had done with the photos. I sat back at the table as he kept talking.

'Just ... I haven't seen any around the house?' He picked up a Christmas card from Dr Lisa with *Silent Night* written in blue glitter. Mum had sworn when she'd got home from work, saying she'd have to buy Lisa a card now. Devon patted the sparkles and put it back.

Uncle Pike shuffled in with mad-professor hair.

'Good morning,' I said. 'Did you get electrocuted?' It slipped out before I could stop myself.

He stopped still and I held my breath.

Devon laughed and stage-whispered to me, 'She's a monster without her coffee.'

Uncle Pike grunted. 'Tippy Chan, I am impressed.'

I grinned and opened my phone and clicked on Sam's first message:

Call me. Its T

Todd? What had he done now; I didn't want to see any more photos or videos of women.

'Tippy, has my espresso machine arrived?' my uncle called out.

I shook my head. I had no idea what an espresso was.

I clicked on the next message:

Where u? Todds fallen

Fallen off what? The jug began to boil, sounding like a volcanic eruption.

'That's the noisiest kettle I've ever heard,' Devon said.

'What?' Uncle Pike said. 'I can't hear without my coffee.' He switched the jug off.

'Thank God,' Devon said. 'I really thought it was going to explode.'

I clicked on the next message from Sam:

CALL ME!!!!!!!!

My stomach dropped; he never did shouty texts.

'So, my parcel hasn't arrived?' Uncle Pike asked me.

'No, sorry.'

I hoped everything was okay. I went to check voicemail, but my phone vibrated. Sam was calling me.

'Shit – answer it,' Uncle Pike said. 'God knows I would if we had our phones.' He and Devon were doing a phone detox. 'My empire could be completely destroyed and I'd have no idea.'

'That's why you pay for managers. That's their responsibility.' Devon put his arms around Uncle Pike. He kissed him and then pulled away. 'Yuck! Have you been eating Bunny Whiskers' kitty litter?'

I answered the call. 'I thought your phone was grounded.'

'Todd's in hospital,' Sam said.

'What?'

'Didn't you get my messages? He fell off the bridge last night.'

Sam's words made no sense. It was like I couldn't hear him properly. Uncle Pike shushed Devon. This had to be a joke.

'Tippy? Are you there?'

'Did Todd put you up to this? It's not funny, Sam. You should never joke about this stuff.' I really needed him to start laughing.

Sam didn't laugh.

Uncle Pike moved over to me.

'I'm not making it up, Tippy, God's honour,' Sam said. He sounded like he'd been crying.

My insides went cold and wormy. Sam was telling the truth – you could never lie about God's honour. I twisted my school shirt until it was tight against my belly. Todd was in hospital.

'Honey, what is it?' my uncle said.

I pressed the phone to my ear. 'Is he all right?'

'Don't know. He was climbing one of the arches. Dad found him. They flew him up to Dunedin Hospital in the chopper.' Sam sniffed.

'What? When? Is this why he wasn't at school?'

'Hang on,' Sam said. In the background I heard his dad talking to someone.

'Sam?' I said.

'Mum says he's on a coma.' I could hear Dr Lisa yelling something. 'Hang on,' Sam said. There was muffled noise as he covered the phone.

Out of the window, the usual morning traffic crossed Riverstone Bridge. I pressed my forehead against the cool glass.

Sam came back, sighing. 'He's *in* a coma. On those breathing-machine things like on telly.'

Just like Dad.

Sam blew his nose. 'I've got to go. Talk later.' He hung up.

'Okay,' I said to no one. I pushed myself off the window and slumped on the couch.

Uncle Pike sat beside me. 'Can you tell me what happened?'

I opened my mouth to speak, and everything blurred. I snapped my phone shut and let it go. It made a soft thud when it hit the carpet. I leaned over onto my knees, hiding my eyes on my arm. Uncle Pike's and Devon's voices buzzed around me. I couldn't do this, not again. My forearm felt hot and wet against my eyelids.

My uncle gave me a squeeze. 'Hey, it's going to be okay.'

I didn't move, trying to keep my sobs silent.

The rest of the morning was a blur. Uncle Pike called school and told them I wouldn't be in. He wouldn't let me go to my room but instead made me a bed on the couch. Devon handed me a mug of sweet, milky tea, and I lay there for ages under a blanket, sipping and watching, but not watching, the TV. My uncle and Devon came in and out from sunbathing on the balcony to check on me and ask if I wanted to join them outside, but I didn't want to move. I wanted to be alone.

My cotton-wool brain kept testing whether I believed Todd had fallen off the bridge and each time came up blank. It felt the same as Dad's accident, except today was super-hot with no clouds, and when Dad had crashed the sky had been grey and the rain hadn't stopped.

I swallowed a lump in my throat. Bloody Lollipop. Why climb

the bridge? I kept his selfie on my phone screen, as if having him there smiling meant none of this could've happened. I read his messages and clicked on the tiny pic he'd sent. The last message I'd got from him. I pressed the button to zoom in. The click of the key seemed really loud. Boobs filled my screen. Why would he even take this pic? And who would let him?

'I'm still trying to get hold of your mother, Tippy,' Uncle Pike said, close by.

I tucked my arms into my sides and turned the phone slightly away, shielding my screen, hoping he hadn't seen anything.

His face appeared above me from behind the back of the couch. 'How you doing?'

'Okay.'

He rolled his eyes and smacked the couch. 'Incorrect answer.' When I giggled, he smiled. 'We're right here. You're not alone.'

I nodded. 'I know.'

When I was sure he had gone, I checked out the pic again. Above the woman's boobs were the ends of her curly brown hair. What had Todd seen? I zoomed out, hoping to find a face, then stopped and lifted the screen closer. Around the woman's neck was a thin gold chain with a heart-shaped pendant, made out of golden twigs or something. I zoomed out but there was no face. I switched back to his grinning selfie and stared at him. *Todd, what did you do?*

Uncle Pike finally managed to get hold of Mum on video chat after lunch. Her cruise ship was somewhere in the Pacific Ocean. When she heard about Todd, she wanted to come home early but was stuck on the ship until they made port in three days.

I had studied her travel brochure a lot. Happy people wore sunglasses and colourful clothes while the crew stood behind them in their white uniforms, smiling. It even had two pools and a movie theatre. I knew she'd be having a great time, and I didn't want to spoil it.

I told her I was okay, Uncle Pike was looking after me. She

frowned and asked to speak with him. I told her again I was fine and that I loved her, before handing over the tablet.

My uncle paced up and down the living room, talking to her in a low voice. At one point I heard Mum saying the word 'trigger' and 'hospital', and Uncle Pike making her a promise.

When he got off the tablet, he sat on the edge of the sofa.

'Can we go see Todd?' I asked.

Uncle Pike patted my blanket and glanced at Devon. 'Your mum wants to take you when she gets back.'

'But why?' I said.

'She thinks it's best.' He kissed me on the head. 'It's after what happened with your dad, honey.'

I fiddled with a button on the couch. 'Oh,' I said, all whispery.

My uncle frowned. 'What do *you* think?'

I sat up a little. 'I want to see Todd. This time it's different.' It wasn't. I was worried he might die.

Uncle Pike nodded and glanced up at Devon, who stood quietly. My uncle smiled at me. 'Sounds like we need a road trip then.' He slapped his thighs and stood up.

Devon crossed his arms. 'What?'

'What?' my uncle said to Devon.

I sniffed. 'Really?'

Uncle Pike crouched down; I had a weird urge to pull his Santa beard. 'Don't tell your mother. She'll kill me.'

I hugged him. 'Thank you!'

He chuckled. Devon muttered something about responsibility. I didn't care. I was going to see Todd.

Lucky for me I didn't get carsick, because Uncle Pike drove like Mum. Devon had stayed at home, off to find a gym or something. As we passed the *You're Leaving Riverstone* sign, I realised this was the first time I'd been alone with my uncle, not counting our weekly video chats, since Dad's funeral in April. Before that he hadn't been to Riverstone for years, not since Grandma died when I was six.

Hunched over the small rental car's steering wheel, he reminded me of a gorilla in a clown car.

'I like Devon,' I said.

My uncle grinned. 'Good. Same here.' He turned down the music – my first classical music lesson was Belinda Carlisle. 'Hey, Tippy, let me know if I'm ever being a dick to him?'

I laughed. 'Okay.'

We drove on for a bit listening to 'Summer Rain' until Uncle Pike paused it. He glanced over. 'How are you really doing, Tippy?'

I put my hands under my legs. 'Good.'

He frowned. 'You do know it's okay not to be okay?'

I nodded. There was some family business I couldn't talk about, not even with Uncle Pike. It wouldn't be fair on Dad.

'Don't forget, I've known you since you were a baby, so you can't try any of that "family business is nobody's business" stuff with me.'

Sometimes he was like a mind reader. 'I'm fine,' I said. 'Promise.'

I pretended to stare out my window but watched him from the corner of my eye.

He glanced over at me. 'That's what you always say. This conversation is not over, Tippy Chan.' He unpaused Belinda and turned her up.

For the rest of the trip we chatted about school, then our favourite Nancy Drew villains. 'I liked the poisonous spider one,' Uncle Pike said.

'Bushy Trott?'

He laughed. 'Yes, that's it. Bushy Trott. And Snorky the hot sailor.'

'Eeew,' I said. 'I don't think he was supposed to be hot.'

'What about you? Who are your favourites?'

'Mary Mason slash Gay,' I said. 'I liked her disguises.'

'Good choice! Nancy's the best, isn't she?'

I nodded. 'I really want to be her – be a detective and solve mysteries.'

'Same here.'

We chatted more about Nancy, then Uncle Pike told me a few stories about his celebrity clients. As well as being a stylist he owned some salons and a nightclub in Sydney. I didn't know any of the people he talked about, but that didn't matter; it was just fun to hang out.

It wasn't until Dunedin Hospital loomed ahead of us that it hit me – this would be my first time back since Dad died. I dug my fingernails into the seat and stared at the ugly building. I hated it. It reminded me of the J. Edgar Hoover Building from *The X-Files*, one of Dad's favourite shows. An orange windsock flapped on the roof: the helipad. How Dad, and now Todd, had arrived.

I went into autopilot as Uncle Pike parked and we walked to the lifts. On the fifth floor we got out. The ICU ward.

My breath hitched.

Nothing had changed. The white walls with the wide navy stripe, steel-grey carpet turning to cream lino tiles by the ICU desk and the patients' rooms behind it. This could be nine months ago, and for a split second I believed Dad would be here. Like the lift was hooked into some wormhole and if we didn't say anything, just went to his room, he'd be there. Everything would be the same but different.

Uncle Pike was looking at me strangely. 'Maybe we shouldn't have come?'

I noticed a Rudolph reindeer cut-out. He'd broken the spell. Dad wasn't here.

The lift dinged and opened behind us, Sam and his dad stepping out. Mr Campbell could have been a movie star, tall with thick blond hair that he combed back, brown eyes and a square jaw. I imagined he would play a lot of squash, if Riverstone had squash courts. Sam, on the other hand, looked like an orange pipe cleaner.

'Tippy?' Sam said.

We hugged for a second or two – until I think we realised at the same time we'd never hugged before. It felt strange, so we let go, repelling like magnets.

Uncle Pike introduced himself to Sam's dad and they shook hands.

'Lucky for Todd you were there,' Uncle Pike said.

'I wouldn't call it luck.' Mr Campbell's deep voice reminded me of a tiger's growl. 'If he hadn't landed where he did...' He patted Sam's shoulder.

'How's Lollipop?' Sam asked me. 'Have you seen him?'

'I was about to ask you,' I said.

Sam shook his head. 'We just arrived. Dad's up for work.'

Mr Campbell was some kind of scientist, but I thought of him as a coroner, like on TV. He went to crime scenes and worked with the actual coroner in Dunedin doing all kinds of tests. Sometimes he worked at the Riverstone Medical Centre too. Sam told me his dad let him play with dead people at the hospital morgue, but I was pretty sure Sam was lying about that. He did make up a lot of stuff.

'Why was Todd climbing the bridge?' I asked Mr Campbell.

Todd's mum, Mrs Landers, appeared behind the ICU desk with a doctor.

Mr Campbell glanced over at her. 'Sorry, excuse me. I better go check on Ange.' He left us and walked over.

'I'll come with,' Uncle Pike said. 'You kids stay here for a minute.' He followed Mr Campbell.

Sam faced the wall and let out a huge sneeze onto it. Snot dripped down.

'Eeew!' I said. 'This is a hospital.'

'Whatever.' He wiped it off with his sleeve.

'That's worse.'

He chased me with his yucky sleeve towards the desk, where Uncle Pike was chatting with a nurse. Behind the ICU desk, Mr Campbell talked to Mrs Landers, her normally jolly face blank.

'Sam,' I hissed, trying not to laugh. 'Stop!'

Mr Campbell put his arm around Mrs Landers' shoulders and gently turned her in our direction. Any laughter in me died. She stared through me and Sam like we didn't exist.

I gave her an awkward wave.

'Dad says Lollipop was videoing himself,' Sam whispered to me. 'For money.'

'From who? Doesn't make any sense.' I turned my back on the adults and leaned into Sam. 'His biggest prank's been filming your parents, you know ... through their bedroom window.'

Sam put his hands over his ears. 'La, la, la, can't hear you.'

Todd had shown us that video on Wednesday. Dr Lisa had her back to the window, sitting on Mr Campbell's lap. He was lying flat on the bed. They were both in the nuddy, and Dr Lisa bounced up and down, her hair swaying. It had seemed weird, but I'd laughed anyway. I couldn't believe that was only two days ago.

'What did you and Todd do after school?' I said. 'Before he went to the bridge?'

'Dunno what Todd did.' Sam shrugged. 'I was at Richard's for a sleepover.'

'Richard F.? Since when have you two been friends?'

'Dad's ratshit idea. With no phone I spent the whole night watching Richard play games.'

'Did he eat LEGO again?'

Sam laughed. 'Wish he had.'

'Did you get to look at Todd's pic before your parents saw it?'

'Are you into boobies, Tippy?'

'Shut up.' My face felt hot. 'No. Just wondering who she is.' It definitely wasn't Dr Lisa; hers were tiny. I glanced down at my flat chest and couldn't imagine having ones as huge as that woman's. Mum's were pretty big though. It freaked me out. Growing them sounded painful, awkward and annoying. I hoped for a miracle, that they'd never change. 'How did he get a photo like that?'

'I don't know. But what I do know is' – Sam smiled at me – '*you're* into boobies. *You're* into boobies.'

I rolled my eyes and ignored his chanting. 'She had on a necklace. I thought you might have seen it before.'

'I wasn't looking at her necklace.' Sam tried to waggle his eyebrows.

'As if.' Sometimes he tried so hard to be a big man like Todd, but he was still a baby. I pushed him into the wall. 'Don't be gross.'

'He's the gross one, sending all those rude emojis after.'

I thought about my blank rectangles. 'Which ones?'

'You know, his usual combo: squirty water, eggplant, cherries.' Sam shook his head. 'My parents saw that as well.'

We stood there watching the adults chatting – well, Uncle Pike and Mr Campbell. Mrs Landers looked dazed.

'How about Todd's phone?' I said. 'Everything will still be on that.' He never went anywhere without it. He was always taking stupid pics or videos of him scaring the cat.

'I wanted to see it too,' Sam said, 'but Dad said it fell in the river.'

Uncle Pike came over. 'Sorry, guys, no visitors today.'

I said goodbye to Sam and Mr Campbell. It felt like me and Sam had been best friends forever, but it had only been since the beginning of the year. His mum had asked me to play with him. Now I couldn't imagine my life without him, or Todd.

Todd had better wake up soon. Not like Dad.

That night it took ages for me to get to sleep. Todd and Dad kept running through my brain. And how much I wished Mum was here. I knew I'd have to be brave and keep busy until she came home; it helped keep my mind off things. When I woke up, the sun was already poking under my curtains. I panicked – I'd be late for school.

I bolted to the living room and asked Uncle Pike if he could drop me off. I'd already missed the bus. Ms Everson was especially mean to kids who arrived after the bell, although recently she'd seemed almost nice. Todd had said she must be 'getting a root'. He was so gross. Then it hit me again: he was in hospital and had nearly died.

My uncle looked at me, puzzled. 'Really? But it's Saturday, isn't it?'

I relaxed, too relieved to be embarrassed; at least I wouldn't have to face my teacher.

After a shower and breakfast, Uncle Pike had us huddle in the garage. The roller door was open, and the sun was out for the fourth day in a row. It was now officially a heatwave – the temperature was supposed to get as high as twenty-nine degrees.

'Be as quiet as you can,' my uncle whispered. 'I don't want those dead people to hear us.'

Devon inched towards the opening, his back flat against the garage wall. 'Is that why you're wearing camo pants?'

I peered around the side of the garage at the Browns' house. 'Pretty sure they're asleep.'

Our car was parked on the road, about four metres down the driveway.

'Let's make a run for it,' Uncle Pike said, just as their bedroom net curtains twitched.

'Curtains!' I said. We ran and jumped in. My uncle started the car, and we shot back in reverse before he spun the wheel and we surged forward.

Mrs Brown yelled and waved out the window at us.

Devon wound his down and hung out, waving. 'Morning, darling, I'll be back to take you shopping. Kisses!'

And then we were round the corner and out of sight. We headed along the golf course and onto the street that would take us to the river.

'I can't believe I'm finally going over the bridge,' Devon said as we turned onto the road by the riverbank.

The sun dazzled on the water, making me close one eye against the glare. Up ahead, the bridge came into view. Which of the six arches had Todd been on? How far up had he climbed before he fell? As we drove onto it, I took a deep breath and held it. Me and Dad used to do this, holding our breath whenever we crossed a bridge. Mum would tell us off for killing our brain cells, then laugh.

'We need to get you sunglasses,' Uncle Pike said to me via the rear-view mirror.

I nodded, keeping my mouth closed and counting the seconds.

Devon wound down his window and stuck his head out. 'This bridge is too cute.'

Uncle Pike snorted. 'Not exactly Sydney Harbour Bridge.'

'That's what I love about it,' Devon said. 'It doesn't need to be.'

The shadows of the thick arches made a strobe-light effect, black then red repeating on my half-closed eyelids. My lungs strained, then we were off the bridge. Nine seconds. I let out my breath as we turned the tight corner onto Main Street, which ran straight all the way to the base of the hills.

'So this is downtown?' Devon said. 'It's like the Wild West with its two-storey buildings and no power poles. Absolute madness!'

'Main Street,' I said.

'They put the power underground years ago,' my uncle said. 'Lipstick, pig, etcetera.'

I leaned between the front seats and tapping Devon's shoulder, I pointed to the right. 'That's the town hall.' Grey metal scaffolding surrounded it and a trench had been dug against the walls, like a moat, with mounds of rich brown dirt. By the footpath an orange plastic-netting fence had been put up with *Danger: Construction Site* signs hanging off it.

'Looks like the foundations are rotten,' Uncle Pike said.

Devon slowed down and craned his neck. 'It's like a governor's mansion with its big pillars out the front. Very fancy.'

'I feel like we exist in different realities,' my uncle said.

'Ooh, a giant Christmas tree,' Devon said, checking out the town's massive founding tree. 'I wish I had my camera.' He turned to me. 'I love it all.'

Christmas decorations also covered Main Street's lampposts. They switched between big bright-yellow stars and large plastic holly wreaths with red berries. Whoever had done the fake snow-making with white spray-paint had got excited, spraying not only the decorations but all over the shop windows too.

'Pub on the corner,' Uncle Pike said, nodding to the left. 'Nothing changes here.'

I pointed straight ahead at the hill in the distance. 'The other pub's up there on the way out of town.'

'You're a good tour guide, Tippy,' Devon said.

I shrugged then realised he couldn't see me. Some of the lampposts still had burst balloons and streamers stuck on them from the Santa Parade last weekend.

Uncle Pike held up Devon's hand and kissed it. 'Sightseeing, that's what we can do.'

Across the road from the pub and past a couple of shops was the Riverstone Medical Centre.

'That's where Mum works,' I said.

Devon nodded.

'That's new,' my uncle said.

'It's been open a couple of years,' I said.

The medical centre was single storey, and tiny compared to the old, abandoned brick hospital on the hill. Mum had taken me and Sam to see it one day on our way to drop him home. It was dero now, empty, with its tall windows broken. Even so, I still liked to pretend it was an exclusive English boarding school filled with rich, stuck-up kids, like the Topham sisters who Nancy hated in *The Secret of the Old Clock*.

We parked two blocks up from the town hall, near the Bank of New Zealand. Dad's office had been down this street, on the corner parallel to Main Street, just across from the *Riverstone Bulletin* office. Shops continued up Main Street for another half block or so, then it was mainly wooden houses painted white like ours but with different-coloured roofs all the way heading south, up the hill and out of town. That is, apart from the cinder-block 'monkey motels', which were painted pink – everyone called them that, but I had no idea why, or why they were pink.

Small trees lined the bank's brick walls, their trunks and branches wrapped in fairy lights for Christmas. I loved this place at night. It glowed and twinkled, turning the corner of the bank into the edge of a magical forest. I used to pretend that hidden somewhere in the walls' shadows was an escape hatch to an enchanted world on the other side. Standing there now I searched the sun-washed bricks, but any magic had gone.

Devon elbowed me with his sudden clapping. He jumped around. 'I can totally work with this.' He pointed to Glory Box across the road. 'Is that a fabric shop? Shut up! Tell me?' He put a finger to my lips. 'No, don't.' He ran across the road and cupped his hands on the shop window, which was filled with bolts of stripey fabric. His shrieks stopped people on the street, who turned to see what was going on. 'Heaven!' He gave us a big, white, toothy smile then disappeared inside.

'Good luck getting him out of Glory's box.' Uncle Pike sighed and rubbed the small of his back. 'I can't survive on plunger coffee. Why are you still in your school uniform?'

'I'm not.' I had on my usual grey trackpants and hoodie. I'd bought them with Mum a couple of weeks after Dad died. I remembered that day telling her I didn't want to shop, but she'd still dragged me around town. Any clothes she'd suggested, I'd hated; they'd all been too bright and colourful, or had babyish writing on them like they were for little kids, or both. Eventually she'd given up and let me get three pairs of grey trackpants and three grey hoodies, all exactly the same. They were comfy and let me disappear. Poor Mum. Dad had been heaps better at clothes shopping.

Uncle Pike put on some imaginary glasses and looked me up and down. 'It simply won't do, Tippy. You have an image to uphold. From what I've seen to date, it's 1950s Soviet factory worker but not in a fun way.'

I shrugged. 'I don't care.'

He crossed his arms. 'Nonsense. I won't have it. Your mother is bad enough. Clearly fashion in the Chan household will have to skip a generation. Plus, what kind of gay uncle would I be if I left you looking like that? It's in my contract.'

'Contract?'

'Yes, with God. We gays have to leave the world more beautiful than we found it.'

Whooping came from across the street. Devon stood outside Glory Box with shopping bags full of fabric. He spun around and lifted them.

I looked down at my comfy grey clothes and breathed in and out. 'Okay.'

Uncle Pike pointed to me and yelled across the street. 'Makeover!'

Devon's mouth dropped. He screamed and ran across the road, nearly getting hit by a slow-moving car.

Suddenly a white van pulled up to the footpath, cutting Devon off and leaving him on the road. The passenger door opened and a tall, blond man unfolded onto the footpath in front of us. I recognised him from TV.

He whipped off his sunglasses. 'Well, well, well,' Horn-blower said. 'Look who ate Christmas.'

My uncle groaned. 'Is it too late to run?'

The van's side door slid open and a woman jumped out. She stretched back inside and grabbed a TV camera. The driver got out and joined her.

Devon appeared around the front of the van. 'You nearly ran me over.'

'Sorry, mate,' the driver said to Devon. 'This idiot wrenched the wheel.' He nodded towards Horn-blower, who ignored everyone except for Uncle Pike.

'How *are* you, Pickles?' Horn-blower asked.

'Hello, Horn-blower,' my uncle said, through clenched teeth.

'H.B. please!' He finally scanned me and Devon. 'What inappropriate company you are keeping. Are you on some kind of "photo shoot"?'

Uncle Pike sighed. 'This is my partner, Devon, and my niece, Tippy.'

Horn-blower shook our hands, his palm lukewarm and clammy.

'Glad to meet you – for a minute there I thought Pickles had a secret stash of children.'

Uncle Pike rolled his eyes. 'Horrendous as always.'

Horn-blower patted my uncle's arm. 'You too! Now tell me, is there any decent coffee in this dump?'

'You say it like I would know.'

The camerawoman shuffled over. 'Come on, let's go get this shot done.'

'Local fat man and children, meet my crew. My crew, meet...' Horn-blower waved in our direction. 'If you want to know all the best places for espresso and food, Pickles can tell you.'

My uncle's face had gone red. 'What are you doing here? Besides being a dick.'

'Dick,' Horn-blower said to Devon. 'That's how we know each other, in case you're wondering. I'm surprised she hasn't told you any of this.'

Devon glanced over at Uncle Pike and crossed his arms.

The camera woman stepped in front of me, straddling the gutter with her camera on her shoulder, filming Main Street. I wondered what the story was. I was about to ask her when Horn-blower's loud, fake laughter interrupted me.

'You *haven't* told her? Really? Pickles, that's so you.'

Uncle Pike's voice softened. 'You know, it was so brave of you to stay here. I often wonder what my life would've been like if I'd done the same.'

Horn-blower stiffened. 'Whatever. I live in Auckland.' He put on his sunglasses. 'Anyway, enough of your fantasy, Pickles. We have work to do. News, murder, et cetera. Busy, busy! Ciao, ciao. Kisses.'

They climbed back into the van and, with a screech, sped off down Main Street.

Uncle Pike went to kiss Devon but he ducked and my uncle got his cheek. Devon lifted his shopping bags and, rubbing the kiss off with the back of his hand, walked away.

Uncle Pike bent towards me. 'Shopping?' he said, in a weird, loud, happy voice.

'Yay,' I said, though it came out more like 'meh'. I patted the top of my uncle's thick springy hair and asked, 'What murder was Horn-blower talking about?'

Shopping was fun, except for the part back home where Uncle Pike and Devon made me model my new clothes in every possible combination.

'Fifteen seconds,' my uncle yelled from the living room. 'That's all the professionals get in a fashion show.' He timed me too. I lost count of my outfit changes. Towards the end I saved time by starting to get dressed in my bedroom then finishing in the hallway. My room looked like a Glory Box robbery, with coloured material everywhere.

When the show finally ended, I put on my new orange shorts and a pink T-shirt Devon had made me buy. It had a unicorn with fairy wings. 'Twinkle' was written underneath it in curly silver glitter.

'It's for little kids,' I'd said at the shop.

'Don't worry, we'll get the biggest size,' Devon had said. 'I'm totally borrowing.'

'It will be too tight.'

He'd thrown it in the basket. 'Exactly, honey.'

After lunch, Uncle Pike and Devon stripped off to sunbathe on the balcony. Devon wore a pair of bright yellow 'budgie smuggler' underpants.

I left them to see if the paper had arrived. The *Riverstone Bulletin*, or the *Bully* as we called it, came out each Wednesday and Saturday. Its motto was 'No stone unturned'. I pulled it out of the mailbox. Todd's accident covered the front page with a huge headline: 'Local Hero Saves Bridge Boy'. A photo of Sam's dad and another picture of the bridge from the riverbank took up nearly half the page.

Yuck. Lorraine Ashton had written it; we hated her. With Mum away, it was my duty to spit in disgust. I read the article. She didn't name Todd but called him a 'twelve-year-old boy' and wrote he had been videoing himself climbing the bridge when Mr Campbell saw him fall from the top of an arch at around 6.30 p.m. At that time, we'd been saying goodbye to Mum at the airport. Todd had landed on a gravel bed in a shallow part of the river, hitting his head. The rest of the story was about his rescue by Mr Campbell and Todd being flown to Dunedin Hospital, where he remained in a critical condition.

I flicked through the paper for any more information. In the middle was a two-page photo spread of the Santa Parade on the weekend. In the biggest pic Rudolph had photobombed Santa and grabbed his beard. I searched for Mum in the costumes behind them – her work always went as Santa's helpers – but it was impossible to tell which one was her. I checked the rest of the *Bully* but couldn't find any other news about Todd.

I rang Sam. He answered in a hushed voice.

'Why are you whispering?' I played with the mailbox flap. 'I forgot to ask, can you come over?'

'Tonight? Hold on.' Sam's parents were arguing in the background. I heard a door shut and then quiet. 'I'll ask them later,' he said. 'Just had to go to my room.'

The glare from the concrete driveway made my eyes scrunch up. 'You okay?'

'Yeah, they're just fighting again.'

I moved into the cool shade of our garage. 'Sorry.' Sam's mum really wanted another baby, and his dad kept trying to make one, but it wasn't working. I had trouble imagining Dr Lisa and Mr Campbell having problems – they seemed too glamorous.

Sam grunted, and I knew that meant he didn't want to talk about it.

'Hey,' I said, 'Todd's never talked about climbing the bridge before, has he?'

'Don't go all Nanny Drew. We're just kids. Ours is not to reason why.' Sam knew I hated that annoying saying from his parents more than anything.

'Why?' I said – my standard response.

When we'd become friends, I had tried to get Sam interested in puzzles and mysteries, but he really just didn't care. He'd said he was happiest not knowing stuff, which made no sense to me. I still didn't know for sure if he was joking when he said he believed in Santa, but his mum had warned me not to say anything about it to him – she liked that he believed.

'And it's *Nancy* Drew,' I said.

'I thought she was a nanny?'

'So she went around solving mysteries while looking after other people's children?'

'Why not?' Sam said. 'She could have a lady robot helper, like a Transformer.'

'For someone whose mum's the town doctor, you're pretty sexist.'

Sam giggled. 'You said "sex".'

I sighed. 'We've got to find out the truth, Sam. Can you ask the Landers for Todd's phone?'

'No. You get all into it and forget about me – it's boring. Everything's already in the *Bully*.'

'Don't believe everything you read,' I said, knowing how much he hated that saying.

He grunted. 'Good, I won't read.'

'Go on. Todd's phone, please?' I said. 'I'd do it for you.' Sam was pretty stubborn but I usually won. 'Their house is just across the street.'

'What's the point?' Sam sounded upset. 'It's not going to wake him up.'

I gasped.

'Shit. Sorry, Tippy.'

'It's okay,' I said, my voice small. I knew he hadn't meant it.

Sam sighed. 'His phone's missing, probably halfway out to sea by now.'

'Tippy!' my uncle called.

'Got to go, Hero-Son,' I said. 'Ask if you can come over.'

'Later, Nanny Drew.'

I hung up and went around to the balcony.

'My espresso machine turn up yet?' Uncle Pike asked from the sun lounger.

'Not yet.' I gave him the *Bully*.

He saw the front page. 'You okay?'

I nodded. It still didn't feel real.

Devon crowded around. 'Who's that? Hot!'

'Eeew, that's Sam's dad,' I said.

'He's even better in real life.' Uncle Pike shook the paper out. 'Do you know this Lorraine Ashton?' he asked me. 'Her tagline says, "Fourth-generation local – as many connections." That doesn't make much sense.'

'Sounds like she designs wallpaper.' Devon rubbed more coconut oil onto his chest. I loved the smell of it.

Mum and Dad had a run-in with Lorraine Ashton about a year or so ago, just before Dad's accident. After that they'd referred to her using the c-word. They wouldn't tell me what had happened, but it must have been bad as they'd only used the c-word around me where Lorraine Ashton was involved – at least twice a week, since her articles were usually on the front page. I told my uncle all about it, and he nodded then burst out laughing. I frowned.

'Sorry, Tippy. I love your mum, and your dad was the best!' He gave me a great big bear hug. 'In that case it sounds like she designs shit paper. Well, we can't call her the c-word but I feel we need to respect your parents' naming system. How about Sea-Hag?'

I giggled and nodded.

'That doesn't start with C,' Devon said.

'Yes, it does,' my uncle said. '*Sea*-Hag it is.' He opened up the middle section. I told him and Devon all about the Santa Parade and how much fun it had been.

'Poor Santa. Is Rudolph drunk?' my uncle asked. I told them how he'd kept lurching from one side of the street to the other.

'Remind me to stay away from him.' Uncle Pike dropped the paper and undid his sweaty orange bandana, mopping his brow and neck. He threw it to one side, just missing Bunny Whiskers lying in the shade. It fell off the side of the balcony. 'Of course.' He pressed his whisky glass against his head, the ice cubes already melted.

Devon didn't seem to sweat. His black fur glistened on his chest from the coconut oil. He stretched out. 'You didn't tell me you grew up in paradise.'

Uncle Pike spluttered. 'Trust me, it's the opposite.' He downed the rest of his drink.

'I can see your Christmas cracker,' Devon said.

'What?' My uncle sat up, covering himself with one hand and putting his glass down with the other. 'Bad boxer shorts.' He tried to stand up, but the sun lounger tipped over and he crashed onto the deck, the lounger landing on top of him. 'Are you serious?' His elbows poked out from under it, and he sprang to his feet. The lounger flew across the balcony, hitting the rails.

'So butch,' Devon said.

'Girl, you know it.' Uncle Pike rambled past me into the kitchen and grabbed some ice. 'I hope you didn't see it, Tippy?'

I was distracted by Mum video calling on the tablet and wandered inside after him. 'See what?' I said as I answered it.

Devon laughed.

'My penis.' Uncle Pike stuck his head under the kitchen tap and drank for ages.

Mum seemed worried. 'Honey, are you okay?'

'Uncle Pike's not wearing pants,' I said.

'What?' Her forehead crinkled.

He shuffled past and grabbed the tablet off me. 'Nice cabin, Lennie.' He pulled his undies' elastic waistband and showed Mum his bum then pinged them back. 'Still got that arse!' He kissed the screen and handed it back to me. 'Tell-tale tit.'

'Pike!' She yelled out, 'Pike!'

My uncle poured himself another drink.

'Relax, Mum, he's wearing boxer shorts.'

He moved back and peered over my shoulder. 'They're called fundies. Devon made them.'

Mum sighed. 'Pike, you can't go walking around Tippy like that.'

He put his hot hand on my shoulder. 'You've got to stop the body shaming, Lennie. It's not okay.'

I lifted the tablet higher so she could see us better. He raised his glass. 'Up your bum!' and walked outside.

'And why's he yelling about his penis?' she asked. 'Is he drunk?' A fair question – it was 2.00 p.m.

'No,' I lied, not wanting to get my uncle into more trouble or to upset Mum. We had only just convinced her to stay on the cruise and not come home early.

'Hmmm,' she said.

Devon popped up behind me. He waved. 'Hi, Helen!'

'Ow!' I said. 'Not so loud.'

She squinted, her brow all crinkly again. She moved closer to the camera until her face took up the whole screen.

'Sorry!' Devon yelled and kept waving. 'Hope you're having a great time!'

I'd had enough and handed him the tablet. 'Bye, Mum. Love you.'

His eyebrows squished together, and he blew out his cheeks as he stared at Mum. She gave him an awkward smile. 'I love you too, honey!' she yelled to the corner of the screen and ended the call.

'Well, that was nice,' Devon said.

'Hmm.' I went out to the balcony.

Uncle Pike was sitting on the rail with a wet purple face cloth on his head, one corner covering his eye. It looked like a starfish was attacking him.

I sat down with my book and got comfortable, while Devon pulled out a block of beige soap and put it to his ear. 'I'm going through withdrawal,' he said.

Uncle Pike raised his face cloth. 'Is that from the Browns?'

'They had a basket of them. I cut off the rope.'

'It doesn't even look like a phone,' my uncle said.

'But it smells nice,' I said.

'Thank you,' said Devon. 'I need to do some more sculpting.' He swiped left on his soap.

I had just finished a chapter when there was a shriek and then screaming, like a woman was being killed.

Devon ran to the rail where Uncle Pike had been. 'Tippy! Phone, quick! Your fat, drunk uncle's fallen off the balcony.'

CHAPTER THREE
Four Kilograms

Uncle Pike lay in the ward at the Riverstone Medical Centre. The room was like a strange waterproof office with random shower curtains. Icepacks covered his ankle, and he was not happy. He glared at me and Devon as we approached his bed. 'Where have you been?'

Dr Lisa came in wearing her white coat, smiling, with Sam in tow. I wanted to be her when I grew up. She was smart, funny and super fit, with beautiful, curly chestnut hair and brown eyes with long lashes. She'd always been kind to me and Mum. Except if I was Dr Lisa then I'd be Sam's mum, which would be weird.

'How's the patient?' she asked.

My uncle roared in pain.

I smiled at her. 'Same, same.'

'I thought you people were supposed to be nice?' she said to Uncle Pike.

'No,' he snapped, 'we're supposed to be funny.'

'Well, that explains it,' she said.

'Hi, Doc.' Devon waved then took a great sniff from the huge bunch of white-and-red-velvet peonies he carried. 'The Browns have such an amazing garden,' he said to no one in particular. The peonies were Mr Brown's A&P Show prize winners. It looked like Devon had picked them all. 'Vase.' He spun off to hunt for one.

Dr Lisa sighed as Devon walked away. 'You're one very lucky man, Pike.'

He snorted. 'Not feeling so lucky today.'

'That will be the hangover, no doubt,' she said with zero sympathy.

'Or the fucking broken ankle.'

'And maybe less of the language in front of your eleven-year-old niece?'

Uncle Pike looked up at me sheepishly. 'Jeepers. Sorry, Tippy.'

'That's okay.' I patted his hand. 'I'd swear too if I had a leg like yours.'

He smiled. 'Thank you.' He grabbed my hand and gave it a little squeeze, then he winced. He turned to Dr Lisa. 'Painkillers. Now.'

Sam and I went back out to the front reception area, a boring rectangular room with glass windows and an automatic door, which opened on to a concrete ramp leading to a small carpark off Main Street. Even the carpet was a boring grey. We sat side by side, watching the traffic go past. On the windows someone had painted strange Christmas decorations.

'Dad's coming,' he said. 'Mum says I can't stay at yours now. I have to go home...'

'Thought that might happen.' I kicked the legs of my chair with the back of my sneakers. 'That sucks.'

'I know. Stupid broken ankle.'

'You did a good job of painting that snowman,' I said. 'Did you use your fingers?'

Sam laughed. 'It looks like a prebert with its creepy stick claws and psycho eyes.'

I giggled. 'And it's going to attack Santa.'

'Is Santa screaming?' Sam said.

Devon wandered over. 'What's so funny?'

We pointed at the window.

Devon's hand reached for his throat. 'What the hell?'

Me and Sam giggled, which turned into a laughing fit. Devon joined in. Finally, I stopped laughing long enough to introduce Devon to Sam.

'What's a prebert?' Sam asked him.

Devon looked shocked. 'What?'

'You know, a prebert?' I said, smiling.

'Why are you asking, kids? Have you been in contact with one? Should I get your mum, Sam?'

Sam looked at Devon like he was strange. 'Told you he wouldn't know.'

'Who's a prebert?' Devon said.

Sam shrugged. 'Just something Lollipop said.'

'Someone called Todd that,' I said, 'and now we say it.'

Before Devon could answer us, the front doors opened and Sam's dad came in. 'Hello.' He padded over to Devon and held out his hand. 'Russell Campbell.'

Devon shook his hand and made a weird strangle-y noise.

'This is Devon,' I said.

'Welcome to Hades.' Mr Campbell smiled. 'I hope these two are keeping out of mischief?'

Devon's mouth was still catching flies when suddenly, for the second time that day, the sound of a woman's screams came from outside.

Out on the footpath two women were fighting: Miss Homer, another teacher from my school, and Ms Everson. I almost didn't recognise my class teacher out of her usual gym gear and ponytail. She wore a black jacket and dress, and her hair was done up all fancy.

'She's so mean,' Sam said.

'Which one?' I said. Ms Everson was a cow, but Miss Homer had accused Sam of stealing at the start of the year.

She yanked Ms Everson along by her black jacket towards the

pub on the corner. Ms Everson stumbled, trying not to fall over. I noticed she wore high heels instead of sneakers. She screamed at Miss Homer to stop.

'This doesn't look good,' Mr Campbell said.

We scrambled out of the doors onto the ramp. Ms Everson saw us and started to yell, but her words got garbled as Miss Homer put her in a headlock. Smokers outside the pub leaned through the windows, calling to the people inside to come out and watch.

Dr Lisa joined us. 'What's going on?' She looked over and gasped as Miss Homer marched my bent-over teacher across the street.

'Shouldn't we do something?' I said.

Miss Homer screeched – a stabbing, wild sound – but the only word I could make out was 'pregnant'.

Dr Lisa shoved Mr Campbell to get him to help, but he just stood there with his mouth open like Devon earlier.

'Stay here.' Devon ran across the carpark and crossed the street.

'Get off me!' Ms Everson sounded frightened. I moved closer to Sam – I'd never heard her scared before. She screamed, struggling to get away.

'You're fucking dead!' Miss Homer yelled and yanked her hard, trying to pull her to the ground.

'Hey!' Devon shouted. 'Stop.'

Miss Homer turned around, freezing when she spotted him and the pub crowd. Ms Everson wriggled out of her jacket and stumbled away. She reached down and took off her heels, then ran along the street in her black dress, crying.

Miss Homer clung to the jacket then sprinted across the road to her car. She sped off in the other direction.

The next day was Sunday and we all slept in. Eventually the noise from Mrs Brown mowing the lawns got me up. It was sunny again; people were already saying it was a record December for sunshine, and we weren't even halfway through the month. Devon kept saying Uncle Pike had obviously lied about how dreadful the weather in Riverstone was.

I wondered how Ms Everson was getting on after last night's fight. 'What do you think they were fighting about?' I asked Devon, who was heading out for a run.

'Probably a man,' he said. I wasn't sure if that was sexist.

Uncle Pike didn't seem to be in too much pain this morning, except when he walked with his crutches, which he hadn't quite got the hang of. He sprawled on the couch and rang an annoying little white china bell he'd found in Mum's room. It had been Grandma's and had pink roses on it and a poem about friendship. With Devon gone, I had to fetch my uncle bits and pieces as he asked for them.

He rang the bell again, and I was about to pretend I had to go to the toilet, when Devon burst into the room. 'You did not tell me! Oh. My. God. Why did you not tell me?'

Uncle Pike dropped the bell in his lap. 'What's wrong, honey?'

Devon stood there, seeming to vibrate. 'Show queens!' He started screaming and jumping in a kind of pogo dance around the room, chanting, 'Show queens, show queens. They have fucking *show queens*!' He pointed towards the showgrounds on the flat.

'I know, right?' Uncle Pike rang his bell until I thought it would break.

I grabbed last weekend's *Bully*. It had a special A&P Show supplement with a two-page 'Show Queen Contestants' spread. I held it up to Devon.

'Shut up!' He snatched it from me then quickly turned and mouthed 'sorry'. 'This is too exciting.' He slammed it down beside Uncle Pike, pointing to the photo of Claire Bates. 'There's the winner.'

She looked like a model: beautiful black hair, blue eyes and a great smile.

Uncle Pike nodded. 'Agreed, and she's eighteen, so the right age to win, compared to the only other attractive one who's ... twenty-four! What? How'd they let someone that old enter?'

I wasn't sure if I should be offended on behalf of the twenty-four-year-old and all the other contestants.

My uncle glanced at me. 'Trust me, Tippy, it's my job to know how these things work.'

I shrugged and went to grab a drink in the kitchen. I remembered Claire Bates from school last year. I'd avoided her – she'd been really loud and always made fun of us younger kids, thinking she was really cool. Todd called her an arse-clown too. I wondered how he was doing.

Devon put the paper up to his face. 'Claire works at Pansy Palace. Oh my God!' He bounced off the sofa and started hopping. 'You didn't tell me there's a gay bar here.'

'It sells plants,' I said.

'Oh.' He stopped hopping and his shoulders slumped. 'Sad face. I was really looking forward to hanging at Pansy Palace. Having a game of pool, listening to the jukebox. I bet they'd have great shows.'

'What the...?' my uncle said. 'Is that Melanie Brown?'

Devon glanced behind him. 'What? Where?'

'Here, in the paper. I can't make out her picture. It's like it's got a filter of doom over it.'

Out the kitchen window I saw the real Melanie skulk around the back of the Browns'. She was smoking while checking her phone. She wore Mr Brown's gumboots and her uniform of tight black jeans and a baggy woollen jersey. I wondered how she got on with the heat.

'Tippy, did you know about this?' Devon said.

'Of course she did,' my uncle said.

'Shut up! Pike, two words: Make. Over.'

'I thought that was one word?' I said. I must have triggered Melanie's spider senses because she noticed me staring. I gave her a little wave and she scowled. She flicked her burning cigarette into the hedge and went back to checking her phone.

Uncle Pike clapped and gave Devon's shoulder a nudge. 'This fucks all over a flower show.'

'She's outside,' I whispered.

'What?' my uncle said.

'Really?' Devon said. 'Come on!' He grabbed my uncle's sunburnt arm and towed him off the couch.

Uncle Pike's moon boot thudded on the floor. 'Ow!'

'Sorry, honey.' Devon handed him his crutches.

'Thanks, and can you get me a little drink?'

We all headed outside, the smell of fresh cut grass still strong. Uncle Pike hopped over to the balcony. 'Hey, Scary Spice.'

For an instant Melanie's expression reminded me of a startled Bunny Whiskers. 'What?' she said. 'If this is about smoking...'

Devon held up the paper with the Show Queen spread. 'About this.'

Melanie mumbled, 'For fuck's sake.' She shoved her phone in her back pocket.

'Relax,' Uncle Pike said. 'We want to offer our services.' He leaned on his crutches. 'Help you win the crown.'

Melanie laughed. She shook her head. 'Why? Because a woman needs a gay man to make her look good? Really living the cliché, aren't you?'

'You know that's the most I've ever heard you speak?' he said.

I think it was the most I'd ever heard her say as well.

'Firstly, we are professionals. This is what we do. There's a reason why clichés are clichés. Secondly, of course a woman doesn't need a gay man to make her look good, but that woman isn't you.'

Melanie smirked and folded her arms. 'You're assuming I want to win.'

'You deliberately mocking or sabotaging it makes sense,' my uncle said. 'I get it – throw blood at the winner or whatever you've planned.'

She stood there, glaring at him. 'The whole thing is so fucked. It's a meat market from the dark ages.'

'Right. But wouldn't it be more delicious to win? Think of it: you'd have a platform for a whole year.'

Devon smiled. 'And it is much more powerful to say it's fucked when you are beautiful and a winner.'

Melanie sighed and went to go.

Uncle Pike put his hand on Devon's arm. 'Not helping, darling.'

She stopped. 'Anyway, you can zhuzh me up all you like with your fairy wands but I know how these things go.' She sighed. 'Chan, tell them.'

I had no idea. And I was pretty sure this was the first time she'd ever spoken to me. 'Because you're the youngest?'

Her lip curled as she stared at me. 'I'm sixteen.'

I felt my face go red. 'Because you've got no hair?'

'Argh! Are you blind? I'm up against princesses – and, worse, they care about it.'

I partially hid from her behind Uncle Pike.

'You mentioned fairy wands before,' he said. 'How many of those princesses' – he pointed to the newspaper spread – 'have two fairy godmothers?'

'Let's be real,' Devon said. 'I'm probably more of a fairy godsister.'

'Why do you even care? What's in it for you?' Melanie crossed her arms. 'I can't pay you. I have zero budget.'

'I'm pretty sure Cinderella didn't get stuck with a bill,' Uncle Pike said. 'Trust us, we're homosexuals.'

'Last time, Santa.' She pulled out her phone. 'What's in it for you?'

'Honestly?' He slumped against the railing. 'We are so bored. No offence, Tippy.'

'Speak for yourself,' Devon said.

'We've already done all the shops,' my uncle said.

Devon's eyebrows shot up. 'Are you for serious? That's it?'

'Yuh-ha. Why do you think I left this piss-den?' Uncle Pike tipped back his drink and grimaced. 'Plus, this is what we do.'

'Literally,' Devon said.

'And we want a backstage ticket to the only show in town,' my uncle said to Melanie.

'Bored, I get,' she said. 'One condition.'

'Name it.'

'I want a bottle of vodka and a carton of cigarettes, my choice.'

'That's two things,' Devon said.

'Deal,' Uncle Pike said.

'Really?' Devon said. 'You're going to give a sixteen-year-old vodka and cigarettes?'

'I gave Tippy a single malt for her birthday, and she's only eleven.' He turned back to Melanie. 'Okay, but I have one condition too: no menthol, and you win. And to win you must do everything we tell you.'

'That's three conditions,' Devon said.

'Two, I think,' I said.

Melanie cocked her head and stared at Uncle Pike, who stared back. Seconds dragged and neither of them moved, until finally she blinked.

'Ha!' he said.

'Whatever. Fine, but no more "Scary Spice". You can do better.'

'Deal,' my uncle said.

Melanie left us, scrolling through her phone. 'Shit.' She stopped and read her screen then glanced up at me. 'Umm.' She walked up the balcony stairs and handed her phone to Uncle Pike. Devon leaned over his shoulder and frowned.

'What is it?' I tried to see, but my uncle passed the phone back to Melanie.

Devon came over and kneeled beside me, and Uncle Pike was serious. 'A murder,' my uncle said. 'Outskirts of town. They think it happened last night.'

I felt numb as we all went inside. It didn't seem real. I'd never heard of anyone being murdered in Riverstone before. What did it mean? I switched on the TV and found a news update. A body, unidentified, had been found five kilometres out of town.

'I know where that is,' Melanie said. 'It's near the only traffic lights.'

'What?' Devon said.

'There's a single-lane bridge with a traffic light on each side, honey,' Uncle Pike said. 'Sydney's not the only place with traffic lights, you know.'

Devon scratched his head.

Michael Horn-blower appeared on camera. His blond wavy hair and red lips would have been pretty on a girl. Behind him was a yellow-and-black-striped traffic light and a tar-sealed road that went up a steep curved bridge over the Clutha. Willow trees lined the other side of the river. Peeking through their green branches were tiny patches of bright blue.

'Well, this is awkward,' Uncle Pike muttered.

Melanie smirked.

'Is he wearing lipstick?' I said, turning up the volume.

'It's a terrible colour,' Devon said.

'...a real Christmas tragedy. With only nineteen days to go, a family has lost a loved one. Christmas will never be the same again. Local police have spoken to an eye-witness who discovered the grisly remains early this morning. In the blue tent behind me forensic investigators are processing the scene.' Horn-blower sounded nothing like he had on the street.

'Why's he talking like that?' I asked. He sounded like he could be the headmaster of my imaginary exclusive English boarding school up at the old hospital.

On screen he pointed across the river. 'It's hard to believe that on Saturday night, just over this picturesque bridge, a gruesome murder took place. On a grassy bank area well known to the locals as "lover's lane", as it were.'

'No, it's not. What a load of shit,' Melanie said, disgusted. 'You go there to smoke weed.'

Uncle Pike looked at her, then at me.

'What?' she said.

'Just say no, Tippy,' my uncle said.

'You didn't tell me he works for the BBC,' Devon said to Uncle Pike.

'He doesn't,' I said. 'Is he allowed to make stuff up?'

My uncle rubbed his face and asked for the remote. I went to hand it to him, but Devon snatched it. 'Well, well, Horn-blower.' Devon stepped towards the TV, clenching the remote. 'I've heard a lot about you, but none of it from my boyfriend.'

'You know he can't hear you?' my uncle said.

Melanie was scrolling through her phone. 'Still no name.'

'At this stage, an act of terrorism has not been ruled out,' Horn-blower said.

'What the fuck?' Uncle Pike said.

There was silence. I stared at him staring at the TV and had the weird feeling the floor had disappeared.

Horn-blower put his finger to his ear and shrugged. Someone off camera said something to him, and the camera turned to one of the officers on the scene. The policeman reminded me of a shaved bull.

'Can you please repeat what you just said?' Horn-blower asked, nodding.

The policeman blushed. 'There's no terrorists?'

Horn-blower waved for the camera to focus back on him. 'There, we have confirmation it was not terrorism. In fact, confirmation this was indeed *not* an act of terrorism as earlier perhaps indicated.'

Feeling dizzy, I sat down.

'You okay?' Melanie asked me.

My head felt wobbly. I nodded even though there was no more okay. How could there be?

'Terrorism ... what a fucking toolbox. Why did you date this guy?' she asked Uncle Pike.

'See?' Devon said to him.

A murder in our small town. It seemed bizarre, like something that happened anywhere else. I glanced out of the window and wondered if they'd already caught the person who'd done it. If they hadn't then the murderer was still out there somewhere, ready to do it again.

My phone vibrated and I flinched.

It was Sam. 'Ms Everson,' he whispered.

I had to put my finger in my other ear to block out Uncle Pike and Devon arguing. 'Have you seen about the murder? It's on TV now.'

'Tippy,' Sam whispered.

'Why are you whispering?' I whispered back. 'It's really annoying.' I kept an eye on the TV, hoping they'd show the crime scene, but so far it was still Horn-blower's face.

'Because I'm not supposed to be telling anyone. Dad's talking to the police.'

'About the fight last night?'

'No,' Sam said.

'What then? Cruelty to animals?' It wouldn't surprise me if Ms Everson had a starving horse somewhere.

'No, you noodle. The body. It's hers.'

'What?' I sat still and concentrated, pushing my finger harder inside my other ear. 'Say again?'

Devon muted the TV, and all three of them stared at me.

'It's her, Tippy,' Sam said. 'She's dead. Hold on.'

'Sam?'

He was breathing against the phone's mic, not saying anything.

My teacher murdered? What the hell? As I stared at the TV, the traffic light behind Horn-blower changed from green to red. 'Sam?'

'Shhh,' he said. 'They're saying something about fingerprints ... Shit.' In an even quieter voice, he murmured, 'She was found nudie-rudie.'

'What? Naked?'

Devon frowned at me. 'Who's naked?'

'Except for a shoe,' Sam said.

An image flashed in my mind: Ms Everson taking off her heels and running down the street.

On the phone I heard men's voices in the background. On the TV, the traffic light changed back to green.

'Sam? Where are you?' I stood up.

'Shhh. Dad's saying something.' The deep sound of Mr Campbell's voice rumbled under Sam's breathing, but he was too far away for me to make out the words.

My scalp prickled and I gripped the phone tighter, pacing up and down. I needed to do something. I needed him to tell me what was happening. 'Sam?'

'Four kilograms?' There was a sharp intake of breath. 'Tippy...' Sam paused for a long time. 'Her head's gone.'

My mouth dropped and it sounded like Sam had burst into tears. His dad called his name, then dial tone.

No. I took a step back. Maybe I'd heard wrong. I cocked my head as if listening to Sam's last words again then flipped my phone shut.

Melanie stood up; her hand reached out but didn't touch me. Devon and Uncle Pike were staring at me as I stood there, not knowing what to do.

'What is it?' Uncle Pike glanced at Devon. 'Is Todd okay?'

I pointed to the TV. 'It's my teacher. Ms Everson.'

'What?' Melanie and Devon said together.

My uncle's brow wrinkled. 'Your teacher is ... dead?'

'Yes.' I didn't move.

'Tippy,' Uncle Pike said. 'Is Sam sure?'

I couldn't remember what I was supposed to be doing. I rubbed my thumb. 'She had no clothes on and, and ... no head.'

Devon gasped. Uncle Pike's eyes bugged out and he choked as he spluttered.

'What? No head?' Melanie said. 'Who told you that?'

I stared at Horn-blower talking on the TV. 'Sam,' I said.

My uncle reached for my hand and gently pulled me over to sit on the couch. He swallowed me up in a hug. 'It's okay.'

Shaking my head, I leaned into him. 'What's happening? Todd ... and now...' My vision blurred. Fat tears clung to my eyelashes.

'I don't know, honey. I really don't know. Shall we try calling your mum?'

I nodded, too afraid to speak in case I started crying and couldn't stop.

I heard Melanie say, 'That's brutal. Sorry, Chan.' Then she must have left.

Devon tried calling Mum on the tablet a couple of times, but she wasn't answering. I dug my fingernails into my palm; she wouldn't be home for another ten days.

Uncle Pike took my hand. 'She's probably playing shuffleboard.'

'What's that?' I said with a shuddery breath, relieved to have a different subject to focus on when my head was feeling all woolly again.

'I have no idea – they just used to say it a lot on *The Love Boat*.'

'What's that?' Devon and I asked.

My uncle sighed and poured a large whisky. 'It was a TV programme where sad people filed onto a boat and found love.'

I wiped my eyes with the palm of my hand. 'Do you think Mum will find a husband?'

'Shit, no,' my uncle said. 'Sorry, honey. No, no.'

Devon looked at Uncle Pike. 'But we hope she finds something that will make her happy. What makes you happy, Tippy?'

I sniffed. My mind went blank and it was impossible to think. 'Reading?'

'Right,' Devon said. 'So we hope your mum finds a good hard book to read on her holiday that she really enjoys and reads a lot of, and then at the end of her holiday she leaves the book behind.'

'She needs a good read,' my uncle said.

'Definitely, but we don't want her bringing that book home.'

'Why not?' I asked, pulling down my sleeve and dabbing my nose.

'Books on holidays can be very different when you are back home,' Uncle Pike said. 'And most likely your mum won't like the book as much.'

'Or the book may belong to someone else, like a library, and it just gets complicated. Your mum doesn't need complicated right now.'

I nodded. 'I hope she gets to read lots and lots of books.'

'That's the spirit!' my uncle said. He switched off the TV and we sat there in silence for a moment.

'Do you want to talk about it?' Uncle Pike said.

I didn't know what to say. 'I haven't seen you guys reading,' I said, my voice croaky.

'I meant your teacher,' he said, nudging me.

I kept staring at the blank TV, rubbing my hands on the couch. All I wanted to ask was, why one shoe? What did that mean?

'To be fair, I probably like to read more than your uncle,' Devon said, breaking the silence.

'Really? I thought we were on the same page.'

Devon jumped up and ruffled Uncle Pike's hair. 'Sure.'

I texted Sam to ask if he could come over, then went for a shower, hoping it would get rid of the thick thud of a headache and my puffy red eyes. It didn't. I put on one of my new dresses. Sam still hadn't replied to my message; I rubbed my temple and hoped he was okay.

When I entered the living room, Mrs Brown was standing there with Devon, near Uncle Pike on the couch. They stopped talking, and she rushed up to me and grabbed my hands. 'Tippy, how are you? I'm so sorry to hear about your teacher. Terrible, just terrible.' The week before she'd told Mum that Ms Everson was a disgrace to teaching.

I was about to say something when I noticed Uncle Pike staring at me, worried. His sunburnt face was pale, his good leg jiggling up and down like mad.

'There's no easy way of saying this.' He asked me to sit beside him. Mrs Brown gave me a small smile and rubbed my arm but avoided looking at me.

My stomach dropped. Please not Todd; Mum always said bad things came in threes. I shuffled over, afraid that if I asked my uncle about Todd he'd tell me. Mrs Brown pursed her lips and brushed the back of the couch behind me. I sat on the edge, staring at the carpet, unable to face Uncle Pike.

'Honey.' He put his hand on my shoulder. 'Ms Everson's ... hair was found this morning.'

I let out a big sigh of relief. It wasn't Todd. 'At the traffic light?'

'No, honey.' He glanced at Devon. 'It was found on Sally Homer's steps in town.'

I turned and frowned. 'Her head?'

Devon shook his head. 'No, her scalp.'

'What?' The fight last evening. Poor Ms Everson. She'd been all dressed up, her hair so pretty. Vomit rose in my throat. I ran to the toilet and leaned on the seat, but it passed. She shouldn't have died, no matter how mean she was. It wasn't fair. Not Todd and not this. None of it was fair.

Devon hovered behind me.

'I just want to wash my face.' I avoided him and my reflection. If only I'd done something, or said something, she'd still be alive.

Out in the hallway Devon gave me a big hug. Mrs Brown handed me a glass of water and some Panadol. 'Drink it slowly.'

I took the pill and swallowed. 'Thank you.' My head thumped.

Devon led me back to the sofa and my uncle. 'I'll make you some sweet tea, okay?'

Mrs Brown took my glass. 'Your teacher's in a better place now, dear.'

Uncle Pike glared out of the window at the town. 'That wouldn't be very fucking hard.' He moved closer, putting his massive arm around me. 'You know I used to pretend Riverstone was River Heights?'

'I still do,' I whispered and snuggled into him.

'And I always wished Carson Drew was my dad. Pretty silly, eh?'

I didn't say anything. I just listened to him breathe.

CHAPTER FOUR
Enter The Nancys

After dinner I left Uncle Pike and Devon, and went to lie on my bed and read.

'Knock, knock.' Devon stood in my bedroom doorway, holding a brown-paper bag.

I put my book down.

He smiled. 'Thought we needed some girl time. May I?'

I nodded. He came in and plopped down beside me. He was checking out my room. The tiger-orange walls glowed in the evening sun while a breeze made my creepy clown curtains breathe lazily in and out. Near the window were puzzles, games and books jammed into a tall white bookcase. Any that couldn't fit were piled up on my dresser and on the floor, along with a couple of T-shirts and a pair of purple shorts. The rest of my new clothes I'd put away.

'I love your walls,' said Devon. 'Did you choose the colour?'

'Yes.'

'Excellent choice. And, let me guess, your mum chose the curtains?'

I nodded and giggled as he rolled his eyes.

'WTF, right? I'm surprised you can sleep at night with those...' He tipped up his brown-paper bag and a sparkle rainbow of nail-polish bottles fell out: lime green, gold glitter, pink, black, ruby red, lemon yellow and more sparkles. Mum never let me paint my nails. Devon grinned. 'Mani-pedi?'

I nodded again, not having a clue what he meant. I chose a bottle of rainbow sparkles in clear polish.

'Good choice,' he said, 'but do you know you can put that over the top of a colour? Pick one and I'll show you.'

I ended up choosing a pretty pink bottle.

'Toes, fingers or combo?'

'Both.' I kicked off my slippers and spread out my toes so Devon could paint them.

He shook the pink bottle. 'The most important rule to remember is: no wiggling.' After unscrewing the top, he leaned over and started to paint my big toenail.

'Do you have any sisters?' I asked – I'd always wanted a sister.

He shook his head.

The smell of the polish was strong, like petrol. 'Family?'

'Not anymore.' He hunched over further to do a second coat of pink, and there was a long silence.

I understood how sad he must be. 'I'm sorry,' I said.

He squeezed my foot. 'Well, that's not true. I do have my gay family.' He blew on my toes, which tickled. 'Nearly there. Remember – *no* moving.' He shook the glitter bottle and after some more blowing put on the rainbow sparkles topcoat.

My toes looked awesome, the coloured speckles bright against the pink. 'Can I wiggle them now?'

He smiled and nodded.

I gave them a big wiggle.

'Never let anyone forget who you are, Tippy.' He was still smiling except his eyes looked sad.

I gave his hand a quick squeeze. 'I won't,' I promised.

He shook his head and cleared his throat. 'I love the smell but probably not the best for your brains.' I noticed tears in his eyes as he stood to open the window. 'Ow!' Devon's foot shot up. He reached down and picked something up from my woolly mat. The shiny gold arm of my old Piggy-Cat.

'What the…?' I said. 'I thought I lost that.'

Devon wiped his eyes. He examined it closely, turning it over in his hand. 'This is porcelain. What is it?'

'It's from Piggy-Cat.'

He frowned and handed it to me.

'Dad gave it to me two Christmases ago.' I held up the paw and demonstrated waving. 'This broke off ages ago.' I told him all about Piggy-Cat. It had been shiny gold with red ears and nails. I'd loved its expression: so happy that its eyes were closed, and with the biggest smile. Its open mouth was where you put the money.

'Ah.' Devon nodded. 'Are waving cats part of your heritage?'

I laughed. 'Maneki-neko's Japanese, not Kiwi.'

'But this is Chinese, isn't it?' He pointed to the red Hanzi on the golden paw.

I nodded. 'Very good.'

He did a half-bow. 'Thank you. What does it say?'

'May a river of gold flow into your pockets.'

'And has it?'

'Nearly.' I rubbed my thumb along the characters. Once I'd saved nearly eight hundred dollars, with help from Mum and Dad. I'd been so close to having enough for a smartphone.

Devon lifted up some jigsaw-puzzle boxes near where he'd stepped on the paw. 'Where's Piggy-Cat? I want to see her.'

'She broke,' I said. 'Her paw's all that's left.' I squeezed it hard.

'Shame. She sounded so happy.' He opened the window and sat back on the bed. 'That's *some* piles of books you have here. Either you like to read or you are great at styling interiors.'

'Both.'

He laughed. 'Okay, now your fingers. Same, same or different?'

I picked up a midnight-blue bottle and a clear bottle with gold flecks.

'Such great taste,' he said. 'Now, don't move.' He painted my fingernails while humming some tune. I was happy sitting still and being quiet, amazed at how cool my nails looked.

When he finished I told him to wait. I gathered up all my Nancy Drew books and spread them around him on the bed.

'That's quite a collection you have there,' he said. 'Her hair is ferocious.' His hand drifted over the books. 'Blonde, red, long, short ... And I'm loving her outfits. Oh my God, check out this fur coat.' He picked up *Nancy's Mysterious Letter* and stroked it. 'Divine.'

'Some of these were Grandma's when she was a girl.' I handed

him my old turquoise hardback copy of *The Secret of the Old Clock*.
'The early ones are the best.'

'Why's that?'

'She's sixteen and isn't afraid of anyone.'

He opened the book and squealed. 'This is too cute!' On the
front page in neat handwriting was Uncle Pike's name; I'd written
mine underneath. Devon opened other books to find my uncle's
name inside. Then Devon held up *The Bungalow Mystery*. 'She
pretends to be so masc for masc, but really she was Nancy Drew.'

'Nearly all of them were his. I love them too.'

He gave me a big smile. 'That's because you both have excellent
taste.'

I grinned then sighed. 'I've always wanted to be like her. You
know, solve mysteries.'

'Why don't you?'

I snorted. 'Besides Mum? I could never do what Nancy does.'

Devon nudged me. 'Seriously, why not?'

'Really? Well ... she's like super-hero brave and always speaks up
for the truth, no matter what.'

He put his arm around me. 'Hello, have you met yourself? You
are so brave and honest. Plus, look at all the resources she has –
fabulous hair and clothes, a car, a gun...' He leaned back and made
a rectangle with his fingers, then closed one eye and peered through
it. 'We can help you with all of those. Fabulous hair and wardrobe,
check. Car, we have one of those. Gun – well, I wouldn't know
where to start with that in New Zealand, but your uncle might?'

I laughed and hugged him. He smelled nice. 'Thank you.'

He gave me a pat and stood up. 'Thank *you* for showing me
Nancy.'

'And thanks for painting my nails. I love them.'

'Anytime, Tippy, anytime.' He was halfway out the door and
turned back. 'Lip gloss? For or against?'

'For.' It was another thing Mum was against.

'Correct answer.'

School on Monday was cancelled because of Ms Everson. I tried not to look too happy when I found out we had the day off.

After breakfast Uncle Pike asked me to fetch Melanie so we could start planning her makeover.

'Best keep ourselves busy, Tippy,' he said. 'Especially when bad things happen. Helps take our mind off things.'

I totally agreed; it had worked with Dad. It still did.

Next door I spoke to Mrs Brown instead of Melanie. Melanie Brown was possibly the coolest person I knew, and I didn't want to face her unless I had to.

'Tippy.' Mrs Brown leaned in and grasped my hands. 'How are you? Have you heard anything from school? That poor, lovely woman.'

I shook my head. 'It's been cancelled.'

She looked annoyed.

Melanie popped up behind her. 'Hey, Chan.'

I tried to give her a raised-eyebrow wave.

Melanie gave Mrs Brown a loud kiss on the cheek. 'Phyllis, you said Jill Everson was a *dirty* bird. That she was quite rooty.'

Mrs Brown dropped my hands. 'Melanie Brown! I did not say that.'

'Yes, you did.' Melanie joined me outside on the doorstep. 'Remember? I told you to stop slut-shaming.'

'What's slut-shaming?' I said.

'Heavens!' Mrs Brown was stroking her throat. 'I never used such language.'

'Maybe not,' Melanie said, checking her phone, 'but that's what you meant.'

I'd never thought of Ms Everson as anything but my teacher. 'Did she have a boyfriend?'

Melanie snorted. 'Boy*friends*, according to Phyllis.'

'Who?' I asked.

'I don't know,' Mrs Brown spluttered. 'Good luck.' She closed the door so hard their Christmas wreath fell off.

Suddenly I was alone with Melanie. I walked ahead of her, trying to think of something to say. My cheeks burned as she scuffed along behind me into the garage.

Uncle Pike was waiting for us on a white plastic chair; his crutches were propped against my dresser, which Devon had dragged out of my room before his run.

'Why are we meeting here?' Melanie said.

'This is now the official war room.' My uncle leaned back in his chair and stretched out his arms. 'And it's easier to hose down.'

She grunted and scrolled on her phone.

'Who do you talk to on that?' he said.

'No one in this shitty town.'

He looked impressed. 'Now you're talking my language. Tippy, can you pass me my hair kit?'

I handed his bag over. He pulled over another chair and gestured for Melanie to sit down.

'How do I know you're not going to cut my head off?' she said.

'You don't,' he said.

I hugged myself and tried not to picture Ms Everson's headless corpse with only one shoe on.

Melanie sat, and he put a black cape over her. 'First, I need to survey the damage and assess what we have left to work with.' He sprayed her hair using Mum's plastic plant sprayer, then started to comb it.

I pulled my chair over near the wall, trying to hide and watch.

Melanie took out a cigarette and looked at Uncle Pike.

'Honey,' he said, 'I own a nightclub. Just try not to get Tippy addicted.'

She lit it and inhaled then blew the smoke away from me.

'What did your hair do to make you hate it so much?' he asked.

Melanie shrugged. 'I'm not into all that hair crap.'

'Clearly. But you care enough to dye it black.'

'Blue-black.'

'And to cut it,' he said.

'Just to stop it annoying me.'

'Poor hair.' He changed to a shiny comb; this one seemed to tug at her hair.

'Okay, tell me everything. Who are the judges?'

'The mayor, Duncan Nunn, and that douche from TV.'

'Duncan Nunn,' he said. 'Why's that name so familiar?'

'Riverstone's number-one real-estate agent,' Melanie and I said together.

'Ah,' my uncle said. 'The wig guy.'

'I never thought of that before,' she said, 'but it makes so much sense.'

'Otherwise we *are* dealing with the paranormal,' he said. 'Who's the TV star?'

Melanie grinned and searched on her phone. She showed Uncle Pike.

He tugged her hair.

'Ow, fuck! I'm attached to this.' She dropped her smoke on the floor and stomped on it.

'Sorry.' He sprayed her hair again.

Melanie showed me her phone. It was Horn-blower.

'That's a weird mix,' I said. 'What do they know about beauty competitions?'

She shrugged.

'I mean, why not Dr Lisa?' Besides being super smart, she knew about being beautiful.

Melanie squinted at me. 'Female judges only. I like your thinking, Chan.'

'We'll need a strategy for the judges,' my uncle said. 'Horn-blower's completely superficial, so we'll have no problems there.'

'Nunn's a bit of a perv,' Melanie said.

'Perfect,' he said. 'And the mayor?'

Melanie shrugged.

'Okay, a wildcard.' Uncle Pike started combing then snipping. 'From what I can see, Claire Bates is your competition.'

'She enjoys netball, skiing and hanging out with her friends,' Melanie said. 'She also volunteers with the elderly at Sunset View. Her bio – I've heard it like fifteen hundred million times.'

'She sounds awful and like bullshit to me,' he said. 'Any of it true?'

Melanie shrugged. 'She can be an asshole.'

'Insecure?'

'That's no excuse.' Melanie lit another cigarette.

'She picked on us younger kids at school,' I said. 'Todd calls her an arse-clown.'

Melanie chuckled and leaned her head back, blowing smoke towards the ceiling. 'Good one, it suits her. Hey, how's he doing?'

'Still asleep,' I said.

She gave me a half smile. 'I'm sure he'll wake up soon.'

Uncle Pike rubbed my back. 'Yes, of course he will.'

I nodded. He'd better.

'Ask your grandmother about Claire Bates,' my uncle said to Melanie. 'She knows everything about everyone.'

'Already have and she doesn't.'

Uncle Pike snorted.

'But she *is* asking around.'

That gave me an idea. 'Does she know who my teacher's boyfriend is?' No one had been arrested yet for Ms Everson's murder.

My uncle stopped cutting.

Melanie held up her phone to me; she was on some kind of news site. 'Negative,' she said. 'But whoever he is, Phyllis already thinks he's guilty. No idea where she gets any of this from. What do you think?'

'Maybe,' I said. 'But wouldn't they have arrested him by now?'

'This is probably a bit gruesome for Tippy,' Uncle Pike said.

'No, it's not.' I actually found it interesting – a real mystery. I hoped that didn't mean I was a freak.

'The rumour going around town is that he is tall and blond,' Melanie said. 'I think Phyllis makes half this stuff up though.'

'Changing the subject,' my uncle said. 'Is your mum excited about Show Queens? Where is she, by the way?'

I shot him a look that he missed.

Melanie's jaw clenched. 'Really? For someone whose sister lives next door, you're pretty disconnected. I thought you fash-hole types were always up with the gossip?'

Uncle Pike tugged her hair again.

'Ow!'

'You're not going to win with a mouth like that. Lucky we're not competing for Miss Friendship.'

'Melanie's mum died,' I said. Her mum's funeral was the first one I'd ever been to before Dad's. 'Two weeks before—'

'Home school's been a bit different.' Melanie stood up. 'I think I've had enough for today.'

'Wait,' Uncle Pike said. 'Shit. I'm sorry about your mum. I'm sorry. I guess I've been up my own arse for such a long time, I'm only starting to open them.'

'Gross, open your arse?' Melanie said.

'No. I think I said my eyes.'

'Um, no, you didn't,' I said.

'You're a freaky Betty Brown-Eye,' Melanie said.

I giggled.

He rolled his eyes. 'They're blue. Now sit down and shut up so I can sort this rat's nest out.'

Melanie gave me a smirk and sat down. 'Thanks for opening your arse, Riverstone's number two.'

'You're welcome, Anal-Lease.'

'Annaliese?' she said.

'Anal-Lease. And we're going to need extensions.'

By the time Devon joined us, Uncle Pike had washed out the black dye and was in the process of colouring. Melanie was wearing a shower cap. Devon was soaked in sweat and breathing hard.

'It's a miracle,' my uncle said. 'We have a spring woman.'

'I knew it.' Devon put his hands on his head and sucked in mouthfuls of air. 'Strawberry blonde?'

Uncle Pike nodded. 'Overall, yes. Creamy blonde with some caramel tones leading to a lighter, almost pinkish blonde. I'm thinking flamingo, I'm thinking cotton candy' – he turned to me – 'sorry, candy floss, or maybe coconut ice. Balayage will be involved.'

Devon circled Melanie. 'Of course, beautiful. Extensions, obviously.' He crept closer to her and she growled.

'I can hear what you're saying,' she said.

'Yes, but can you understand it?' Uncle Pike said. 'Lee is couriering from Paddington tomorrow. I told her you'd call later with a shoe order.'

'Shoes,' Melanie said. 'And I have to make a speech.'

'Topic: "Intersectionality of an A&P Show Queen"?' Devon said.

'Perfect,' my uncle said. 'Your platform is representation, or lack of it. You'll spend your reign as queen working as a beauty ambassador for everyone, encouraging them to join the competition next year. I'll speak to Vagi – she'll work with you on public speaking and your speeches.'

'Who?'

'Only one of the top PR people in Australasia. She'll work with you online.' He checked his watch. 'Devon will give your grandma the details. However, just to be sure, we're going to go full Hollywood starlet.' He peeked under her shower cap. 'A few more minutes. We'll make you shine so bright they won't even remember what you said.'

Melanie frowned and Devon backed away, framing her with his fingers. 'Yellow, who knew?' He pushed a finger towards her. 'Shhhhhh. I need to sketch.'

Her lip curled as Devon skipped off inside.

We waited for Melanie's dye to work. Soon Uncle Pike took off her shower cap and finished treating her hair, giving her step-by-step instructions on how to take care of it while Devon went next door to design with Mrs Brown in her sewing room. I helped Melanie take off the cape, her hair now a caramel blonde. It was amazing how much the colour changed the way she looked. Her eyes seemed bigger and greener.

She raised her eyebrows. 'That bad, huh?' She checked herself out with her phone and I detected a little smile. 'Whatever, I don't care.'

'This is just the base,' Uncle Pike said. 'I'll do the cut and colouring once the extensions are in. Try to keep undercover.' Uncle Pike took off his disposable gloves and patted the seat beside him. 'Tippy Chan, you're next in the chair.'

'In case it rains?' Melanie asked.

I imagined her standing in the rain in Mr Brown's gumboots, a cigarette dangling from her lips with hair dye running down her face.

'No, we don't want the competition seeing you,' he said. I sat in the chair and he wrapped the cape around me. He placed his hands lightly on my shoulders. 'Tippy, how do we feel about red?'

An hour or so later I went with Uncle Pike and Devon to the supermarket. The huge carpark was strangely empty, and we drove right up to the front door. My uncle stepped out on his sore leg, forgetting his crutches. He swore just as a young mother and her son were going past. 'Santa said "fuck",' the little boy told his mum. She grabbed his hand and dragged him away, glaring at Uncle Pike.

'Ho, ho, ho,' he bellowed after them in his best Santa voice. 'Bloody crutches,' he muttered.

As the doors opened, 'Jingle Bells' blasted us and my uncle swore again. Devon ran off to get a trolley. He smiled and waved at a woman with a screaming kid standing in front of a large Duncan Nunn Real Estate poster, then bobsledded back to us.

I scuffed along behind, giving them some alone time like Mum had asked. They'd told me I was allowed to choose anything I wanted. A week ago I would've gone nuts and filled the trolley with chocolate and chips and ice cream and sausage rolls – all year we'd been eating boring pasta and rice – but right now I didn't want anything, except Mum.

My neck felt cold, like a breeze was blowing on it all the time. I guess I'd had black shoulder-length hair forever, and my new pixie cut would take some getting used to. That, and it was plum with bright-red streaks. Mum was going to freak.

'You okay, Tippy?' my uncle yelled over his shoulder – he hadn't yet mastered turning around with his crutches. 'What do you want to do today?'

Devon was swirling through the bread aisle. His tight crimson tank top had *Tourist* written on it in sequins that sparkled under the fluorescent lights. He seemed to be on a mission to read every label in the supermarket. This was going to take forever.

I thought of what Devon had said last night about being like Nancy Drew. 'Can we pick up Sam and go to the traffic light?'

My uncle did a sixty-point turn and stared at me blankly.

Devon stopped reading.

'I thought we could look for clues,' I said.

Devon spoke very slowly. 'You do realise her body isn't there anymore?'

'I'm not stupid.'

'Of course you're not. You're my niece.' Uncle Pike glared at Devon. 'And quite frankly the chances of dying of boredom in this dump are much higher than being topped by some small-town murderer. I can't even drink with these poxy things.' He lifted his crutches and yelped as his moon boot hit the floor.

'Poor pussy cat!' Devon patted him on the face. 'But that's not strictly true. You were drinking last night.'

'I meant in an enjoyable holiday way,' my uncle snapped.

'Someone's got her cranky pants on,' Devon said to me.

'You seemed pretty happy when you were singing,' I said.

Uncle Pike growled.

Suddenly Mrs Kent appeared with her brontosaurus high-school son, Nathan. She stopped while he lumbered on, pushing their trolley, music leaking out of his headphones. Sam and I reckoned that if a furless panda and a pink spider had a giant baby it would look like Mrs Kent.

'Hello, Jess,' she said.

'Hi, Mrs Kent. It's Tippy,' I said. 'Tippy Chan?'

'No, I'm sure it's Jess.' She gave Uncle Pike and Devon the full up-and-down. 'And you are?'

My uncle smiled but it looked a bit fake. 'I'm *Tippy*'s uncle. And this is my boyfriend, Devon.'

'You're not Asian.' Mrs Kent turned her back on them and bent over to me. Her soft pink folds rearranged into a smile. 'I'm sorry. I get you all mixed up.' She giggled. 'You know what I mean.' She straightened and followed Nathan. 'Have a great day.'

'Is that fucker on glue?' my uncle said.

'She always confuses me with Jess Chung,' I said, which was weird since Jess was way older and looked nothing like me.

Uncle Pike's eyes narrowed and met Devon's. There was a slight nod between them.

'What's wrong?' I asked.

Devon climbed the shampoo and conditioner shelves and looked over at the next aisle.

My uncle beamed at me. 'Nothing with you, my dear. You're perfect.' He patted me on the arm. 'Sometimes Karma just needs a little hand.'

I had no idea who Karma was.

'And you know what? Fuck it, I've changed my mind. I think looking for clues is genius. Devon gets to do her sightseeing and we can all hang out. Think about it – we'll be like Nancy Drew and the Hardy Boys, with our very own mystery to solve.'

Devon threw a bottle of shampoo over the aisle and I heard Mrs Kent squawk.

'Someone has just died,' Devon said, jumping back down, 'and I don't know if it's appropriate for Tippy—'

'It was your idea,' I said, kicking the trolley wheel.

'I didn't mean investigate a murder.'

'What?' Uncle Pike frowned at Devon then shook his head. 'What-ever.' He turned to me. 'You know what, Tippy? You need a win.'

I thought my eyes were going to pop out. I couldn't believe he was agreeing to it.

'And anyway,' he said to Devon, 'don't be so sexist. You wouldn't say that if she was a boy.'

'Umm, hello, yes I would. She's eleven.'

'Exactly! When I was eleven I was driving a Land Rover.'

'With dinosaurs,' Devon said.

'Why were you driving a Land Rover?' I asked.

'Tippy, do you promise not to tell anyone we're doing this, especially not your mother?'

Devon smacked him in the head with some bread.

'What? Oh my God.' Uncle Pike rolled his eyes. 'You should never keep secrets from your parents.'

I nodded. There was no chance I'd tell Mum.

Devon bounced ahead of us, pulling the trolley. We skipped the next aisle, where Mrs Kent was scratching her head. Nathan was slouched over their cart, ignoring her and the shampoo on the floor.

'I know!' I said. 'This can be our Mystery Club.'

'And the first rule of Mystery Club,' Devon and Uncle Pike said together.

I looked at them blankly. 'Everyone's a suspect?'

'Not where I was going,' Uncle Pike said.

'Me neither,' Devon said.

'But I like it!' my uncle said.

I couldn't help but grin.

Devon stopped and stared at me. 'Tippy, you have such a beautiful smile!'

I felt awkward and great at the same time.

'Do I get to design the logo?' Devon asked.

'Sure,' I said.

'Then I'm in! All of those in favour of calling the club "The Nancys"?' Devon said, throwing both hands in the air.

'What?' I said.

'Carried!' my uncle roared.

Shoppers ducked and looked for the noise. Mrs Kent scuttled past, giving us a wide berth.

'Ooooh! Fabric paint!' Devon pointed down the aisle. 'Best. Day. Ever!'

My phone vibrated and I flipped it open.

'Who's that?' Uncle Pike asked.

'Text from Sam.'

'He better not be sending you rude pics. Never take rude pics of yourself.'

'Yes, Tippy, not until you're an adult,' Devon said. 'And then make sure your face isn't in shot.'

'Eeew,' I said. 'My phone isn't smart, remember?'

Devon laughed. 'Neither is falling off a balcony.'

Uncle Pike picked up the nearest cereal box and threw it at Devon's head, missing him.

'Sam can't go with us to the traffic light,' I said.

'Good,' said my uncle. 'We need to have a planning meeting first if we are going to do this properly. Also, from now on Nancys business is members only – okay, girls? High five!' He raised his hand.

I jumped up and slapped it. Sam wouldn't get it anyway; he'd hate The Nancys.

Devon went to high five Uncle Pike then whipped his hand away. 'Too slow.' He pushed my uncle into a shelf of Weet-Bix, making him let go of his crutches. They clattered against the lower metal shelves. Losing his balance, Uncle Pike grabbed hold of a Christmas chocolates display, pulling it over and crashing to the floor.

'Shit – sorry, honey! I keep forgetting.' Devon reached down to help him up. Spread all around my uncle were chocolate advent calendars.

Finally, I knew what I wanted.

CHAPTER FIVE
Everyone's a Suspect

When we got back home after our supermarket adventure Uncle Pike had needed a nap. I sat with him now at the dining table while Devon cleared the last of our late-lunch dishes. After saving my advent calendar for dessert I ripped open the first seven doors to catch up on the month, tipping the tiny present-shaped chocolates onto the table.

'Ready?' Uncle Pike asked us.

Nodding, I swept all the chocolates into my hand and stuffed them into my mouth all at once. Mum would freak if she knew what we were doing.

'I call this inaugural meeting of The Nancys Club to order.' My uncle banged a teaspoon on the dining table, denting it. 'Fuck, fuckity, fuckhole!' He grabbed his hand and blew on it.

Devon rubbed my uncle's arm. 'You okay, whale pie?'

He nodded and sucked in some air. He shook his hand again and hit the tips of his fingers on the edge of the table. He let out a high-pitched scream.

Devon leaned in and kissed him on the cheek. 'Please stop hurting yourself for attention.'

I sucked on the chocolatey goodness in my mouth.

'I've been thinking.' Devon paused and frowned. 'My glasses would be perfect for this meeting. Anyway, like I tried to say in the supermarket, why don't we start off with something small, like a missing clock?'

'Really. That's a thing?' Uncle Pike asked. 'Who the fuck would steal a clock?'

'You know, like in the book,' Devon said.

'Nancy stole it,' I said, my mouth still full.

'Ah, that's right,' my uncle said. 'And then in the end she keeps it as a trophy.'

Devon tilted his head. 'Like a serial killer?'

I swallowed the delicious lump. 'You need to read the book,' I said, the roof of my mouth still sticky. I pulled out my scrapbook and flipped it open. Before lunch I'd glued in all the news clippings on the murder I'd collected from the internet and local paper.

'Okay, that's not creepy,' said Devon looking over my shoulder.

'No judgements,' Uncle Pike said.

'The victim,' I said. 'Female, thirty-five years old.'

Devon's eyes widened. 'You sound exactly like the cops on telly.'

'Thanks,' I said. 'That's what I was trying to sound like. Why don't you give it a go?'

He cleared his throat. 'Now listen up, people, we have a killer on the loose. Chan and Pike, I want you to cover the east side. And Mahoney' – he pointed to Bunny Whiskers, who was snoozing on the balcony – 'I want you to cover the west.'

We clapped, and Devon took a bow.

'Okay, what else?' Uncle Pike said.

'School,' I said.

'What?'

'School – Jill Everson was my teacher.'

Devon frowned and scratched his head. 'I need optics.' He snapped his fingers. 'I'm a very visual learner.' He went over to the far living-room wall and pulled open the curtains to the view of the neighbours' blue concrete wall and black-tinted windows.

'Do you ever see the Hoares?'

'Pike!'

I shook my head. 'Not anymore.'

Devon took out a black marker and pulled off the cap with his teeth. He drew a line across the window, the pen squeaking.

'Are you sure you can rub it off?' Uncle Pike said.

Devon spat out the cap. 'Of course.' Under the line he wrote *Time*.

I helped Uncle Pike up and we moved closer, sitting on the couch.

'And then we have the murderer,' Devon said.

'Mrs Brown said he was tall,' I said. 'And blond.'

'If town gossip is right,' said Uncle Pike. 'And if it is the boyfriend.'

Devon drew a really long stick man holding a blade, then covered his head in a black cloud.

'He's really sinister.' I didn't like looking at him.

'Hold on.' Devon drew him holding a balloon on a string.

'That's probably creepier now,' I said.

Devon drew a cat beside his feet. The cat looked dead.

I got up and put my hand on his. 'Maybe just stop drawing now.'

'Okay.'

Uncle Pike rang his little china bell. 'Any men at the school tall and blond?'

I shook my head. We had two male teachers – they were both bald; and the caretaker had grey hair.

At the beginning of the timeline Devon wrote *Saturday*, the night Ms Everson was killed, and then *Sunday*, when her body was found and her hair showed up at Miss Homer's.

I shuddered, and gave my head a pat and a rub.

'You okay, Tippy?' my uncle said.

I gave him a thumbs-up. I didn't want the mystery to stop.

Devon grabbed a chair, and at the top of the window he wrote a heading: *Victim: Jill Everson*. He leaned back and checked his work, like an artist painting a canvas, then jumped off the chair; under *Sunday* he wrote *Sally Homer*.

'Put a circle around Sally's name,' said Uncle Pike, 'and draw an arrow to Saturday night. We all know Jill was alive then. What time did you see them?'

'Around 6.00 p.m.,' I said. 'Not long after we'd seen you.'

Devon drew the arrow and wrote *fight* under the time.

I picked at the gold glitter on my thumb. In my head, I saw Miss Homer screaming, 'You're fucking dead!' We should've followed Ms Everson and checked she was all right.

'Hang on,' Devon said. Already the window was getting covered. He tried to rub off a line. 'But it's glass!' He looked worried, licked his finger and tried again, rubbing hard. The black mark stayed where it was.

Uncle Pike asked for the pen and read it. 'Permanent.' He took a big sniff and then chucked it back. 'Well, it was a shit view anyway.'

I shrugged. Mum kept those curtains pulled, although she liked to clean the windows. A lot.

'Okay,' Uncle Pike said, 'what time was Jill Everson's body found?'

I held up my scrapbook. 'Sunday morning – that's all the police say.'

Devon wrote *time* and a *?* under Jill Everson's name. He looked at the tip of the pen then banged it against the glass.

'Are you okay to talk about this, Tippy?' my uncle asked.

In a weird way it felt like playing *Cluedo*. And even though Mum taught me never to say anything bad about the dead, Ms Everson had been mean. She used to make all the kids cry. She'd left me alone, though, especially after Mum had talked to her. If anything, now that she was dead I actually felt sorry for her.

I nodded. 'I really want to find this monster and stop them.'

Uncle Pike squeezed my hand.

Devon gave me a big hug. 'You just let us know anytime you want to stop, okay? We can choose a different mystery.'

I really didn't want that. I smiled to show them I was fine, then flicked through my scrapbook. 'There's no other times mentioned, except Sunday morning when Miss Homer found ... you know, on her steps.' Maybe this wasn't as easy I'd thought – *Cluedo* didn't have missing body parts.

Devon pressed the pen hard against the glass beside Miss Homer's name. As he scribbled, the marker screeched and squeaked but no ink came out. 'Sad face. I think I've broken it.'

'Are you speaking emoji?' Uncle Pike said.

'Tippy, do you have another marker?' Devon said.

I shook my head.

His shoulders slumped. 'I didn't even get to draw my *suspects* box.'

'It's okay,' I said. 'We can buy another one.'

'Perfect, but I think I'll need at least three. And different colours.'

'Green?' I said.

Devon shuddered. 'Only for my traffic light. Maybe.'

Uncle Pike grabbed his crutches to stand up. 'Sounds like we need to fill in the gaps of our investigation timeline. Let's interview Sally and also find out who stumbled on Jill Everson.'

I grabbed the tablet and took a picture of the window.

My uncle rang his annoying bell again; I was *so* going to throw that off the balcony. 'Something else,' he said.

Me and Devon stared at him.

'Sally and I used to go to school together,' he said. I'd totally forgotten; Mum hadn't talked about it for ages. I still hated Miss Homer for lying about Sam stealing from her at the start of the year. And now also for being a murderer, maybe.

'Is that all?' Devon said. 'Hold on, one more order of business before we go.' He ran out of the room and quickly came back with a bag. 'A little something I prepared earlier.' He reached in and pulled out a fresh white T-shirt, stripping off his old one. Heaps of muscles moved in his back as he put it on.

'How did you have time to design—' Uncle Pike said.

'Tada!' Devon spun around. On his white T-shirt was *Nancys* in blood red with splatters around it.

'Never mind, makes sense now,' my uncle said.

'What do you think?' Devon posed. 'My first prototype.'

My uncle pursed his lips. 'Too literal. Taste level is very questionable.'

'I don't think you can wear that in public without someone attacking you,' I said. 'And not even the murderer.'

Uncle Pike raised his eyebrows. 'Tippy Chan, very impressive. I agree. It looks like a trophy. Wouldn't surprise me if they arrested you and DNA-tested the fabric paint.'

'Hmm, good feedback.' Devon turned around. 'What about our first logo? Logo number one?'

On his back, in the same blood paint, was what looked like an Egyptian eye, or maybe a flower, or a heavily made-up drag queen. Devon craned his neck around to look at us.

'I don't understand,' Uncle Pike said. 'Do they have conjunctivitis?'

'Is it Nancy's eye?' I said.

'Or the victim's?' Uncle Pike turned to me. 'Sorry, Tippy.'

I shrugged.

Devon rolled his eyes. 'No. Well, yes, maybe it was a play on that, but also like a private eye.'

'Hmm ... More like someone's privates grew an eye.' My uncle scratched his beard. 'Do I also detect an homage to Georgia O'Keeffe?'

Devon turned back to us. The room was quiet. Uncle Pike tapped his chin. Devon shifted from one foot to another. Uncle Pike frowned then crossed his arms in the shape of an X. 'I'm sorry, but it's a no from me.'

'Sorry, Devon.' I copied my uncle's arms. 'But it's a no from me too.'

Devon lowered his head and nodded. 'Okay. Well, thank you for the opportunity.' He pulled off the T-shirt and walked away, head down, dragging his bag.

Miss Homer's place was a five-minute drive across the bridge and on the flat, just a block off Main Street. It was one of the old teachers' cottages owned by the school. She was waiting for us at the front door in a purple tracksuit. Her face looked puffy and blotchy from crying. 'Pike? Oh my God! Look at you! I heard you fell off the balcony.' She grabbed his arms and held them. 'I couldn't believe it when you called. You've got so ... so...'

'Fat?' Devon said. 'Old?'

'And you are?' Miss Homer asked. 'Oh, wait, let me guess. Are you Pike's "friend"?' She clapped. 'You are! Well, you are yummy.'

Uncle Pike's lip curled. 'Air quotes? Really, Sally?'

I stopped at her concrete steps, which looked small and ordinary. On the bottom one I could make out a dark-brown patch about the size and shape of a fried egg. Was it a bloodstain?

'Hi, Tippy. How are you?'

I glanced up and my scalp prickled. She was studying me.

'Hi, Miss Homer.' I tried to smile but the first rule – 'everyone's a suspect' – came into my head. She was the prime suspect. I really hoped her stare was just the usual pitying look the town supplied for me and Mum – or maybe it was about my haircut.

'Please, call me Sally. I trust your uncle and his "friend" haven't been leading you astray?' She frowned and turned to Uncle Pike. 'You haven't, have you?'

'In this dump? Hardly. She' – he pointed with his thumb – 'is Devon.'

Devon smiled and waved in front of Sally.

'Come in, come in. Shit, how long has it been, Pike?'

'Long enough for your hairstyle to come back in fashion.'

'Trust me, it's never been out in Riverstone,' she said, patting her short blonde mullet.

Inside was a small open-plan room. It reminded me of a motel I'd stayed in once with Mum and Dad, except that room hadn't been filled with dirty clothes and didn't smell like a rubbish bin. The adults sat at a little round dining table that looked even smaller with Uncle Pike hulking over it.

I found a safe spot on Sally's two-seat sofa among used tissues, a towel and what may have been some green undies. In front of me was a large TV. I watched Devon in its reflection as he scanned the room, his smile slowly turning into a frown. I tried not to laugh when he recoiled at a large poster of two dolphins leaping from the sea and kissing in front of a giant full moon.

'I've got a bone to pick with you,' Sally said to Uncle Pike. 'You never accept my friend requests. I have to stalk you through your sister.'

'Really?' he said. 'I'll have to fix that straight away.'

'You better,' Sally said.

'You seen Horn-blower?' my uncle asked.

Devon muttered something then smiled.

'*We* are friends on Facebook – see how that works?' she said. 'You know he's on the telly now? Always promises to visit but doesn't, and still a complete dick-fuck. Sorry, Tippy.'

I shrugged.

'Was I ever as bad as him?' my uncle said.

Sally laughed. 'Pike, you were worse. Where d'you think he learned it from?'

My uncle shuddered. 'Ghost of Christmas Past.'

'Or future,' she said. 'Imagine if you two had stayed together.'

'Wow. Then I'd be an even bigger monster.'

'Hardly.' Sally reached over and grabbed his hand. 'It's so good to see you.' She turned to me. 'Tippy, do you know I used to date your uncle?' She shook her head. 'What was I thinking?'

'What was I on?'

Devon cocked his head.

'Relax,' Uncle Pike said to him, 'it was for one second.'

'Did you guys … you know?' Devon asked.

'Once, but it was awful and, like Pike said, lasted for one second. But you were really good at—'

'I don't think Tippy wants to hear about our sex life – do you, Tippy?'

I turned to find somewhere to hide but accidentally kicked an empty wine bottle and put my hand on a wet ball of tissues.

'Oh my God, Tippy, I'm so sorry!' Sally started to laugh but it turned into crying with big heavy sobs and gross snot dripping out of her nose.

Uncle Pike put his arm around her. 'Tippy, grab Sally some tissues and water, please.'

I wiped my hand on the sofa and got up. I pretended like it was a game of *Where's Wally?* except with a tissue box. Hopefully it wasn't underneath anything I needed to touch.

'When I came back, at first I thought…' She wailed.

I glared at the back of her head. Her sudden crying was over the top, if you asked me.

I found a plastic beer jug and filled it with tap water, trying to drown out her snivelling. When she'd dobbed in Sam to Ms Everson for stealing, he was a newbie and didn't have any friends. After that none of us really trusted him – and none of us wanted to get on Ms Everson's bad side. My cheeks burned; I'd avoided him like everyone else.

Sally blew her nose loudly on some toilet paper then wiped her eyes with it. She took a deep breath. 'At first I thought that horrible cat next door had left me something dead.'

'Don't even get me started on next-door cats,' my uncle said.

'Hey,' Devon said. 'Don't go hating on B.W.'

Above the sink were some clean-ish glasses. They'd do; *I* wasn't drinking out of them. I took them to the table. I couldn't find any tissues, and Sally already had her roll of toilet paper, so I went back to her weird-smelling sofa.

She wiped her nose. 'It's always meowing.'

I muttered, 'That's the noise cats make, you arse-cl—'

'What's that, Tippy?' she said.

I froze. *Crap.* 'Um. Cats go miaow?'

Sally sniffed. 'Yes, that's right.' I was off the hook.

Uncle Pike glared at me. I shrugged. Whatever. She was faking it anyway.

'I grabbed the broom to sweep it off. That's when I realised.' She tipped over her chair, ran to the sink and vomited.

Gross – maybe she really was upset. Still, glad I'd filled the jug before she spewed.

Devon ran to get a face cloth from the bathroom, and Sally cleaned herself up. 'I can't get it out of my head, it was so, so...' She hiccupped and her eyebrows scrunched together.

'It's okay,' Uncle Pike said. 'We're here now. Just take a deep breath.'

The cottage was quiet except for the hum of the fridge and the low swish of cars on the main road.

Uncle Pike poured her a glass of water. 'You said, "When I came back" – where had you been?'

'Church. I left just before 10.00 a.m. and everything was fine. Got back around eleven-thirty and...' She breathed out of her mouth. 'The step and then...' She took a sip of water and put down her glass carefully, giving my uncle a small smile and wiping her hands on her thighs. 'And then the news about Jill.'

I thought she'd start crying again but instead she just sat there staring at her glass.

He reached over and held her hand. 'Horrible.'

Nodding, she dabbed her eyes.

'What about your neighbours, did they help?' he asked. 'Did they see anything?'

She barked a laugh. 'No, the shunts. But if I go outside after a few drinks without my pants on, everyone sees it and makes a big fuss.'

'Where were your pants?' Devon asked.

I tried to slide out of view down the sofa, but the lower I went the worse the smell.

'I'm so scared. Why me? Am I next?' I heard her sniffing then blowing her nose. 'This ... and that kid falling off the bridge. What's going on around here?'

I dug my nails into her stinking sofa. *First she fights with my teacher and threatens to kill her, and now she can't even remember Todd's name.* 'His name is Todd Landers and he's my friend. And he's in a...' I bit down hard on my lip to stop from swearing.

Sally burst into more tears. 'I'm so sorry.'

I turned my back on her and pushed against the sofa. I wished she'd stop saying sorry; I didn't believe her. And I wished Sam was here, but I knew he'd hate even knowing I was sitting in Sally's house. I double-checked for new messages, but there were none. I flipped my phone shut and listened as Sally blew her nose again.

'If it's any consolation, Tippy,' she said, 'the night of your friend Todd's accident was the worst break-up of my life.'

I took a breath and turned, trying to give her a sympathetic smile. I had to get my Nancy on. Sally was the prime suspect and I needed to focus on our investigation. I didn't want this to be our first and only interview. If that meant putting Todd and Sam out of my mind for the next couple of minutes, then that's what I'd have to do.

Sally wiped her nose. 'Why else do you think the place looks like this?'

Devon blinked a couple of times then sighed with relief. 'I did think the overall dolphin theme was pretty distasteful, and the curtains...' He put his fingers in his mouth and pretended to vomit.

'I meant the mess!'

'Sorry, Sally.' Uncle Pike placed his hand over hers. 'Bad taste happens to good people.'

Devon nodded. Sally just looked dazed.

I wanted to ask about the fight. 'What about Ms Everson?'

Sally burst into tears again, and my uncle shook his head at me before he spoke to her. 'Okay, Sal, I think you've had enough for today.' He picked up a bottle of pills and read the label. 'Good old Dr Lisa. Have you had any of these lately?'

Sally shook her head. 'She came after the police to check on me.'

He opened them. 'Two for you and two for me.'

'Nothing changes.' She laughed and took her pills.

He passed them to Devon who waved them away. 'I'm driving.'

Uncle Pike popped his and tipped back his water.

Devon read the label. 'It says take one.'

'Whoops,' my uncle said, smiling. He hopped up and put his

arm on Sally's shoulder. 'Come on, honey, let's get you lying down over here.'

Devon looked at the sofa. 'Yuck.'

Uncle Pike glared at him, and they helped Sally over.

As I got up out of the way, I spied a tissue box poking from behind the television. 'Yes!' I said.

They all stared at me. I tiptoed through the litter, grabbed the box and waved it over my head.

My uncle sat on the edge of the sofa; the arm moved outwards, and I thought I heard it crack. He got up and shot us a quick look. Sally didn't seem to notice the new sag. He held her hand. 'Do you want to stay with us?'

'Thanks, but Mum's coming over. Do you want to see her?'

'Hmm.' He kissed Sally on the forehead.

We left her rugged and drugged on the sofa. Uncle Pike crunched and smashed hidden objects with his crutches as we waded to the door and showed ourselves out.

'What do you think?' I asked when we got back to the car. I didn't believe her; she was hiding something.

'There's no excuse for dolphins,' Devon said.

'Very true, my dear, very true,' Uncle Pike said. 'Tippy, take note.'

Sally hadn't told us anything – what she'd done after the fight, or even what the fight was about. My teacher may have had a blond, tall boyfriend. Someone may have dropped her hair on Sally's steps.

As we drove away, there were only three things we knew for sure: Ms Everson had been murdered, her head was still missing, and Sally Homer was the prime suspect.

CHAPTER SIX
The Crime Scene

I timed the drive from Sally's to the crime scene, as this seemed like something an investigator would do. It took eight minutes and twenty-seven seconds. The route followed the river with its grassy floodbanks and willow trees. We drove past the turn-off to my house then around the corner, under the railway bridge and past the dump. From there on it was farms either side of the road – flat rectangular paddocks lined with tall poplars and the occasional house or shed. Uncle Pike's music education today was Cher. 'Gypsys, Tramps & Thieves' belted from the stereo while outside black-and-white cows ambled along muddy fields.

At eight minutes and five seconds, we turned a corner.

'There it is,' my uncle said.

The yellow-and-black traffic light was like something out of Narnia. Beside it a small, pretty bridge the shape of my school protractor rose up steeply over the river. Willows lined the far bank just like on the TV news.

Devon pulled off onto a short road that led to the traffic light and stopped, waiting for the red light to change. The curve of the bridge was so high, I couldn't see past its middle. There was no way of knowing what, or who, could be waiting on the other side.

'How exciting!' Devon said.

'Only traffic lights in South Otago,' Uncle Pike said.

I wound down my window and stuck my head out. Spatters of bright, white, fluffy clouds reflected off the ripples on the river. The traffic light changed to green, and I held in a deep breath as Devon drove slowly up the steep bridge. When we reached the top I scared myself by thinking it was going to collapse. Then we were over and off the bridge. I let out my breath.

Past the traffic light on this side, the road curved around a tight bend and onto a single sealed lane. On the inside corner was a rough patch of long grass about the size of our garage, outlined by white-and-blue police tape. The river and main road beyond were hidden by the willows along the riverbank.

The crime scene. *This is where it happened.*

The marked-out shape reminded me of a parallelogram, something Ms Everson had taught us to calculate. I felt sad for my teacher but also really excited to be here – did that mean I was a bad person? I kept a poker face, something I'd got very good at.

A police car was parked across from the crime scene, near the turn-off to the Pratts'. At the end of a long gravel driveway you could see their old wooden house and lean-to tin shed, surrounded by trucks and farm equipment that had stopped working a long time ago.

Devon pulled off to the side of the road, parking just in front of the police car. I turned around and watched through the back window as the driver's door opened and a policeman came out. He was the same one from the telly who'd said there were no terrorists – the one who looked like a shaved bull.

'Hello,' my uncle said, hopping out of the car with his crutches.

Outside the air stank, a sweet rotting smell. For a split second I thought it was from the crime scene.

Devon wrinkled his nose. 'Yuck, is this what the country smells like?'

I laughed, a little too loud. 'It's silage. Animal feed?'

'Oh.' He did a back stretch. I was sure he still didn't know what I was talking about. It was so quiet you could hear the river flowing around the feet of the bridge, only broken by the random baaing of sheep.

He lowered his orange sunglasses and squinted. 'There's so much green. Everywhere.' He put his sunnies back on and shuddered.

I patted his arm.

'Watch out, Tippy,' Uncle Pike said. 'She may burst into flames any second.'

The policeman was staring at Devon's bike shorts and sparkly *Tourist* top. 'Can I help you?'

'No thanks. Just looking,' he said.

The policeman frowned. 'This is a crime scene, nothing to see here. You better be moving on.'

Inside the police tape was a patch of grass stained a dull brown. That had to be dried blood. There was so much of it. I tried not to think of Ms Everson bleeding.

Uncle Pike spoke to the officer. 'My friend here is a psychic and would like to look at the area to see if he can help the police find the killer.'

Trying not to look surprised, Devon nodded. 'I guess I do feel a lot of things.'

'A melange?' my uncle asked.

'Yes, but more than that. I can tell, for instance, this policeman has had homosexual encounters before.'

The officer turned red and started stammering.

'Really?' Uncle Pike hopped closer to him.

I wandered over to the edge of the tape. Blowflies buzzed across the flattened grass where I guessed her body must've been. Around it was a brown halo, almost like a snow angel – except instead of snow it was dried blood. I crossed my arms and held on to my T-shirt. Being here made it real, but a part of my brain still refused to believe this had happened to my teacher. I let out a deep breath and shook my head, trying to focus on finding clues. I wished I'd brought Mum's tablet to take pictures.

The policeman raised his voice, denying he was a 'shirt-lifter'. Uncle Pike smiled and told him it was okay – it was natural to be defensive when you were discreet, non-scene and straight-acting, and we wouldn't tell his co-workers.

The policeman finally calmed down and sat in the car with Uncle Pike, who gave me and Devon a thumbs-up all clear.

I ducked under the tape. Crouching, I noticed all the grass surrounding the flattened area seemed normal. I couldn't see any tracks or a clear path for how the body or murderer had got there.

Devon came over. 'What do we do now?' he asked from the other side of the tape.

I turned my back on the policeman and whispered, 'Is he okay?'

'She'll be fine. It's always a little hard coming out the first time.'

'So he's gay? How did you know?'

'Puh-leez!' Devon headed towards the bridge.

'Where are you going now?'

'I don't want to walk in all that blood.'

I hopped across the crime scene, trying to avoid trampling the grass and the brown spots. Then climbed under the tape, joining Devon at the base of the bridge. I kept staring at the ground, looking for clues, but all I could see were pebbles and broken glass.

'You find anything?' I asked.

'Like what?' he said, stretching.

'You know, clues?'

'Like what?' he repeated.

I left him stretching, went under the bridge and crouched. It was cool down there in the shade, and still a little smelly from the nearby silage. Flies hung around a stick poking out of the river. Something was snagged on it; it looked like a dead sheep.

I grabbed Devon and showed him. He stared at it blankly. 'I am not understanding.'

'Look at it closely.' I threw a rock at it and missed. 'Is it her clothes? Or just a dead sheep?'

'Why would a dead sheep be in the river? Don't people drink this water? Eeew! What is wrong with this town?' Devon pretended to wipe his tongue.

'The murderer may have dumped her clothes in the river,' I said.

He sighed. 'Okay, fine, but I'm not touching it.' He started wading out into the water.

'Be careful,' I yelled. 'Dad said there's a strong undertow, even when it looks calm on top.'

Devon nodded, but he didn't get far before he splashed back. 'So gross. Definitely a sheep.'

We headed back to the car. Uncle Pike and the policeman were now sitting on the bonnet, laughing. The policeman got a call on his radio and walked away to take it.

Once he was out of earshot, I whispered as loud as I could, 'We thought we found a clue in the river.'

My uncle double-checked the policeman couldn't hear. He winked. 'Just like our Ms Drew, Tippy. Well done.'

'But it was just a dead sheep,' I said.

'Oh.' He frowned.

'Shouldn't we let the police handle this?' Devon asked.

Uncle Pike snorted. 'Why? Then they'd get to solve it before us.'

'Or not,' I said. 'If they're anything like the police in Nancy's early editions.' I didn't want us to stop now.

'Quite right,' Uncle Pike said. 'So cynical. So young. So proud.'

'Um, *hello*, has everyone gone mad?' Devon said. 'They were books – this is a police investigation.'

My uncle shrugged. 'Sometimes you need to drive through a red light.'

Devon looked confused again.

'Listen,' I said to him, 'if we find something really important, we'll let...'

'Barry,' Uncle Pike said.

'We'll let Barry know straight away.'

Devon folded his arms.

'Yes, yes, of course,' my uncle muttered. 'Straight away. Now, Devon, my love, more important matters ... Barry and Stevie H.?'

Devon lit up and did a star jump. 'Yes! OMG, how perfect would they be? I wonder if we can get Stevie H. to visit.'

'We can at least hook them up online.'

Devon clapped. 'I love it.'

Barry finished his call. 'I have to head off. Good to meet you, Pike.' He held out his hand.

'Come here.' Uncle Pike gave him a big hug. 'What's your number? We're going to be in town for a while and you should come over for dinner.'

Barry paused and then smiled. 'I'd like that.'

It took us five minutes and thirty-seven seconds to get home, but it didn't really count as we got stuck behind a tractor with a mower for one minute and twelve seconds. As we drove up our street I saw

Mrs Brown lurking, peering around the corner of her house. A police car was parked by our mailbox.

Devon pulled up behind them. 'Surely not another one?'

'Finally arresting Mr Brown?' Uncle Pike said.

A woman and a man got out; neither in police uniform. The woman nodded in our direction.

Our car felt too stuffy. I wiggled in my seat and wound down the window. Last time the police had been here was when Dad crashed. I repeated, *Please don't be Mum*, over and over in my head.

'Tippy? Tippy?' Uncle Pike's tattooed hand gripped my forearm and gave me a gentle shake. 'Tippy?'

I looked up. He and Devon were staring at me, their foreheads all crinkly.

'Honey, it's all right,' my uncle said. 'Everything's okay. They're probably here to ask about your teacher, that's all.'

I tried to nod and take a deep breath, but I was all shuddery. Devon got out and opened my door. He leaned over and unbuckled my seatbelt, taking me into his big arms. His shorts and legs were still a bit wet from the river. I hugged him back as he lifted me out of the car and placed me gently on the footpath.

Mrs Brown joined us. 'Cops are here.'

'Really?' Uncle Pike said. 'Where?'

'Tippy, look at your hair!' Mrs Brown said.

I ignored her and watched as the policewoman came towards us. Suddenly I felt winded, like I'd fallen off the monkey bars.

'Another beautiful day in paradise,' she said. 'I'm Detective Sergeant Graham and this is Detective Melon. Tippy Chan?'

For some reason I couldn't stop shaking. I sucked in some air.

'Are you okay?' Detective Sergeant Graham asked.

I shielded my eyes from the sun. I had to be brave. 'Is it my mum?'

She gave me a weird look then shook her head. 'No, no, we just want to have a chat about your teacher, Ms Everson.'

Uncle Pike kneeled-squatted awkwardly, clutching one crutch, his sore leg poking out in front of him. He one-armed hugged me.

'Oh, honey, is that what you thought?' He gave me a squeeze. 'Your mum's fine, trust me. It would take more than a murderer to kill her.' Detective Melon cleared his throat, and my uncle shot him a look. 'What? You know what I mean.'

I flopped against Uncle Pike and giggled. Mum was okay. He kissed me on the forehead. As we headed inside, he hopped along on one crutch and held my hand until we sat on the couch.

Devon got changed and came into the living room wearing a dark-blue sarong patterned with fluoro-pink watermelons. He fetched me a drink of water then busied himself organising tea and plunger coffee. I watched as he cut up a small round Christmas cake a patient had given Mum. Hiding under the thick white icing was the yucky brown fruitcake.

'So, Tippy, can you tell us where you were Saturday night?' Detective Sergeant Graham said.

I told them about Uncle Pike falling off the balcony and us being with him in the medical centre and then coming home.

'Did you see Ms Everson?' she asked.

I nodded.

Devon brought over a plate with the pieces of Christmas cake. As he bent down, his pecs popped out of his sarong. 'Oops, there go my melons.' He stood up and adjusted his sarong to above nipple height.

The detectives looked confused.

'Used to happen to her at the club all the time,' Uncle Pike said.

'They're from Sydney,' I said, and the detectives nodded.

Devon came back with everyone's drinks and sat near Detective Melon. Devon had made me another mug of sweet, milky tea. I cupped it in my hands and blew on it.

'Mm, this icing is delicious,' Detective Sergeant Graham said.

Devon smiled and patted his breast. 'Thank you.'

Detective Melon glared at him then turned to me. 'What time was this? When you saw Ms Everson.'

'Around six?'

'Did you speak with her?'

I shook my head. 'We were inside the medical centre, at the reception. She was outside, arguing.'

'Arguing with who, Tippy?' Detective Sergeant Graham asked.

Uncle Pike squeezed my hand. 'Sally Homer,' he said.

I bit my lip and watched Detective Sergeant Graham move forward in her seat. She wrote something down and glanced at her partner. My uncle was peering over at her notes; she spotted him and covered them up. 'Do you know what they were arguing about?'

I shrugged. 'They were yelling, then Ms Everson ran away.'

'Did you speak with Sally Homer?'

'No. She got in her car and drove off. We went home after that.'

'Did she drive off after Ms Everson?'

'No, the other way.'

'And you were here with her?' Detective Sergeant Graham asked Devon.

'I certainly was,' he said, tickling Uncle Pike's beard. 'She was a lot to handle that night.'

My uncle raised his moon boot. 'Well, I had just broken my ankle.'

'I meant Tippy,' she said.

'I remember it was after my usual bedtime,' I said.

'Which is?'

'Nine,' I said.

'Really?' Uncle Pike said, surprised.

'That seems way too early,' Devon said.

Detective Sergeant Graham sighed.

'What time did it happen?' I asked.

The detectives shifted in their seats. 'We're not at liberty to say,' Detective Melon said. 'But it seems likely around the 11.00 p.m. to 2.00 a.m. range.'

Detective Sergeant Graham cleared her throat and glared at him.

'That's very specific,' Uncle Pike said.

'Like he said,' she said, 'we are not at liberty to discuss it.'

Detective Melon glanced at her as he sipped his coffee.

'Tippy,' Detective Sergeant Graham said, 'can you think of anyone who might have wanted to hurt your teacher?'

Sally Homer dragging her across the street in a headlock came to mind. I shrugged. 'I never saw Ms Everson outside class. She could be pretty mean.'

'To the kids?' the detective sergeant asked.

I glanced at Uncle Pike.

'It's okay, Tippy,' he said.

'She'd tell us that she'd pull out our fingernails if we upset her.'

'What?' Uncle Pike said.

'Really?' Devon said.

'That's so fucked,' my uncle said. 'Did anyone say anything to her?'

'No,' I said. We were all too scared, except maybe Todd.

'Surely that's a crime?' Uncle Pike said to Detective Sergeant Graham.

'Jill Everson is dead.' She sat up straight, as if my uncle had said something really rude.

'Cake?' Devon said, holding the plate up to her.

She waved him away. 'How about visitors?' she asked me. 'Did anyone ever come in to class to see Ms Everson? An adult, maybe someone who didn't work at the school?'

'Parents, I guess, sometimes after school. Other than that I don't remember anyone.'

'Thanks, Tippy. If we need to ask any more questions, we'll let you know.'

They got up to leave.

At the door, Detective Melon turned to me. 'Did Sally Homer spend much time in your classroom? With your teacher?'

I thought about it. 'Sometimes.'

'How often would you say? Every day?'

'Usually at lunchtime. And after school sometimes I'd see them together.'

'Did you see Ms Everson with any other teachers?' Detective Sergeant Graham said. 'As much as Sally Homer?'

'Only at assembly, really.'

'Thanks, Tippy, you've been very helpful,' she said.

After the detectives left, Uncle Pike and Devon gave me a big hug. I went to my room and video-called Mum on the tablet. I got through to her, but our call kept dropping out and freezing her in unflattering poses.

'I wish you were here,' she said. 'They have an amazing library.' The screen went garbled and then clear with her smiling. 'I miss you and love you so—'

I touched her frozen face. 'I miss you,' I said.

I sat for a while holding the tablet, then headed back into the living room.

Devon had already stripped off into his tiny yellow togs. He glanced up from his drink-pouring. 'You okay?' Outside Uncle Pike was sunning himself on the balcony.

I nodded and came over, leaning against the kitchen bench. I stared at Mum's handwriting on the wall calendar. She'd circled the sixteenth and written her flight number and time, 4.20 p.m. In caps she'd written *DON'T BE LATE!!!* I smiled and gripped the bench: nine more days and she'd be home.

Devon screwed the cap back on the bottle of gin then offered me some Christmas cake. I took a piece, even though I hated fruitcake, and picked at the almond icing, trying to separate it. 'Why'd you think the police asked so much about Sally?'

He shrugged. 'Maybe because she did it.'

CHAPTER SEVEN
Kissing Dolphins

The next morning Uncle Pike gave me a choice: I didn't have to go to school if I didn't want to. It was a no-brainer. Finally I was living the Nancy Drew life – with a mystery to solve and no annoying classes to get in my way. After breakfast Devon made us go out on the drive for a runway show. He modelled a new, tight Nancys T-shirt. 'Tada!'

This one was black with *Nancys* in white writing. Forming the letter N was the silhouette of a long-haired, busty woman bending over slightly, hands on hips and spreading her legs in stiletto heels.

He walked to the mailbox, did a model turn, then came back to us and posed.

'First off, nice work on the graphic. Very crisp,' Uncle Pike said.

I agreed and leaned back on my white plastic chair. I felt the legs begin to buckle and shot up again.

Devon smiled and puffed out his chest.

'I also like how you've brought in the mystery element,' my uncle said, 'as it raises many questions.'

'Is she trying to find her clothes?' I said.

'Where's she put her magnifying glass?'

'And her torch?'

'Is this Nancys the same club where Bunny Whiskers works?'

Devon pursed his lips and put his finger to his chin. 'Not where I was going at all, but very good questions.'

Back in the living room I pulled open the curtains covering Devon's window, so we could start our next Nancys meeting.

'So, looking at the timeline...' Devon tapped a new red marker on his bottom lip. He wrote *11.00 p.m.* on *Saturday* and *2.00 a.m.* on *Sunday*, then drew a line between them, thickening it by going over it several times. Above it he drew several small downward arrows, then above that a sad face with a teardrop. 'I think we all know what this part is.'

We nodded. Poor Ms Everson. We had to find out who did this.

Under *Sunday*, Devon drew a cross. 'What time does church start, or go for?'

'Why?' Uncle Pike said. 'Sally didn't do it.'

'She's the prime suspect,' I said. 'Our only suspect.'

'And the only one the police asked about,' Devon said.

'What's up with them.' My uncle shook his head and sat back in his seat. 'It's *not* Sally.'

Devon paused his drawing and the room went quiet.

I took a deep breath. My palms were sweaty. 'She told Ms Everson she'd kill her the same night she was murdered, and there's no witness for her alibi.'

'When you put it like that.' Devon wrote *Suspect* and underneath wrote *Sally Homer*.

'No,' Uncle Pike said. 'It's not Sally. I refuse to believe it.'

'We have to follow The Nancys' rules,' I said. 'I hope it's not her.'

Devon agreed and drew a fancy picture frame, like one of those antique gold ones, around the new suspect list.

'Fine.' My uncle focused on rubbing his palm. 'But it's not her.'

'Okay, it's not her.' Devon underlined her name twice. 'Back to church. When does it start?'

'Ten a.m.,' I said. 'Me and Mum went to it once.'

Uncle Pike looked over and raised his eyebrows.

We went earlier in the year, one Sunday morning after Dad had died. But in the car afterwards Mum had been so angry, muttering something that sounded like 'heaven's fucking entry criteria'. Back home she'd been about to cry, so I had just gone to my room.

On the tablet I searched for Sally's church and found its website. It confirmed Sunday service was from 10.00 to 11.00 a.m. I passed this to my uncle.

'Good work, Tippy.' He handed the tablet to Devon. 'Verified.'

Devon beamed at me and handed it back. 'You're really good at this.' On the window under *Sunday* he put a tick and circled the timeline from 10.00 a.m. to 11.30 a.m. 'This is the window, get it? Window.'

We stared at him.

'Anyway,' he said, 'this is the time the killer had to drop off the...' He paused.

'You can say scalp,' I said.

'Okay, drop off the scalp at Sally's steps before she says she returned.' Beside 11.30 a.m. he drew a spiky bush.

'What's that?' I said.

'It's her ... hair?' he said, looking at me like I was strange.

I frowned. 'It was really curly.'

Devon scribbled over it. He put the pen up to his face. 'Red's not working for me. Never thought I'd say that about you, red.' I swapped him a blue marker. Beside the scribbled bush, he drew a cup and saucer. 'That's much better. Thanks, blue.'

'We need to look for the head,' I said.

Devon swung around. His and Uncle Pike's eyes bugged out at me.

'What?' I said. 'Isn't it our biggest clue?'

My uncle tapped his lip. 'She does have a point.'

'Oh my God, are you serious? We can't have Tippy seeing that.'

'Tippy, you're not to look at the head.'

I shrugged. 'Sure, I don't mind.' Part of me would've liked to have seen what it looked like, though.

Uncle Pike turned to Devon. 'Happy?'

'I'm speechless with words.'

I pointed to the window. 'You need a missing items list.'

Devon sucked on the end of the pen.

'Missing items,' I said, louder.

He sighed. 'How did we get here?'

'Remember to add her other shoe to the list,' Uncle Pike said.

'And her dress,' I said.

'Fine, fine, just hold on.' Devon stood on the chair and drew a rectangle. At the top he wrote *Missin List*. 'Get it? The missing list is missing a G.'

We ignored him.

'Head,' I said. 'Phone. Bag, if she had one.'

'Shoe,' my uncle said. 'Clothes.'

Devon wrote everything down. 'Anything else?'

'We need more information from Sally,' Uncle Pike said, sipping his tea. 'Like what she was doing on Saturday night.'

'What they were fighting about,' I said. 'And whoever found the body.'

'Isn't it "whomever"?' Devon said. 'Should we talk to Jill's neighbours?'

'They're the same ones as Sally's,' I said.

'Let's leapfrog and scale up this investigation,' Uncle Pike said. 'Dinner with Barry? We can find out more from him.'

Devon squinted at the pen tip and nodded slowly. 'Leapfrog and scale up – *so* corporate.'

'Can Sam come too?' I asked.

'Of course,' Uncle Pike said. 'The more the merrier.'

'I'm cooking,' Devon said.

'Thank God for that. Tippy's cooking is awful.'

'Hey!' I said.

I took a picture of the updated window with all my teacher's missing things, including her poor head. Imagine even though you were dead your head was missing? So unfair. And how could anyone in Riverstone be such a monster? My brain struggled to believe it was anyone I knew. But if they lived here then it meant it had to be. Everyone was a suspect. And if not Sally, then who?

'We come bearing wine,' Uncle Pike yelled at Sally Homer's front door.

'And orange bubbles.' Devon lifted my hand attached to my fizzy drink. I really hoped Sally wouldn't want any.

You could hardly see the bloodstain on her step anymore. I traced the outline with my toe and wondered if she'd been scrubbing it.

She peered through a curtain before opening the door and hugging Uncle Pike on her tiptoes. I couldn't imagine them as a couple: he was so huge and she was so little. It was like the ballerina from my plastic jewellery box going out with Big Ted. Sally gave Devon and me a wave. 'Hi, guys. Come in.'

The state of her cottage was about the same. 'Mum helped clean up.'

Uncle Pike and I looked at each other.

Devon seemed upset. 'Really? The dolphins are still here? At least let us help you with a mini-makeover.'

'I'm fine.'

'No, really,' he said. 'You'd be doing us a favour.'

I hid my fizzy drink up my T-shirt and waded over to the sofa, which was in the same state as I'd left it.

'How've you been?' Uncle Pike said as they sat back around her little table.

'Besides being suspended from school pending the investigation? Even though I'm innocent?' She stopped and glanced over at me, but I pretended not to notice, playing with my phone. I didn't want her to stop talking because of me. 'But that's not the worst of it. The cops have been around...' She lowered her voice. 'Maybe this isn't the best for Tippy?'

'Tippy?' Uncle Pike said, trying to get my attention. 'Tippy?'

I looked up. 'Sorry, just a sec.' I pretended to pause my phone's imaginary game. 'Yes?'

He winked at me. 'She gets in the zone with those bloody things.'

'Okay,' Sally said. 'Tippy, you want a glass or anything?'

'No, thank you.' I opened my bottle and took a big swig, the sweet orange fizzing on my tongue. I didn't trust anything in this house, including her.

'Let's crack open one of these.' Uncle Pike unscrewed the cap on the wine bottle.

'It's eleven o'clock,' Devon said.

Sally got up and grabbed some glasses. 'Pubs are open.'

'Surely the cops can't think you did it?' Uncle Pike said.

'I don't know what to think anymore.' She sat back down as he poured the wine. After another glance at me, she continued. 'I'm really worried this is going to be pinned on me.'

I shifted around on the sofa so I could keep a better eye on the adults over my phone.

'But have they been talking to anyone else?' my uncle said.

'Not that I know of.'

'What possible motive could you have?'

She finished her half a glass of wine. 'That bloody argument.' She poured herself another. 'I so wish I hadn't done that.'

'It must've been bad to have a scrag fight in public?'

'Yes, but not bad enough for me to kill anyone. I would never do that. Never.'

I stared at her and snorted, thinking about when she had screamed, 'You're fucking dead!' The adults all swung around to look at me. *Uh-oh*. I banged my chest, pretending my drink had gone down the wrong way.

Devon jumped up. 'Are you okay?'

I nodded and took a swig. Sally went back to her drink, but Uncle Pike shook his head slowly at me. I gave him a blank look and scooched back down the sofa, my face on fire. 'Do you have an alibi for the murder?' my uncle asked.

I popped back up and studied Sally. This was when she'd lie if she was guilty.

'That's the problem,' she said. 'I was drunk at home, watching TV.'

I took another swig of my fizzy. I couldn't tell if she was lying; she seemed drunk now.

'How depressing,' Devon said, looking around the room.

'I was thinking more *Bridget Jones*,' she said.

'Even worse,' Uncle Pike said. 'So you were actively supporting the heteronormative paradigm?'

She laughed bitterly. 'If only you knew.'

'Tell me,' he said, topping up her glass again.

She stopped and stared at him.

It became so quiet my breathing sounded noisy. I stayed still, not daring to move.

Wincing, my uncle shifted his sore leg then gave her an encouraging nod.

'Pike...' Sally said. 'I'm a dyke.'

'Ha! I knew it,' Devon said. 'Hold on.' He disappeared from the room.

'Thank God,' Uncle Pike said, reaching for her hands. 'Why didn't you say?'

'I wasn't ready. This is ... *was* my first relationship with a woman.'

'Oh my God.' My uncle pulled back and rubbed his face. 'You and Jill were together?'

Unnoticed, I slowly shook my head. What was Sally up to? Mrs Brown said Ms Everson had a boyfriend, not a girlfriend.

Devon came back in holding up a large dreamcatcher. 'I knew it. The signs were here all the time.'

'What?' Sally said. 'Mum gave me that – and no, Mum's not queer.' She sighed. 'Anyway, yes, we *were* together. Jill broke it off, the day after the bridge accident.'

'I'm so sorry,' Uncle Pike said.

'Sorry,' Devon said. 'That sucks.'

'As much as my decor?'

'Let's be realistic, your decor is worse.' Devon waved the dreamcatcher. 'Sadly no dolphins died in this driftnet.'

Sally started crying. 'She told me life was too short. She was seeing someone else and had been for most of the time we'd been together. And she was pregnant – that's why the fight ... I was driving past and saw her all dressed up like that. For him.' Sally sank into Uncle Pike, who held her as she cried big, heavy sobs.

If that was true, it was pretty crappy. I almost felt sorry for Sally – except she was a liar and maybe a murderer.

To give them some space, Devon moved away and sat beside me on the sofa arm. I heard something wooden break, and he shot up. The sofa arm sagged outwards a lot more. He looked at me and grimaced. I shrugged, trying not to laugh.

Sally didn't seem to notice. She managed to slow her crying enough to blow her nose. 'I'm so sorry.'

'Don't be ridiculous,' Uncle Pike said. 'You cry as much as you want to, honey.'

Devon wandered back to them, past the kissing-dolphins poster.

The dolphins. *Shit.* I sat bolt upright. Fumbling with my phone, I clicked the pictures folder then opened Todd's boob pic again, zooming in to get a better look.

I peeked over my phone at the adults. Devon hugged Sally. 'If anyone deserves to go full-on leaky, it's you,' he said.

She glanced over at me and I flinched. I tried to give her a little smile and pretended to go back to my phone game. On my screen the heart-shape necklace was clearer: two dolphins touching, nose to tail.

'Who's the bastard?' Uncle Pike asked.

I sat still, wondering what to do, the dolphin poster creeping me out. Did this mean Sally did it?

She gave a half-laugh. 'The bastard who knocked up my girlfriend?' She started crying again and shook her head. 'I never got to find out.' She wiped her face. 'Jill blocked me on Facebook. That night I kept calling and texting her, but...' She shook her head again and put her hands over her face.

'So the person who could help confirm your alibi is now the person who the police think you...' Uncle Pike pulled his beard. 'Fuck.'

Sally looked lost.

I jumped up from the sofa. 'Just one question.'

My uncle said, 'I don't think now—'

'Did you give Ms Everson any jewellery?'

Sally sniffed. 'What? Why?'

'No reason.' I snapped my phone shut, finished my drink and stuffed the bottle down the back of the sofa. I knew we couldn't trust her.

She raised her hand to fend off Devon. 'I gave her a dolphin heart necklace.'

He gasped.

I'm the arse-clown. She was telling the truth. My orange drink left a sickly sweet aftertaste, and for a second I thought I could smell silage again. I got up and patted her hand. 'That sounds beautiful, Sally. It's okay, we believe you.'

'Thanks, Tippy.' She started to cry again.

A weird urge to laugh came over me. Todd had seen Ms Everson's tits for real.

CHAPTER EIGHT
The Case of the Missing Necklace

Back at home it hit me: I hadn't thought once all day about Dad. I snuck off to my room and shut the door while Devon made lunch.

I felt bad and reached under the pillow to grab my Piggy-Cat paw. 'Sorry, Dad. Love you forever.' I closed my eyes and squeezed the paw. I tried to picture his face and got as far as his sticky-out black hair, but the rest of his features blurred.

Noises came from the kitchen. I promised Dad I wouldn't forget him again, then slipped Piggy-Cat's paw back under my pillow. I picked up the tablet to check out Sally's Facebook profile.

So far I'd kept my Facebook spying a secret, even from Sam. His parents weren't on it anyway. A couple of months ago I'd woken up to find Mum had taken down and hidden all of our family photos in the house. She wouldn't talk about it, but for a while that was okay because I could always sneak onto her Facebook and see Dad there – plus, I knew she'd put the photos back up when she wasn't so mad-sad.

Then one day I logged on and all her pics of Dad had been deleted. My heart pounded in my ears, my hands shaking as I logged out and back in again to check. No pictures. None of it made any sense. When Mum finally came home from work I ran out holding the tablet, nearly screaming at her. I had to bite the sides of my tongue so hard until I could feel my poker face was back on, then I asked if we had any digital photos of Dad. Mum glared at me for ages, until I started to think she'd somehow caught me on her Facebook. Then, in a low, growly voice, she said, 'Not. Now.'

Later she apologised for being tired – but she never answered my question. I asked her a couple more times about the photos of Dad, and she always changed the subject. I searched everywhere, including under the house and in my parents' old phones, but I didn't find anything, not even the framed photos. All my fingers and toes were crossed that Mum had stored them somewhere safe and I'd get to see him again soon.

'Lunch,' Uncle Pike called out.

'Coming!' I rubbed my face and quickly logged onto Mum's Facebook. I found Sally in Mum's friends and clicked on her. She had a terrible profile photo, taken inside her house with all her rubbish in the background. She didn't have many friends, and Ms Everson wasn't one of them.

I did a quick search for Jill Everson and found her, but she had her settings on private. In her profile pic she wore black sunglasses and a straw cowgirl hat, and was holding up a glass of wine.

I went back to Sally and scanned through her photos. All of them were of her and her family – except for a selfie with Ms Everson, who was in her black dress and coat from the night of their fight. It must've been taken just before Sally had chased her down the street. Sally had her arm around Ms Everson's shoulder, but it didn't look friendly, more like she was gripping her. Ms Everson wasn't smiling. Sally had posted it that night at 11.57. She must have been drunk or had trouble with the keyboard, because she had written, 'Good Luck C@#t!!!!!!!!!!!!!!' No one had commented or liked it.

I saved it to my pictures folder, a lesson I'd learned after losing Dad's pics, then zoomed in on Ms Everson. Close up, the dress had a black lace collar with roses, and I could easily see the gold chain against the dark fabric. I moved the pic until I got on to the pendant, then expanded it as much as I could. Two dolphins kissing.

This confirmed it: the pic Todd had sent me was definitely Ms Everson.

I chucked the tablet on my bed, then joined Uncle Pike and Devon in the kitchen. Devon had made me a Christmas-ham sandwich, and 'carb-free' sandwiches for him and Uncle Pike. These had no bread or ham and I suspected were just salads.

'So do we think it's definitely the boyfriend?' my uncle asked.

I bit into my sandwich; it was delicious. 'It's a lead. And she was going to meet him.'

'We need to interview Barry tonight,' Uncle Pike said. 'Ask about the neighbours and Sally. And the kissing-dolphins necklace while we're at it.' He stabbed a cherry tomato with his fork and stared at my sandwich.

'How's your sandwich, honey?' Devon asked my uncle, who grunted.

'Mine's delicious, thank you,' I said.

Uncle Pike narrowed his eyes at me, and I smiled, taking another bite.

Uncle Pike played with his fork. 'This is getting serious for Sally. We need to look at the evidence again – all of it. We need to look at connections between the victim and the murderer.'

I put up my hand. 'Hold on.' I set down my sandwich and scrolled through my phone. 'Wednesday afternoon, the day before Todd's accident, he sent me this.' I showed them the boob pic.

'What is it with your generation?' Uncle Pike said.

'Wait. Look at the necklace. Todd saw Ms Everson's tits for real.'

Uncle Pike and Devon stared at me, then at each other. In the quiet someone's dog barked.

My uncle put down his bowl and shook his head. 'How...? Can you zoom in, Tippy? Do you recognise where he took it?'

I zoomed in and clicked up to get the view behind her shoulder. It came up as white pixel blocks.

Devon leaned over. 'Maybe the classroom?'

'No, we have heaps of stuff on the walls. Ms Everson even put posters over the windows.' Where had Todd been when he took this?

'Would there be any reason for Todd to have seen her breasts at any stage up until now?' my uncle asked.

I shook my head. 'None of us have ever seen Ms Everson's breasts.'

'Not even accidentally plopped out?' Devon said.

'I don't think women's breasts accidentally fall out in front of classrooms of children,' Uncle Pike said.

Devon tapped his fork against his chin. 'It doesn't need to be in front of the whole class.'

'No, none of us at school ever saw her breasts,' I said. 'Trust me, Todd would've told us.'

'Hold on.' Devon cleared the magnets and postcards off the fridge, then held up a blue marker.

'Remember the window?' Uncle Pike said.

'Relax, the fridge is literally a whiteboard that keeps drinks cold.' Devon cracked his knuckles and stretched. 'Right.' He drew a woman with big bosoms and a scribbly blue triangle between her legs.

My uncle sighed. 'Really?'

'What? The bush is back.'

I shrugged. 'It kind of looks like her.' Something nagged in my head. I grabbed my phone.

Devon was drawing the stick man with the cloud head again. 'And then we have the murderer.'

I still didn't like looking at him. 'Yuck.'

'I know, right?' Devon drew the dead cat beside his feet. 'Is that better?'

I shook my head.

Devon drew a speech bubble coming from the murderer and wrote *I heart pandas*.

I grabbed the pen, drew another speech bubble and wrote *I eat snot*.

'Eeew,' we both said, and giggled.

Uncle Pike clapped. 'Focus, please.' He pointed at Ms Everson's boobies. 'Tippy, why didn't Todd just tell you he saw them? Surely that would be big news?'

My body felt cold but my scalp had hot prickles.

'Tippy?' he said. 'You okay? You've gone pale.'

I suddenly felt sick. I went to the sink and poured a glass of water, gripping it hard as I drank. 'I didn't see him again.'

Outside, Bunny Whiskers sunbathed. The kitchen clock ticked. I knew I was right but I didn't want to be. Taking a deep breath, I turned around and asked Devon for the marker. On the fridge I drew another stick man, this one with huge hair. 'Todd Landers,' I said. 'The murderer's first victim.'

'That was an accident, Tippy,' Devon said. 'In the paper the police said—'

Uncle Pike snorted.

'I thought maybe Todd had ... Never mind,' Devon said.

'What?' I said.

'You know, taken his own—'

Uncle Pike's shoulder knocked Devon, who grabbed at the wall to stop himself from falling, accidentally ripping off the calendar. 'Hey!'

'Sorry, I slipped,' my uncle said, giving Devon a weird look.

'This is serious,' I said. 'If I'm right, then Todd's in danger.'

Devon ran his hand through his hair. 'Okay, I need to auto-correct here.' He took the marker off me. 'So let's run with this for a minute. You're saying that Todd' – he put the tip on Todd's eye and drew a line to Ms Everson's boobs, which he circled – 'saw Jill Everson's breasts and somehow' – he drew across to the murderer's cat – 'the murderer knew and wasn't happy about it?'

I nodded.

Devon sucked on the pen. 'But why? Why wasn't he happy?' His lips were blue.

'What if Todd didn't just see her boobs,' I said, 'but also saw her with the murderer?'

Uncle Pike picked up a tea towel and gestured at Devon. 'You've got pen on your mouth.' He tried rubbing Devon's face. 'But she died three days after Todd fell.'

Devon grabbed the cloth and squinted at his reflection in the jug. 'Yes, but what if he's married?'

'Seems a bit far-fetched to try and throw Todd off a bridge and then get rid of your girlfriend,' my uncle said. 'When you could just get a divorce.'

Devon soaked the tea towel in some water. 'Right, so how does Todd know Jill?' He tried rubbing his mouth again but the blue wasn't budging.

My uncle sighed.

'From school,' I said.

Devon chucked the tea towel in the sink. 'So she was Todd's teacher, and Todd was her pupil.' He went back to the fridge and drew more lines between them.

'No, he's in a different class,' I said.

Uncle Pike bounced his fork off his salad. 'We have three people – well, two and one monster – but what was their relationship?'

'What do you mean?' Devon said.

'Well, what tied them together instead of what they had in common?' my uncle said. 'You're my boyfriend and Tippy is my niece and the three of us are together. I'm what we have in common, but I'm not this relationship.'

'So the murderer and Jill were boyfriends and Todd was the nephew?' Devon said.

'We've got to get Todd's phone,' I said. 'He might have pictures of the murderer.'

'What about Russell?' Uncle Pike said. 'He was there and at the crime scene.'

I thought about Sam; he wouldn't be happy if we asked his dad. 'Maybe. He saw Todd fall. But can we try asking Barry first? Sam hates me investigating.'

'Really?' Uncle Pike said. 'Why?'

I shrugged. 'He likes not knowing. Todd accidentally told him the ending of *Se7en* and he cried.'

My uncle frowned. 'You guys watched *Se7en*?'

'Spoiler alert,' Devon said. 'Hang on, should we be looking for a box?'

'Maybe?' I said.

Uncle Pike pinched the pen from Devon. He read its label and frowned. 'No wonder you can't get it off your face.' He tried to rub a line from the fridge. 'This is a permanent marker ... again.'

'I liked the shape of it,' Devon said. His tongue was blue as well. 'You got it off last time.'

'Bitches!' Melanie yelled from the front door.

'Shit.' I grabbed the wet tea towel and tried to clean the fridge, but it only smeared the ink a little.

'Coming!' Uncle Pike said. 'Fix this,' he growled and hobbled out of the kitchen.

Devon grabbed the magnets and postcards, putting them over the drawings of the murderer and Todd, while I tried to wipe off the marker. I gave up and put a postcard over naked Ms Everson, clicking on a tiger fridge magnet to keep it in place.

Devon let out a big sigh. We did a silent high five then started giggling. We covered our mouths and tried to keep quiet, but that only made it worse until we both snorted with laughter. My stomach muscles ached; I bit down on a tea towel. Devon kept his hand over his mouth, his eyes nearly popping out. With a final snort he shook his head and ran outside.

Sam's dad dropped him off for dinner. As soon as he got out of the car, he started taking the piss out of my hair – and not very well. 'Whoa! You look like a rock chick, or one of those matchsticks.'

'Whatever, Hero-Son.'

We waved goodbye to his dad. I noticed green jelly smeared on the back of Sam's knee.

'When did you have jelly?' I asked.

He shrugged. 'Why? Are we having some tonight?'

'You've got some on the back of your knee.'

He wiped it with his sleeve, smearing jelly on his clean, pale-blue hoodie.

'How's Todd doing?' I said.

Sam shrugged again. 'Mum says he's the same. Still can't have any visitors.' He kicked a stone into the garden. 'Man, this sucks.'

'Yup.' Me and Sam had hung out a lot, just the two of us. But now it always felt like Todd was missing, like he'd show up any moment and tell us it was all a prank.

Bunny Whiskers jumped off the Browns' car and nibbled on some grass.

'Let's follow the cat.' Sam loved Bunny Whiskers. He wasn't allowed a pet because his mum said he was allergic, but whenever he played with the cat here, he was fine. He ran through the bushes onto the Browns' lawn. I spied Bunny Whiskers at the end of the house, near Melanie's smoking spot. Sam ran ahead and I followed, then stopped when I saw movement in the Browns' bedroom. I crouched in the shadows beside their window and peeped in.

Mr Brown sat naked with his back to the window, a beach towel wrapped around his shoulders. His skinny arms poked out from underneath, his skin loose and baggy. Laid out on the bed beside him were his pyjamas. He was on one of those shower chairs with wheels. Me and Sam had played with them at the medical centre while we waited for our parents to finish work. Usually those games ended with one of us ramming the other into a wall.

Mrs Brown appeared from the hallway. She came over and smoothed down her husband's half-dried, sticky-out white hair then leaned over and, struggling, lifted him off the chair and onto the bed. She smiled, saying something to him, and went to take his towel. He smacked her arm away. As she flinched, he grabbed her forearm and yanked her towards him.

'What's going on there?' Sam called out.

I ducked down and put my finger to my lips, crab-walking past their window and joining him in the sun. 'Nothing,' I said. 'And not so loud.'

Bunny Whiskers squirmed in his arms.

'Let her go,' I said.

Sam kissed her head and dropped her on the lawn. She bolted into the hedge but then came out again and stalked back towards us.

I heard a car pull up. I ran back up the slope, leaving Sam with the cat. As I passed the Browns' bedroom the curtains were pulled.

Barry was standing by our mailbox. He seemed nervous, holding a bottle of wine like it was an expensive antique vase. He was out of his uniform, in blue jeans and probably his best going-out shirt, which wasn't ironed very well. He carefully handed me the wine bottle. 'Hello.'

'Thanks.' The glass felt a bit greasy from sweat.

'Not for you, though,' he stammered. 'You're a minor.'

'That's okay.' I smiled at him. 'Please, come in.'

Inside, Uncle Pike opened the wine while Devon got the glasses.

I left them and joined Sam out on the balcony, handing him a lemonade.

'Did Todd have any enemies?' I asked after a moment. I'd tried but couldn't think of anyone who'd want to hurt him.

'Only everyone,' Sam said.

We laughed; Todd did love to annoy people.

Sam bent down and picked up a twig, throwing it over the side. 'Dad says Ms Everson's head should show up anytime now.'

I thought of the box from *Se7en*. 'Why? What makes him so sure?'

Sam leaned on the balcony rail. 'Dunno. 'Cause her hair showed up, I guess.'

I rested on the wooden rail too and looked down at the town. The river glowed golden from the low-lying evening sun. Lights in homes and orange streetlights were just starting to turn on. Across at the showgrounds, the Ferris wheel was nearly complete. I found it hard to imagine anything sinister happening here.

He half turned, squinting against the light. 'She would've needed shoes, so her body could walk around after her head had gone.'

Talking rubbish was one of our things. It felt good that after everything, and with Todd gone, we could still talk crap. 'You don't need shoes to be able to walk,' I said.

'There's lots of prickles and stuff.'

I sighed. 'Your head's more important than your shoes.'

'Only if you're a matchstick.' Sam laughed, and I groaned.

'Have you walked on prickles in bare feet?' he said. 'Maybe that's what the killer thought too.'

'Really? Why? Did your dad say something?'

'Why do you keep asking that? You promised no boring Nanny Drew.'

I never promised Sam that; it was just his sign he was getting sick of my questions and would soon stop answering.

'Hang on,' I said, ignoring his bait. 'She did have a shoe on. So, according to your theory, she could still hop.'

'True, as she clutched her Emily Watson flowers.'

I giggled. 'You love those flowers.'

'You do.' Sam leaned over the rail. 'No, he doesn't think it's a local.'

'Why not?'

He shrugged and dropped a spit ball over the side.

'Gross,' I said.

He was quiet. Question time was over.

Devon came onto the balcony, wheeling the barbecue. He stopped to take in the view. 'This light is fabulous. Entrée is ready.'

Sam pushed himself up off the rail and we went inside. On the table were two bowls of dips and a basket of pita bread. One dip was hummus and the other had a funny name – baba ghanoush – which Sam kept saying. I tried only a little bit of it on some bread; it tasted kind of smoky. Uncle Pike loved it.

'What's this called again?' Barry said.

'Baba ghanoush,' Sam said and dipped more bread into it.

'It's very good,' Barry said.

Devon grabbed a plate of meat from the kitchen. 'Thank you. The lamb and chicken skewers won't be long.'

'Do you want me to do anything?' Uncle Pike yelled out.

'No, honey, just look after our guests and your foot,' Devon called back.

'More wine, Barry?'

The policeman put his hand over his half-full glass. 'I'm driving, so better not.'

'Terrible business what happened,' my uncle said to him.

'What business?'

Uncle Pike glanced at Sam. 'You know ... what happened. Where we met.'

Barry blushed. 'You said you wouldn't tell.'

My uncle frowned. 'Wouldn't tell what?'

'Are you talking about the murder?' Sam said. 'Baba ghanoush!' He drummed his fingers on the table.

'Yes, and don't do that,' Uncle Pike said.

Barry leaned back in his chair. 'Ahh.'

Sam stopped drumming and stood on his chair. As he crawled over the table to grab a piece of pita bread, he spilled his lemonade. 'Sorry.'

I jumped up to get a cloth as Devon came back inside. He opened the fridge and took out two salads. 'Something I prepared earlier – tabouleh and fattoush.' He put them on the table and went back out to the barbecue as I mopped up Sam's mess. The fried pita bread in one of the salads looked like corn chips, and my mouth watered.

'Yes,' Barry said. 'A very terrible business.' He glanced over at me and Sam.

'Did her neighbours see anything?' Uncle Pike asked Barry.

He shook his head. 'And that old fella in the front unit is blind anyway.'

'You haven't talked to him?' My uncle frowned. 'But he may know something.'

We stared at Barry, who was frowning too, like he didn't get it.

'He may have even heard something?' Uncle Pike said.

'Ah, okay,' Barry said. 'Good to know.'

I tried not to look shocked, and my uncle's eyes widened. He took a large drink. 'And that poor witness who found the body.'

'Suzie Pratt,' Sam said, before stuffing his face with more pita bread.

We all stared at him. Suzie was only like five years old.

'That's not public knowledge,' Barry said.

'What?' Sam shrugged. 'Dad works with you guys on crime scenes. I hear things.'

I wished he'd tell me all of those things.

'Tippy!' Devon called. I poked my head out, and he asked for a dish to serve the skewers on.

Poor Suzie. Her classroom was near ours. Sometimes Sam's dad was late to pick us up after school, so we'd play outside. If Suzie's mum was late we'd keep an eye on the little girl until she arrived. She was late a lot.

I grabbed a metal server from near the hot oven and went back while Devon piled it up with delicious-smelling lamb and chicken skewers.

'Is the oven supposed to be on?' I asked him.

'Shit. Thanks.' He switched off the barbecue and ran inside.

As I put down the serving dish, Devon came over with a hot platter.

'Careful,' he said. 'This is kibbeh and also falafel.' He set it down far from Sam's reach. 'Dinner is served. *Bon appetit.*'

We all clapped, and he took a bow. When he sat down, we heaped up our plates.

'So, is it true Sally Homer did it?' Uncle Pike said, attacking a chicken skewer.

Devon nodded. 'That's what I heard too.'

'This is delicious, by the way,' Uncle Pike said. Devon grabbed his hand and kissed it.

'If by that,' Barry said, 'you mean are we looking for anyone else, then the answer would be no.'

This time I couldn't hide my shock.

Uncle Pike shot Devon a look, while Barry lifted up a lamb skewer. 'These are delicious.'

As we ate, Uncle Pike and Devon talked with Barry at the other end of the table about gay things. I asked Sam if he remembered Ms Everson wearing a necklace.

'She had no head,' he said.

'Did your dad and the police say anything?'

Sam gave me a strange look then smiled and nodded at Barry. 'Let's ask.'

'No, Sam—'

'I told you. No more Nanny.' He put his hand on my wrist and yelled, 'Hey, Barry, did you find a necklace?'

The adults stopped talking.

'On the body?' Sam said. 'Tippy wants to know.'

'Dick!' I hissed and stomped on his foot under the table.

'Ow!' He let go of my arm.

Barry frowned at me. I quickly tried to think of something to say that wasn't creepy. 'I just remember her wearing a pretty gold one, that's all.'

Devon winked at me and turned to Barry. 'Gold can be very pretty.'

The policeman stammered, 'Not that I could say if a necklace had been found anyway.'

'So there wasn't a necklace?' Uncle Pike said.

'I didn't say that—'

'There *was* a necklace?'

'Not on the body,' Sam said. 'Not at the crime scene. Just like her phone.'

Barry stood up. 'The missing necklace and phone is not public knowledge. You can't keep saying these things.'

Sam laughed. 'I didn't. You just did.'

Barry turned red, and Uncle Pike managed to convince him we had no idea what any of it meant.

'That was mean,' I whispered to Sam.

'I told you, no more,' he said. Once Sam said something, he usually followed through. He shrugged then grinned at me, doing breakdance arm waves.

I found it hard to stay mad at him, even when he did Todd-stunts like that. Todd was a bad influence. I missed him; he would've loved Sam's performance tonight. *Todd better wake up soon.*

'Peace?' Sam asked me.

'Help me clear the table and I'll think about it.'

He did, even drying the dishes and wiping the bench, while Barry had a coffee then said goodnight. Sam's dad arrived soon after. As I walked Sam out, we laughed about how freaked out Barry had been.

'Poor Barry,' I said.

'Why? We all know what was there.' He jumped in the car, and Mr Campbell gave me a wave. I waved back as Sam wound down his window. 'Bye, Matchstick.'

'It's not going to catch on,' I said. 'Hero-Son.'

After they left, Devon pulled open the curtains. Under *witness* he wrote *Suzie Pratt* and under *missin* he wrote *gold kissing-dolphins necklace*.

'We should code name this "The Case of the Missing Necklace",' I said.

'Better than the scalped school teacher,' Uncle Pike said.

Devon stood on his tip-toes and in big letters at the top of the window wrote, *The Case of the Missin' Necklace*. He pointed his marker to *Missin'*. 'Get it?' he said.

We ignored him again.

Out the other living-room windows the lights of Riverstone twinkled. Somewhere, out there, was a murderer. Were they keeping Ms Everson's kissing-dolphins necklace as a trophy? And her head? I shuddered as I lifted my tablet to take another photo for our case file.

CHAPTER NINE
What Suzie Saw

The Pratts' living room was what Uncle Pike described as 'shabby shit' and 'depressing'. Wafts of vomit came out of the sofa, making my nose wrinkle as I sat on it. I rested my head and noticed what I hoped were dried milk and chocolate stains. I sprang forward and turned around; where my hair had been were worse-looking stains.

Devon couldn't hide his shock. 'The horror. What colour are these walls? Armpit stain? Yellow teeth? I just don't understand it at all.'

A big picture window overlooked the front yard and the driveway. Covering the bottom half of the window were cloudy smudges, streaks and what looked like snail trails. I could also make out small handprints. Out in the garden Suzie Pratt played with a large beachball. Her matted black hair looked like a bad-tempered bird's nest. She wore a red puffer jacket and a grubby grey tutu that might have once been pink.

Uncle Pike watched her. 'How old is she?'

I shrugged. 'Five.'

'Really? At five you were playing the violin, not running around the garden like a troll.'

'She started school last term – and I don't play the violin.'

He tried to get comfortable in his tiny chair. 'You should've kept practising. What a terrible waste.'

'I never played the violin,' I said. A blowfly buzzed past and banged against the glass. It reminded me of the crime scene. 'She can be a bit angry.'

Suzie glared at us; her fists were clenched and snot ran into her open mouth. She kicked the ball at the window but didn't get enough grunt and it fell short.

'Rabies?' Uncle Pike asked.

Devon was rocking back and forth, staring straight at the wall, his eyes wide. 'Awful, just awful.'

Suzie's bulky jacket got in the way of her picking up the ball; she kept leaning over and accidentally kicking it. She screamed.

'And Mrs Pratt and Mr Pratt aren't brother and sister?' Uncle Pike said.

'I'm not sure that's appropriate,' I said.

Mrs Pratt came into the room carrying a spotless silver tray with teacups, milk, sugar, a teapot and chocolate-chip biscuits. 'What's not appropriate?'

My face started to burn. 'Smoking.'

'Hear, hear,' my uncle said. 'And plenty more of it too.'

This bewildered Mrs Pratt, who carefully placed the tray on the coffee table.

Devon snapped out of his trance and flashed his super-white teeth. 'What a beautiful tea set.'

She licked her lips and sat down. 'Thank you. It was my mother's. One day it will be Suzie's.'

That seemed a bit creepy but at least the cups were clean – of course, Suzie could have licked the teaspoons. Even though it was twenty-eight degrees outside, the heater was on full blast. Beads of sweat shone on Uncle Pike's pink face.

'Suzie likes it warm.' Mrs Pratt rolled up her sleeves. She smiled and waved at Suzie, who frowned and tried to boot the ball into the window again. 'Did you ever want to have kids?' Mrs Pratt asked my uncle.

'I always thought I'd be good at baking pies.'

She poured the tea. 'You don't need to have children to do that.'

'What a very odd thing to say,' Uncle Pike said. 'Did you ever want children?'

She smiled at him. 'Milk? Sugar?'

We helped ourselves to biscuits – well I did, anyway.

Devon used his Serious Police Voice that we had practised. 'How's Suzie been since the incident?'

'She won't go to school.' Mrs Pratt tried to smile then looked down at her hands. 'She won't talk about it. Anytime I try to raise it with her, she tells me to eff off.'

'Is that normal for Suzie?' Uncle Pike said.

'She can get a bit upset sometimes. Other than that she's just been Suzie.'

From outside, the little girl spotted my biscuit. Her face screwed up and she started screaming. I took it out of my mouth and she stopped. I slowly put it on the table and she cocked her head, following it. She began banging on the glass and shouting.

'Is she okay?' Devon asked, his turn to be bewildered.

I couldn't make out Suzie's words, though I suspected 'biscuit' may have been one of them. I lifted my biscuit up again, and sure enough her banging and shouting increased.

'Oh, the poor darling,' said Mrs Pratt. 'I better let her in.'

Uncle Pike looked horrified, and Devon had his mouth open. I couldn't help smiling, and covered my mouth with my hand. Laughter bubbled up from my tummy.

'Mummy's coming, honey.'

I sucked in my cheeks and bit them, but Devon and Uncle Pike's expressions were just making it worse. My uncle mouthed, 'What the fuck?' and I couldn't stop a laugh escaping.

Mrs Pratt turned around.

'Sorry, burned my mouth,' I said, waving my hand in front of it.

She nodded and went back to her possessed daughter.

I pinched my nose. I had to get out of here before I had a complete giggling fit. Definitely before Suzie came in, as she would set me off. 'Toilet,' I said to no one in particular and quickly ran out of the room.

The hallway was dark and cool after the heat of the front room. Suzie's half-open bedroom door was easy to spot, with wooden clown letters spelling her name. I peeked in. It was a complete mess, like a tornado had just been through – a tornado that had wet the bed, by the smell. On the walls were some of Suzie's drawings. They all seemed pretty normal. A picture of her and a yellow lion. One of her and I guessed her mum and a rainbow. One with a green scribble mess on one side, Susie in the middle, and on the other side a stick prince with a jagged red crown – well, I hoped that's what it was and not her dad with his head exploding.

It gave me an idea. I went back to the living room.

Suzie was stuffing her face with biscuits and gulping milk. She refilled her glass, emptying the milk jug, then yelled for more. Mrs Pratt smiled and picked up the jug, excusing herself. Suzie took turns glaring at Uncle Pike and then Devon.

'Do you like to draw, Suzie?' I asked.

She stared at me then slowly nodded. I felt like she was trying to work out my angle.

'How about we draw some pictures while the grown-ups talk?'

'Splendid idea,' my uncle said. Suzie whipped her head around to face him. 'Disconcerting to say the least, my little piranha.'

Mrs Pratt came back into the room.

'Is it okay if Suzie and I do some drawing,' I said. 'Please, Mrs Pratt?'

She looked relieved. 'Yes, of course. Suzie, can you show Tippy where the paper and crayons are?'

'No!'

'Please, darling?'

Suzie started screaming at a pitch so high it made my teeth hurt.

My plan wouldn't work if we couldn't draw. 'It's okay, Mrs Pratt, I'll get them for Suzie.'

Mrs Pratt told me where to find the paper and crayons. I grabbed them, and took Suzie, with her fistful of biscuits, to sit at the other end of the living room, hopefully out of earshot of her mum. The carpet was damp. I tried not to think about why as I handed Suzie some paper and a book for backing, then put the crayons in the middle. I drew a picture of the traffic light and grass where Ms Everson's body had been found. Suzie watched me then started to draw the same.

I quickly got a plate of biscuits and more milk from the adults' tray. I mouthed 'more time' to Uncle Pike; I wanted to keep Suzie drawing for as long as possible.

He asked Mrs Pratt if she had any photos of Suzie. Mrs Pratt was only too happy to show them all the photos she had.

'That's great, Suzie,' I said, sitting back down. She had just finished the traffic light and grass. 'Do you think you can draw this the same as when you found the body?'

The room had gone quiet. I hunched over, waiting for Mrs Pratt to start telling me off. Suzie stared at me. The loudest noise in the room was her mouth breathing. The adults started to speak again, and I exhaled.

Suzie snatched the biscuits and was stuffing them into her mouth while she began to draw with a black crayon. Crumbs covered the carpet and got mushed into the picture with her scribbling. She pressed so hard she broke the crayon and screamed.

'You kids all right?' Mrs Pratt called out.

Suzie threw the black crayon at the yellow wall.

'Yes.' I didn't want Mrs Pratt coming over. 'Suzie's a good drawer, aren't you?' She ignored me, as she smashed in another biscuit. Mrs Pratt turned back to my uncle and Devon.

Suzie's drawing had the traffic light, grass, sun and now a headless stick figure. She drew a tree in the middle, then grabbed the red crayon and went wild, scribbling over the stick figure and the grass. I glanced up, worried Mrs Pratt would join us. Devon noticed and asked her if he could have some more tea. She got up and looked over. I smiled and waved, and she went to the kitchen.

I rushed over to Devon and my uncle. 'I need five more minutes.' They nodded, and I went back and crouched by Suzie.

She had drawn a brown car and a stick figure beside it. Antlers were coming out of its head.

I shuddered and felt a chill despite the blasting heater. 'Is this a man?'

Suzie didn't look up but nodded. She drew circles at the ends of its arms.

'What are those, Suzie?' She ignored me. 'Are they bags?' She nodded and started to get up. I needed more time. 'Suzie, was this ... man there when you saw this?' I pointed to the body.

She cocked her head at me and pointed to the man with her crayon. 'Slay.'

I gasped, stumbling away from her. She tipped over the empty biscuit plate and got up. I reached for her drawing but she snatched it away. 'Can I have it, please? It's such a good drawing.'

She stared at me as she slowly tore it up then scrunched it into a ball. I copied her, crumpling mine as well. She stopped and watched me, breathing heavily.

I reached out my hand. 'Swap?'

She jerked hers away and started screaming again.

'Suzie?' Mrs Pratt shot up out of her chair. 'Mummy's coming, darling.'

I plucked Suzie's crumpled-up picture from her hand. It drove her wild; she lashed out and scratched my face. 'No!'

I threw my picture at her.

Mrs Pratt hurried over. 'I'm sorry but I think you better go.'

Suzie screamed even louder, which I hadn't thought was possible, and started slashing the walls with the red crayon.

'Go, now!' her mum said.

We got out fast and clambered into the car. My ears were still ringing. I held up the crumpled, damp ball and told them about the picture.

'Outstanding, Tippy Chan,' my uncle said. 'Well done.'

'That's amazing, Tippy. You're so clever.' Devon started the car and reversed.

I locked my door, worried Mrs Pratt would uncrumple my picture and get mad.

'We managed to get the time she saw it,' Uncle Pike said. 'Twenty to eleven, when Sally was in church. And then we got the Suzie birthing story, in every excruciating detail.' He and Devon shuddered.

'Possibly more excruciating for Mrs Pratt,' Devon said.

'That's debatable,' my uncle said.

As we drove down the driveway, Suzie pressed her nose against the window like a pig. I could make out the snot snail trails over the bottom half. She smacked her hand on the glass.

'Wow, she's one creepy mother...' Uncle Pike said. 'Are we sure the killer isn't Suzie?'

I shrugged. 'Not one hundred per cent.'

Devon shuddered again. 'I can see why the murderer left her alone.'

'Speaking of alone,' I said, 'how come she was over there by herself?'

'Her mother couldn't find her,' my uncle said. 'Apparently that's just Suzie.'

'Lucky she wasn't run over,' Devon said.

'Seen any cars around here?' Uncle Pike said. 'Besides the ones surrounding the house.' It was true – not one car had driven past the whole time we'd been at the Pratts, or the last time when we visited the crime scene.

'So the killer must be local,' Devon said.

'Why?' I asked.

'How else would you know there's no traffic here?'

We drove around the corner to the crime scene and parked where we had last time.

I flattened Suzie's torn-up crime-scene sketch on my thigh and got my pink plastic Sellotape snail out. Dad had given me a new snail tape dispenser every Christmas, except for the year he gave me Piggy-Cat. I didn't know what had happened to the ones from the years before; they'd just kind of disappeared. He would hand me his terribly wrapped present, and I'd pretend not to know what it was. 'Surprise!' he'd say when I opened it. The only surprise really was what colour plastic snail it would be. I loved getting them.

I pushed my thumb down hard on the jagged plastic edge

between the pink snail's stalks. This year I wouldn't get one. Never again. My body suddenly felt very heavy.

Uncle Pike turned around in his seat. 'You carry sticky tape?'

'It's part of a detective kit.' I cleared my thick throat and concentrated on sticking the picture together. 'It's handy for fingerprints.' I paused and held up *The Know-How Book of Detection*, which I'd brought with me just in case.

'My God, that was one of my favourite books!' my uncle said.

I passed it over. He showed Devon his name written on the inside cover.

'Who was going to steal your books that you had to write your name inside each of them?'

'Clearly it worked, because here we are.' Uncle Pike waved the book in front of Devon.

We got out of the car. The air still stank of silage; I breathed through my mouth to try to not smell the sweet rot. I heard a vehicle approaching in the distance. Through the willow branches and across the river I got a glimpse of the main road. A milk tanker drove past. I waved but doubted they could see me. I patched together the rest of Suzie's drawing and spread it on the car bonnet. I glanced up and caught Uncle Pike mouthing something to Devon.

'What?' I said.

Uncle Pike balanced on his good leg, using Devon and the car as makeshift crutches. 'I said "fucking hell", which seems appropriate as this thing with horns looks satanic.'

'It creeps me out,' I said. 'Suzie even said "slay" when she pointed at it.'

'Holy shit!' He pushed himself off the bonnet. 'What's the female name for Damien?'

'Diamante?' Devon said.

'I'd stay away from balconies if I was Mrs Pratt.'

I held up the picture to the road, trying to work out where the car would have been.

My uncle leaned over. 'So we're looking for a brown car and something from *The Omen* on a shopping spree.'

Devon lifted his big black purse. 'Man bags?'

'She did say it was a man,' I said.

'Okay, a male horned demon with bags,' Uncle Pike said.

'I thought demons were genderless?' Devon said. 'How about I run up the road with my man bag?'

My uncle gave me a nod. 'Great idea. Run until you hear Tippy yell.'

Devon bounded up the road. I waited until he got to where the thing in the picture appeared to be. 'Stop!' He froze, then posed with his purse.

'It's hard to tell from the scale in this masterpiece,' Uncle Pike said, 'but it looks like Suzie's bags are bigger.'

'Rubbish bags?' I said.

'Genius.' He waved for Devon to come back.

'What do you think the bags were for?' I said.

'Well, one would be for her head.'

I lifted up the drawing again. 'And her shoe, and maybe clothes?'

My uncle pulled on his beard. 'Hmm. I mean, why have bags, unless he's collecting the evidence?'

'Worried about littering?' I said. 'And why leave a shoe behind?' Suzie was so lucky the murderer hadn't seen her. 'Didn't the police ask her this?'

'Mrs Pratt said Suzie didn't want to talk to the police, but she pointed out where the body was.'

Devon was still in the same spot, doing some kind of dance.

I walked over to the side of the road, next to the edge of the taped-off area. Here the riverbank was closer and willow branches hung over the fence. 'Also, if the killer was here at the same time as Suzie, he may have seen her. She could be a target.'

Uncle Pike leaned on the car. 'I don't think he saw her, otherwise would she still be alive?'

One of the fence posts was broken at the base and the wires sagged to the ground. It was easy to climb over; Suzie would've had no trouble. On the other side I moved the picture around, picking a willow tree. I climbed under its branches. From beside its trunk, Devon still appeared to be in the right position. He was checking out something in the grass on the side of the road. As I circled the tree, the brown-stained grass came into view. *Poor Suzie – this must be where she hid*. I searched the area around the roots and found a little yellow plastic lion. 'Over here!'

On one crutch, Uncle Pike shuffle-hopped along to the fence. I stood on the wires, pushing them down even further for him, and he sort of pole-vaulted over, trying not to squash me.

I showed him the views from the tree and what I'd found.

'She saw everything...' my uncle said, shaking his head. 'Poor sausage.'

Devon joined us and I filled him in. 'She needs counselling,' he said. 'Like, she needed it anyway, but this...' His eyes were teary. I put my hand on his shoulder, and he gave me a big bear hug, lifting me off the ground. As we headed back he wiped his eyes with the back of his fists. 'Does anyone drive brown cars anymore? I mean, is that a thing around here?'

Uncle Pike dumped himself in the passenger seat. He tried to stuff his crutches in beside him but they got caught around his legs. I grabbed them as Devon started the engine.

'The Browns' car is fawn,' I said, shoving the crutches into the back seat and shutting my door.

'Yuck,' my uncle said. 'Code Brown.'

I giggled. 'Code Brown is what they say at the pool when there's a floating poo.'

'Hmm,' Uncle Pike said. 'I know.'

I thought about Mrs Brown lifting Mr Brown; she was strong. Devon turned around and held out his closed hands for me to pick one. When I tapped his fist nearest me, he opened it. 'I found this by the road,' he said. 'Clue!' On his palm was a rectangular silver case engraved with the initials D.N.

CHAPTER TEN
A Bully at the *Bully*

Back home I checked the mail while Uncle Pike and Devon headed inside. I pulled out the *Bully*. Evil Sea-Hag, Lorraine Ashton, was on the front page again, this time interviewing Ms Everson's next-door neighbours on what the TV and newspaper were now calling the 'Christmas Tragedy'. I quickly read Lorraine's article. One neighbour, who didn't want to be named, used to hear a male voice with Ms Everson, often late at night. In the rest of the article, neighbours shared memories of my teacher, like how she took her own bins out. Nothing we didn't already know.

Checking the mailbox again I noticed something white at the back. I crouched down. It was a white paper version of Emily Watson's delicate flower.

I plucked the origami out, twirling it in my fingers. It wasn't mine. Thanks to Sam's story from last night's dinner, an image of my naked, headless teacher popped into my mind, lurching along on one high heel towards the traffic light, her fists stuffed with these white paper lilies. I shuddered and held it away from me as I went inside to double-check it wasn't my flower and that I wasn't going mad.

In my bedroom, my red origami lily lay on the windowsill where I'd left it. I held up the white paper flower and relaxed. Sam's idea of a sick joke – he must've planted it last night.

'Tippy!' Uncle Pike called out from the living room.

'Coming.' I ripped the flower up and put it in the wheelie bin; I'd make Sam pay later.

I joined my uncle and Devon on the couch. After handing Uncle Pike the *Bully*, I told them about the neighbour hearing a man.

'At least someone finally spoke to the neighbours,' my uncle said, scanning the front page.

'The mysterious boyfriend.' Devon went over to his window. 'So much to fill in.' He picked up a blue marker and put a tick beside

Suzie's name. On the *Sunday* timeline he wrote *10.40 a.m.* and above it drew a traffic light.

My uncle was flicking through the paper. 'Wouldn't a Christmas tragedy happen, I don't know, on Christmas Day?' He folded the paper and frisbeed it into the wall.

Devon pulled over a dining chair and stood on it. 'But wait, there's more.' On the murderer's black-cloud head he drew some horns and gave him a pitchfork tail. I hadn't thought it was possible for Devon to make it any scarier, but he had. He drew an arrow pointing between the murderer and the traffic light. In the suspect box under Sally's name he wrote *boyfriend* and under that he wrote *D.N.*

Uncle Pike massaged his temples. 'For fuck's sake, cross off Sally.'

I shot Devon a look and gave him a little nod. I might not like her, and her alibi sucked, but she hadn't done it. Devon put a line through her name, leaving only *boyfriend* and *D.N.* in the suspect box.

'Duncan Nunn?' I said. 'He's the only D.N. I can think of.'

'Seems to be the right demographic for an engraved-silver business-card holder,' Uncle Pike said. He shook his pill bottle and opened it.

'And he does hand out his cards a lot.' I got my uncle a glass of water. 'He isn't tall, though.'

'And I wouldn't call his "hair" blond,' my uncle said, swallowing his painkillers.

'More like taupe or overflowing-ashtray,' Devon said. 'Also, what is his...' He wrote *Motive?* on the window and pointed to it.

I shrugged. 'Melanie says he's a perv.'

Devon wrote *pervert* under *Motive?*

'Rejection, maybe?' Uncle Pike said. He tapped his forehead with his finger. 'Let's park this for now.'

Devon wrote *rejection* and drew a fluffy cloud around *Motive?*

'What about Mrs Brown?' I said.

They stared at me.

'She's the one who talked about the boyfriend – he might not exist.

The male voice could just be a friend. And their car is brown, and she didn't like my teacher. Also she is strong enough.' When I told them about what I'd seen through the window, they seemed upset.

'That is not okay,' Uncle Pike said. 'Not about you looking through their windows, though that's probably not okay either.'

'I'm going to say something to them,' Devon said.

'Good, let me know if you want me to come with you.' My uncle turned to me. 'Number one Nancys rule and all, but how about we keep her as a runner-up for now?'

'Fine.' I didn't know why her name wasn't on the window.

Devon sniffed the pen. 'There is someone else.' In the suspects' box under *D.N.* he wrote *Horn-blower* then drew a penis with big hairy balls and water squirting out of it.

I giggled.

My uncle's mouth dropped open.

'Questions?' Devon said.

'So many...' Uncle Pike said.

'He's tall and got blond hair,' I said. 'Unlike Duncan Nunn.'

Devon nodded. 'And he's a...' He drew around the penis, pressing hard enough to make the pen squeak.

'Not great for Tippy,' my uncle said.

I shrugged. 'Todd always draws them, or makes them out of emojis.' I wondered how he was, if he was awake yet.

Uncle Pike shook his head. 'Wow. Okay ... there is no way, but let's go with this for a moment. Why would he kill Ms Everson?'

'Career,' I said. 'He's on TV all the time now.' On screen Horn-blower was trying to interview Ms Everson's blind neighbour through his wedged-open front door.

'He's horrible,' Devon said. 'And he makes bad makeup choices.' He covered his eyes and pointed to the TV. 'Again with that ugly red lipstick.'

'He talks different on TV as well,' I said.

Devon nodded. 'Like he is two people.'

'Hmmm,' Uncle Pike said. 'But a murderer?'

'And he lives in Auckland,' I said.

My uncle looked at me.

'What?' I said. 'He was in Riverstone when it happened. And he said "murder", remember? Before there was any murder.'

'Still...'

'First rule,' I said.

'Why are you defending him?' Devon said. 'You still have feelings for him?'

Uncle Pike sighed. 'This is ridiculous.'

Devon smacked the cap back on the pen and shook his head. 'I can't believe this.' He handed it to me. 'Why won't you talk to me about him?'

My uncle sat frozen, staring at Devon.

'Anything?'

Uncle Pike bit his lip and shrugged.

'Unbelievable.' Devon went to the kitchen.

I glared at Uncle Pike. 'What?' he said.

'Remember what you told me in the car about being a dick?' I shook my head and left him on the couch.

In the kitchen, I gave Devon a hug. 'Thanks,' he said.

'Now, Tippy,' Uncle Pike said in a stern voice from the couch. Devon turned on the kitchen taps full throttle, but I could still hear my uncle over the waterfall noise. 'There's someone we'll need to meet if we're serious about solving this mystery.'

'Duncan Nunn?' I could only see Uncle Pike's moon boot as I grabbed a tea towel off the oven handle.

'I like how you call it a mystery,' Devon called out, turning off the taps. He started washing the lunch plates. 'It makes it sound so much nicer than hunting down a killer.'

'Thank you, darling,' my uncle said.

I was still trying to work out whether he was being sarcastic or not.

'And yes, Duncan Nunn,' he said, 'but I was thinking of someone else as well.'

I frowned. 'Horn-blower?' I checked Devon. He stopped washing and grabbed the tea towel off me.

He dried his hands. 'Are you kid—'

'Definitely not.' Uncle Pike popped up above the back of the couch. 'But, Tippy, I understand if you don't want to meet them – it's your choice.'

Devon nodded at me. 'Remember, you always have a choice.'

'Okay,' I said. 'Who?'

'Sea-Hag,' my uncle said.

As I stared at him, Devon dropped a plate on the bench.

Uncle Pike held up his hands. 'Listen. We need to interview her and find out what she knows. Unfortunately, she's probably the most informed out of anyone, including the police.'

Lorraine Ashton's bio pic glared up at me from an old *Bully*.

Uncle Pike grabbed his crutches and hoisted himself up. 'Totally understand if you want to sit this one out. Maybe we could ask Mrs Brown to look after you?'

I didn't know what Sea-Hag had done to my parents, but I didn't care as long as we got clues to stop the monster and save Todd and anyone else from dying. Plus, solving the murder had been my idea. And I was not about to hang out with Mrs Brown.

Devon stopped washing the dishes and leaned his hip against the sink. Uncle Pike shuffled to the dining table. They stared at me, waiting for an answer.

'I'm in,' I said. 'We can't just keep interviewing Sally, and we at least need the name of the boyfriend. Sea-Hag can go—'

The tablet on the bench lit up and beep-bopped with an incoming video call. It was Mum, and suddenly I felt very guilty.

Her face loomed on the screen and she frowned at me. 'Have you dyed your hair?'

Shit. 'Uncle Pike cut it,' I said, avoiding the dye question. Mum humphed and was about to say something else, but I cut her off. 'Can I see out the porthole?'

She asked me what I had been up to as she showed me the

different shades of blue out her cabin's porthole. I didn't mention Lorraine Ashton and definitely nothing about our mystery club.

'How's school?'

Uncle Pike rang his annoying bell behind me. 'Cancelled it,' he yelled out. 'I needed an assistant.'

I turned and held the tablet up so Mum could see us both.

'What? Did you get that from my room?' Mum yelled back. 'And stop pulling Tippy out of school. She needs routine.'

I smiled. 'Miss you.'

Mum shook her head at my uncle then gazed at me and kissed the screen. 'Can't wait to get back and see you. Until then, keep wearing the red jacket.'

I laughed.

She frowned. 'I'm not joking.'

'It's too hot.' I showed her the sunny day outside the kitchen window.

'Is Melanie Brown smoking?'

Whoops. 'Bye, Mum.' I couldn't believe her trip was nearly half over; it had gone so fast. She'd be home in eight days, which was great, but it would also mean the end of The Nancys. I tried not to think about that. We just needed to solve this mystery fast.

From across the road we watched Lorraine Ashton through the *Riverstone Bulletin*'s large windows. She was charging around the open-plan office with a phone stuck to her ear. Her face was red, but it wasn't from the shouting she was doing. She stopped and held a piece of paper close to her face and then further away. I remembered her having squinty eyes like small black beads. She shoved the paper in front of a mousy-haired blob slumped at a desk; he visibly shrank, and I fully expected him to slide off his chair and hide. But then Lorraine was off again, bouncing around the room like a pinball.

'Looks like we're dealing with a bully,' my uncle said. 'We have zero tolerance for that kind of nonsense, Tippy.'

I nodded. 'A bully who works for the *Bully*.'

'I'm still stuck on the wardrobe,' Devon said. 'Where do these people shop? I don't recognise any of these fabrics from Glory Box. It's acid-wash denim but it's not?' He drew a frown in the air. 'Upside-down happy face.'

We waited on the footpath while Uncle Pike crossed the street. Across from the *Bully*, on the other corner of the intersection, was Dad's office. His name had been painted over and the wooden blinds were gone. Placed in the window were some knitted Christmas handicrafts. I chewed my bottom lip. Nothing about it was the same. It was like his work had never existed.

Uncle Pike entered the newspaper office. He talked to a receptionist, then Lorraine spied him and sauntered to the front. It was hard to tell how the conversation was going, as her body language seemed to be permanently aggressive.

Lorraine watched Uncle Pike leave before turning her gaze on us. She came up to the window and glared, nodding slowly towards me while saying something to the receptionist behind her without turning around. It creeped me out.

My uncle jerkily shuffled back across the road like a zombie on crutches.

'Take a picture. It lasts longer,' Devon yelled to Lorraine, and she turned her back on us.

Uncle Pike was struggling to get up from the gutter to the footpath. I grabbed his arm and Devon went behind my uncle, helping him up.

'Did she tell you anything?' I said.

'No, she was predictably rude and aggressive. She also knew who we all were and how long we'd been in town.'

'Did you ask where she got that pageboy haircut?' Devon said.

'No, that didn't come up. But she has agreed to meet us for dinner at Lyndells in half an hour.'

Devon raised his eyebrows.

Uncle Pike pretended to be reading from a notebook. 'I quote:

"I gotta eat anyway and you..."' He glanced up. 'It seems a word got rubbed out. "You blanks are buying me steak." End quote.'

'Charming,' Devon said. 'Oh! What am I going to wear? Lyndells sounds so exotic.'

'Did someone say exotic?' Duncan Nunn hurried across the street from the newspaper office, waving his hands for us to wait. He seemed shorter in real life. 'Pike, Devon! Duncan Nunn, real estate.' Before Uncle Pike could make a move, Duncan had cornered them, shaking their hands. 'A little birdy told me you'd be here.'

Inside the *Bully* Lorraine was smirking at us, her arms crossed.

He moved closer to my uncle, tapping his chin. 'Now, is it true you gays have a lot of money to spend?'

Devon seemed hypnotised by him. 'Do you mean like the mayor?'

Duncan put his arm around him. 'See, am I right?'

'Someone needs a breath mint,' Uncle Pike said.

Duncan circled behind them and put his hands on their shoulders. 'Have I got the perfect home for you.'

Uncle Pike squirmed, trying to get away, whereas Devon studied Duncan, like a scientist examining some odd metallic insect that may, or may not, sting.

'Renovators' delight,' Duncan said.

'You're not doing too badly,' Devon said, turning to survey him. 'Actually, it's quite a nice suit. As for your hair, I think you're making the most out of a bad situation.'

Duncan's mouth tightened and his jaw clenched, then he relaxed and gave a toothy smile.

'Teeth whitening, maybe?' Devon said. 'And would you consider working out?'

'Not me,' he said in a high-pitched voice. He cleared his throat. 'No. Not me.' He flattened his tie against his belly.

'Okay, well, who then?'

'Not *who*, but *where*...' He spread out his arm.

Uncle Pike gave me a 'let's go' head tilt and shuffled on his crutches towards the car. I grabbed Devon's hand and dragged him with me.

Duncan followed closely behind. 'May I ask what you are doing right this second?'

'Breathing,' Devon said.

'Dying,' my uncle said, not looking back.

Duncan loomed over me.

I shrugged. 'Silently screaming.'

Uncle Pike doubled over laughing, and Duncan drew back.

'Incorrect. You're all coming with me to view number four Ronsdale Place, perhaps the best house I've ever had the pleasure of listing.'

My uncle stopped and faced him. 'Does this approach ever work?'

'Of course, and I'll not take no for an answer.' He shoved business cards into my uncle's and Devon's hands.

'Tomorrow,' Uncle Pike said. 'Right now we have somewhere to be.'

'I'll take that as a yes.' Duncan Nunn rubbed his hands together. 'It's a date.' He trotted across the street and up past the *Bully*. He unlocked his car.

It was a brown convertible.

CHAPTER ELEVEN
Off the Record

We argued about Duncan Nunn all the way home. I wanted us to follow the murder car, Devon needed to get changed for the pub and Uncle Pike said we had to stick to meeting Lorraine. I even tried asking, 'What if he's got someone in the boot?' but it didn't work.

'Tomorrow,' my uncle said from Mum's bedroom. 'I promise. We are going open-house undercover.'

'I love an open house,' Devon said, quickly changing T-shirts.

'True,' Uncle Pike said. 'They are fun.'

'Ready,' Devon said. He wore a tight, light-blue T-shirt with a V-neck that went nearly down to his bellybutton, showing off his furry chest, and so thin it was see-through.

'Woof,' my uncle said. They started kissing, so I left and waited in the car.

Riverstone had two pubs, but only one had a fancy restaurant – called Lyndells, after the owner's wife. It was packed for twelve-dollar steak night.

'Where's the apostrophe?' Uncle Pike said. 'Unless I am to believe there are many Lyndells involved in this place?'

'It is possible...' Devon said. 'I imagine Lyndell is a very common name here.'

'She's the only one I know of.' I checked out the plastic holly and tiny pine cones in the middle of the table; I hadn't eaten out since my tenth birthday.

'Does she do the cooking?' Devon asked excitedly.

'No, she does the drinking,' Lorraine said, menacing from above us. She wore a large, white linen shirt untucked over tight green moleskin pants. She grabbed a chair and slammed herself down. 'Right. Which one of you bitches is buying me a drink?'

Devon tried not to look repulsed.

Uncle Pike fake-smiled. 'What a lovely idea. I hope you pick me.'

Lorraine stared at him, clearly used to her gaze intimidating people.

'Seems like someone has the stare bears.' Devon smiled, giving her 'full wattage'. He had explained his charm system to me while we sunbathed on the balcony. There was 'shy girl', where you looked up and fluttered your eyelashes; 'smiley cat', where you showed lots of teeth and gave blinky cat eyes; and 'full wattage', where you shone like a diamond. He said there were others, but they were probably for when I was older.

For a moment Lorraine looked off balance and then she turned her black shark eyes on me, the weakest. 'Tippy Chan,' she said.

My insides went cold. I couldn't hold her gaze and felt my face go red. I shifted in my seat and accidentally kicked Uncle Pike's moon boot.

'Fuck!' he roared, startling Lorraine.

'Sorry, sorry!' I said.

He moved his leg from under the table and rubbed it. He tried to give me a smile. 'That's okay,' he said in a high voice.

A waitress popped up. 'Can I get you all some drinks?' I recognised her as one of Claire Bates's friends. Like Claire, she'd finished high school last year; unlike Claire, she was nice. She stared at Devon and put the pen in her mouth.

'Honey, do you know where that's been?' Uncle Pike said.

She ignored him and licked its end.

'Don't mind if I do – vodka and tonic, and make it a double,' Lorraine said.

The waitress took our drink orders then Lorraine waved her off. 'So, what have you got for me?'

Uncle Pike leaned forward. 'What have you got for *us*?'

'Why would I have anything for you?' She eyed him as he spoke. 'What's your angle, Pike? You said you had information. Information the cops don't have.'

'You're the investigative journalist. You tell me. Surely you have a theory.'

She smirked. 'Either you saw something...' She studied us. 'No, that's not it.' She homed in on me again. 'What do you think your parents would say about you poking around a murder investigation?'

I looked down at the table, playing with my napkin.

'Oh my God, you *are* investigating this? I don't think her parents will be very impressed,' she sneered. 'Sorry, guess I shouldn't be using plural.'

I took a deep breath and raised my eyes to hers. 'They already think you're ... They call you Cunt-Hooks,' I blurted out.

It was as if I'd punched her in the face with lemon-coated boxing gloves. She sucked in her thin lips and pulled back as if yanked by an invisible rope. Uncle Pike and Devon laughed, though it sounded muffled and my ears felt hot. I couldn't believe I'd said that. I had just stood up to a bully. When my uncle held up a hand for a high five, I slapped it on autopilot.

'Looks like you're all having a good time,' the waitress said, smiling. She put down everyone's drinks.

Lorraine looked dazed.

'What can I get you all?'

Uncle Pike ordered us each steak and chips, except for Devon who instead of chips got a salad and instead of dressing got balsamic vinegar in a little jug.

'So, Lorraine,' Uncle Pike said, 'great pieces in the paper.'

She glanced at me, then focused on him. 'I think you're bluffing. What do you have, Pike? I'll show you mine if you show me yours.'

Devon dry-retched.

She glared at him. 'I'm sitting right here.'

'Off the record?' Uncle Pike said.

She snorted. 'Okay, Deep Throat.'

'That's a funny name,' the waitress said, going past.

'Well,' my uncle said, 'we know it's not Sally Homer.'

Lorraine's expression didn't change. She stared at him. 'Go on. Why not?'

'She has an alibi for Saturday night.'

'Being a lonely drunk is not an alibi.' It was like a tennis game between the two of them, with me and Devon the spectators.

'There's a witness who can corroborate,' Uncle Pike lied.

Lorraine lifted an eyebrow.

'Ha!' he said. 'You didn't know? One to us. Now it's your turn, Lorraine.'

'I agree it's not Sally Homer.'

'Why not?' he asked.

The waitress brought our meals. 'Here we go!' She smiled at Devon. 'And I'll just go and get yours.' Her gaze dropped to his muscly chest and arms.

Uncle Pike waved her off. 'Thank you.'

She smiled and bounced away.

'The murder weapon,' Lorraine said, her mouth already full of steak. I suddenly didn't feel hungry and put my fork down. She hacked off another mouthful, sawing hard against the plate.

My uncle hadn't touched his food. 'What about it?'

Devon swung his head in Lorraine's direction, while seagulling my uncle's chips.

'There's no way Sally Homer would have access to one, or would even think of using it. Come on, she's a pretty basic kind of girl. You should know...'

'Access to what?' my uncle said.

Lorraine sneered at him. 'Not so fast. Who's this witness?'

I stared at him, willing him not to tell her anything. We could find out about the murder weapon some other way. Maybe Sam could sneak a look at his dad's case files ... but that would mean either lying to Sam or telling him about The Nancys.

'You work it out,' my uncle said. 'We all know Sally didn't do it.'

Lorraine shovelled in the last of her meal, chewing with her mouth open. 'Like I said, I agree, but the police...' Bits of steak were stuck in her teeth. 'Open and shut, all the evidence they need is there. There's nothing else.'

'What about the fact she was at church when the scalp appeared on her steps?' he said.

Lorraine gave a half-shrug. 'No one else saw it. She could've gone to church for an alibi, come home and put it there, then called the cops.'

'But she couldn't dump Jill Everson's body at the traffic light and be at church at the same time,' I blurted out.

With a smirk, Lorraine leaned back in her seat, pointing her thumb in my direction. 'I'm beginning to like this one.'

Our waitress came back with Devon's meal. Lorraine was watching me like a hawk. I returned her stare and smiled in what I hoped was a creepy-clown way. The waitress lingered around Devon until Lorraine shooed her off again.

'Okay, Chan, spill. The public think Everson was killed at the traffic light on Saturday night.'

Uncle Pike gave me a nod.

I took a sip of my drink. 'A witness saw the murderer that morning at 10.40. He left the body but took the clothes and head with him.'

'Who's this witness?'

'Sources,' Uncle Pike said. 'You know, can't reveal and all that.'

Lorraine put her elbows on the table and rubbed her hands together. 'Suzie Pratt. Has to be.'

None of us said anything. I had to look away.

'Ha, it *is*, isn't it? How did you make her talk? The cops got nothing out of her, and her mother won't let me see her.'

'Couldn't think why,' Uncle Pike said.

Lorraine ignored him. 'Chan, you said "he". She's sure it was a man?'

I nodded. 'In a brown car.'

She didn't move. 'Have you told the cops?'

'Not yet – an exclusive for you,' Uncle Pike said.

'I'm flattered.' She used her fork as a toothpick. 'Look, I understand why you haven't. Something about this doesn't add up. This investigation doesn't make sense.'

'How so?' my uncle said.

'Off the record?' she said, staring at him.

'Of course.'

Turning in her seat, she checked the dining room behind her.

'Are you after the waitress?' Devon said.

'No, not that halfwit.' She finished her inspection and faced us again. When she spoke, her voice was lowered. 'Timelines are skew-whiff.'

'Are reporters allowed to make up words?' Devon asked.

'All the evidence points to one suspect,' she continued. 'But someone with no form at all is suddenly decapitating people? They're focusing on the wrong person, which means the murderer is still out there.'

'What are you doing about it?' I said.

'Publicly? Nothing. I don't know who I can trust or where this goes.'

'You mean the police?' Uncle Pike said.

She looked smug and shrugged. 'Incompetence, corruption – it's either or both. They just need it to go away.' Part of her was enjoying this.

'But you trust us?' I asked.

'Strangely, yes. Circumstance makes for strange bedfellows, Chan.'

Devon frowned. 'What did she say?' he asked Uncle Pike.

'Can you get us a copy of the police report?' Uncle Pike asked.

'And Todd's,' I said. If anything was missing, it should be in there.

Lorraine burped and grabbed my napkin to wipe her mouth, her own now a disgusting, brown-stained crumpled ball. 'You'll keep me updated on anything you find?'

Uncle Pike swallowed his mouthful and nodded. 'Deal.'

'And a bottle of Scotch and a carton of cigarettes,' she said.

'If you drop calling it the "Christmas Tragedy",' he said.

'Deal.' She stuck out her hand and they shook on it. 'That was my genius editor anyway.'

'What is it with this town and its deals?' Devon said, just as the waitress reappeared.

She winked at him as she cleared Lorraine's plate. 'I know, right?'

'Grown-ups talking,' Lorraine said.

'I mean,' Devon said, 'shouldn't you be doing this for justice, truth and the story?'

'I am.' She shoved her chair back hard. 'It just doesn't pay that much.'

'How do we know you're not in with the murderer?' I said, thinking of the first rule.

She stood up, sculling the last of her drink. Her tiny black eyes narrowed as she loomed over me. 'Because, believe it or not, I don't like anyone fucking with my turf.'

I could believe that.

She went to leave but turned back and leaned on the table. 'A surgical saw. That's what he used.' She banged the tabletop. 'Adios.' She tromped off, nearly colliding with the starstruck waitress.

Nancy Drew had been knocked unconscious and had rocks thrown through her windows, but she'd never had to deal with a surgical saw. I shuddered and tried to block out how it had been used on my teacher – this was getting next level.

'I've got to hand it to Lorraine,' Uncle Pike said. 'She certainly knows how to make an impression— Shit, hide!' He covered his face with his menu but it was too late.

Michael Horn-blower strode across the restaurant towards us. 'Hello, von Trapps.' He rested his hands on the back of Uncle Pike's chair and leaned towards Devon. 'How are you, Maria? Still making clothes out of curtains, I see.'

Devon looked confused and upset.

Uncle Pike's face went red. 'Come on...'

Horn-blower laughed.

I was so sick of arse-clowns. 'Why'd you say "murder" on the street before my teacher was killed?'

He stopped mid-laugh.

'Did you do it?' I was trying hard not to yell at him.

He stared at me and glanced down at Uncle Pike.

Suddenly I felt hot and my heart was banging. Horn-blower was standing way too close to me; he was mean and I wanted him gone. 'Did. You. Do. It?'

He snorted. 'Now, listen here...'

'No, *you* listen, you old, fake vampire.'

All three mouths dropped open.

My vision narrowed like I was inside a dark tunnel looking out. 'Her blood was everywhere. Everywhere. Blood all over the grass.'

Horn-blower looked like he was going to be sick.

Our waitress sprang into view inside my black frame, whipping her hair. 'Can I get you guys anything else?'

'This man' – I pointed my thumb at his crotch – 'out of my face.' Blood pounded in my ears, making my voice sound muffled.

Horn-blower stepped back. 'What?' He looked down at his pants then back up.

'Monster!' I clawed at my napkin, trying not to scream.

His eyes bulged and he put up his hands. 'Hey, hey. I'm going.'

Uncle Pike wrapped his arms around me. 'It's okay, Tippy, it's okay.' I was shaking. He glanced at Devon; they both looked worried.

'No, it's not.' I slumped into my uncle and didn't feel brave anymore – just really, really sad. My tears were hot, and even in Uncle Pike's embrace I felt completely alone. I wanted Mum. I didn't want to feel broken anymore. I wanted everything back the way it was, to wake up at home and go into the living room and find Dad sitting there.

Uncle Pike stroked my hair. 'No, you're right. It's not, you're still going to have a lot of anger coming up. Grief's like that. It's a bleak-headed beast.' He rocked me. 'I'm so sorry you have to go through this.' He handed me a napkin. 'But do you know what?'

I tried to stop crying and swallowed hard. Managing to slow it down, I shakily wiped my face with the napkin and rubbed my runny nose. 'What?'

'At least you are using it for good.'

'Girl, she had *no* idea that was coming.' Devon shook his head, smiling. 'Wow. "Old, fake vampire" ... Thanks, Tippy.' He gave me a hug and we had a chuckle. 'Looks like Lyndells brings out the beast in you.'

I wiped my face with the napkin again and gave my uncle a big hug and kiss on the cheek.

'PS,' he said. 'That was Lorraine's napkin.'

CHAPTER TWELVE
Dead-End Street

Thursday morning Uncle Pike called my school and told them I wouldn't be back in for the rest of the year. I jumped around clapping. *I'm so lucky. Poor Sam – sucks to be him*. Mum would freak if she found out but it was totally worth it. We had a quick Nancys meeting before our undercover open house with Duncan Nunn. As Devon cleared the last of the breakfast dishes, I opened The Nancys scrapbook and headed up a new page: *Murder Weapon*.

'Hear ye, hear ye! I call this meeting of The Nancys to order.' Uncle Pike slammed down a wooden spoon, snapping it in half and denting the dining table again. 'Fuck!'

'Really?' Devon snatched the broken spoon handle from my uncle and sat beside me. 'Did you put extra stickers on the scrapbook?'

I nodded. 'To stop anyone thinking it was about the murder.'

Devon picked it up. 'Love the penguin, and the lion.'

'I must admit the lion is my favourite,' Uncle Pike said.

'Thanks.' I tore open door ten of my advent calendar – fifteen days till Christmas. Time was running out. I tipped it over, smacking the back of it to release the tiny chocolate, which I popped in my mouth.

Devon handed my scrapbook back. 'Anyway, first things first.' He unzipped his gold jacket to reveal a black T-shirt with *Nancys 3.0* written across it in bright pink.

'Simple yet complicated,' my uncle said. 'I like the reference to the third prototype.'

I nodded. 'Also the number of members in The Nancys.'

'Exactly!' Uncle Pike said. 'You're getting very good at this, Tippy Chan.'

Devon beamed. 'And now for the logo.' He slowly slipped off the jacket like he was dancing.

'Woof!' Uncle Pike said.

Devon turned around to reveal a pink triangle with smoke curling out of it. This was the best T-shirt so far; at least it didn't look like it was painted in the victim's blood.

'Is it the Bermuda Triangle and there's been a plane crash?' I asked.

Devon tapped his finger on his chin. 'That's one interpretation.'

'Love it on so many levels,' my uncle said. 'A homage to our culture, Nancy's privates and smoking.'

Devon smiled and nodded.

'Great,' Uncle Pike said. 'The mystery of Nancy's triangle.'

'Things disappear in there,' I said.

My uncle laughed. 'Indeed.'

Devon blew us kisses and took a bow.

'Thank you, Devon and Tippy,' Uncle Pike said. 'For our next order of business: the murder weapon. A surgical saw. Let's brainstorm.'

'The Nancys Club is so corporate,' Devon whispered to me. 'This is great work experience for you, Tippy. I keep forgetting my executive glasses for these meetings.'

My uncle cleared his throat. 'Parking the *why* for now, where would our suspect get hold of a surgical saw?'

'Hospitals,' Devon said. He hopped up and went to his window; in the bottom corner he wrote *weapon*.

'There's two here: Mum's and the old hospital,' I said. 'What about funeral homes? There's Barron's Funeral Parlour in town.'

'Good points, Tippy. Write those down,' my uncle said.

'Online,' Devon said. I added that to my list in my Nancys scrapbook.

'Not much we can do about that one,' Uncle Pike said. 'Do vets have surgical saws?' He glanced at Devon, then winked at me. 'Do they have to chop off puppies' and kittens' legs?'

Devon shrieked and danced around with his fingers in his ears.

'I think so,' I said, trying not to smile.

Devon cocked his head and pulled out his fingers.

'But you probably wouldn't need a saw for a kitten,' I said.

He jammed them back in again.

Uncle Pike smiled. 'Nice work.'

'Thanks,' I said. 'The freezing works might use a saw?'

'Maybe, though the weapon sounds a bit more surgical.'

Devon pulled his fingers out again.

'Okay.' I read from my list. 'So medical centre, old hospital, funeral home, online, vet clinic and maybe the freezing works.'

'First off we need to find out if any of the locals are missing a surgical saw,' my uncle said.

I called Dr Lisa and handed my phone to Uncle Pike. He spoke with her, but she had no idea what he was talking about. He shook his head and I crossed *medical centre* off the list.

Next he rang the freezing works. 'Same again. They laughed at me, said a machine cuts up the meat.'

I crossed *freezing works* off the list. 'What are we going to do about the funeral parlour?'

Uncle Pike picked up the tablet and waved it. 'Let our fingers do the walking.' He did a search for 'mortuary equipment suppliers'. 'Doesn't look like it's standard equipment – doesn't mean there isn't one stashed away, of course.'

'How are you going to ask the vet?' I said.

Devon glanced up from his murder-weapon drawing; it looked like a chainsaw.

My uncle scratched his beard and spied Bunny Whiskers out the window.

'No!' screeched Devon and ran out the door. She froze mid-lick as he scooped her up. 'No cutting Bunny Whiskers' legs off!'

'Undercover Bunny Whiskers?' I said.

'Oooh!' Devon immediately lifted the cat into the *Lion King* position and started singing. She let out a little meow and licked her nose.

'Awesome.' I snapped an updated window picture as well as several of Devon and Bunny Whiskers while Uncle Pike called the vet. He finished his call, threw the cordless onto the couch and shook his head. 'Worst one yet. I think they'll call the police on me.'

Devon was still singing 'Circle of Life' when Uncle Pike clapped, startling the cat. She jumped from Devon's arms and bounded for the door.

'Focus, children,' my uncle said. 'Okay, so even though we don't know where the murder weapon is, at least we know *what* it is.'

'That's all you need in *Cluedo*,' I said.

Devon tapped his pen on the chainsaw drawing, near the murderer's dead cat. 'But don't you need to know *where* it is as well?'

'No,' I said. 'More like where *the murder* happened, like in the library.'

'Good, we've got that one,' Uncle Pike said. 'And, darling, a surgical saw doesn't look like a chainsaw.'

Devon took the marker out of his mouth. 'What?'

'Never mind. Close enough,' my uncle said.

We drove across the bridge on our way to the open home. Main Street was busy today; as we passed the shops I counted seven people on the footpath. Up ahead I recognised someone at Skinny Genies. I patted Devon's shoulder. 'Slow down.'

'That's new,' Uncle Pike said, checking out the cafe. 'Tables on the footpath ... al fresco dining in *Riverstone*?'

I leaned in between them and pointed. 'Claire Bates.' She was sitting outside by herself, sucking on a milkshake.

'Oh my God, in the wild!' Devon said. 'Is she in a marching band?'

'I don't think so,' I said.

'White fuck-me boots,' Uncle Pike said.

'Ah,' Devon said. 'I've got to get the name of her photoshopper.' He craned his neck as we drove past. 'They did a remarkable job.'

We continued up Main Street towards the pink monkey motels. Devon gasped when he saw them. 'Dusky salmon? Why?'

'Exactly,' Uncle Pike said.

Devon covered his mouth as we passed, heading to the bottom of the hill. He indicated right and turned off onto Old Hospital Road. The road went up a small hill then dipped down and wound back up, wrapping around the side of the hill. Poplars and silver birches lined each side of it. We came to a fork.

I wriggled forward between the front seats and pointed to the road straight ahead. 'Up there's the old hospital.'

'Let's check that out on the way back,' Uncle Pike said.

We took the left bend up into Ronsdale Place. It was a cul-de-sac, like home except one side had no buildings, just bush covering the hill. The bottom side had four large houses built below the road, their roofs and half their walls visible from the street.

We pulled up behind Duncan's brown convertible.

'Do you think it's the same car?' I said.

My uncle held up Suzie's picture and compared it. 'Maybe, if the top was up. Her car does look bigger.'

Devon undid his seatbelt and leaned over, trying to get a better look at the picture. 'Just to be sure, we *are* talking about a five-year-old's drawing?'

Uncle Pike tilted the picture. 'She's also drawn the car from the front.'

'Anyway,' Devon said, 'the murderer's wearing antlers, and I don't see Mr Nunn doing that, do you? His rug would rip off.'

'You may be onto something there,' my uncle said. 'But he is a professional headpiece wearer, so a suspect until proven otherwise.'

'And he's a creeper,' I said.

'Great observation and point, Tippy.'

'Melanie certainly hates him,' Devon said.

We got out. A massive *For Sale* sign, which was mainly a picture of Duncan Nunn, leaned against a white wooden mailbox painted with a black number four.

'Smouldering,' Devon said.

'One for the bank,' Uncle Pike said. He looked at his moon boot then at the steep slope of the driveway versus the narrow stairs leading down to the red front door. I hadn't known Ronsdale Place was so hilly.

'I really do love an open house,' Devon said. 'This could be our first home.'

My uncle frowned. 'Hmm.'

Devon's smile disappeared. 'I was just kidding.'

Duncan was waiting for us at the front door. 'Come on, peoples!'

Devon headed off and Uncle Pike looked at me.

'Mean, remember?' I said.

He sighed. 'Fuck it! Okay.' He handed me one of his crutches and hopped after Devon using the other. 'Wait. I'm going to fall down these stairs.'

Devon leaped back up and grabbed him around the waist.

'Of course this could be our first house,' Uncle Pike said. 'We'd need to tint the windows to stop the sun bleaching everything.'

'I love sun-bleached,' Devon said, beaming.

'Like hair?'

'Exactly, and Ronsdale Place sounds so glamorous.'

I followed them slowly, waiting on each step for them to move.

'Trust me, it's not,' my uncle said. 'Dr Ronsdale was the town's first hospital's boss. He went mad and killed his family.'

'What?' Devon said.

I'd never heard this story. So there had been murders in Riverstone before. As we slowly made our way to the front entrance, I wondered if the house was haunted.

'We'll need to take money off for accessibility issues, Duncan,' Uncle Pike said.

The real-estate agent ignored him and gave two loud claps. 'Peoples, listen up.' He was looking into the distance.

'Who's he talking to?' Uncle Pike said.

'Concentrate!' Duncan put his hands above his head then brought them down like a bird flapping his wings. In a loud voice, he said, 'Number four Ronsdale Place ... Is. For. Sale.'

We waited for him to say something else but that was it. We started to clap.

'No need, no need.' He waved us away but was obviously pleased with our response.

'Is this the house where Dr Ronsdale killed his family?' Devon said.

Duncan ignored him again. He unlocked the large red door and threw it open, hitting the wall inside. He swept his arm. 'Please come in and experience.'

In front of us was a plain hallway with doors off it.

Uncle Pike shuffled in. 'You should've been a magician. It's like I'm in paradise!'

'You haven't answered my question.' Devon gave Duncan a half-bow, which he returned.

'Come through, come through. Plenty of time for questions later.'

I checked behind the door and found a large dent in the wall. Duncan quickly appeared behind me, slammed the door shut and leaned against it. He was creepy.

'Friends,' he boomed, pushing himself off the door, 'the entrance hallway. This door leads to the garage – no more wet feet!'

'I need earmuffs,' Uncle Pike said.

'Why would you have wet feet?' Devon said.

Duncan tilted his head back, eyelids fluttering. 'Here...' he pointed to the door on the other side – 'the master bedroom!' He flung open the wooden door, which shuddered, hitting the doorstop. Inside was a large, empty room with worn olive-green carpet. It smelled damp.

After taking a step inside, Devon grabbed his throat and went back out to the hallway, shaking his head.

Uncle Pike stared at the white ceiling. 'Is that mould?'

Duncan looked up too. 'Where?'

'Exactly,' my uncle said. 'Why does it smell so pissy-pants in the middle of summer?'

In the hallway Devon pulled out his soap phone. He covered the bottom of the bar and whispered to Duncan, 'Sorry, it's a dental emergency.'

Duncan stared.

Uncle Pike shrugged and pushed past him. 'She's the boss.'

Devon stayed on the 'phone' in the hallway while Duncan

showed us the other two bedrooms. They were all the same. I wondered which room Dr Ronsdale had done it in.

'Nice wallpaper frieze,' my uncle said. 'I'm starting to understand why the previous family abandoned this place.'

'And now for the money shot,' Duncan said.

'Hey!' Uncle Pike said. 'Inapprops.'

Duncan spun around and blocked the door. It was like he was in his own music video. 'The piece of resistance.'

We followed him into a big open-plan living room. It had an incredible view out of its large sash windows. From here I could see the old hospital below and all the way across Riverstone, the river and the bridge and even the hill where we lived. With binoculars you'd be able to see our house.

'Sconces!' Devon pointed to the wall. 'Faux wrought iron, circa 1995. Why? I can't. I simply ca—'

I flicked on the light switch.

With a shriek, Devon ran out of the room and down the hallway.

'Wow,' Uncle Pike said. 'I'm sorry – I'm confused, Mr Nunn. Why are you torturing us? Did we do something to upset you?'

Duncan gestured towards the view. 'I think you're missing the point.'

My uncle headed back out to the hallway. I followed him to the front door. Devon had already disappeared, and we still needed to ask Duncan about Sunday morning.

'But I haven't shown you the rest of the house,' Duncan said, behind us. 'Or the garage yet.'

'Is it creepy?' I said. 'Is that where it happened?'

'What?' he said.

'Like *Blair Witch*,' Uncle Pike said. 'You know, standing in the corner?'

Duncan's face was blank.

'Wasn't that a basement?' I asked my uncle. 'Remember, all the kids' handprints?'

'Where did you watch that?' he said. 'Was this with Todd and Sam again?'

Duncan grinned and beckoned us to follow him, opening the door to the garage he'd shown us earlier. 'This way, this way!' A dim light bulb at the end of a short cable swung from the low ceiling in the middle of the garage, casting shadows on the short flight of wooden stairs in front of us. It smelled stale, like under our house; dry and airless. But unlike under our house, which was crammed with stuff, it was empty except for a deep-freeze and Devon, standing beside it with his back to us. He must've bumped his head on the bulb on the way over, or this was his special-effect lighting.

'There you are,' Duncan said to him, heading down. I helped Uncle Pike hop down the stairs.

We were running out of time, so I jumped in. 'Did you lose a silver business-card holder?'

'What?' Duncan said. 'How do you know about that?'

'Any reason you'd be at the traffic light?' Uncle Pike asked.

Duncan started laughing. It was creepy. I glanced back up at the hallway door.

'What's so funny?' Devon asked, joining us, alarmed.

'Of course, I wondered where that got to. I thought I was losing my mind.' He patted his hair. 'That was fun.'

'What?' Devon said slowly.

Duncan chuckled. 'Location, location, location.'

We stared at him.

'Come on, really?' Duncan said. 'Lover's lane? Cops and robbers? Karen was the cop and I was—'

'We get the picture,' my uncle said.

I had no idea what any of them were talking about. 'Who's Karen?' I said.

'My lovely lady. She's married, so of course I have to be discreet. A gentleman never tells.' Duncan winked and nudged Uncle Pike in the ribs. 'You know how it is.'

My uncle grimaced. 'I'd hoped Tippy would be older before she lost all faith in mankind.'

'Were you there on Sunday morning?' I asked Duncan.

'Mmm.' He played with his lips. 'We have a standing appointment on Wednesday.' He chuckled. 'Hump Day.'

My uncle pulled me against him, trying to cover my ears, but I could still hear.

'Shame about that teacher, though,' Duncan said. 'I heard she was like a rabbit with her lady-whistle. Caretaker caught her once with some tall blond drink of water in the classroom, bare arse and all.' Reaching out to the wall, Duncan pressed a button and the wide roller door lurched upwards, stalling halfway.

I wondered if the caretaker was where Mrs Brown had got her info from as well. That, and why Duncan would say 'lady-whistle'.

Uncle Pike sighed heavily. 'Some respect for the dead, eh? She was my niece's teacher.'

Duncan beamed. 'Nothing but respect! I'm "sex-positive", as the young ones say.'

I wriggled out from under my uncle's hands. 'I don't say that.'

Duncan recoiled, giving me a look like he'd just eaten a cockroach.

'I've seen quite enough,' Uncle Pike said. 'This house brings up a lot of horror for me.'

'It's a total horror show for me,' Devon said. 'I can see why Ronsdale went mad. What's been seen cannot be unseen.'

Duncan stabbed the button several times. 'Wait!' When the roller door ground upwards again, Devon bounded out under it and up the drive, like Bunny Whiskers.

My uncle shook his head. 'We'll think about it.' He shuffled outside, back to the cul-de-sac. 'Dead end, literally.'

I followed him, then it hit me. I'd lived all my life in a dead-end street too.

CHAPTER THIRTEEN
An Arrest

The drive to the old hospital took one minute and twenty-seven seconds. We pulled into the empty carpark. Roots from the surrounding trees had split the concrete driveway, weed islands growing up among the cracks and bumps. The whole place seemed a bit sad and lonely to me. Mum had said hundreds of babies had been born here, including her and Uncle Pike. I thought about all those happy families chatting and taking their babies home. Today it was silent except for the odd squawk of a seagull.

I opened my door and got out. 'First thing, I guess, is to check if the power's on. That, and if we can find Ms Everson's head.'

'Whoa on the head,' Devon said.

His drawing of the sad face with a teardrop came to mind.

'I don't care,' Uncle Pike said. 'Anything that proves Sally didn't do it.'

'But her head, really? And why are we checking the power?' Devon said. 'I thought we were just looking for a saw?'

My uncle made an ungracious exit from the car. 'Lucky I wore underpants today.'

'Eeew,' I said.

He laughed and straightened himself out. 'Does anyone know we're here? After that last horror show...'

'Ummm, you're the oldest,' Devon said to him and smiled at me.

'I've texted Sam,' I said.

'Okay,' Uncle Pike said. 'I wonder if we should tell anyone else? I assume the police aren't bothering to find the killer.'

A killer on the loose. My mouth felt dry. 'Sam's pretty reliable.'

'I guess,' my uncle said, completely unconvinced. 'He's not the sharpest tool. Are you sure he's not adopted?'

'Mr Campbell is his stepdad.'

'Still doesn't explain it,' Uncle Pike said, settling into his crutches.

The old hospital's dark windows had gone from sad to scary.

There were lots of places someone could hide and watch us. I was glad for the warmth of the sun.

At the front entrance, the panes in the main double doors had been smashed in. Pieces of broken glass were scattered on the ground and crunched under my sneakers as I pushed against the doors. They were locked. The gaping bottom panels looked big enough for me to climb through, but before I could, Uncle Pike snaked his arm through a jagged hole and unlocked the door. 'Looks like someone worked out how to get in.'

We walked into a foyer with a large, green-marble reception desk. Jumbled leaves and rubbish covered the floor. Faded light filtered through the front doors and grimy windows, but further ahead the main corridor was dark. Devon's voice boomed in the silence. 'It reminds me of one of those places in a zombie movie.'

My heart pounded. 'Thanks for that,' I whispered.

'Shit – sorry, Tippy,' he said. 'Didn't mean to spook you.'

'It's okay.' I found some switches and flicked them on and off but nothing happened. I turned on my torch. Its beam cut a short path down the corridor. Halfway along were the remains of a small party: beer bottles, some smashed, a blue-and-red beanie and a white sock. On further investigation they didn't seem to have belonged to Jill Everson.

'Let's see if we can find the operating theatre,' Uncle Pike said.

We continued on and came to an intersection. I shone the torch at the walls and found black plastic signs with white lettering pointing to the wards, kitchen, X-ray and finally operating theatre. I gestured to the sign.

'Eureka,' Devon said. He wrinkled his nose. 'I hate the smell of hospitals.'

'That's funny, 'cause I hate the sound of clichés.' My uncle was being mean again.

Devon walked ahead, and I gave Uncle Pike a frown.

He sighed. 'Really?'

I nodded.

He hopped forward, caught Devon and put a hand on his shoulder, leaning his head against his boyfriend's. 'I'm sorry.' They were wandering into the darkness.

I pointed with my torch. 'This way.' We moved down a hallway with less rubbish and fewer leaves on the floor until we came to a large door.

'Here goes nothing.' Uncle Pike covered his hand with his sleeve to open the door. 'In case of fingerprints.' We both nodded.

Inside was a stainless-steel trolley and some weird shower curtain, but otherwise it was empty. Except for the dust.

'Kind of makes sense, I guess,' my uncle said. 'They weren't just going to leave hospital equipment lying around.'

I shone my torch on the dust-coated floor and swept it around our feet. Only our footsteps stood out clearly. 'No one's been here for a very long time.'

As we pulled back into our driveway, Mrs Brown rushed over, wearing a brown fern-and-kiwi apron.

'Not again.' Uncle Pike sighed.

Devon hopped out of the car while I pushed open my door with my foot.

'Have you seen the news?' Mrs Brown said.

Uncle Pike hauled himself out. 'What news?'

'There's been an arrest.'

'Who?' the three of us said at once.

Mrs Brown nodded towards me. 'That teacher, Sally Homer.'

Uncle Pike moaned. He slapped the roof of the car. 'Sally? Are you sure?'

Mrs Brown took a couple of steps back. 'Apparently they found that poor Jill's shoe in her cottage.'

I ran inside ahead of them and pulled the curtains over Devon's window. Uncle Pike crashed down on the couch. I switched on the TV and found a 'breaking news' segment. Sally was being put in a police car, a white puffer jacket over her head.

My uncle pushed back into the couch then leaned forward. 'I don't believe it. It can't be Sally.'

Mrs Brown perched on the edge of the couch.

'How?' I said. It felt all wrong, like when Horn-blower had said 'terrorism'. I couldn't believe they had arrested her – she was innocent.

Horn-blower appeared with a microphone in front of Sally's cottage.

Mrs Brown clasped her hands to her chest. 'Oh look, there's your little friend.'

'Change the channel,' Devon said.

I tried the other channels but none of them had the story yet.

'Change it back,' Uncle Pike said, stressed.

Mrs Brown rested her chin on her hands. 'Isn't he handsome? Have you met Michael yet?' she asked Devon.

His nostrils flared. 'Unfortunately...' I thought about our run-in at the restaurant and my face burned.

'Shhh.' Uncle Pike waved his hand in my direction for the remote. I handed it over. 'Please,' he said to Mrs Brown and turned up the volume. She huffed and smoothed down her apron.

Horn-blower stood near Sally's steps, a police car parked out the front behind him.

'...an exclusive with the arrest of Sally Homer for the alleged murder of Jill Everson, bringing an end to the Christmas Tragedy, but not for Jill Everson's parents and family.'

Devon muttered, pacing up and down, as Horn-blower walked around Sally's cottage talking through the details of the arrest. A high heel flashed on the screen, then a policeman issued a statement saying items of clothing belonging to Ms Everson had been found in Sally's cottage that afternoon. Behind him stood a group of people; I recognised Barry, Detective Sergeant Graham and Detective Melon.

'Fuck.' Uncle Pike rubbed his head, making his hair stick out even more. 'What is wrong with these fuckwits? She's fucking innocent.'

Poor Sally. I didn't think the police were very good, but I hadn't realised they were this bad. In the early books, Nancy had been right to treat them like bumbling fools.

'Well, they wouldn't arrest her if they didn't—' Mrs Brown said.

'Really?' Uncle Pike pointed to the screen with the remote. 'Because it looks like they have.'

An image of a pair of green ladies' undies flashed on the screen.

'Yuck!' Devon said. 'Who'd wear green lace panties?'

I shrugged. Undies were undies to me. 'I think they're the same ones that were on her sofa.'

Melanie waved to me from the balcony. I went over and let her inside.

'Looks like we're in this together.' She pointed to her head. 'I'm talking about your hair. It looks good.'

I told her about Sally's arrest.

'Phyllis is all over it. You okay, Chan?'

I shook my head. I still couldn't believe it. I whispered, 'Uncle Pike's really upset.'

Mrs Brown came over to join us as my uncle held the remote up and away from Devon's snatching hand.

Horn-blower did an arrest recap, and the green undies flashed back up.

Uncle Pike tried to stand but lost his balance. He grabbed the telly stand and the flat screen wobbled. His face pressed against it. In the background Horn-blower droned on in muted silence.

'Oh my God, are you kissing him?' Devon said.

'At least you're not bored,' Melanie said to my uncle.

He pulled back from the TV. 'Touché. I won't ever complain about that again.'

CHAPTER FOURTEEN
Sad-Sack Chimp

The next morning I woke up early and couldn't get back to sleep. Even though I didn't have to go to school I didn't want to get up. My stomach ached. No worse than any other time over the past nine months, but today I thought about staying in bed and chucking a sickie, at least for the morning. So many things were going on: Sally's arrest, Todd in a coma and my teacher's funeral today. I wanted Mum; she should've called. I hadn't heard from her since Wednesday and I no longer cared if she was having fun – I needed her now, not in six days' time. I reached under my pillow and felt the cool, smooth hardness of Piggy-Cat's paw. Clutching it, I curled into a ball. Maybe we should stop investigating – what was the point when the police didn't want to?

Muffled sounds of Uncle Pike and a female voice, who I guessed must be Melanie, came closer. There was a knock on my door.

I groaned. 'Come in.'

Uncle Pike and Melanie crammed in my doorway. She was in her usual oversized black jersey and jeans. 'See? Chan has the right idea. You old people get up way too early.'

'Rubbish, it's 7.40 a.m. Sun's been up for hours. Morning, Tippy.'

I nodded. Melanie was in my bedroom, just when I thought today couldn't get any worse. My ears burned and I was sure my face was turning red.

'Like my mullet?' She bent her head and shook it. She now had long blonde hair but just at the back – amazing and also a bit creepy.

Uncle Pike sighed. 'Beauty pageant, remember?' He tapped her head with a brush. 'And if you're going to Jill Everson's service, please wear a hat and your clown makeup. We don't want the competition suspecting anything.'

Melanie swiped at the brush. 'Nah, I'll give it a miss.'

I wondered if she wasn't going for the same reason as me. Actually, I had felt sadder at her mum's funeral than at Dad's, which I knew didn't sound right. I remembered Melanie reading out a poem about her mum and I'd lost it completely. Maybe Dad's had been different because of all the people whispering and watching me.

Melanie gave me a sympathetic nod. 'We can hang instead.' At least she understood about today. 'Just warning you, Grandad's sick so Phyllis will be around. She's so gutted she's missing this funeral.'

I squeezed Piggy-Cat's paw. Not going to the funeral was pretty tempting but being alone with Melanie was still scary.

'Your choice, Tippy,' Uncle Pike said. 'But I do think it'll be good for you to go.'

'Have you heard from Mum?' I mumbled.

'Not yet – but she'll call, honey. Probably just out of range.' He pointed his thumb at Melanie. 'If you do decide to stay, she'll teach you how to smoke.'

She nodded. 'Properly.'

I pulled my duvet up to my chin. 'Thanks.'

'Come on,' my uncle said to Melanie, lifting up her new hair. 'Let's get this mess sorted. Tippy, we'll see you soon.' They shut my door.

I lay there, my feet prickly hot. I kicked at my duvet. Sam would be going. I wondered if he'd be upset if I didn't turn up. He would be alone without me and Todd, but my classmates would be there. I sighed; I couldn't do that to Sam. I sat up. The murderer might be there. If the police didn't care, that meant it was left to us to investigate.

Focusing on our mystery, I got up and searched for my grey trackpants but couldn't find them. I suspected they'd been chucked out, so I put on my new black leggings and rainbow T-shirt and headed to the garage-slash-salon.

Melanie sat, smoking. She now had long hair except for one side above her ear. She looked so different, older somehow. She tried to blow smoke rings while Uncle Pike hunched over an old TV dinner table he'd covered with tin foil. He picked up a blonde hair extension. 'These are called wefts, Tippy. Real human hair, none of that fake stuff.'

I got a sour taste in my mouth and stepped back. For a second I imagined it was Ms Everson's bloody hair from Sally's step. I needed to keep busy like Uncle Pike had said, so I got Mum's tablet and plugged it into the speaker. Today's classical music lesson from my uncle was Madonna; as instructed, I looked up 'Into the Groove' and pressed play. The music sounded familiar.

Uncle Pike began putting the extensions in above Melanie's ear. He was separating her short hair using his hand and a long-handled comb, with black plastic clips to keep it in place. She waved her phone at him. 'I've checked you out online. You're the real deal.'

I leaned over her phone. There were pictures of Uncle Pike and Devon in the Sydney society pages. I'd always known my uncle was successful, but I hadn't really thought about it much. He was just my Uncle Pike. I was really proud of him.

'Stalker,' he said to Melanie, starting to brush her hair. 'These days my team usually handles the clients. I only do it on special occasions, like now at Christmas. That's why I can't stay, Tippy. Once your mum's holiday's over, we have to head back for the party season.'

I hoped he would change his mind – maybe over the next week I could convince him and Devon to stay longer, at least for Christmas.

'Thank you,' Melanie said.

'Don't go soft on me, Anal-Lease. I need you to win this.' He paused his brushing and gestured to Grandma's tiny china bell. 'Like the bell says, "Accept your faults." Can't argue with Isabel Meekings on that.'

'I think you're taking that out of context.' Melanie grabbed the bell off the dresser. 'It says, "To know a friend accepts your faults and loves you 'cause you're you."'

'Ha! It doesn't say anything. It's a bell.'

'Fuck, you're annoying.'

'You know, Anal-Lease, I was a bit older than you when my dad gave me a couple of hundred and a ticket to Sydney and I took off.'

He combed a section of hair, running it through his fingers. 'The next day I got a job in a Paddington salon sweeping hair.' He picked up a weft and peeled off the tape. 'I still felt a bit creeped out by it. This song reminds me of that.'

'Why didn't you do your apprenticeship here, then go?' Melanie asked, flicking her ash.

'Shit, I'm sorry, I forgot you're not from around here.' He pressed another weft against the first one.

'I'm serious. Why not?' she said.

He drained the last of his coffee. 'It just wasn't done, at least not in those days.'

'What, the eighties?'

Mum never talked about this time of her and my uncle's life.

'It may as well have been the 1950s. Dad didn't want a hairdresser for a son. How was he going to look people in the face and explain he had a big gay son?' Uncle Pike picked up a pair of pliers and squeezed along where the tape was. He then removed a clip and began another section. 'And then AIDS came along. It was much easier for Mum and Dad to accept my supposed "lifestyle choice" from across the Tasman. They never visited me.'

'Sounds like my dad,' Melanie said. 'Out of sight, out of mind.'

Uncle Pike grunted.

Each time they mentioned their dads, it felt like a stab in my lungs. I wished I could think of something to change the subject, but I kept coming up blank.

Soon enough, my uncle put on the last weft. 'I think some people find it too hard to open up, so they put it off.' He picked up the pliers and pressed hard on the tape. 'I thought I had more time...' He took out the remaining clips then gently brushed her hair. 'We'll do some cutting and styling on the day.'

She stared at herself in the mirror. 'Sounds good,' she said, distracted. I helped her out of her cape, and she moved her head from side to side. 'Feels weird.' She lifted up her new long hair and twirled it.

'Drop it.' He smacked her fingers. 'Take care of yourself today. You've got a chance with your father. Keep trying.'

She stretched. 'Who knew? Betty has a heart.'

'And you have a moustache,' he said.

Melanie rubbed her forehead with the rude finger. 'Later.'

Uncle Pike paused packing away his equipment. 'You've got this. You're beautiful.'

She half turned and smiled, tucking a loose strand of hair behind her ear.

I realised my mouth was open. I closed it and felt my face go red.

My uncle chuckled. 'You ain't seen nothing yet, Tippy Chan.' As Melanie headed out, he hoisted himself up on his crutches. 'It might seem strange, Tippy, but sometimes we do these things, like helping Melanie win, because it makes us feel good. Because we are good at them.' We walked slowly inside. 'Just like you and The Nancys – you are such a good investigator, I'm sure you'll have it solved in no time.'

I looked down at my feet and smiled. '*We* will have it solved in no time.'

'Quite right.' He shuffled into Mum's bedroom with his bag. 'Now, we have a funeral to get ready for.'

I went to my room and lay down on my bed, trying to think what to wear. I still hadn't moved, or made a decision, half an hour later when there was a knock on my door.

I turned, and Uncle Pike was standing there. 'Mind if I come in for a minute?'

'Sure.' I sat on the edge of my bed, hoping he wouldn't ask about Dad again.

'Listen, I just want to check in. I know today's a big day, and I just realised most of this morning Melanie and I talked about our dads. I'm sorry.'

I shook my head. 'I'm fine.'

He snorted. 'Of course you are. So because you've said that, I'm now going to have to sit down and have a chat. And no eye-rolling.' He backed up to my bed then kind of fell on it. The wooden frame made a loud creaking-moaning noise that I'd never heard before. He sank into the mattress, his butt nearly pushing it to the floor. Alarmed, he glanced around my room. 'This is a lot lower than I expected.'

I tried not to laugh as I slipped down the mattress-vortex towards him.

He stuck his moon boot out in front of him, off the floor. 'You know, when I was your age, Tippy, your grandparents and I went to Wellington Zoo. I don't know where Lennie was. It was the seventies. No, early eighties. Kids kind of did their own thing back then. Anyway, it was drizzling and we came to this outdoor enclosure, like a big sunken pit. Sitting alone on the concrete ground below was a chimpanzee with a damp sack pulled over its head. I don't know where the other chimps were, maybe out of the rain in a shed or something. My parents made fun of it, their loud laughter making it flinch.' He bowed his head. 'I should've stopped them. I still feel ashamed about it. I kept trying to catch the chimp's sad brown eyes to let it know I wasn't like them, I wasn't laughing, but it just pulled its sack down lower, covering its face.'

I reached out and held my uncle's hand. 'Poor monkey.'

'Even now there are some days when I feel like that chimp.'

I couldn't imagine Uncle Pike sad like that. I squeezed his hand and thought about Mum after Dad had died. It had been much easier alone in my room than out there with her.

'But the point is, Tippy, we're not always fine. None of us, and that's okay. Sad? Fuck yes. And never, ever do you need anyone's permission to feel what you're feeling. That's all your own. You got it?'

I twisted at my duvet cover. 'Got it,' I mumbled.

He gently lifted my chin. 'But it is also your job to find the beauty in life, and sometimes, on a day like today, that's not easy. So I need you to listen.'

I glanced up at his blue eyes and nodded.

'Good, because on days like these that's when it's the most important to find it, and also what makes it so beautiful when you do. Can you remember all of that for me? Especially today?'

'Yes.' I buried my head in his chest.

'You are never alone.' He rubbed my back. 'Never. And you are loved, Tippy Chan.' His voice rumbled against my ear. We sat there for a minute, quiet. 'I miss your dad too. He was so brave. And the kindest person I've ever met. And so much fun.'

'Really?' I said.

'Absolutely. I'll tell you the "fun" part when you're a grown-up, I promise.'

Devon jogged past clutching a black Glory Box bag.

I hopped up off my bed. 'Love you, Uncle Pike.'

'I love you too, Tippy Chan.' He held out his hand for me to help him up. I pulled really hard. He groaned and pushed and somehow managed to get upright without breaking my bed or hurting his foot.

We joined Devon in Mum's bedroom.

'I am declaring a memorial wardrobe crisis,' Uncle Pike said. He opened Mum and Dad's closet. Hanging inside were Mum's dresses and jackets. 'Where's your dad's clothes?' he asked me. 'Not that I'll fit them.'

I shook my head. After Dad died, on TV I'd seen a character smell the clothes of someone they had lost. I had gone to his closet and tried it, but all his clothes had smelled like lemon washing powder; Mum had washed everything. The next day, after school, his clothes were all gone. Now every time I tried to remember how Dad smelled, all I got was lemon washing powder – the only bonus was that whenever I hung out the washing, I thought of him.

Uncle Pike shut the closet. 'That's a real shame. Your dad had great taste.'

I gave my uncle a big hug, my ear pressed against his belly; that meant a lot coming from him.

He flopped back onto Mum's bed. 'I still have nothing to wear.'

'What about Mr Brown?' I said.

Devon handed me the black Glory Box bag.

My uncle frowned. 'I can't tell if you're being serious.'

I looked inside the bag and pulled out a purple dress. It was perfect. 'Did you make this?'

Devon nodded. 'Do you like it?'

I hugged him. 'I love it, thank you.'

He squeezed me. 'You are very welcome.'

'Campbell,' I said to Uncle Pike. 'Sam's parents always look like they've just stepped out of one of those sticky magazines at the dentist's office.'

'Really?' my uncle said. 'Again, how did they end up with Sam?'

Sam had nice clothes but by the time he left home he'd either spilled something, got mud on them or ripped them. Sometimes all three.

'And why are those magazines sticky?' Uncle Pike said.

Devon cracked up. 'I know, right?' They both burst out laughing.

I shrugged. I didn't think it was that funny. I went into my room, got changed into my new dress and came back.

Devon was in a black jumpsuit, sitting on the edge of the bed lacing up big, black steel-cap boots. He stopped and played with his bottom lip. 'I bet Mr Campbell's got great taste.'

Uncle Pike shook his head. 'Have you looked at where you are?'

'Mr Campbell and Dr Lisa are officially my favourite Riverstone couple,' Devon said.

'How many do you know?' Uncle Pike said.

'Well, there's the Browns...'

My uncle put up his hand. 'Enough.'

I made an emergency phone call to Sam, who checked with his parents. 'His dad says you can borrow whatever you like.'

Uncle Pike howled like a wolf, and Devon jumped up and down on Mum's bed. They seemed pretty excited about checking out Mr Campbell's closet.

'Do you think the murderer will be there?' I said.

'At the Campbells' house?' Devon said.

I laughed. 'No, at church.'

'Good thinking, Tippy,' Uncle Pike said. 'Let's keep a close watch.'

CHAPTER FIFTEEN
A Service not a Funeral

We drove over to Sam's. Dr Lisa answered the door, perfectly made-up. She wore a sleeveless black dress that my old Barbie would have loved; it seemed to flow off her. 'Too much?' she said to Devon.

'For you, never enough,' he said.

'Hello, you two,' she said to me and Uncle Pike. Her eyebrows shot up. 'Tippy, your hair! Sam said you had a new do.'

'Do you like it?' I asked.

'I love it. It's very cool.'

I smiled and felt sunshine in my tummy. I had found today's beauty in life: Dr Lisa.

'And how's the patient?' she asked.

My uncle gave her a big, fake smile. 'Did you say pain relief?'

Before she could reply, Sam bowled past her. 'Hi.' He was all dressed up in black pants with a white shirt, which he'd already spilt something red on.

'Sam!' Dr Lisa said. He ran back inside. She turned to us again. 'Please come in, and excuse me while I sort out my son.' She chased after him.

'Thank you so much,' Devon said, eyes wide.

I loved Sam's house; it was like an art gallery. It had concrete floors and white walls with lots of cool paintings, and even their family portrait looked like something out of a magazine. At the end of a wide hallway was a big sunny room with the lounge, kitchen and dining room combined. But the best thing was the back wall, all glass from the floor to the high ceiling. It was like being in their garden. Trees and bushes hid the town and you could pretend you were anywhere – and often me, Sam and Todd did.

New in the corner, blocking the view to the garden, was a tall, large, white Christmas tree with strings of silver pearls and red shiny baubles spaced perfectly on it. Everything was so symmetrical.

Had they measured between each ornament? I doubted Sam would have had anything to do with decorating it.

Mr Campbell padded barefoot towards us. 'Hello.' He wore a dark-blue pinstripe suit and a white shirt that made him look even more tanned. A lock of hair fell over his eye, and he swept it back into place while holding out his other hand to Uncle Pike.

'My hero, thank you,' my uncle said. 'Seriously, you're a lifesaver.'

Mr Campbell slapped my uncle on the back. 'No, that's my wife. I'm just a forensic scientist.'

Sam appeared shirtless and playing air drums. 'Ba-dum-bum-*chsh!*'

We laughed and Mr Campbell winked at Devon, who had his mouth open. 'Good to see you again.'

Devon stammered, and Uncle Pike elbowed him in the ribs.

'What's wrong with him?' Sam asked me.

'He's got a crush on your dad,' I whispered.

Sam giggled and made kissing noises as the adults headed off to the bedroom. His mum appeared with another white shirt and chased him back into his room. Why did she keep buying him white clothes?

I sank into their huge white leather couch and gazed out the window. With today's sunny blue sky I found it easy to pretend we were on a tropical island, with the beach just beyond the trees. My thoughts shifted to church and my dad's funeral. I pushed myself off the sofa and hunted for the remote. It took me a minute to realise the melted silver shapes by the TV were a nativity scene. Baby Jesus looked like two ball bearings. I guessed it would be harder for Sam to break.

'Looking for this?' Dr Lisa handed me the remote. 'Drink?'

I thanked her and sat back down. 'Yes, please.'

'How are you doing, Tippy?'

'I'm okay.'

She brought over a glass of lemonade. 'It's a relief that murderer is off the streets. I couldn't believe it was her.' She shook her head. 'But then again, after she called my son a thief ... Karma's a bitch.'

I nodded. There was that name again, Karma.

For a second I thought about telling Dr Lisa what we knew. Maybe she could help – she was super clever and used to keeping secrets as a doctor.

She studied my face. 'Are you really okay about today?'

I knew she was just trying to be nice, but I wished people would stop asking me that.

Sam jumped over the back of the couch and landed beside me, making me spill my drink.

His mother sighed. 'I'll grab a cloth. Let me know if you ever want to talk about anything, okay?'

'Thank you.' I turned to Sam. 'You think all our class will be at the funeral?'

'It's called a service – a funeral has a body.' He poked his tongue out the side of his mouth as he finished buttoning up his shirt.

'But they've got her body,' I said.

'Yeah, but not all of it.'

Dr Lisa threw over a tea towel, hitting Sam in the face.

We laughed and I wiped up the spill.

'Dad says because it's public there'll probably be heaps of people,' he said.

'I'm glad we're going together,' I said.

Sam smiled and nudged my shoulder.

'Wish Bridge Boy was here,' I said.

'Yeah.' Sam laughed. 'Lollipop's going to hate that name. His mum says he's still asleep. They don't know when he'll wake up.'

'But he will wake up?'

Sam shrugged. 'Why wouldn't he?'

I played with the hem of my purple dress and avoided his eyes.

'Oh crap. Sorry, Tippy, I—'

'I really want to see him.' I missed Todd, even more so here with Sam at his house. The three of us had always hung out here. I wanted to know he was safe.

'Me too,' Sam said. 'He would've been fun today.'

I giggled. That's why Sam was my best friend – he knew when to drop it.

'Have they found Todd's phone yet?' I asked.

He shrugged. 'Don't think so.' He looked up as his dad came in, laughing with Uncle Pike, who had on one of his white shirts. It was way too small.

'Pretty cool your dad's a hero,' I said.

Sam grinned and glanced over at him. I loved seeing Sam so happy. 'And they've locked up that psycho,' he said.

'What if she didn't do it?'

'Are you serious, Nanny Drew? They found the shoe and all that stuff.' He frowned. 'After what she did to me ... Are you on her side or mine?'

'Yours, of course.' I slapped him on the leg. 'Hero-Son.'

Dr Lisa took the tea towel from Sam. 'Drink?' When he nodded, she took my glass. 'I'll get you a refill.'

I smiled and waited until she went into the kitchen. 'Thanks for the Emily Watson flower you left me. I loved it.'

'What?' Sam acted like he didn't know what I was talking about.

'Sam, your drink's on the table,' his mum said. 'Please be careful...'

Uncle Pike, Devon and Mr Campbell joined us at the table. The white shirt my uncle wore was so tight it was see-through. All his colourful tattoos on his back, shoulders, chest and arms stood out, like the material was patterned. I don't know how he'd managed to do the buttons up over his belly but the shirt was so stretched that I expected it to burst open any second. He had to roll up the sleeves as well because they were too short. None of Mr Campbell's pants had fitted, so he ended up wearing a pair of black trackies.

Sam came with us in our car. He spent the whole trip asking Uncle Pike what each of his tattoos meant. Outside the church, news vans were parked all down the street. Camera crews and reporters hung around the fence on the footpath, near the gate and on the steps leading inside. I passed Horn-blower's camerawoman but didn't see him in the pack.

Inside, Sam and I sat together with our class in the middle pews on the left side. In front of us was Ms Everson's family. They had come down from the North Island and were short and fat. Her sister or cousin – I didn't know which – had curly brown hair and the same big boobs as my teacher. Uncle Pike, Devon and the Campbells sat two rows behind us with our classmates' families.

Nothing had changed since my last time here with Mum. Up front the huge wooden cross still hung at a dangerous angle from the wall above the pulpit. On either side were arched stained-glass windows. In one, Mary cuddled the baby Jesus under the Christmas star, while the other showed man-Jesus holding a lamb by its tummy while his other hand held a long stick with a curly top. Sunlight made the windows' colours dazzle. They hadn't shone like that at Dad's funeral. It had been pouring with rain and the glass had been dark, almost black.

Up near the pulpit, between two massive white flower arrangements, was a large colour photo of Ms Everson on an easel. Instead of her usual ponytail she had her hair out, and it was curly. It took me a while to work out what else was different about her.

I nudged Sam. 'Look, she's smiling.'

'She looks weird,' he whispered. 'And creepy.'

I giggled then felt bad for not feeling sad about her.

During the service the minister didn't say Sally's name but instead called her the evil that had claimed Ms Everson's life. I didn't understand why, as this was Sally's church.

'As it is written in Luke, Chapter Eight, Verse Seventeen: "Whatever is hidden away will be brought out into the open, and whatever is covered up will be found and brought to light."' If only the minister knew how in the dark we still were. Her murderer was probably inside the church right now. I looked behind me for a tall, blond man in the sea of adult suspects. Across the aisle, near the front was Horn-blower.

I craned around Sam, trying to see what Horn-blower was up to, when Sam elbowed me. 'Sit back,' he hissed.

The minister introduced the Mayor of Riverstone, Aroha Jones. She walked up to the pulpit. She nodded at Ms Everson's parents then spoke to them in te reo Māori. She paused and looked at us all, before continuing.

I kept my eye on Horn-blower, trying to spot any tell-tale monster signs.

Mayor Jones then spoke in English. 'Good morning. Our thoughts and prayers are with Jill Everson's family and friends. As a community we've faced one of the worst things that can ever happen.'

Horn-blower's head was cocked to one side. His lips were pursed, and he was nodding like he did when he interviewed people on TV.

'With the arrest today, as a town we get to move on,' Mayor Jones said. 'But not Jill. Not her family.' She focused on them again. 'I just hope this quick arrest helps bring some form of closure and justice for Jill. An end to this Christmas tragedy in our safe town.'

Horn-blower smirked and put a hand over his mouth.

My leg bounced up and down. I wanted to kick something.

'As a town,' the mayor said, 'we say goodbye to a wonderful, caring teacher, and we start a new chapter. We begin to heal.' She nodded to Ms Everson's parents and sat back down.

I clamped my mouth shut, biting hard, and started grinding my teeth. It wasn't fair. I wanted to shout, 'Sally's not the murderer – he's still out there. Probably right here!' At least then people would know the truth, but then so would the murderer.

Sam blocked my view of Horn-blower and put his hand on my knee to make it stop jiggling. He whispered, 'Do bats poo upside down?'

I exhaled and smiled. I nudged him. *Thank God for Sam.*

Next, people got up and talked about how kind Ms Everson had been to children and animals. I tried not to look surprised. At Dad's funeral I'd tried to hug her and she'd pushed me away. But that had not been the worst thing my teacher had done. It had taken NaiNai ages to get her visa after Dad's accident. She had missed saying goodbye to him at the hospital. By the time she'd arrived, Mum and Uncle Pike had arranged everything for the funeral, and NaiNai had not been okay about any of it, but especially not the cremation. After we'd scattered Dad's ashes into the water off Riverstone Bridge, she'd flown straight back to China. I didn't know if I'd ever see her back here again. When I'd got back to school Ms Everson used my family scattering Dad's ashes into the river as an example of cultural in-sensitivity and blamed it on my grandma being Chinese. I'd sat in class embarrassed and confused, trying not to cry. By the end of school I had the biggest headache. When I got home I kept it to myself; Mum already had enough to deal with.

Sam nudged me. 'Remember the guinea pigs?' he whispered. He sniggered and I tried not to laugh. Ms Everson hadn't cared about them – in fact, she used to make the class look after them on the weekend. We'd never taken them; Mum always said, 'Fuck no to that shit.' Then one day, after school holidays, we came back and they were dead. No one had looked after them. Ms Everson waited until we'd all sat down, then she picked them up by their tiny feet and dropped them into the rubbish bin, blaming us 'cruel children' for their deaths. Emily Watson had cried for most of that day. Today she wasn't crying at all, which was really strange.

Horn-blower chatted to the woman beside him. I scanned the room again. This service was bigger than Dad's or Melanie's mum's, and they had both been pretty huge. My chin trembled and I pressed my lips tighter to stop it. Being here made me feel like it had only happened yesterday. My throat squeezed itself and I swallowed. The minister was droning on, but hard as I tried, I couldn't stop everything blurring up. I shut my eyes and tears rolled down my cheeks. Wiping my face with my hands, I quickly pulled out my tissues, blowing my nose. I didn't turn around in case Uncle Pike got worried. The church was so packed there was nothing he could do anyway.

Sam put his arm around me. He whispered that his parents had been fighting again. I knew this was his way of making me feel better, by distracting me. I asked him what the fights were about and he shrugged, whispering, 'Usual baby-making sex stuff.' I was sure he was mashing up his parents' problems with Todd's video teasing from the other day, but it made me smile. It helped.

Finally the service ended. It took ages for us to get out of the church as we shuffled in the crowd. A small, hot, sticky hand grabbed mine. I looked down at Suzie Pratt staring up at me, snot running into her open mouth. She had on a purple-and-shiny-green *Little Mermaid* costume that strangely worked with her bird's-nest hair. I was glad to see her, and also glad she didn't seem upset about the funeral. I smiled and squeezed her hand. 'I really like your outfit.'

She didn't move, and her expression stayed the same.

Mrs Pratt wasn't with her. I stood on my tiptoes and searched for her among the forest of adults. Suddenly her panicked face popped up over some shoulders behind Suzie. I waved and pointed at the little girl. Mrs Pratt nodded, looking relieved, and pushed through the crowd. I passed Suzie's hand to her mum and said goodbye. I didn't want to hang around in case Mrs Pratt asked me any crayon-related questions.

'Thank you, Tippy,' she said. Suzie kept staring at me even as her mum kneeled in front of her; I didn't think she had blinked once. Mrs Pratt stoked Suzie's hand. 'You can't leave Mummy, remember?'

'No!' The little girl snatched her hand away and ran back through the crowd towards the front of the church. Her mum got up and hurried after her.

I looked for Sam but he must have already gone. Up ahead Uncle Pike and Devon waited for me, not caring about going against the flow of people.

'You okay?' my uncle said, peering at me.

'I'm fine. Sam looked after me.'

'Good.' He gave me a hug. 'Well, let's get out of here and have some ice cream – what do you say?'

I nodded and held both their hands like I had in the airport, which seemed like ages ago now.

'Sticky hand,' Devon said, swinging my arm. 'You been eating lollies?'

I shook my head and Devon frowned. I wished I had but I was pretty sure it was Suzie's snot.

Outside, Duncan Nunn was near the fence handing out business cards to a news crew.

'I'm surprised he hasn't organised a bus for an open home afterwards,' Uncle Pike said. 'Oh God, surely he's not trying to sell Jill Everson's house here?'

'I'm going to say goodbye to Sam,' I said.

He was standing beside his dad, who'd now been cornered by Duncan. They hadn't seen me so I hung back a little, listening. I searched for Horn-blower but couldn't see him.

Duncan touched Mr Campbell on the elbow. 'So what do you think?'

He looked down at his arm. 'Nice power move, Duncan.'

The real-estate agent laughed. 'You know, it's a sweet investment. You and the wife don't have to live there. Maybe take a second look?'

'Let me talk to Lisa,' he said, trying to get away.

Over by the church steps, Dr Lisa had her back to us. She reached out and touched Ms Everson's mum on the arm. She reminded me of a Greek goddess, the folds in her dress catching the sun.

Duncan patted Mr Campbell on the shoulder. 'Bring Lisa again.'

Sam was playing with his phone.

'See you later?' I said.

He didn't look up. 'Yep.'

I didn't want to leave him. 'Weird, right?'

He put his phone in his pocket. 'Emily Watson didn't even cry, and she cries at everything.'

I gave him a big hug. 'Thank you.'

He smiled then looked at his shoes.

'Why do you carry those paper flowers around?' I said. 'Do you have a crush on Emily?'

'What are you talking about? *You* have a crush on her. You go on and on about those flowers all the time. I couldn't even make the stupid things.'

I frowned. Was he kidding? Before I could ask, Uncle Pike and Devon came over.

Mr Campbell excused himself from Duncan. 'Fellas.' He gave them a group hug. 'Am I glad to see you! Please let me introduce you to Duncan Nunn, real-estate agent extraordinaire.'

'We're old friends.' Duncan pumped Devon's hand then spun to shake Uncle Pike's. 'My best gays!' He swept his arm out in dramatic fashion, hitting one of Jill Everson's family members in the chest.

'Ow!' She burst into tears.

An angry relation put their arm around her. 'Pervert!'

'Sorry!' Duncan called after them. 'Not sorry – am I right, boys?' He held up his hands like he was squeezing some imaginary tennis balls.

'Good luck,' Mr Campbell muttered into Uncle Pike's ear and gave a little laugh.

'You're evil,' my uncle said.

Sam was standing in front of his dad, playing on his phone again. I tried to think who else could've put that flower in our mailbox. Emily Watson? She was wacky enough to do it, and they were her invention. I couldn't see her in the crowd outside.

'So, have you decided?' Duncan asked my uncle, linking his arm though Devon's.

Mr Campbell chuckled and held Sam's hand, raising it like a boxer's. 'The winner! Have fun.' Sam glanced at me and waved, then they were gone before I could ask him about the flowers again.

I felt a little bad for thinking of Emily as weird; knowing her, she probably meant it as a nice thing for everyone in our class.

'Alone at last,' Duncan said. 'So? Don't keep me in suspenders.'
He laughed.

Uncle Pike grabbed my hand. 'Remind me to organise a
memorial service for Russell Campbell once we escape this
madness.'

We walked as fast as we could through the media pack, with my
uncle hopping and lurching along on his one crutch, trying to
outrun Duncan to the car.

But Duncan beat us and leaned against the front passenger door.
'Tell me,' he said, 'how amazed were you by the house?'

'Totally amazed,' Devon said, staring at him.

'Those views, am I right?' Duncan elbowed Uncle Pike in the
ribs. 'Are we ready to sign?'

'That sounds like a great idea.' My uncle put his hand on
Duncan's shoulder and walked him away from the car. 'But there
are so many reasons why we never will.' Uncle Pike opened his door
and got in while Duncan stood there with a smiling-confused look.
'Namely because we hate everything about it.'

'Kisses.' Devon drove off and left Duncan there smiling.

We'd been back home for a minute when: 'Cooee!'

Mrs Brown stood in our balcony doorway with some fruit mince
pies. Her sundress had big chocolate-coloured flowers on it and was
a lot shorter than I remembered. She came inside and set the pies
on the table. I liked licking off the icing sugar but hated the filling.

Uncle Pike was lying on Devon's lap on the sofa with the tablet,
trying to get hold of Mum.

'Anyway,' said Mrs Brown, 'just wanted to check on you, Tippy,
and see how the funeral was. I thought it might be nice to have a
cuppa and I can fix you lunch. Don't get up. I know where
everything is.'

'*Quelle surprise.*' Uncle Pike chucked the tablet beside him.
'Sorry, Tippy, no Lennie yet.'

I shrugged. The worst of it was over now anyway.

Mrs Brown patted Devon's arm, and he gave her a loud air kiss. 'So I spoke to my friend Raelene at the rest home, and she's never heard of that Show Queen fraud, Claire Bates.'

'So Bates lied about her volunteering,' my uncle said. 'Interesting...'

'I have a mind to report her.' Mrs Brown turned to Devon and smiled. 'Your Devon is a very talented designer.'

'You are!' He kissed Mrs Brown on the hand.

It turned out they were already on to the pattern-cutting stage for Melanie's Show Queen dress; I couldn't wait to see it.

Melanie called out from the hallway. 'Bitches, where you at?' She came into the living room.

'I was just making a cuppa,' Mrs Brown said.

'Party,' Melanie said. 'Notice anything different?' She twirled around.

Devon gasped. Uncle Pike squinted and his jaw dropped. '*No.*'

She broke into a big smile, something I hadn't seen before. She did look taller.

'By George, you've done it!' My uncle put his hands together and kissed his fingers.

'What?' I still couldn't see anything different.

'Tippy Chan, our duckling has become a swan. Glide for me, swan. Glide!'

Melanie walked up and down the living room and twirled. I looked at her feet. She was wearing heels. 'I took your advice and cut school. Who knew practice made perfect?'

Devon put his arm around Uncle Pike, who fanned his eyes with his hands and blinked back tears. 'So ... proud.'

'Are you crying?' Melanie asked.

'As if.' Uncle Pike wiped his eyes. 'Nails, show me.'

She waggled her fingers. Her nails were long and pink with white tips.

He inspected them. 'French manicure. They did a good job. Don't eat them until after you win.'

'They're a little bit fucking annoying.' She tapped on the screen of her phone. 'But I do like doing that with them.'

'Just don't break them,' Mrs Brown shouted over the noise of the jug.

Melanie rolled her eyes then zeroed in on me. 'Chan, how was it?'

I shrugged. 'Okay, actually.'

She nodded. 'Good.'

I mumbled thanks and checked out the carpet.

'Isn't that nice?' Mrs Brown said. She started emptying our fridge of all our food for lunch. I kept waiting for her to notice the drawings under the postcards. She stopped and turned to me. I held my breath. 'Now tell me everything that happened at the funeral.'

CHAPTER SIXTEEN
The Return

After lunch I was humming along to Madonna's 'Holiday' as I vacuumed the living-room floor. Uncle Pike was resting on his bed while Devon sunbathed on the balcony. Part of my mind was running through who in my class, besides Emily, would give me an origami flower when I felt a poke on my back.

'Hi, honey.'

'Mum?' I turned around and there she was: tanned, relaxed and beautiful. I gave her a huge hug. I'd forgotten how good she smelled.

'Surprise! I couldn't wait.'

I hugged her again. I couldn't believe it was her.

She laughed. 'I need to go away more often. That's such a pretty dress!'

I gave her a twirl. 'Thanks, Devon made it for me. It's asymmetrical.' It was so good to see her. It felt like it had been forever.

Mum grabbed me and gave me heaps of kisses. 'Your hair looks so much better in real life, thank God.' She held my face. 'I'm sorry, I wanted to be here for the funeral.'

Uncle Pike shuffled into the living room clutching the *Bully*. 'Tippy, I think I've found...' He glanced up. 'Good lord! When did you arrive?'

'About five minutes ago. Surprise!' She gave him a big slap on his shoulder.

'Ow!' He rubbed it.

'Sook,' she said. She took my hand.

'I've been trying to call you,' I said.

'On the second-last island I made a run for it. Twenty-six hours...' She shook her head. 'Never again.'

'You look great,' Uncle Pike said.

She did. Just like my old mum, before her and Dad had started fighting over money.

'Don't sound so surprised.' She punched my uncle on the arm. 'You didn't burn down the house.'

'Ow! No, but I did have sex in your bed.' He nudged her with his elbow. She grimaced then started picking up the newspapers beside the couch.

Devon came in from the balcony in his tiny yellow Speedos. He wore his towel as a cape. 'Oh hi, Helen!'

Her mouth dropped, as did her gaze.

'Mum,' I said, 'these are called budgie smugglers.'

'Did you do a lot of reading on your trip?' Devon said. 'It looks like you did.'

I'd never seen Mum speechless before.

'You look fabulous, BTW,' he said.

She nodded, still staring at his yellow togs. 'Um, thanks...'

Uncle Pike waved a hand in front of her.

When she glanced up, her cheeks went pink. 'I'm...' Her voice sounded weird and she cleared her throat. 'I'm just going to put my bags away.'

Devon smiled, but as soon as she left he turned to Uncle Pike and mouthed 'fuck'.

My uncle whispered to me and Devon, 'What about the fucking window?'

I distracted Mum in her room while Uncle Pike and Devon cleaned it with nail polish remover. I wasn't sure about the fridge. Even though she'd just got back, I managed to convince her to take me to see Todd at Dunedin Hospital. I may have played on her feeling bad about missing the funeral a bit more than I should have, but this was important. Besides seeing him, I really wanted to get his phone and make sure he was safe.

After unpacking and a quick nap Mum called Mrs Landers and I listened in. It didn't sound good. But, after Mum hung up, she said he was fine. I asked if that meant he was awake, but she shook her head.

Uncle Pike and Devon walked with me and Mum to the car. They were giving us some alone time, while taking advantage and having a date night away.

My uncle waited until Mum was in the car before he asked me, 'You've got our hotel number? We're only away one night.'

I nodded.

'Keep an eye out in the hospital and be careful – whoever did this is still out there.' Uncle Pike frowned. 'Maybe we shouldn't go...'

I laughed. 'You sound like Mum.' I told him it was fine. 'Nancys meeting when we get back,' I said.

Devon gave me a squeeze. 'Remember, don't trust anyone.'

'That's a good rule for life,' Uncle Pike said. 'And the first rule of The Nancys?'

'Everyone's a suspect,' we all said together.

I gave them a quick hug then jumped in the car with Mum. She took off, tyres screeching.

On the drive up to Dunedin it was her turn for questions. She kept asking me what we'd got up to when she was away.

I was pretty hazy. 'Shopping, sightseeing, hanging out at home. With Uncle Pike's ankle we couldn't do much...' I filled her in on all the local news, which was a lot, and luckily she stopped asking me things when we got into town. I had definitely got my questioning from her DNA.

In Dunedin the footpaths were busy with cruise-ship tourists. We drove past the brick Allied Press building with its witchy turret, and up ahead Dunedin Hospital loomed. I pressed my bare feet against the glove box, something Mum hated, though today she didn't say anything.

Inside the hospital lift she squeezed my hand. 'We can go home if you want to. Anytime, okay?'

I squeezed back and nodded. I felt guilty – I should've told her about my visit with Uncle Pike, but I didn't want to get him in trouble. Anyway, it was too late now, and there was no point getting her upset.

We got out on the fifth floor; it was decorated now with silver-and-red tinsel along the walls and under the desk. On Sam's sneeze-wall they'd put up a large paper Christmas tree with 'get well' wishes as decorations. Mum spoke to the ICU nurse at the desk, and this time we were allowed to see Todd.

Through a window we saw him hooked up to life-support machines. It felt so good to look at him but horrible at the same time. With his head shaved he seemed a quarter of his size. His mum was sitting by his side. Mrs Landers had lost a lot of weight; her happy, round face was now hollowed out and saggy. She gave us a weak smile and got up. Her eyes were puffy and red, and I wondered if she'd slept since the accident.

As she came to meet us, I realised she could blow our cover and tell Mum I'd been here before. I picked at the nail polish on my thumbnail, praying she had forgotten.

'Good of you to come again,' she said. 'I know how hard this must be for you both.'

Shit. Mum shot me a look and my breath hitched. 'Of course,' she said, hugging Mrs Landers. 'I'm so sorry, Ange.'

I watched Todd behind them in the window. When Mum gave me a smile, I relaxed a little.

'How is he?' I asked, scared to hear the answer.

Mrs Landers gripped my hands tightly; hers felt hot. 'Where

there's breath there's hope, Tippy.' She shook them up and down. 'We'll hear his voice soon. You know Todd, can't keep quiet for long.'

I smiled and avoided her headachy-eyes, staring instead at the gold crucifix around her neck. Todd didn't have a filter; you always knew what he was thinking. Is that what had got him in here?

'Have they found his phone?' I had to ask.

She let go of my hands. 'No.'

Mum gave me a weird, questioning look.

I jumped in. 'Mrs Landers, did Todd ever mention selling his videos?'

She frowned. 'He did say a video was going to make him a lot of money. I thought he was just being silly.' She glanced at Mum. 'Have you heard something?'

'Do you know what the video was about?' I asked.

Mum put her hand on my arm. 'Tippy...'

'No, no, it's okay, Helen. Really.' Mrs Landers smiled at me. 'You know, I wish I'd asked. Do you know?'

I shook my head and avoided Mum. I wished I knew as well.

'Would you like to say hello?' Mrs Landers said. 'Some of the doctors think he might be able to hear us.'

I tried to be brave and smile back, but I'm not sure it came out the way I wanted. Part of me felt relieved Mrs Landers hadn't said any more about me and Uncle Pike visiting. Maybe the days had blurred for her like they had for me when Dad was in that room. Except some stuff I'd never forget.

Mum put her arm around me.

'It's okay, Mum,' I said. 'I can go alone.'

She nodded but came in with me.

Todd's room was quiet, aside from the beeping of the monitors and the noise from the breathing machine. For a second it was my dad lying there after his car accident, his head bandaged, arms by his sides. The warmth of Dad's hand – surely it wouldn't have been warm if he wasn't going to wake up. I remembered thinking he must be able to feel my touch. Pleading with Mum to wait for NaiNai, to wait until Dad got better. And then the silence when the doctor turned off the machines. My ears had been hot and muffled, straining to hear any sounds of life. I'd been numb. Mum had clutched my arm, crying. The bruises from her fingers had lasted for days, but in that moment I'd felt nothing. I had kept my head bowed to hide my dry eyes from her and the hospital staff. I'd tried desperately to cry, if only to prove nothing was wrong with me, but no tears came. Nothing. Starting to panic, I'd hid further behind my hair, embarrassed and guilty I wasn't feeling the right things at the death of my father. A monster in daughter's clothing.

'Tippy? Tippy?' Mum touched my cheek. 'You okay, honey? We can come back later if you like.'

The doorhandle of the bathroom behind her came into focus. 'It's okay.' I cleared my throat.

'No, it's not, honey,' she said. 'But it's good you are here. Do you want some time alone with Todd? I can wait outside if you like.'

'Thanks, Mum.' I sat down beside him and grabbed his hand. It was kind of weird – we'd never done this when he was awake, even though classmates teased us about being girlfriend and boyfriend. No doubt he'd give me crap about it later. 'Hey, Bridge Boy. Like your new nickname? Lollipop isn't going to work anymore without your mop, unless maybe Lollipop Stick? Sorry, spoiler alert – you're bald.' I tried to laugh but sniffed instead. I missed the three of us so much. Todd had to get better and I had to be brave for him. I cleared my throat. 'Wake up, Todd. Wake up, Todd.' I repeated it over and over, hoping to annoy him awake, but his monitors didn't change, so I shut up.

'Get well soon' cards covered his bedside table.

I held his hand with both of mine and rubbed the back of it with my thumbs. 'I need you to wake up, Todd. Wake up. I think you're still in danger. You need to tell me – what did you see?'

One of the cards had a gross clown on it. I reached over and opened it, recognising Sam's writing.

'I guess Sam's ahead of me. No one's as annoying as him. Except you.' Poking out from behind Sam's card was a white origami lily.

As we said goodbye to Mrs Landers, I asked if Emily Watson or her parents had been to visit.

Mrs Landers shook her head.

'Who gave Todd the paper flower?'

'Isn't it sweet?' Mrs Landers hugged me goodbye. 'I wish I knew.'

CHAPTER SEVENTEEN
What Would Nancy Do?

It had been a huge day, but I couldn't let the mystery of the origami flowers go and I couldn't sleep. Who was doing it? Was it connected to the murder? In my bones I felt Todd was in danger. Before going to bed, while Mum was in the bathroom, I'd called the hotel where Uncle Pike and Devon were staying. But they'd gone out. I left a whispered message with the receptionist.

In bed everything we'd done and seen was on repeat in my head. There had to be something we'd missed. What would Nancy do? It niggled at me in the dark like a wobbly tooth or the answer to one of Ms Everson's surprise tests. A slow freight train rattled in the distance. Staring at my clown curtains, I thought of Devon – and it hit me. I knew what I had to do.

The time was 12.54 a.m. If I was going to do it I should do it now. I lay there, my heart racing. I could just stay in bed, safe and warm. And let someone else die? I got up and peeked in on Mum. She was 'lady snoring', as she called it. I texted Sam, asking if he wanted to meet me at the old hospital in half an hour. I told him it was to go ghost hunting, which was kind of true. *Please answer.* I crept out to the garage and grabbed my bike. The roller door was down so I had to go back through the house, my wheels making a quiet *snick-snick*. I pulled open the sliding door onto the balcony. Next door, the Browns had put up their Christmas tree. Tiny red and green stars twinkled, lighting up a corner of their dark living room, the only lights on. I carried my bike down the balcony stairs and quickly walked it along the side of the house until I was out on the road. It was not too late to go back to bed. I shook my head.

My phone buzzed. It was Sam. *Not now. Go tomorrow afternoon.* He was such a baby. Todd teased Sam heaps that Dr Lisa still wiped his bum.

I texted back: *Has 2 b now – ghosts nite etc.* Then I sent a follow up: *Plse?????*

Sam sneaking out was a long shot but I'd hoped he would, just in case anything happened. I waited. My phone buzzed:

DON'T GO!!!! BE CAREFUL!!!!!!!

I flipped my phone shut and dropped it in my backpack. I was trying not to be disappointed; at least he knew where I was. Besides what was the worst that could happen? I shuddered and tried not to scare myself out of going. Nancy would be gone already. Jumping on my bike I coasted down the hill among the hum of the orange streetlights.

Though brightly lit, the town was asleep, the streets empty except for the late-night travellers passing through. Even the pubs had been closed for a couple of hours. I rode across the bridge on the pedestrian walkway, and was glad I did when a logging truck and trailer rumbled past. Below me the river was a mixture of streetlight orange and browny black. Then I was off the bridge and onto Main Street. A total of three cars passed me before I got to the Old Hospital Road turn-off.

After biking uphill most of the way I was puffed. At one point I had to get off and walk. When I reached the old hospital its carpark was deserted. I leaned my bike against a tree in the shadows near the front entrance. The empty hospital had turned creepy. My day thoughts about babies turned to all the people who had died here. My arms got goosebumps and I spun around to check behind me, scraping gravel over the concrete. I needed to get in and out before I completely spooked myself. I pulled out my torch and ducked through the gap in the broken front door.

Inside I stood still and listened. Nothing. I crept towards the main corridor with my torch switched off. The deeper in I went, the darker it got. I could just make out the far doors to the ward and really wished I had Bunny Whiskers' eyes. Up ahead was the signpost for the kitchen. Maybe I should've waited and gone with Sam. I checked my phone: no messages. It was not as bright as my torch so I left it flipped open for its soft light.

Around the corner and halfway down the next corridor were the kitchen's double doors with their round windows. I tiptoed towards them in big, exaggerated steps, but old leaves crunched under my sneakers, making me freeze each time. My hands were clammy by the time I peered through the cloudy, scummy glass portholes. I couldn't make out anything inside but a black mass. I pocketed my phone and, as quietly as I could, I gingerly pushed open one of the doors. The spring hinges *tick-ticked* over my breathing.

The smell of bleach was strong. I switched on my torch. Stainless steel bounced the light around the clean benches, except for a large sink, which looked rusty. Under one bench were grimy pots stacked on dirty oven trays. I shone the torch on the floor and it gleamed back.

'Bingo,' I said, my voice sounding way too loud.

Devon had been right when he said he hated the smell of hospitals. It had been nagging at me until I realised we shouldn't have smelled any hospital smells, just an old building. We'd been so busy looking for the murder weapon that we hadn't searched for any other clues.

I turned around slowly. The hair on my neck prickled. My muddy footprints stood out on the freshly mopped floor. I flicked off my torch and froze, holding my breath, listening for any sound. The silence hummed as my eyes adjusted to the night. Through the large windows above the sink, shapes outside came into fuzzy focus. *Crap*. I ducked down. Anyone out there would've seen me plain as day. *Fuck*.

Crouched there, my heart pounding and body tense, I was ready to run. I let out my breath and took a big gulp of air. The smell of bleach burned my nose and throat. I was too close to leave now. Bleach stung my eyes. I forced myself towards the sink bench, blinking and clutching at my stomach. I didn't want to look up, I really didn't, but I needed to know if anyone was out there.

I took out my phone but slammed it shut as light flared from it. I inched myself up. Hot and cold prickles crawled over my scalp as my ghost-like face stared back at me from the window. I scanned outside: nothing but the overgrown courtyard and empty windows staring back from the opposite wing. I exhaled, realising I'd been holding my breath.

Suddenly movement flashed across one of those windows. I bolted, flying through the kitchen doors and down the hallway, forcing myself to stop at the end. Blood pounded in my ears. I peered around the corner and tried not to scream. The far doors to the ward were swinging. I leaned back against the wall then launched myself forward, sprinting in the dark towards the front entrance and through the foyer, shooting through the gap in the door.

Outside, the carpark was still empty. I ran to my bike, glancing over my shoulder, but everything was in the shadow. I jumped on and pedalled as hard and fast as I could, not sitting on the seat, gulping mouthfuls of fresh air, hoping to stop the burning from the bleach. I wanted to check behind me but was too scared of losing control of the bike downhill. Instead, I listened hard, but the wind and my banging heart blocked my ears.

I was alone. The only person alive out in the open.

I hit the dip. I was close to Main Street and pushed on up the short hill. Behind me came the sound of a car. I reached the top of the hill and sped down past the stop sign at the intersection with Main, taking a left. No traffic in sight. After the darkness of the road, the orange streetlights were like spotlights.

I leaned in around the corner. My tyres slid on the loose gravel and the bike tipped. I wrenched it back up. On my left was a steep drop down a clay bank, maybe two metres. I pumped the brakes and jumped off. Headlights shone behind me from the dip in Old Hospital Road. I chucked my bike down the bank and slid after it.

I heard the car over the streetlights' hum. I listened to it slow down at the stop sign and then rev up and turn onto Main Street. I froze, too scared to move. Gravel from the roadside crunched and popped under the car's slow-moving tyres. It was directly above me. I squeezed my eyes shut and prayed for it to keep moving, but it stopped, the engine idling. I hadn't caught my breath from the bike ride, and now I was breathing so fast I couldn't get enough air. I worried they would hear me panting from up there, which only made it worse. The car door opened, and I let out a tiny squeal. I put up my hands to cover my mouth, but they were shaking out of control.

Tears ran down my face. This was it – I was going to die.

From downtown came the sound of another vehicle heading this way. Above me, the car door shut and the engine revved as it took off down the road. I needed to get up and see who it was, but instead I slid down, crying and holding my knees.

When my breathing finally returned to normal, I wiped my eyes and nose on my sleeves and stood up. The dull thud of a headache was coming. I pulled the neck of my T-shirt over my face to stop any glare and checked my phone underneath: 2.48 a.m. and a new message from Sam asking where I was.

I texted back: *Home safe :)* and stuffed it in my pocket. I didn't want him to worry. He couldn't come and get me anyway.

For a while I stayed down against the bank, pressing myself into it each time a car passed. The smell of dirt seemed safe – and was preferable to bleach.

A car drove past slowly again. I grabbed my phone to call Mum, but as I pressed my contacts button it died. *Shit*. I crouched, feeling the ground for a weapon to protect myself. Drunken laughter echoed out and the car sped away. My teeth started chattering. I stamped my feet and hugged myself to keep warm. Although I was freezing, I didn't want to leave my safe spot.

I shivered there until dawn, when the noise of traffic had become more regular. Then, in the early light, I pedalled home. I dumped my bike in the garden by the garage. All the lights in the house were off. I crept along the side of the house and snuck inside through the sliding door.

As I shut it, the light blinded me.

'Tippy Chan, where the *hell* have you been?' Mum roared. 'You answer when I ring you. I was about to call the police.' She threw the cordless on the couch. I must have looked terrible, because she went from angry to concerned in less than a second. 'Oh my God. Are you all right?' She held on to my snot-mud-caked arms.

Fuck. I nodded. 'I'm fine. No one's touched me.' Then something burst in me. I started crying big, hot tears and hugged Mum, never wanting to let her go.

It all came out. I told her about The Nancys.

She just sat there, and at the end calmly thanked me for telling the truth. She told me not to worry, that I hadn't done anything wrong.

'Neither did Uncle Pike or Devon,' I said.

'They're adults, honey. It's their job to know better.' Her smile was gone. 'Shower and sleep.'

I stood under the hot water for ages while Mum came in and out speaking to the police, finally she sat at the edge of the bath, holding the phone.

'Don't worry, honey. They're sending someone out to the old hospital to check it out. It's going to be okay.'

My mind still raced. I needed to warn Uncle Pike and Devon about the murderer, and now about Mum and the police knowing everything. She handed me a towel. After I dried off, she helped me into my nightie like she used to when I was little.

In my bedroom she gave me a massive cuddle and kissed me on the head. 'I love you, Tippy.'

'Love you too.' She felt warm and safe.

Mum shut my door. I let out a massive sigh and went to crawl into bed, when I saw the white paper flower on my pillow. I started screaming.

CHAPTER EIGHTEEN
Leave

I woke up to murmuring outside my bedroom door. The sun peeked around the sides of my curtains. I grabbed the tablet to check the time, but it was flat. I had no idea how long I'd slept. I shivered as last night came back to me. Had the murderer been in my room with that flower? I hadn't been able to tell Mum. When I started screaming, she'd burst into my room and I'd just stood there, ripped paper on the floor. She'd held me for ages and wanted me to sleep with her, but then the phone had rung, and it was the police. I'd sat on my bed while Mum listened. She covered the handset and whispered, 'Nothing there,' then she put the call on speaker. I heard an annoyed man's voice.

'...just a little girl scaring herself silly with ghost stories. We have the killer in gaol, Mrs Chan. Please stop wasting our time.'

Mum had hung her head and ended the call. When she finally looked at me, I could tell she believed the police. I sat there, twisting my duvet, not knowing what else I could say. She'd asked again if I wanted to sleep in her room, but I didn't. Instead, we'd gone around the house checking all the doors were locked and the windows shut before finally I fell asleep.

Lying in bed now, I could make out snatches of conversation.

'...out all night,' Mum was saying.

The smell of bleach was still in my nose. I wondered who she was talking to.

'She thought she was going to be murdered.'

'She's all right, though?' It was my uncle. I felt relieved to hear his deep voice.

'She's fine, no thanks to you.'

I got out of bed. We needed an urgent Nancys meeting. I had to tell them about the old hospital.

'She's sleeping.' Mum's voice was close now.

'I just want to see her,' he said.

My doorhandle turned.

'No.' She sounded stressed, which usually did not end well. 'She's told me everything. The whole lot. Me being pissed off with you doesn't even begin—'

'Come on.' The turning stopped.

'Seriously,' she said, 'I can't even look at you right now. I'll tell her you dropped by.'

'Come on, Lennie.'

'Fuck you, Pike. She was out all night because of you. Anything could have happened. You didn't see her. She was terrified. Terrified.'

I had a sinking feeling in my gut as my hand hovered near the doorhandle.

'Firstly,' he said, 'thank God she's all right. Secondly, she's an amazing girl. How about getting out of your fucking helicopter and trusting her?'

I needed to stop this. This was my fault, and we needed to talk about the murderer, who was still out there. I grabbed the handle when tapping started at my window.

'How fucking dare you?' Mum's voice was getting louder. 'Are you really saying that to me right now? Trust? You pulled her out of school. You promised not to take her to see Todd.'

'Look, I'm sorry, okay? Just let me see her and I'll go.'

The tapping started again, so I went over and peered outside. Devon waved furiously. I pulled open the curtains with a big, silly grin on my face. The bright sunshine made me blinky as I opened the window.

He leaned in and grabbed my face, smooching my forehead. 'Oh my God. Hello, Tippy-Tippy.' His voice sounded weird, and he gulped. 'It's so good to see you.'

Bunny Whiskers jumped up on the windowsill and put her tail under Devon's chin.

'Come in,' I said.

He nodded towards my door. 'I think they need a moment. Come out here – I'll grab you. I used to sneak out my window all the time when my parents fought.'

I hadn't climbed through the window for ages but first I needed to clear things up and stop the fight. 'Maybe if I go see them...'

'Trust me, honey, there's more going on here than last night. Just give them some time.'

'Okay.' I guessed five minutes wouldn't hurt. I grabbed my chair, and Devon held out his arms to help me over. 'Hang on. I should get dressed first.' I was wearing the Piggy-Cat nightie Devon had made me: his interpretation of my money box. Like my Piggy-Cat, the one on the nightie had its eyes closed and a big smile, but everything else was different. He'd made it orange with blue polka dots and given it a pink candy-floss wig. Plus it had no arms.

'Rubbish,' he said. 'You look fabulous.'

I pushed myself up and was halfway out when Bunny Whiskers scrambled against me to get inside. 'Really, puss?' I gently pushed her head.

'Stop being so fucking proud and open your eyes,' Uncle Pike boomed from the hallway.

Bunny Whiskers startled at the sound and tried to turn around, slipping off the windowsill and clawing Devon's arm on the way down. 'Fuck!' he said. 'That really hurt.'

The cat sprinted off into the garden.

'She didn't mean to,' I said.

He lifted me down and gave me a big hug. 'I know. It's okay.'

The Browns' living-room window opened, and Mrs Brown popped out and waved excitedly. 'Devon. Devon! Over here!'

I rolled my eyes. 'Your number-one fan.'

'Phyllis, my love.' He blew her a large kiss, which she caught and held to her breasts.

'Tippy?' Uncle Pike had opened my door and was gaping at my empty bed.

Mum pushed past him. 'You can't just barge into our house...' She froze when she saw I wasn't there.

'Hello.' I waved like Devon, hoping they weren't going to be too mad.

Mum balled her fists. 'Get inside now!'

'Go easy,' Uncle Pike said.

'Just leave, Pike. That's what you're good at.' She walked out of the room.

'Sorry, Tippy,' he said, following her.

Devon put his arm around my shoulders. 'Come on. It'll be okay.' We walked past the front of the house to the garage.

My tummy was sore and I rubbed it. 'It's my fau—'

Mrs Brown ran up to Devon and gave him a hug.

Mum was still shouting at my uncle. 'You go on about how much this town hates you, but it's bullshit, Pike. You're the only one who hates you.'

Devon frowned. 'Maybe you should go back inside, Phyllis. This might take a while.'

Mrs Brown nodded and patted my arm. Somehow I doubted she'd miss this show. She stepped through the garden, avoiding Mum and Uncle Pike, who had burst out of the house and were now on the footpath at the end of the driveway. Devon put his arm around me, and his other hand over his heart.

'You could have just fucking come out!' Mum was going nuclear; her eyes bulged and her fists clenched. 'Mum and Dad would have dealt – instead you ran away. How could you leave us?'

Uncle Pike leaned on his crutches. 'What are you talking about? You went to uni. You had Joe.'

She gave a short, hard laugh. 'You think that was easy? Where were you when I needed you?'

'I live in Sydney.'

'You fucking left—'

'I'm not your husband!' It was the loudest I'd ever heard Uncle Pike roar.

Mum gasped, and put her hand to her stomach.

He sighed. 'Shit. I'm sorry, Lennie, but this is a conversation you really need to be having with Joe, not me.'

Seeing Mum's tears run down her red, splotchy face made my lip quiver. I felt the hot flush of my own tears prickling. Her shoulders slumped, and all at once she seemed small and sad and lost and alone. I wanted to be brave and tried blinking to stop crying. Out of the corner of my eye Mrs Brown lurked, and in that moment I wanted to scream at her to fuck off.

Devon's arm was too hot around me. I shrugged him off and moved away.

'Joe was the best,' my uncle said. 'And it's fucked he's not here, but you can't take that out on me, or anyone else.'

Mum wiped her eyes with the back of her hand. 'You put my daughter in danger. Now get the fuck away from us.'

'I'd never let anything happen to Tippy.'

Mum snorted. 'She could've died last night, or worse.'

'Under your watch,' Uncle Pike said.

'From ideas you put in her head!'

'Come on.'

'Leave! Go!' Mum screamed at him. 'I'm not going to lose Tippy too. Go!' she shrieked, the cords in her neck sticking out.

Devon was in my ear telling me, 'It's going to be all right.'

I ran to Mum as my uncle headed towards the white rental car.

'Don't go, Uncle Pike.' I turned to Mum and hugged her. 'This isn't fair. It's my fault.'

She held me tight. 'Not now, Tippy. Not now.'

'Mum!' Her grip didn't change.

Uncle Pike's face was pale. 'I love you, Tippy. This is not your fault.' He got in the car.

Devon went past and squeezed my hand. 'Sorry about this,

Helen.' He opened the driver's door and turned to Mum. 'Pike just wanted to give you a break and spend time with Tippy.'

Mum didn't move. He got in the car and they drove off.

'Pike!' she yelled after them. 'Pike!' But they had gone. 'That's right, fuck off. Leave.' She crumpled, holding on to me in my nightie, our crying the only sound on the street.

Later that afternoon, Mum took me down to buy a Christmas tree from a paddock near Riverstone Bridge. We drove in silence; neither of us had really spoken since the morning's fight. I'd always looked forward to getting the tree with Dad. This year, as we wandered around the pine trees, it was easily the most awkward and least fun time ever. Near the back of the makeshift forest, I found a wonky, lopsided one, missing most of its needles. 'This one,' I said, feeling sorry for it.

Mum shrugged behind her dark sunglasses. 'Less mess.'

We drove back in silence. Dad and I used to decorate the tree as well. We had a routine: he would do the tinsel and I'd hang the ornaments, a jumbled collection of reindeer, shiny red, green and silver balls, and three woollen snowmen. Also there was a bunch of crappy craft I'd made when I was really little, which now made no sense at all. Every year Dad would threaten to chuck them in the wheelie bin and I'd laugh, telling him he couldn't 'cause I'd made them especially for him. When we'd finished hanging the decorations he would lift me up and I'd put the Christmas angel on top. She was a Beijing Opera doll NaiNai had sent me from China when I was really little. Dad had helped me make her fairy wings out of pipe-cleaners, but I don't remember that.

This time Mum gave decorating a go, but we didn't get far before we started crying. We sat on the floor surrounded by the decorations and the smell of pine, Mum stroking my hair.

A random memory popped up and I pulled back, wiping my eyes. 'Remember that Christmas lamp I made at school, and Dad nearly killed himself when he plugged it in?' I laughed.

Mum gave me a weird smile. She got up and left the room.

CHAPTER NINETEEN
The Monkey Motels

Being grounded on a Sunday sucked. Mum went to work, leaving me with a long list of chores and Mrs Brown as my prison warden. Mrs Brown said she'd keep an extra-close eye on me. At least Mum was working the day shift so I wouldn't have to spend the night at the Browns'.

As I vacuumed under the dining table I started thinking there were probably two sides to the Cinderella story. Sure, she didn't investigate a murder in the middle of the night, but she'd probably done something dodgy to deserve her punishment, like her stepmother catching her smoking and drinking. My mind drifted back to the sound of that car idling above me and the door opening.

The home phone rang, and I jumped. No doubt Mum checking up on me. I answered it – there was silence on the other end, then a *click*. My heart started to race. I slammed it down and ran out to the balcony.

Melanie was in her usual spot, having a cigarette. She wore a Nirvana T-shirt instead of her normal baggy jersey, but still had on black jeans and gumboots. Her new long hair was in a ponytail. 'Chan.' She squinted up at me on the balcony. 'You okay?'

I nodded and glanced back inside. I didn't want to go in there and thought about asking Melanie to come over, but the call had probably just been a wrong number.

'Your mum's awesome, Chan. Always remember that.'

Inside, the phone started ringing again. I gripped the wooden railing, my knuckles going white. I pictured the white flower on my pillow.

Melanie took a drag and blew the smoke up in the air. She shielded her eyes with her hand. 'First Christmas, you know?'

The phone stopped ringing. I let go of the railing and exhaled. 'It sucks.'

'Sure does.' She took another drag then flicked her cigarette into the hedge. 'See ya, Chan. Take care of yourself. You've got my number if you ever need to, you know...' She started back up the side of the house.

'Why don't you ever stub it out?' I called.

She stopped but didn't turn around. 'This place wouldn't burn to the ground if I did that.' She gave me a wave with the back of her hand. 'Merry Fuck-mess, Chan.'

Back inside, the home phone rang again. I flinched; it seemed louder than normal. Scary thoughts raced along with my pounding heart. *I am here alone. The murderer knows where I live.*

I forced myself to answer it. There was long silence again, then a woman said, 'Tippy?'

'Who is this?' I said in a strange, high voice.

She laughed. 'Sally. It's Sally Homer.'

I sagged against the kitchen bench. She wanted to talk to Uncle Pike. I told her I didn't know when he'd be back, which was true. I hoped he hadn't gone to Sydney. I became aware of how much I'd been sweating. My T-shirt clung to me.

'Can I ask you a question?' I said.

'No, I didn't do it,' Sally said.

'We know that.' Well, I really *did* now, after hiding from the murderer in a ditch. 'After Ms Everson died, who came into your cottage?'

'My lawyers asked me that too.'

I fanned myself with the power bill. 'We just want to help you and stop him before anyone else gets hurt.'

Mrs Brown poked her head in. *Shit.* 'You all right, dear?'

I covered the mouthpiece. 'All good. It's Mum.'

'Oh.' Mrs Brown frowned. 'Really? I just tried to call her. Can I have a word?'

Crap. Sally was still talking.

'...police, you know after the steps on Sunday morning, family, you guys...'

'Hold on please, caller.' I covered the phone again and turned to Mrs Brown. 'Mum says she will call you back.'

'But how does she know I'm here?' Mrs Brown said.

'Thank you.' I smiled. 'Thank you.' I usually found if I did this enough, it freaked people out. 'Thank you.'

Not Mrs Brown. 'It's okay. I'll just wait here.' She sat at the dining table.

'Horn-blower?' I said.

Mrs Brown cocked her head.

'Mike?' Sally laughed. 'He wouldn't have the guts. Plus his clothes would get dirty.'

'But didn't he come to your place?' I remembered him outside her house when she was arrested.

She sighed. 'He did. He always promises and never does. It was so good to see him. But now I know it was just for the scoop. He showed up just before the police came – he must've known about the arrest.'

'Did he come inside?'

Mrs Brown shot up. 'What?'

'You're just like Devon,' Sally said. 'My place is a tidy mess, thank you.'

More like a filthy mess. 'No.' I fake-laughed. 'He could have planted the shoe.' I avoided eye contact with Mrs Brown.

The line was silent except for Sally's breathing. 'Shit. But no ... I mean, he did come in, but why would he do that?'

'To get away with murder and get a story with a million views?' I said.

Sally's time was up. She had to go. 'Tell Pike I'll call back when I can. And tell him thanks.'

'Will do. We'll see you soon.'

Mrs Brown screeched. 'Wait!'

I hung up as her hand reached for the phone.

'Whoops,' I said.

'Who was that?' she asked. 'And why were you talking about Michael Horn-blower?'

'Would you like a cup of tea?' I switched on the jug, hoping its noise would soon make talking impossible.

'I still remember when your uncle left,' she said. 'He never got over it.'

I switched the jug off. 'Uncle Pike?'

'No, Michael. I used to see his mum at bowls.' Mrs Brown fixed her hair. 'Your uncle left for Australia without a word. It broke that poor kid's heart. His mother's never forgiven your uncle. I don't think Michael's had a relationship since.'

Leaving did seem to be a theme with Uncle Pike. I really did hope he and Devon were still in Riverstone.

'Like a bad fairytale.' Mrs Brown cocked her head. 'Who was on the phone?'

I moved away from her, not wanting her to read my eyes.

She grinned. 'Was it the boys?'

Sam and Todd immediately came to mind, which made me sad. I shook my head and switched the jug back on.

'Devon wanted me to tell you, in case your mum ... well, in case she was too busy to tell you.' Mrs Brown got up and went to the balcony door. 'They're staying at the monkey motels.'

I nearly jumped up and down. 'Thank you, Mrs Brown.' I wanted to hug her.

She winked. 'Just passing on a message.'

Devon opened the door wearing either the hand towel or a small bathmat around his waist. 'Tippy Chan, is that lip gloss? Come here.' He gave me a big hug, pushing me into his black hairy chest. 'How'd you get here? Is your mum around?'

I was still catching my breath from the ride. 'No, she's at work. I rode over. Mum doesn't know.'

'Tippy!' he said.

'It's okay. I don't plan on sneaking around. I just wanted to see you guys.' I shrugged off my backpack.

'And we want to see you too, honey. We just don't want your

mum worrying. Come in. I'll give her a quick call and let her know where you are.'

Inside was a small cream cinderblock room with blue-grey swirly lino. Uncle Pike sat up at the end of a double bed, his moon boot resting on an ugly violet-and-mustard floral quilt cover. The curtains matched the cover. He'd been reading the *Bully*, which he chucked across the room.

'How you doing, Tippy?' He groaned as he got up and grabbed a crutch.

'You are so old,' Devon said, cradling the phone.

'Been better,' I said to my uncle. I tried smiling but it didn't feel very real.

He shuffled over and gave me a bear hug. 'She okay?'

'She's been better too,' I said, wrapped inside his arms.

'I'm sorry.' His voice vibrated.

'Voicemail,' Devon said.

'We don't have much time,' I said. 'We have to do something.' I filled them in on the old hospital, and the two origami flowers I'd found.

'No wonder your mum was upset. You sure you're okay?' Devon asked.

I smiled. 'I am now.' I grabbed my Nancys scrapbook and the tablet out of my bag. As I crouched, I noticed the floral curtains weren't quite long enough to cover the grey net-curtained window.

'You know, I've been thinking,' Uncle Pike said. 'Something about the timing doesn't fit.'

'The Nancys is over,' Devon said. 'We can't do this.'

'There's a monster out there,' I said.

'Who nearly caught Tippy,' my uncle said.

'And knows where I live. And Todd.'

Uncle Pike nodded. 'And Sally's in prison.'

'She says hi and thank you,' I said, sitting on the bed.

'When did you talk to her?' my uncle asked.

'No, no, no.' Devon waved his hands. 'This is a bad idea.'

'Rubbish!' Uncle Pike said. 'What, are you going to trust the police? The Nancys were never over, and clearly we're the only ones in this dump who can catch a killer.' He put his arm around Devon. 'But this time we'll let Lennie know.'

'Another Nancys member?' I said.

My uncle snorted. 'Obviously not.'

'Thank God,' Devon said. 'No offence, Tippy, but this is an exclusive club.'

'Great.' Uncle Pike clapped. 'The Nancys are back in business.'

'Fine. It's not like I can stop either of you.' Devon leaped up on the bed and grabbed my hand. I climbed up too and we started jumping up and down.

'Really?' my uncle said. 'Okay, first order of business.'

I jumped off the bed.

Devon threw a pillow at my uncle's head. 'Wait!' He leaped off and opened his suitcase, pulling out three black T-shirts. He threw a small one at me and a massive one at Uncle Pike. They were the *Nancys 3.0* versions in bright pink with the smoking triangle on the back. 'Put them on,' Devon said. 'We can't have a team meeting unless we're dressed as a team.'

'Well, that's probably not tr—' my uncle began.

'Put. Them. On.' Devon pulled on his T-shirt.

'Okay.' I went into the small bathroom and got changed. The T-shirt actually looked really cool.

Uncle Pike's T-shirt hugged him around his big pecs, and the tight sleeves made his tattooed arms bulge.

'Perfect size.' Devon patted my uncle's chest. 'And, Tippy, look at you!'

I smiled and curtseyed. 'Thanks.'

Devon put on a pair of square black glasses. 'You all look so beautiful.'

'You remembered your glasses.' I gave him a quick cuddle.

My uncle fanned himself with my scrapbook. 'Yes, thank you, honey. Let the minutes reflect the excellent job our chief marketing officer has done on the uniforms.'

Devon yelped and blew kisses to us and an imaginary crowd.

'Okay, Tippy, what have you got?' Uncle Pike said.

I told them why I'd gone to the old hospital, and Devon's clue about the smell. 'When I arrived, the kitchen had just been bleached,' I said. 'Why? Was it a coincidence?'

'There's no such thing, Tippy.' Devon climbed back on the bed – standing on my uncle, who groaned. 'Sorry, honey.' Devon patted him on the face. 'Who did you tell you were going there?'

'Sam,' I said. 'But it can't be him.'

'No, poor kid,' Uncle Pike said. 'He's more likely to cut off his own head. Anyone else? Lorraine?'

I shook my head. 'No one. But there's more. Today Sally called me from gaol – well, she called the home phone wanting to speak to you. Turns out Horn-blower was inside her place just before the police arrived. He had the chance to plant the shoe.'

'It can't be him,' Uncle Pike said.

Devon picked up a pillow and shoved his face into it. There was a muffled scream.

'Now, hold on,' my uncle said, all business.

Devon lifted the pillow above his head, ready to strike.

Uncle Pike held up his hand. 'It can't be him. Mike has haemophobia.'

'What?' Devon and I said together.

'Fear of blood. He faints if he sees it. He's had it since he was a kid.'

'He could've got over it,' I said.

'Even if he got treatment, why do something with so much blood?'

Devon dropped the pillow. 'He's still a penis,' he muttered. 'And you're calling him *Mike* now?'

Uncle Pike ignored Devon. 'So it's back to Sam and the hospital.'

'Not Sam,' Devon said. 'But someone with access to Sam's phone.'

We both looked at Devon.

'I check your phone all the time,' he said to Uncle Pike. 'And who is Kelly?'

'What? Trust me, you've got nothing to worry about. Kelly's a woman.'

I thought about Sam's parents; they were awesome. 'It can't be the Campbells.'

'First rule, remember?' Uncle Pike said. 'Could anyone else access his phone?'

I shook my head. 'It's been grounded, not allowed to leave their house. Unless someone hacked it? Like on the TV shows?' As unlikely as it sounded, I hoped I was right.

'Damn it!' my uncle said. 'Why does it always have to be the well-dressed people?'

'I really liked them,' Devon said sadly. 'He is so hot.'

Uncle Pike sighed. 'Okay, putting the hacking to one side, let's say it is them. Which one? Do we know what they were doing at the time of the murder?'

I tried to think. My phone buzzed. With my free hand, I flipped it open. A text from Sam: *Where are you?*

'Okay, so Dr Lisa was at the hospital,' Devon said. 'The afternoon you broke your ankle.'

'And Suzie Pratt saw a man,' I added.

'True,' my uncle said. 'But the doc could've had her hair in horn-shaped pigtails.'

'But Sam was with his dad that night,' I said. 'And his mum was working.'

'Russell is tall with blond hair,' Uncle Pike said. 'Did you ever see him with Jill Everson?'

I shook my head. 'Never outside of school. He always picks me and Sam up in the afternoon.'

'And at school?' my uncle said.

'Sometimes they'd talk for ages while me and Sam played outside.'

'Inside the classroom?' Devon said.

'I guess so,' I said. I thought about what Duncan Nunn had told us about the man's naked butt and the rabbits. The posters she'd put up on our classroom windows – were they there to stop people looking in?

'Right,' Uncle Pike said. 'And when Todd had his accident, Russell was on the bridge.'

My legs felt like jelly, and I sat on the corner of the bed. I thought of Sam's grinning face and how proud he was of his dad, and burst into tears.

'Hey, hey, it'll be okay.' Devon put his arm around me. 'Sam will be okay.'

'How?' I said, pulling away. 'Todd lives across the street from them.'

'We don't know it's his dad yet.' Uncle Pike handed me a tissue box from the bedside table. 'He's got a pretty good alibi for Jill Everson: he was with Sam that night. And the doc was working.'

I took a couple of deep breaths and tried to clear my head.

'You okay to continue?' Devon asked.

I nodded and blew my nose.

Devon bent over, his butt poking out of his towel as he rummaged in his suitcase. 'Watermelons, where are you? Tada!' He tied his sarong around his waist. 'I wish I had my window.' Devon started hunting around the room.

Uncle Pike clawed at the bed as he watched him. 'I'm not going to ask ... Okay, let's backtrack.'

'Found it.' Devon held up a lipstick.

'Not on the window,' Uncle Pike said. 'The afternoon of Todd's accident, was Sam with them?'

'That was the night we took Mum to the airport,' I said.

Devon jumped up on the bed and walked over my uncle, lifting off the large painting of a roaring stag in a forest above the bed and passing it to him. On the cream cinder blocks Devon drew a timeline in bright red, starting with Todd's name.

Uncle Pike groaned. 'That is not going to come off.'

'Duh, ever heard of makeup remover?' Devon drew four arches of the Riverstone Bridge on top of the line.

My uncle rubbed his face. 'Of course, how silly of me.'

'There's six arches,' I told Devon. He added an extra two but they were much smaller and on a downhill slope.

'Anyway,' Uncle Pike said, 'back to business. Russell was on the bridge. Where was Sam?'

'He went to Richard F's after school for a sleepover. It's weird because he's never done that before. He doesn't even like Richard F.' I stood up and threw my snotty tissues in the bin. An ache was growing in the back of my throat. I pictured Sam again, happy. I would give anything for it not to be his dad.

'Hold on.' I picked up The Nancys scrapbook and flicked to Todd's accident news clipping.

'What is it?' they said.

'Doesn't say there was anyone else but Mr Campbell on the bridge,' I said. I felt cold again. 'What if he made it all up? He said Todd's phone went into the river.' I rubbed my wrist, my thumb burning my skin. 'Todd was working on a video for money. What if he was black-mailing Mr Campbell, and Mr Campbell took Todd's phone?'

Uncle Pike patted a spot beside him on the bed. 'Let's try to work out what we do know first. We definitely know Todd was taken away by the helicopter. Do you know where he'd been after school?'

Devon drew a helicopter above the bridge. It was actually pretty good. 'When did they fly him to hospital?'

'Six-thirty-ish,' I said. I sat beside Uncle Pike, the bedspread shiny and bobbly under my legs.

Beneath the timeline Devon drew an arrow from Todd's name to the second arch of the bridge and wrote *6.30 p.m.* In the arch he drew a big question mark.

'Me and Sam don't know where Todd went that day,' I said to Uncle Pike. 'Usually he'd hang out at Sam's until dinner.'

Devon examined the red lipstick and dotted it on his lip. 'Drawing really uses this up.'

Uncle Pike twirled his moustache. 'Can you show me your teacher's pic on the phone?'

I opened my phone and pulled up the photo on my screen, handing it over.

Uncle Pike studied it. He clicked and zoomed in behind Ms Everson's shoulder again. 'I don't think Russell was working that afternoon.' He pointed to the background. 'I think this is the Campbells' bedroom.'

I squinted but couldn't tell. Todd had perved in Sam's parents' window before, down the side of their house.

Devon gasped and leaned over. 'OMG. It is. Same shade of white.'

'We need to get to your mum,' Uncle Pike said. 'Trust me, Devon knows her colours. We spent long enough in Russell's room trying on everything he owns.'

'Literally,' Devon said.

'White's not a colour,' I said, calling Mum's work from my phone. Becky on reception told me she was out. Our home number went to messages.

'Does this mean I don't have to return his shirt?' Uncle Pike asked. He tried Mum's mobile; it went to voicemail.

I started to panic. What if Mr Campbell had Mum?

My phone vibrated with another text from Sam: *Are you home alone?*

Sick rose in my throat and my skin crawled. I swallowed hard and passed my phone to Devon and Uncle Pike. 'I don't think this is Sam.'

CHAPTER TWENTY
The Emily Watsons

We ran into the medical centre's waiting area and up to the reception desk. Becky gave me a little wave then covered her handset. 'Hi, Tippy, love your hair. You after Mum?' When I nodded, she dialled a number and murmured something. 'She's on her way.' Becky checked out our T-shirts. She stared at my chest. 'Nancys 3.0,' she read slowly. 'Is that the name of your touch team?'

'Sure,' I said.

'Do you like mine?' She giggled, showing off her pale-green T-shirt that had elves playing leapfrog. *Elfs are fun!* was written in red letters with snow on them.

'Great.' I tried to smile and wondered about the spelling mistake.

'What's a touch team?' Devon asked me.

'Touch rugby.' I dragged him away from a frowning Becky.

Mum came out looking worried and confused. I let out a big breath and my body relaxed. She was safe.

'Tippy? You're supposed to be at home.'

'Lennie, we need to talk,' Uncle Pike said.

She marched over, her fists clenched. 'You can't just go and take my fucking child when you want to,' she said in a low voice. 'That's called kidnapping.'

'Mum.' I tugged on her sleeve to get her attention. 'Mum, it's okay. I visited them at the motel.'

'Over here.' She jerked her head towards a consulting room, and we bundled inside. She shut the door. 'Tippy, you've got to stop this. You're going to get yourself killed!'

I tried to focus on Mum but behind her Dr Lisa came to reception; she hadn't seen us. All I could think was that her husband might be a murderer.

'We're all in danger,' Devon said to Mum.

'What?' She was angry, like she'd bite the next person who spoke. 'What have you fuckers done?'

I moved between them, just in case. 'Mum, it's okay. We're the good guys.'

'What the fuck does that mean? And what are you wearing?'

Devon gave her a double thumbs-up.

'Listen,' Uncle Pike said. 'We'll sort our shit out later, I promise. I really am very sorry. For everything. I love you.'

Mum snorted and crossed her arms.

My uncle held up his hands. 'But right now we need you to listen as this is literally life-and-death stuff.'

Someone knocked on the door, and Dr Lisa poked her head around. She looked surprised to see us. 'Hi, guys. I didn't know you were here. Family reunion?'

I smiled but couldn't look her in the eyes. She was so nice; I didn't want her to be involved in this. But there was the first rule: everyone's a suspect. Plus, if Mr Campbell had been seeing Ms Everson, and considering the type of murder weapon, it didn't look good.

Devon smiled and waved at Dr Lisa.

Uncle Pike tipped an imaginary hat. 'Doc, good to see you as always.'

She smiled. 'Sorry, I just need Helen for a patient.'

'Of course,' Mum said. She turned to us. 'I'll be home for lunch in half an hour.'

'See you there, Angel Puff Pants.' Uncle Pike patted her on the head, something Mum hated.

'Kisses in the wind.' Devon blew her a big air kiss.

Mum glared at us and left the room with Dr Lisa, flipping Uncle Pike the rude finger behind the doctor's back.

'She'll come around,' he said to me. 'I see this...' he raised his middle finger '...as a sign of progress.' As we walked out of reception, he stopped. 'Oh my God, did Francis Bacon paint this Christmas window display?'

Mum dropped her keys on the kitchen bench.

'We need to talk,' Uncle Pike said. 'And I mean *really* talk.'

She sat down at the dining table. 'Tippy, we need the room.' Mum loved White House dramas.

'Yes, POTUS,' I said, trying to lighten the mood, but neither of them laughed. I stepped out into the bright sun on the balcony.

Devon was around the corner with Bunny Whiskers. I hid beside the doorway, peering back in and listening.

'I know we're not a touchy-feely family,' my uncle said, shuffling over to the table on one crutch.

She leaned back, folding her arms.

'But I am really sorry.' He pulled out a chair and dropped onto it. 'I'd never let anything happen to Tippy. I would rather die.'

'I'm listening.'

'It started out as a bonding opportunity. Todd had hurt himself, and her teacher had died, but then we really did start solving this thing. When Sally got arrested, we knew it couldn't have been her.'

Mum snorted. 'All the evidence seems to disagree.'

'Come on, you know Sally. The killer's still out there, and I think we can put together the last pieces.'

Mum leaned forward, her elbows on the table. 'But why, Pike? Why put Tippy in danger like that? Why not just let the police handle it?'

'The police can't or won't handle it. Sally's arrest makes no sense – evidence was planted on her. They've never even looked for anyone else. A key witness wasn't interviewed because he was blind, for fuck's sake.'

'But again, why Tippy?'

'It was her idea...'

Mum shot back in her seat. 'What?'

'Wait.' He held up his hand. 'Let me finish. You know how we both love Nancy Drew?'

Mum nodded. 'You used to make me buy them from that old cow.'

'She was a homophobic old mole.' He stared out of the window at the town below. 'She'd ask me why I was reading – not what but *why* – and she owned a fucking bookshop.'

'She was a mole. I think she always knew Nancy was for you.'

'Anyway, it all seemed like a harmless idea at first.' He turned back to the table. 'Tippy sees worse things, like *Blair Witch*.'

Mum's eyes bulged and she clenched her fists.

He waved his hands. 'Okay. Maybe, maybe not. But it became a way for us to get close, to talk about Joe...'

'You didn't?'

'No, of course not. That's not my place. But, Lennie, you'll need to soon.'

Mum's back arched up.

'Hey.' My uncle raised his hands again. 'I'm not telling you how to parent, just saying it will come out.'

'I know.' Mum sighed. 'But it's going to break her heart.'

What were they talking about ... what would break my heart? Something Dad did? What could he have done that would upset me that much – something bad? Had he hurt people? But it's Dad. He wasn't some monster. Was he...?

Uncle Pike nodded. 'This adventure helped us talk to Tippy about grief. What started off as a sightseeing distraction snowballed into something else. The thing is, Lennie, we're really good at this. *She* is really good at this.'

Mum drummed her fingers on the table. 'You know she was only four when she busted me and Joe for Santa? She'd staked out the living room.' Mum shook her head.

Before I was a monster's child ... Whatever Dad did, it could not have been that bad, or we would have heard about it. Riverstone didn't keep secrets for long. Inside it was quiet. I shifted my weight onto my other foot. Squinting against the glare from the white walls was beginning to give me a headache.

'People are still in danger,' Uncle Pike said. 'Todd could still be in danger.'

I clutched my phone and glanced at the bridge down below. Todd had to be okay.

Mum released another big sigh and stretched her arms out on the table. 'You know, sometimes I wish for those nothing days. You know? Rushing to the bank, going to the post office, doing the grocery shopping ... even work.' She sat back up and gave my uncle a small smile. 'Those days ... you don't know they're gold until...' She inhaled a shuddery breath. 'They never come back.' Big wet tears ran down her face.

My hand went to my chest.

Uncle Pike got up and hopped over.

'Everything's destroyed. There's nothing left.' Mum wiped her face with her hands. 'Tippy...'

'Hey, hey, it's okay. You're okay. Tippy will understand.' He placed his big hands on her shoulders.

She grabbed them and sobbed. 'I fucked up and I miss him so much ... I'm so fucking angry at him. Who chooses to do that?'

'I know, Lennie. I know.' He stood holding her as she cried. 'Don't kill me, but you need to get counselling. Both of you.'

I thought I heard Mum hiss.

'Hey,' he said softly, 'you've removed Joe completely. Tippy needs her dad. You need him.'

Mum was quiet. She wiped her eyes, and I thought she nodded slightly.

'You and Joe were the real deal,' he said. 'Hold on to that. You know some people never get what you guys had.'

Mum shook her head. 'He was fine. You knew him. Nothing to worry about. Then last year...' She blew out a big breath. 'And that nosey cunt started investigating, accusing him of stealing clients' money.'

I yelped and covered my mouth, pressing myself flat against the wall. My brain was going to explode. Dad stealing other people's money? What had Lorraine found out?

Inside it went quiet. I wondered if they'd heard me.

Eventually Uncle Pike spoke. 'What happened?'

'Joe never did it, of course. If he had I would've heard about it by now, but you start to wonder ... I hated her for planting that doubt. That mistrust stayed with us until the end.'

I peered in again. So that's why they'd called Lorraine the c-word.

'Shit, Lennie.' My uncle held Mum's hands across the table. 'That's rough.'

She gave a short laugh. 'Don't worry, it gets worse. Joe did take all *our* money. Not only that but he took out loans, even mortgaged the house.'

'But that was freehold from Mum and Dad,' Uncle Pike said.

Mum shook her head. 'Not anymore. I don't know what he did with all of it – well, I guess I do have a pretty good idea how he spent it, but it's all gone. Except the debt, that didn't go when he died.'

All that time this was what they'd been fighting about. I'd known it had to do with Dad spending money, but now I got why Mum had screamed at him, asking how he could keep losing it when he was an accountant. I'd thought she was just being mean, saying Dad was bad at his job.

Uncle Pike stood up. 'Why didn't you tell me all this? You've got to let me help.'

Mum smiled. 'You're here now. That's what I need.' She pointed to Devon talking to Bunny Whiskers. 'You've got a chance, Pike, but it takes work. Joe was no saint, and you know I'm not. But you've got to stay the distance. No running away, no matter how painful it gets.'

'Charming,' my uncle said.

'I'm serious. This one seems like a keeper – just the right amount of madness to survive this family.'

Devon imitated the cat, pretending to lick himself clean with his paws.

'All this Horn-blower stuff...' Uncle Pike sighed. 'This is already the longest relationship I've ever had. What if I fuck it up?'

Mum got up and put her hand on his shoulder. 'Then say sorry and don't do it again.'

'Sorry,' he said.

She rested her chin on his head. 'Me too.'

Devon came around the corner holding Bunny Whiskers. His smile faded when he saw me. 'Sweetie, what's wrong?'

I shook my head and wiped my nose with my hand. 'I think everything is going to be okay.'

He hugged me, Bunny Whiskers squashed between us. She batted my face with her paw and growled. 'Naughty puss-puss!' He held her up to his face. 'Remember what we talked about?' She stared at him and gave a tiny meow. 'Correct,' he said and let her go. She bounded down the stairs then loped off into the dahlias. 'She is out of control.'

Inside, Mum and Uncle Pike laughed.

'Looks like the war is over,' Devon said to me. 'Shall we?' He held out his hand and I took it. 'Knock, knock,' he called.

'Why don't you actually knock?' Mum said.

'Exactly, right?' my uncle said.

We went inside and sat down. Mum reached for my hand. Uncle Pike gave Devon a kiss and rubbed his cheek.

Mum sighed. 'I can't believe I'm saying this, but show me.'

I pulled The Nancys scrapbook out of my backpack and gave it to her. She flicked through it.

Devon sat beside me at the table. 'Love your tree. It's so sparkly.' He frowned. 'Kind of. Is it deconstructed?'

'Thanks,' I said, I didn't know what deconstructed meant. 'We ran out of tinsel.'

'And decorations?' he said.

'And interest?' Uncle Pike said.

She shut the scrapbook and asked me, 'The Case of the Missing Necklace ... You worked all this out on your own?'

'No, we worked it out together.' I pulled up all The Nancys pics on the tablet and slid it over to her. Then we talked Mum through everything we knew.

'Do you think you could get us security footage from the hospital?' Uncle Pike said.

'Maybe.' She scrolled though the photos and got to the drawings on the window. She went over and pulled open the curtains, peering at the glass. 'Who cleaned this?'

Uncle Pike raised his hand.

'You did an exceptional job.'

'Thank you.'

I jumped up and showed her Todd's text and the pic of Ms Everson on my phone.

Mum's eyebrows knitted together. 'Has Todd sent you photos like this before?'

'No,' I lied. 'We think this is Ms Everson in Mr Campbell's bedroom. Todd may have been blackmailing them.'

'What?' Mum roared. 'That's it. Enough. I've got to work with these people. Delete that picture now.'

'But—'

'No buts. And no tit pics!' She snatched my phone and handed it to my uncle. 'Pike, you need to be on top of this. I expect my daughter's phone to be porn free.'

My heart sank. I'd really thought we'd convinced her.

'You're accusing my best friend's husband of not only being a murderer but also having an affair. A man who, by the way, is a local hero.' She headed towards the kitchen. 'Based on what?'

'Mum, he could be a murderer! The background colour's the same.'

'No, Tippy. Seriously, not another word about this. You can't just go around accusing people of these things.' She grabbed the jug and filled it at the sink. 'And white is not a colour.'

'Heard that before.' Uncle Pike nudged me. 'Don't worry,' he whispered and gave me a wink.

Devon frowned at him.

'Cuppa?' Mum called, switching on the jug. 'I can't believe I nearly bought in to all that Nancy Drew busi— What the fuck have you done to my fridge?'

'I took down the magnets,' I said.

Uncle Pike rolled his eyes. 'That was Devon.' He got up and shuffled to the couch. 'Reminds me, we need to buy nail-polish remover.'

Mum licked her finger and tried to clean the marks, but nothing rubbed off. 'Devon!'

He pretended to get a phone call, covering his imaginary cell. 'Sorry, long distance.' He put his finger in his other ear and nodded. 'Yes, this is she, how may we help?' He stepped out onto the balcony.

'Is that a bar of soap?' Mum asked.

After lunch Mum went back to work, leaving Uncle Pike and Devon to look after me. I was still grounded – even after I'd shown her everything. Mum had told us off again and made us swear we wouldn't do any more sleuthing. We'd all agreed but I'd had my fingers crossed behind my back and noticed my uncle doing the same.

I couldn't stop thinking about Sam. What would happen to him if his dad was guilty? But Mr Campbell was nice. And I thought he liked Todd. It made my brain ache. The whole thing didn't make any sense. Nancy Drew never had to investigate Bess or George's parents for murder.

My phone vibrated: another text from Sam, asking me to come over.

I showed Uncle Pike, who was getting his hair 'sculpted' by Devon in the kitchen.

'What do you think?' my uncle said.

I shrugged. 'I don't know anymore. I hope it's from Sam.' I hadn't seen or talked to him since Ms Everson's memorial service, and I was getting worried. 'I want to check on him, make sure he's okay.'

'Invite him over,' Devon said.

I tried calling Sam, but it kept going to voicemail. A text came through: *Sorry can't talk but come over.*

I showed it to them.

'This stinks of catfish,' Uncle Pike said.

'Ewww, sounds gross,' Devon said. 'Cover eyes.' He doused my uncle's mane with hairspray he'd borrowed from Mrs Brown, shaking the can between sprays. It stank. 'Tippy, this is called eighties soap-opera hair. Notice how big it is?'

I nodded, coughing and waving away the fumes. 'I need to see Sam. I'm worried he might be...' I didn't want to say it.

'Okay,' my uncle said, lurching up on one crutch. 'First, let me call Sea-Hag and organise a meet-up for the police report.'

'What?' Devon said.

'What about Mum?' I said. She'd crack it if she knew we were investigating again *and* talking to Sea-Hag.

Uncle Pike found the cordless. 'You're with us; it'll be fine. Tippy, grab a bottle of whisky from your mum's liquor cabinet. I can't remember if I drank it or not.' He dialled Lorraine's number. 'And remind me on the way that we need to get a carton of cigarettes.'

'On it,' I said. 'Remember Todd's report as well.' Worried as I was about Sam and Todd, I still had to hide my grin. The Nancys were back on the Case of the Missing Necklace.

'This is so not a good idea,' Devon said.

After a quick phone call, we headed off. At the old hospital carpark Lorraine met us in a small silver hatchback. I really wanted to know why she'd harassed Dad, but I guessed it would have to wait. For now.

I got out and leaned against the warm metal boot of the car. Suddenly I felt thirsty. Last time I'd been here I was running for my life.

Devon stood beside me. 'You okay?' He squinted.

I smiled and rubbed my arms.

Lorraine wound down her car window. 'Hand them over.' She wiggled her thick fingers. A tiny diamond sparkled on her ring finger.

'Aren't you going to get out?' Devon said.

She snorted. 'Not if I don't have to.'

Uncle Pike handed her the carton of cigarettes, which she chucked on the passenger seat. She was more careful with the bottle of Scotch.

'Anyway,' Devon said, 'isn't this illegal?'

'Not if you're eighteen,' Uncle Pike said. 'Sixteen for cigarettes.'

'Eighteen,' Lorraine said. 'For both.'

'Really?' My uncle made an *eeek* face. 'Whoops.'

Lorraine handed him a manila folder. 'Copy, of course, never came from me. Couldn't get any crime-scene photos though. Long story but it seems this time the police actually do care about them being made public.' She nodded in my direction. 'Chan, your friend Landers' accident report is in there too. Want to tell me your theory on that?'

'I'll let you know when I see it,' I said.

'Come on,' Uncle Pike said, 'there's more. We want to show you something inside.'

Lorraine sighed. 'Better be good.' She wound up her window and pushed herself out of the car.

We made our way through the old hospital to the kitchen. I filled Lorraine in on everything that had happened on Friday night. She listened, taking down notes. In the kitchen the smell of bleach seemed even stronger than I remembered, and my muddy footprints were gone.

She crouched down to examine the floor, rubbing it with a finger. She grunted and stood up. Over by the sink, she peered out the window. 'Have you been over there?' She tapped on the glass at the other wing across the courtyard.

Inside my shorts pockets, I clenched and unclenched my fists. 'No. And there's something else. This sink's cleaner, if that's possible. I remember it looked rusty that night.' As if on cue, sunlight beamed through the windows and the sink gleamed.

'Spooky,' Devon said.

Lorraine took photos. 'Okay. Let's go see what the murderer was doing over there in the wards. You' – she pointed at Devon – 'stay put. I doubt any chemicals could hurt your brain.'

He gave her a salute. 'Thanks!'

We walked down the corridors, keeping close to the walls in case we mucked up any footprint evidence. It was a relief to be away from the bleach. I wasn't sure if it was just the smell, but my heart pounded like it had on Saturday night. I stared hard at the floor for any clues; it wasn't easy to tell with all the rubbish everywhere. Across the other side of the courtyard, however, the ward's floor was clean, with no sign of footprints or dust. Windows ran along one side of the ward's hallway, their frames identical to those in the kitchen. On the other side were doors to the patients' rooms.

From here I could easily see Devon in the kitchen. He waved at me then pretended to whisk something in a large mixing bowl. My scalp prickled and I shuddered.

Lorraine tapped her pen against her notebook. 'You all right, Chan?'

I pointed out the window. 'They must've seen me.'

She shrugged. 'Maybe, maybe not. You're here now, aren't you?'

Uncle Pike joined us. 'You know research has found that spiders are maternal?'

She ignored him. 'But why would the killer be here?' she said to herself as much as to us. 'It's looking more and more like a medical professional pulled this one off. Surgical saw, head removed...'

Mr Campbell was a medical professional. I pulled open the police report. Uncle Pike leaned on the window beside me. The hairs on my forearms rose. Sam hadn't been joking – Ms Everson had been clutching white paper flowers.

My uncle looked at me. 'The Emily Watsons?'

I nodded and concentrated on my breathing.

'What are you talking about?' Lorraine said.

It got worse. I pointed something out to Uncle Pike.

'Fucking hell,' he said.

Lorraine nearly headbutted me, checking where I had pointed. 'Yeah, washed her in bleach. Sick fuck.'

He took the file off me, and I slid to the floor. The smell of bleach came back strong, and I panted, my heart racing.

'Tippy?' he said.

Poor Ms Everson. I put my hands over my head and tried to take in a deep breath. That could have been me.

Lorraine squatted in front of me. 'All right?'

I exhaled, took in another breath then blew it out slowly.

'Want to go home?' Uncle Pike said.

I shook my head and pushed myself back up. This had to stop. We had to stop it.

'Can I?' I held the side of the report and looked again. Her phone was listed as missing but there was no mention of the kissing-dolphins necklace. I scanned down further. 'It doesn't say she was pregnant. Unless I'm missing something?'

Lorraine eyed me, pursing her lips. 'No, that's right. According to the autopsy report, she definitely wasn't pregnant. Why are you asking, Chan?'

I shrugged, still breathing in through my nose and out through my mouth. 'Who would do those tests?' Somehow, breathing through my mouth helped fade the memory-smell of bleach a little.

'Forensic pathology in Dunedin manages all that.' She moved closer. 'You know, where your friend Sam Campbell's dad works?'

I tried not to flinch when she mentioned Mr Campbell.

'Russell's probably done these labs.' Her breath stank like a wet ashtray. She stood up, grabbed the file off Uncle Pike and flipped over a couple of pages. 'There.' She punched her finger at a signature at the bottom of the report. 'Russell Campbell. He did the testing.'

'That's nice.' I smiled and took the file back off her. I still wasn't sure about sharing everything with Lorraine.

Uncle Pike squeezed my shoulder and shuffled off up ahead.

'What aren't you telling me, Chan?' Lorraine said.

I shrugged, turning my back on her. Then I sucked in a breath. Had Mr Campbell covered up the pregnancy?

'Over here!' Uncle Pike called out from the end of the corridor.

Lorraine strolled up the hallway. 'I'm not finished with you, Chan.'

I waved Devon over to join us. He waved back but then got busy riding a pretend escalator. I jogged up to Uncle Pike and Lorraine, who were standing in front of an open exit door.

Outside, a broken concrete path wrapped around the building. Rusted metal beds, clumps of tall grass, and years' worth of brown beer bottles, broken and whole, littered the side of the hospital, along with the odd faded cigarette packet. In front of us, a steep clay bank with a muddy track trailed up the hill, disappearing into some large macrocarpas.

Devon finally joined us, and we headed up the hill, leaving behind Uncle Pike on his crutches. We were careful to walk beside the track in case of any footprint clues. Although it was steep, it was a short climb to the top.

'I hope he's okay,' Devon said.

'Good luck to whoever runs into him,' Lorraine puffed.

'Isn't it "whomever"?' Devon asked.

We cleared the trees and came out into the middle of a cul-de-sac, the street empty except for three parked cars. Number four still had its *For Sale* sign out the front. It was Ronsdale Place.

I felt clammy even though the sun shone brightly. 'Devon, did you look inside the deep-freeze when you were in the garage?'

He shook his head.

'Shit,' Lorraine said.

CHAPTER TWENTY-ONE
Deep-Freeze

'Well, I must admit I was surprised to hear from you, Pike.' Duncan Nunn licked his palm and flattened his hair. Having a convertible was possibly not the best choice for him. 'Lorraine.' He nodded.

She lifted her chin at him. 'The house was locked, and we couldn't break in.'

He gave a short laugh. 'Good one.'

Ignoring him, she wandered off round the side of the house.

He rubbed his hands together then held them out, like he wanted us to hold them. 'I thought you hated this place for all kinds of "reasons".'

'That's true.' Devon put his arm around Uncle Pike's shoulders. 'But we discussed it, and we think we could make it work, for the gay lifestyle.'

'I knew it!' Duncan stabbed his finger at the sky. 'I knew I was on to something there.'

'That's the spirit,' my uncle said. 'And as you told us, Duncan, kitchens and bathrooms sell houses.'

'I don't remember saying—'

'And we didn't see the kitchen or the bathroom. So sell away.'

'You don't have to ask me twice!'

'Well, technically...' Uncle Pike said.

Devon and I followed the others, but when we reached the hallway we ducked through the door to the garage and closed it behind us. I rubbed my hand over the wall, finding the light switch. We hurried down the wooden stairs and over to the deep-freeze. It was padlocked.

'Shit!' Devon said.

'Can we break it?' I said.

'Then whomever will know that we know, you know?'

He was right. 'Sometimes other keys work in them.' Sam had a padlock on his schoolbag and was always losing his key; mine opened his every time. I pulled it out and tried it in the lock; after only a couple of seconds of twisting, it popped open.

I nudged Devon. He grinned and nudged me back. Slowly, he lifted the lid, the rubber seal making a sucking noise as it popped open.

I heard the sound of the door to the hallway opening. I turned, hearing Duncan say, 'No, no, we should definitely see the garage again.'

Devon yelped. 'You can't see this, Tippy.' Before I had a chance to look back, or reply, he shoved me. I stumbled, nearly falling over. pushed me.

'Hello? Excuse me?' Duncan said to us. 'Please stick with the tour.'

I pretended to do a fancy dance move. 'Just practising. This garage is a great dance studio.' I glanced at Devon; his eyes were wide and his hands shaking. The lid to the deep-freeze closed.

'Glad to hear it!' my uncle bellowed. Duncan raised his hands to his ears. 'That's a plus right there, Duncan, if my niece likes it. And we gays, as you know, need to dance.'

'That's right.' Duncan nodded. 'Good, good.'

I danced over to Devon, and he put his arm around me; he looked pale. The padlock was back on the deep-freeze, locked.

'Do you want me to open the garage door again?' Duncan asked.

'We've seen all we need to see here.' Devon tried to smile but his eyes were filled with tears. His teardrop emoji drawing came to mind.

Lorraine and Uncle Pike agreed with Devon.

'Let's take one more look at the piece of resistance, then I'll leave you to decide.' Duncan clasped his hands and waited until all of us had moved into the hallway before he switched off the garage light and closed the door.

I whispered to Devon, 'Are you all right?' He nodded but didn't say anything.

We headed into the open-plan room, except for Devon, who waited by the door in the hallway. When Uncle Pike switched on the lights, Devon jumped. I went back and held his hand.

'Duncan, how come the electricity's on?' my uncle asked.

'Oh, that's pretty normal,' Duncan said, heading over to the windows. 'Look at this million-dollar view. Let me show you...'

My uncle stood with his back to the windows. 'So that's something everyone knows?'

The real-estate agent tried to hide his irritation. 'Yes, yes, everybody knows that.'

'Even Russell Campbell?' Uncle Pike said.

Duncan laughed. 'Especially him! He's looked at this property a couple of times. In fact, just before that terrible murder happened. When I got back I couldn't find the keys anywhere ... Lorraine, don't tell anyone that!'

She grunted. 'Where were you?'

He waggled his eyebrows. 'Dirty road-trip weekend with you-know-who.' He nudged Uncle Pike in the ribs. 'You know how it is.'

'And the keys?' she said.

'When I got back on Monday I couldn't find them. Had to ask the owner's son for a new set. Never a good look.'

'Who's that?' she said.

'Drysdale. They don't live around here anymore. Had to courier the keys down from Christchurch. Don't worry, I've made plenty of copies now. Lorraine, don't print that.' He laughed.

She curled her lip. I hoped she would snarl.

Duncan dangled the keys in front of my uncle's face. Uncle Pike tried to snatch them, but the real-estate agent was too fast. 'You'll have to be quicker than that.' He pointed his toe like a ballerina. 'I'd say, if you *are* interested, Russell Campbell is your biggest threat.'

Outside, Lorraine got into our car and waited while Duncan Nunn locked up. She seemed to have the ability to take up all available space, covering most of the back seat. I felt the heat radiating from her, so I tried to get some room by squashing myself against the door. I heard a noise in the boot as Devon chucked Uncle Pike's crutches in and then a slam.

'So, genius, was the head in there?' she asked Devon when we were all in the car.

He nodded, and Uncle Pike leaned over and put his arm around him.

Lorraine let out a noisy breath through her nose. 'So, are we telling the police?'

'Why wouldn't we?' Devon said. 'I just found a frozen scalped head in that freezer thingy.'

Uncle Pike rubbed his arm but Devon flinched and moved away from him, leaning against the driver's door.

Poor Devon. I'm glad now he saved me from seeing my teacher's head. Sam's voice saying 'four kilograms' popped into my head. I shifted back into my seat and hugged myself. Through the windscreen, number four Ronsdale Place creeped me out. It really was a murder house.

'Can we trust them?' Uncle Pike asked Lorraine.

'Maybe,' she said. She turned to me, her thigh wedged against my leg. 'Chan, you definitely think it's Campbell?'

I caught Uncle Pike's eye.

'It's okay, Tippy,' he said.

'Yes.' And I told Lorraine everything, this time not holding anything back: Mr Campbell spending time with Miss Everson after school, the caretaker witness, our visit to the Campbells', Sam's phone and the paper flowers, everything, all our clues.

When I finished Lorraine grunted. 'So, he was banging her. I'd heard the rumours but didn't believe ... And you think he changed the pregnancy test results to cover his arse?'

I nodded.

'She got knocked up and he killed her.' Lorraine was shaking her head. 'Men are disgusting.'

'No arguments here,' Uncle Pike said.

'Were there any other witnesses on the bridge?' I asked Lorraine.

'Landers?' she said. 'You think Campbell tried to kill him as well?' She leaned on me like a drunk on a boat. 'Why?'

I desperately wound down my window to get some air, then stuck my head out on an angle. 'Todd saw Mr Campbell and Ms Everson...'

'He took photos and video,' Uncle Pike said. 'We think he tried to blackmail Russell.'

'And Campbell was the only witness to the accident, and Landers' phone was never found.' Lorraine moved off me and opened her door. 'Give me some more time to check Campbell out, and then we'll reconvene. He *is* the town hero, after all.'

'Which you created,' my uncle said.

She smirked. 'Don't worry, I can cancel as well.' She smacked Devon on the shoulder again and he flinched. 'No blabbing to anyone,' she said. 'Deal?'

'Air freshener, anyone?' Uncle Pike shoved it in her direction, giving Devon a kiss on the cheek.

Duncan Nunn had left the house, and I watched as he drove off in his brown car. I thought of Suzie Pratt's picture. Then it hit me – the car!

'The car was black, not brown,' I said. 'It *is* him!' Suzie Pratt had thrown the broken black crayon away and had to use the brown one to draw the car.

All three adults were quiet. They looked at each other then back at me.

Lorraine shut her door.

I told them about the crayons as I brought up my photo of Suzie's picture on the tablet. 'Dr Lisa's car's red, and Mr Campbell's is black.'

Lorraine leaned in so close her hair tickled my cheek. I tried to breathe out the side of my mouth so I wouldn't smell her stale ciggy breath.

I held up the tablet to show Uncle Pike and Devon, but also to try and get some space back from Lorraine. 'We've been looking at this wrong.' I remembered the picture of the frog and the prince in Suzie's bedroom. 'We thought the murderer was leaving the crime scene with clothes and the head. But Suzie's drawing was a two-fer.'

Devon clapped. 'I can't believe you said two-fer! So grown up.'

Lorraine pursed her lips and nodded.

'Go on, Tippy,' Uncle Pike said.

'She's drawn her two views from her hiding place at the tree.' I covered half the picture with my hand. 'This half' – I showed the car, murderer and bags – 'is her view from the side of the tree when the murderer first arrived. He was bringing something in, not taking it away.' I shifted my hand to the other side, showing the grass, stick figure and traffic light. 'This is the view she had of the body after the murderer had left.' I moved my hand away completely. 'A picture of both views.'

'That poor kid,' Devon said.

The car was quiet – except for Lorraine, who hummed.

Uncle Pike tapped his finger against his chin. Then he spoke slowly, like he was thinking out loud. 'So, the murderer staged the crime scene in the morning.'

I nodded.

'We know the murder happened in the early hours. Most likely in the old hospital's kitchen,' Lorraine said. 'Which means those bags were probably filled with blood, which he used to stage the crime scene...'

All the dried blood around the flattened grass, making that headless snow-angel pattern. I squeezed my tablet and thought about Susie, what an unlucky, and lucky, little kid. Maybe she would forget. I hoped so. And Devon too.

Uncle Pike continued. 'He drops the scalp off at Sally's first so the police will be distracted while he stages the body at the traffic light.' He squinted. 'After that public fight, Sally was the perfect fall woman.'

'Really?' Devon asked.

'No, honey,' Uncle Pike said. 'Not a "fall woman" like Melanie's a "spring woman".'

'Ahh,' Devon said.

'Lorraine,' my uncle said, 'it's time the police got involved. Again.'

'Tippy, you've solved it!' Devon said. 'And just FYI, the picture's also called a "before and after".'

'Thanks,' I said. '*We* solved it, but we haven't caught the monster yet.'

'You all better be right. If this goes south with the police I'm throwing you all under the bus.' Lorraine pushed against me as she got out of the car.

'Would expect nothing less,' Uncle Pike said, as the door slammed.

I watched her get into her silver hatchback as Devon drove us away.

'Can we go faster please?' I asked, no idea if Sam and Dr Lisa were safe, or even still alive.

CHAPTER TWENTY-TWO
A Murderer's House

I put on my phone's stopwatch and timed the trip to Sam's house. Two minutes thirty-eight seconds. Devon drove past the house and parked up the road, out of sight. Uncle Pike stayed in the car, speaking to Barry on the phone.

I opened my door and got out – I needed to make sure Sam was safe.

'Tippy, wait.' Devon chased after me. 'Stop.'

'Crutches,' my uncle called out.

I ignored them both. I'd been down Sam's path a million times, but this felt different. My mouth went dry as I rang the doorbell. We waited and I rang it again. No sounds came from inside, but through the frosted glass I thought I saw a shadow of movement.

'I need to make sure Sam's okay,' I whispered to Devon.

He shook his head at me. 'Let's go back to the car.'

I gestured around the side of the house, made a walking sign with my fingers and pointed to my eyes. Devon looked confused.

'Let's look in the windows,' I said.

'No!'

I ran around the side of the house, flattening myself against the wall.

'Tippy,' Devon hissed, waving at me to come back.

The first window had the curtains drawn so I continued, racing to the back of the house. The large wall of windows reflected the garden. Inside, a faint, faraway glow came from down the hallway, maybe near the front door. I'd need to risk pressing my face against the window if I wanted to see inside. I hoped no one would be staring back at me. I held my breath and, cupping my hands, peered in.

No one on the white couch, or in the living room or the kitchen. I breathed out. The hallway had dark shadows; impossible to tell if anyone was lurking there. I needed to get across to the other side of the wall of windows without being seen. I sprinted, worried that at any second Mr Campbell would bang on the window and I'd be the next target.

I reached the other side and pressed myself up against the wall. The gap between the neighbours' wooden fence and the wall was less than two metres wide. This side of the house, dark and cool, never got the sun. The first set of windows belonged to Sam's room. The curtains were drawn, and the light was off. Next was the bathroom, which had bubbly glass so you couldn't see in anyway, and with no lights on inside I couldn't even make out any shapes.

So far, nothing.

The last window was one I knew well: the master bedroom. The window where Todd had videoed Sam's parents doing it, although it had turned out that it wasn't Dr Lisa bouncing up and down but my teacher. Being here, it struck me that this was real. Ms Everson and Mr Campbell had had sex, and Todd had seen it. I felt so sorry for Sam and Dr Lisa.

I slowly peeked through the corner of the master-bedroom window. The curtains were open. I exhaled; Mr Campbell wasn't there. A tiny crack of light from the hallway shone from the bedroom door. The room was dark, but I could make out a giant bed in the middle. Surrounding it on the floor was a Sally-Homer-style mess of white sheets, screwed up balls of rubbish and clothes.

Devon came around the far corner and, crouching, ran towards me. I put my finger to my lips and pointed up towards the window.

The bedroom door opened wider. I ducked down, squashing myself into the wall. The light came on and shone on the wooden fence. My heart leapfrogged into my throat. I crawled on hands and knees to the corner of the house, a ruler's length from the edge of the window. I stuck to the wall, scared my banging heart was going to burst. I glanced back at Devon. He'd pressed himself to the wall under the bathroom window, watching me. I pointed up and mouthed, 'They're home.'

A shadow loomed against the fence. It became bigger the closer it got to the window. I shrank into the smallest ball I could manage. The curtain closest to Devon was pulled, cutting the bedroom light on the palings in half. Though it was hard to tell, the shadow looked like it belonged to Mr Campbell. He started to pull the second curtain, nearest to me, but stopped.

I put my hand over my mouth and froze. His shadow seemed to stare at me. Every part of me wanted to run. I worried I might accidentally scream. From this angle I didn't think he could see me, but I wasn't going to check in case I looked up and his eyes were boring into mine. Finally, he pulled the other curtain all the way across and the light was gone.

I bolted around the corner and hid beside the front door. Devon joined me and we caught our breath.

'At least we know he's home,' Devon said.

I nodded. 'But I still need to see if Sam's okay.' I rang the bell again before I got too scared. Inside, a blurry shadow headed towards the door.

'Tippy,' Devon said, 'we should wait for the police.'

Mr Campbell answered the door in an old T-shirt and stained grey trackies. His usually perfect hair was greasy and messed up, and he smelled like he'd been drinking. I'd never seen him this rough before.

'Hi, Mr Campbell. Is Sam home?' He bowed and swept his arm towards the living room. The hallway was a mess. The paintings were gone except for the family portrait, which was crooked.

'Come in. Sam should be through in a minute.' I glanced at a frowning Devon as Mr Campbell shut the door behind us. We walked down the hallway towards the large white Christmas tree, which now leaned against the wall, most of its red baubles scattered on the floor. The living room was empty except for the white couch. Were they moving? Where to?

'I wasn't expecting visitors.' Mr Campbell joined us in the big room. 'Drink?' He grabbed his glass from the kitchen counter and topped up his whisky. The sink was overflowing with dirty dishes and food containers, the dishwater a greasy grey.

'No thanks,' I said, checking out the empty space. I wondered where ball-bearing Jesus and melted Mary and Joseph had gone.

'Sure,' Devon said to Mr Campbell, shrugging at me.

'Go check the rooms,' I whispered. He shook his head violently and I pushed him. 'Quick, please!' I hissed.

Devon growled at me then ran quietly down to Sam's room.

I sat on the couch and watched Mr Campbell. He looked in the cupboards for a glass then stood still, staring at me. I pretended to play with my phone but kept an eye on him. He didn't move.

It began to creep me out. I texted Sam: *Where r u?*

Mr Campbell sipped his drink. A phone vibrated on the kitchen bench. I put mine down. He smiled and started to hum.

'Sam's not here?' I tried to sound normal.

'No?' Mr Campbell slunk behind me. 'Maybe he left with her.' He picked up Sam's phone. 'We grounded his phone.' He went to put it back but dropped it on the bench, where it skidded into the sink. 'Shit!' He set his drink down in slow motion, then plunged his hands into the greasy water, shuffling around pots and plates to find Sam's phone.

Devon snuck on down the hallway, checking out the bathroom.

After a moment Mr Campbell stopped for a quick drink then plunged his hands back in, swearing under his breath. We needed to get out of there. I checked on Devon's progress. He came out of the bathroom and shook his head.

Mr Campbell pulled some dishes from the sink and clomped them on the bench. Finally, he fished out Sam's phone. He shook it and pushed its buttons, but its screen looked dead. He sighed. 'Now look what you've made me do.' His eyes focused on me, like those of a shark. 'Sam's going to be very upset.'

My mind went blank, and my tongue stuck to the roof of my dry mouth.

He circled around the couch and towered over me. 'I think you'd better come back later.' I scuttled across the cushions to get away from him, and he gave me a strange look, filled with hate, one I'd never seen from him before. His mask was slipping. He shook his head and laughed bitterly. 'She's got to you too.'

I stood up, trying not to run. Where was Devon? 'I'll come back later.'

Mr Campbell stared at me as I moved towards the hallway. He turned and padded ahead of me, heading to the front door. I kept as far from him as I could, scrambling to think how to get past him and get out.

'Devon?' I called in a wavery voice.

Mr Campbell lashed out, punching the family portrait. 'Fuck!'

I jumped. The glass smashed and sprinkled on the concrete floor. I so didn't want to cry, but my vision was getting blurry. I took a gulp of air.

His hand bleeding, Mr Campbell staggered back against his bedroom door, which was ajar, and fell over, landing on the messy floor inside. Devon was standing by the bed, eyes wide. Covering the floor wasn't rubbish, but hundreds of white origami flowers.

I was going to vomit. Mr Campbell really had done it.

He lay on the floor, not moving, and for a second, I thought he'd passed out – but then he started laughing. Sam's dad was gone, replaced with this monster.

There was banging on the front door, then it opened. Barry and Detective Melon stood there, with Uncle Pike leaning against the wall behind them.

'Tippy?' Barry said, staring at me. As they came inside, I pointed to Mr Campbell, unable to speak.

'You?' Detective Melon said to Devon, who waved at him while stepping over Mr Campbell to get to me.

'I'd like to leave now,' I said, not recognising my high-pitched voice.

I didn't wait to hear what Uncle Pike or the police said. Instead, I ran, Devon streaking up the garden beside me, calling my name. Mr Campbell's drunk laughter followed me all the way up the hill to the car. My hands still shook as I opened the car door and slammed it shut. I wanted to get away fast. 'Quick,' I said. 'Let's go.'

Devon got in and held my shaking hands, as Uncle Pike finally made it back without his crutches.

'Sorry, Tippy,' my uncle said, out of breath. 'In hindsight, perhaps taking you to a murderer's house was not the smartest move. Let's not tell your mum about this one.'

Devon let go of my hands and punched Uncle Pike's arm. 'Told you!'

'Ow! *You* let her go inside.'

I smacked the back of the driver's seat. 'Please go!' I expected to see Mr Campbell on the street any second.

We'd solved a murder, but this wasn't how I thought I'd feel: scared, empty and black-hole sad all at once. I never wanted to feel like this again.

Devon sped off. As we drove past, I couldn't see Mr Campbell outside. The front door was shut. I took a couple of deep breaths and wiped my eyes.

CHAPTER TWENTY-THREE
Banoffee Pie

It was over. By the next morning my feelings had totally changed. I hugged myself and got a big, silly grin on my face. We'd actually

solved a murder. Stopped a monster. The Case of the Missing
Necklace was officially closed. Now I understood why Nancy Drew
took on so many cases – the feeling was addictive. The police had
taken Mr Campbell away and everyone was safe. Todd was safe.
Sam and Dr Lisa were safe. Sally would be free. I had left Sam a
voicemail and texted him on Dr Lisa's phone but hadn't heard back
from him yet. I knew his mum would tell him I'd done a good
thing, and we would be okay. He was still my best friend, even
though his dad was a murderer.

And as if today couldn't get any better it was also the start of the
school holidays. I was home alone. Uncle Pike and Devon had gone
off for a daytrip, and Mum was working a double shift. She didn't
know about Mr Campbell yet, and we had decided – well, Uncle
Pike and me mainly – that waiting until it came out in the *Bully*
might be the best approach. Hopefully she'd be so happy we'd caught
a murderer that she'd forget it happened while I was grounded.

My phone rang. *Shit*. Unless she had already heard it from Dr
Lisa.

I relaxed – it was Lorraine. 'Chan, you around?' It sounded as
though she was eating something wet and sticky, like peanut-butter
cheesecake. She didn't wait for my answer. 'My office, now.' She
hung up. Hopefully she had a new case for The Nancys.

I jumped on my bike. It was another blue-sky summer day with
some fat purple clouds in the distance. I sped down to the *Bully*
office and arrived out of breath at reception. The woman behind
the front desk gave me a smile.

'Chan!' Lorraine was sitting in a small glass-walled meeting
room off to the side. She shuffled along in her office chair and
poked her head around the door. 'In here.'

The receptionist raised her eyebrows.

'Answer the phone,' Lorraine yelled at her.

I didn't hear any ringing as I went to join Lorraine. Inside, a small
round table was pushed against the wall, taking up most of the
space along with three blue, padded office chairs.

Lorraine shoved her laptop aside and poured me a glass of water. 'Banoffee pie?' She shoved a yellow-brown piece of pie into my face. I shook my head, and she gulped it down like a pelican eating a fish. Her open mouth made a smacking noise. 'You know we're the same, Chan. We both want the truth.' She licked her fingers. 'Everson's blood work results came back negative. Again.'

'Negative for what?'

'She wasn't pregnant.' Lorraine wiped her hand on her chair.

I felt a twinge in my tummy. Leaning back, I nearly tipped onto the floor.

'Oh yeah. Chair's broken.'

I got up and changed seats. 'She really wasn't pregnant?'

'Keep up, Chan,' Lorraine said. 'That's not what I wanted to show you.' She clicked some keys on her laptop. The room smelled of sickly-sweet banana.

My stomach started to ache. Mr Campbell hadn't got Ms Everson pregnant. He hadn't covered up the test results. I licked my lips.

The screen split into two. It was security-camera footage from Riverstone Medical Centre. The top half showed the front entrance. Over the creepy snowman and screaming Santa paintings, I could see to the carpark and as far as the footpath along Main Street. The bottom half of the screen showed a long hallway ending at the back exit.

'Cameras cover the exits because of the drugs,' Lorraine said. 'This video is from the Saturday night of Jill Everson's murder.'

Lorraine scrolled through the footage until Sam and I appeared in the top screen. We were soon joined by Devon. She put it on fast-forward.

6.05 p.m. – Mr Campbell came in the front entrance and joined us.

6.09 p.m. – in the corner of the screen, two figures sped past on the footpath.

Lorraine stopped and rewound. She paused. Ms Everson and Sally were mid-tussle. It felt weird seeing my teacher again, after everything and all the time we'd spent solving her murder. Almost like seeing a celebrity or an old friend. I wished I could go back and warn her.

Lorraine hit fast-forward again and they disappeared off screen, and our group went outside on the ramp. Dr Lisa sped through the front entrance, joining us. Devon then disappeared from the screen, as he had run across the road.

6.15 p.m. – we all came back inside the front entrance. Dr Lisa headed back in to work.

6.23 p.m. – Mr Campbell left with Sam. Devon and I headed inside to see Uncle Pike.

9.20 p.m. – we exited.

Lorraine fast-forwarded.

2.07 a.m. – Dr Lisa left.

'This is now Sunday morning,' Lorraine said. She fast-forwarded and then played.

9.45 a.m. – a black car pulled up into the carpark outside: Mr Campbell's. He entered carrying a gym bag. I shuddered. Something didn't look right.

'Looks like he was called in,' she said.

'Wait,' I said. 'Pause please?'

Lorraine paused.

'Can I?' I pressed rewind until Mr Campbell came through the door. Then I played it frame by frame. 'There – can you see that?' He glanced up directly at the camera then looked away. The eyes of a killer.

'That doesn't mean anything,' she said. She cut another piece of pie.

'But it shows he knows the camera's recording him at this time.'

Lorraine shrugged, licking the knife.

I fast-forwarded.

11.37 a.m. – he left through the front entrance. I stopped, rewound and played again from when he entered, this time watching the bottom screen. But nothing unusual happened.

'He was at work at the time Suzie Pratt saw the murderer,' Lorraine said. She grabbed the laptop back.

I felt sick. What had we done? Sam's dad. The town hero.

'Earth to Chan.' Lorraine waved in front of my face. '*This* is what I wanted to show you.' She plugged white earbuds into the laptop. 'Put these in. You need to listen.' She handed them to me; they had browny-orange earwax on them. I tried not to grimace as the headphones touched my skin. They dangled dangerously from my ears, just waiting to fall out. How could there be any more to show me?

She swivelled the laptop back around so I could see the screen. She pressed play. It took a second or two before I realised what I was watching.

'How?' I said.

'They found his phone this morning.' She turned up the volume.

I heard wind against the phone's microphone. The image shook and blurred as Todd lifted his phone to his face. 'Proof, Sam, that I'm doing your dare.'

He pulled the phone back. He was lying on his stomach on one of the bridge's concrete arches, his other hand gripping the side. Then he moved the phone outwards and showed the bridge below; a logging truck passed underneath. Judging by the distance to the road, it looked like he was three-quarters of the way to the top.

'This is going to be the easiest hundred dollars.' He passed the phone to his other hand, the video wobbling as he let go of his grip on the bridge. I heard him panting, then the slap of skin on concrete as he held on. He pointed the phone down to the footpath on the other side of his arch, then up higher to show the back of the town hall and the founding tree on the flat, then back down to the footpath. He grunted as he stretched further out to show the slow-moving green river below. The image suddenly jerked around.

I gasped.

'Just kidding,' Todd said. His face filled the screen. I exhaled – he was such a dick. 'Next stop, the top.' A close-up of grey concrete filled the screen.

I could make out yelling.

'What the...?' Todd said.

'Get down!' a man shouted over the noise of traffic and the wind.

'For fuck's sake.' Todd's face came into view. 'Sam, why's your dad here? You better not have told...' He pointed the phone down to the walkway.

Directly below was Mr Campbell, his hands cupped on his forehead as he stared up.

'Be right down,' Todd yelled. He turned to face the camera and winked. 'After I win a hundred bucks.' The image jerked around again and filled with concrete and sky as Todd climbed upwards.

'You better not have...' Mr Campbell shouted. I couldn't make out the rest except the end. 'Just come down now. Please!'

'What? Like I want— Shit!' Suddenly jumbled images of sky, town and a shrinking Todd losing his balance on the concrete bridge flashed by as his phone fell in windy silence. Todd screamed and on screen a glimpse of him falling.

'No!' The phone tilted and a flash of Mr Campbell standing on the railing, before everything changed to a watery light green. A loud gurgling, rushing noise turned into silence as the phone sank into darkness.

The video file stopped.

The meeting room came into focus. It felt stuffy, like there was no air. I realised I'd been gripping the side of my chair. I ripped the earbuds out and pushed back from the table.

'So, Chan, what do you think of all that?' Lorraine lifted another piece of pie and offered it to me again.

I shook my head. The bananas smelled rotten and made me gag. My mind was spinning. I kept seeing Todd fall. I hated her for putting that in my brain and had to resist shoving the pie in her face.

'It was an accident,' I said. I wanted it to be a question because the truth meant Mr Campbell was innocent. That was why Lorraine had shown me the videos. I clutched my sides.

'Looks like it,' she said. 'There's texts from Sam Campbell daring Todd to climb it for a hundred dollars. Campbell's no longer a person of interest to the police. Sally Homer's the prime suspect again.'

I rocked in my seat. We'd been wrong. About everything. Mr Campbell wasn't a killer. Todd wasn't a blackmailer. The murderer was still out there.

'He's still a cheating arsehole,' Lorraine continued. 'I'd show you Todd's other videos and photos but you're a bit young for that.'

'He's only six months older,' I said.

'Nice try, but it's not going to happen. Let's just say there's no doubt Campbell was screwing your teacher.' She unplugged the headphones from the laptop and stuffed them in her pocket. 'I'd steer clear of him. Can't imagine he's too happy with any of us.'

I groaned. We had framed my best friend's dad for murder. I bit my nails. Riverstone suddenly felt very small. Mr Campbell would be at school, Mum's work, everywhere. Shit. Mum ... Then there was Sam.

Lorraine shut her laptop. 'Those tractor dollies might get washed out tomorrow – that would be a Show Queen first.'

I stood up. She kept talking, but I was no longer listening, Todd's screams as he fell played in my head. I needed to get away.

I fumbled for the door and then I was out. Lorraine called after me. I stumbled down the stairs. Outside it was raining. My cheeks burned and I wanted to vomit. I grabbed my bike and pushed off hard. I had ruined everything and solved nothing.

Curled up on my bed, I twirled Piggy-Cat's paw in my hand. 'Dad,' I whispered, 'I've screwed up. Really, really bad.' I tapped my nose with the paw. I missed my Piggy-Cat and her big, happy smile.

Dad used to surprise me by putting money in Piggy-Cat while I slept. In the morning I'd check and my savings would have grown, sometimes by as much as fifty dollars and once even a hundred. The first time it had happened, I had no idea where it had come from.

I'd asked Mum, but she denied it and glared at Dad. He smiled at me and shrugged, saying maybe the tooth fairy had got drunk. For ages I kept trying to stay awake to see if it would happen again, but it wasn't until the fourth time that I saw Dad creeping in and putting cash in Piggy-Cat. He patted her head and tiptoed back out.

One night he must have been drunk; I could smell whisky. It took him a couple of goes to get the money into Piggy-Cat's mouth. He nearly lost his balance and there was a crash. 'Shit!' He looked over at me. I pretended to be asleep – I didn't want the money to stop. He put the stuff back on my dresser then tried to get out of my room but went the wrong way and banged into my window instead. I squashed down my giggles, listening as he thumped and scratched his way around the walls until finally he found the door. There was a big sigh of relief. 'Night, Tippy,' he said in a loud whisper as he opened the door. 'Love you forever.' He closed it as quietly as he could, which was still pretty noisy. The next morning I'd found Piggy-Cat's broken paw on my rug.

All of that now seemed like another lifetime. I lay there listening to the rain hit the roof, wishing I could slip back into that everyday-normal again – before Ms Everson, before Todd and Dad, even before my parents fighting and Melanie's mum dying. But instead, I was stuck here, alone on the other side, looking in. I kept trying Dr Lisa and even Sam's stuffed phone, calling and texting him that I was sorry, but so far not even one reply.

I spent the rest of the day in my bedroom, only coming out when Mum came home from work for lunch and then again at dinner. Each time I waited for her to blast me about Mr Campbell but she hadn't yet. Luckily for me, Dr Lisa hadn't shown up for work. I still had to pretend everything was all right, which was hard as I didn't want to look Mum in the eyes.

After she'd left for her night shift, I had just got into my pyjamas when Uncle Pike and Devon arrived, laughing and soaked from the rainstorm.

I waited until they had dried off then joined them in the living room, sitting beside my uncle on the couch. 'Mr Campbell's innocent,' I said. I filled them in on my visit with Lorraine, and on Mr Campbell, Todd, the pregnancy results and the security-cam footage.

'Wow,' Devon said.

Uncle Pike put his arm around me. 'I don't know why she'd show you Todd.'

'Not okay,' Devon said, sitting on my other side.

'At least we know what happened now,' I said. 'It was a stupid dare.'

My uncle sighed. 'Yes, true. But you still shouldn't have seen it.'

I nodded and snuggled against him as a gust of wind knocked about the sun loungers on the balcony. At least Todd was safe from being stalked by a killer; it really had been an accident. That was the only silver lining in all of this.

'Do you think we could get a copy of the phone's photos and videos?' Devon said.

Uncle Pike glared at him.

'What? It's research.' He mouthed to Uncle Pike, 'He's so hot.'

'Eeew, that's Sam's dad,' I said.

'That's not his fault,' Devon said. 'He's like a hot Hannibal Lecter – except he doesn't eat people or kill them.' He nudged me. 'That's good news for Sam.'

My uncle shook his head.

I played with my pyjama button. I'd probably lost my best friend and now had an enemy. 'I don't think we should try to solve any more mysteries. We didn't even find the necklace.'

'Have you been drinking?' Uncle Pike said. 'Russell will get over it.'

'Of course he will,' Devon said unconvincingly. I didn't think Sam would, or the Campbells. Devon continued: 'And at least now the police have all the clues we found.'

I rubbed my foot on the carpet. 'Maybe it's sometimes better not to know the truth.'

Uncle Pike glanced at Devon. 'Well ... look on the bright side. Fewer people to buy Christmas presents for.'

I pulled on my sleeves. I wanted to hide and never go outside again. With the storm, it looked like I wouldn't have to. 'What do I tell Mum? She warned us not to. She's going to find out – Dr Lisa's her best friend.'

'You haven't done anything wrong,' Devon said.

'We did frame someone for murder,' Uncle Pike said. 'Let's not sugar-coat that.'

'And I promised not to sleuth. And I was grounded.'

Devon gave me a big hug.

'She'll get over it. Plus, we had our fingers crossed. I think you're very brave.' My uncle clumsily stroked my head. 'Pat, pat.'

'Stop it.' I laughed, moving forward out of his reach.

There was another huge gust and rain spat against the windows. 'Finally,' he said, as it poured harder.

Devon looked glum. 'So you weren't lying about the weather.'

'Hold on.' My uncle put his finger in his ear then nodded several times. 'Mm-hmm, aha!' He beamed at Devon. 'Correct!' Uncle Pike hadn't been this happy when it was sunny. 'Now, where did I leave that "I told you so"? I'm sure it's around here...' He picked up Grandma's friendship bell and rang it.

'So awful,' Devon said.

'Will they cancel the Show Queens tomorrow?' At least then I wouldn't have to be in public.

My uncle shrugged. 'Team Melanie will be ready.' He kissed me goodnight.

'Have a good sleep, honey,' Devon said. 'And don't you worry. Whatever happens, we'll face it together.'

'Remember, we're The Nancys,' Uncle Pike called out. 'No one fucks with us.'

CHAPTER TWENTY-FOUR
Nancy Next Door

'It's summer, baby!' Devon tipped his orange sunglasses. It was a beautiful morning – the sun was back out and the concrete was already dry after all the rain last night. 'The show must go on.' He headed next door to finish Melanie's dress with Mrs Brown.

I was in the war room with Uncle Pike and Melanie. Mum had gone to bed. She had another shift today as well. I was worried about her working so much. She still didn't know about what we'd done to Mr Campbell. When I woke up this morning I'd felt worse than I had the morning of Ms Everson's funeral. At least then I hadn't been responsible for ruining everything.

Melanie sat in the salon chair, jiggling her leg. She wiped her palms on her jeans and seemed nervous. Uncle Pike sat behind her, spraying her hair.

'Drink?' I asked.

He raised his full glass.

'Vodka, thanks,' she said.

I nodded. At least today I could help Melanie.

I ran inside and poured her a big glass of Mum's vodka. I figured if Mum noticed she'd just blame my uncle. Hopefully this would help Melanie's nerves.

When I came back in, they were quiet.

I passed her the glass. 'Did I miss something?'

'Melanie was just fan-girling about Claire Bates,' Uncle Pike said.

She laughed. 'As if.' She smelled her drink and glanced up at me.

I held my breath, not sure what my uncle would say if she outed me.

Melanie winked and sculled it back. Her eyes watered and she blinked with her mouth open, her face going red.

I froze.

Behind her Uncle Pike didn't seem to notice. He kept snipping and combing.

She started coughing and spluttered. 'Sorry, water went down the wrong way.'

'Would you like some more?' I asked.

'Yes, please,' Melanie croaked. She handed me her glass with a crooked smile. Finally, I was doing something right. She pulled out her cigarettes.

I went and refilled her glass. I thought about Mr Campbell glaring at me, his face filled with hate. And that was before the false arrest. How was he going to be now? My hand trembled as I screwed the bottle cap back on. I just needed Sam to know how sorry I was. I'd been so wrong about his dad and Todd and everything. The murderer was still out there but I couldn't find them. Why did I ever believe I could? Sam was right – I wasn't Nancy Drew. I was just some kid.

On the way back I stopped and checked Suzie Pratt's picture again. Something about it nagged at me. As I stared at the murderer's face I took a sip, forgetting it was vodka. It burned my mouth and my face felt hot.

'Tippy!' my uncle called out.

Shit. I hurried back to the garage.

'More ice, please,' he said.

An hour later, Melanie had been 'styled' and 'blown out' and looked like a movie star. A quick cigarette break, and then Uncle Pike was on to her makeup.

'Tippy, please check on where they're up to next door with the dress. In fifteen minutes, we'll be ready for them, and then we need to go.'

I ran over to the Browns' and knocked on the door. Mrs Brown bustled me inside. 'This is so exciting. Come and have a look.'

Inside her craft room, Devon was hand-sewing sparkles onto a filmy sunshine-yellow dress. The colour made me happy, and I broke into a big grin. It reminded me of butterfly wings. 'Nearly there,' he said, balancing pins in his mouth.

The plan was for Mrs Brown and Melanie to arrive at the show after us, so we didn't blow our cover with Horn-blower. Luckily no one seemed to have noticed how loud and bubbly Melanie was. I just hoped she would get through the competition without spewing on her dress or on the crowd.

At the showgrounds I led Uncle Pike and Devon from the carpark to the rides. We passed Dr Lisa's red car on the way. I searched for Sam and at the same time hoped I wouldn't see Mr Campbell. There was no way I could face him. So far, no Sam, but I did pass a few classmates and their families; they'd already found balloons somewhere.

Devon demanded we go on the Ferris wheel before doing anything else. I lined up for tickets and sent Dr Lisa a quick text to let Sam know where I was just in case he wanted to meet. I watched as Uncle Pike and Devon talked to a man beside a large green tractor. Well, my uncle talked while Devon stared. The man looked a bit like my old Ken doll but with his hair rubbed off.

'Heard you were rat-arsed and fell off your balcony,' Ken doll said.

'Seriously?' Uncle Pike said. 'Everyone knows that, yet no one in this fucking town knows who's cutting people's heads off?'

Devon laughed a little too long, and Ken raised his eyebrows. 'They got that lady, didn't they? That schoolteacher.'

'What if it wasn't her?' my uncle asked.

Ken shrugged. 'Don't know about that – they found all that stuff.' He moved closer. 'They say she was obsessed.'

I felt a tap on my shoulder and turned around. It was Dr Lisa. 'Hello, Tippy.'

I was happy to see her, but then I remembered Mr Campbell. My cheeks burned.

'Where's Mum?' Dr Lisa said.

'At work.' I took a sudden interest in my sneakers. 'Is Sam here?'

She grabbed my arm. 'Come with me for a sec.' It wasn't a question. She glanced behind me. Uncle Pike and Devon moved around the other side of the tractor, out of sight. She led me the short distance across the grounds to the grandstand. I had to trot to keep up with her. We entered the players' entrance underneath, the tunnel dark and cool after being in the sun. She checked we were alone. 'Have you seen him?'

'Who? Sam? I haven't seen him for ages.' My throat felt thick and I cleared it. 'Is he here?'

She gave a little laugh. 'No, I meant Russell. Is *he* here? Have you seen him?'

I shook my head. 'I think I'm the last person he wants to see.'

She tapped her fingers against her thigh.

I didn't know what to say about Mr Campbell. 'I'm so sorry. I didn't mean to cause any trouble.'

She laughed again; it sounded strange. 'Don't worry, Tippy. He deserved it. Listen, Sam and I are leaving today, for good. He wants to see you and say goodbye. I don't know what happened to his phone, so I'm glad I ran into you.'

My heart went from happy that she didn't hate me to a shrunken ball in less than a second. 'You're going?'

'This town destroyed my family.' She cleared her throat. 'Meet me back here under the grandstand with Sam in an hour – can you do that for me?'

'Of course. I wish you'd stay.'

She squeezed my hand. 'Not an option. I told Russell next time he drank, we'd be gone. I'm just glad Sam gets to say goodbye to you.' She pointed to a changing room. 'Stay there and I'll send him in. Sorry for the secrecy. Just need to make sure his dad ... well, never mind.'

I went inside the cinder-block changing room and waited for a couple of minutes. It smelled of wet concrete and liniment. Then I heard Sam's voice. 'I don't want to see her. Not after—' He stopped at the changing-room door and stared at me, Dr Lisa behind him.

'Go on then,' she said, giving him a gentle shove.

'Mum, I don't want—'

'Listen to me, Sam Campbell. This is your best friend. I'm sure she has plenty she'd like to say to you.'

I swallowed and nodded.

'Meet me back here in an hour.' She gave Sam some money. 'Now go have fun.' She left us alone.

Neither of us spoke for ages.

I found it hard to look at him. 'Sorry about your dad.'

'Yeah, well now Mum says I can't see him. Thanks to you.' Sam booted an empty lemonade can across the room. The clatter seemed extra loud against the concrete.

'I'm so sorry. I thought we were right.'

'That's my dad, Tippy. Just so wrong.'

My tummy was all hard knots. 'What can I do to make it up to you? Anything.'

'Whatever,' he said. 'Let's just get this hour over with.'

I followed him outside. Noise came from all directions: children laughing, fairground rides and a loudspeaker commentary on the dressage.

'Over here.' I tugged on the back of Sam's white T-shirt but he refused to turn around. I left him and lined up for the Ferris wheel again, keeping an eye on him. He stopped and dragged himself towards me but hung back in the queue, eventually standing behind me. I stared down at the grass. 'All the clues pointed to him. I'm so sorry.' I turned around.

He glared at me, shaking his head. 'What the...?'

Uncle Pike and Devon joined us.

'Tractor-man's so pretty,' Devon said.

'I didn't think men could be pretty?' Sam said. He seemed relieved not to have to talk to me anymore.

'Of course they can,' my uncle said. 'And women can be handsome, like your mother.'

Sam looked confused. He saw me watching him and turned his back on me.

Uncle Pike smiled. 'Be sure you tell her I said that.'

We bought tickets from a dirty-looking man – Devon described him as being 'off his tits' – and finally got on. I sat beside Sam but he still wouldn't talk to or look at me.

The wheel barely turned, and when it did it jerked. I was no longer sure this was fun. We stopped at the top. I searched for my house and saw a tiny Mrs Brown hanging out her washing. From here I could see the whole town, all the way to the traffic light where Jill Everson's body had been found and then further out to the sea. On the other side was my school and Main Street snaking up the hill past the old hospital and out of town.

The carriage swayed. I wanted to get down.

'Everything seems greener up here,' Devon said sadly.

'I guess.' Sam kicked at the cage.

It was a good spot to see the show. Below us were the rides, vans selling hot dogs and candy floss, and the farm machinery. Sheds at the edges of the showgrounds were filled with cows and sheep being judged, and on the rugby field were horse-jumping and dressage competitions. In front of the grandstand was a makeshift stage made of two old trucks parked butt to butt. This was where the Show Queen final would be. On it now was a local band from high school, playing versions of top-twenty songs. I didn't recognise the girl singing.

'Seriously?' Uncle Pike shook his head. 'Sounds like her pussy's down a well.'

'I think she's lonely,' Devon said.

My uncle checked his watch. 'Have you heard from Melanie?'

There were no new messages on my phone. I avoided my uncle's gaze. 'I'm sure she'll be here.' I pictured her groaning beside the toilet with vomit in her hair extensions. I crossed my fingers; I hoped I hadn't ruined this too. Over at their house, tiny Mrs Brown had disappeared.

'Better be,' Uncle Pike said. 'I think I'd like to get down now.'

'Maybe it's broken,' Sam said matter-of-factly, and my uncle shuddered.

'Are you afraid of heights?' I asked Uncle Pike, relieved I wasn't the only one hating this.

'No, honey.' He smiled and rubbed my arm. 'Just fair rides badly put together by people on drugs.'

'That sounds reasonable,' Devon added absently. 'I wish I had binoculars.'

'Why did we agree to a phone detox?' Uncle Pike said.

Devon frowned. 'I really don't know.' He pulled out his soap and took a selfie with us. My uncle rolled his eyes, gripping tighter on to the safety bar.

We did three more loops before the ride finally ended.

'Worst ride ever,' Devon said to the operator, who ignored him.

I was glad to be off it too. 'Let's go see the animals.'

We made our way across the grounds, weaving in and out of families, groups of kids and farm equipment, until we got to a shed with white wooden yards covered in an old, rusty corrugated-iron roof. It smelled of hay and dust. In the first pen were a couple of brown and cream alpacas. When we moved to the rails, a faded-brown one came over to visit.

'Look, it's Devon,' Uncle Pike said. 'What are you doing in that pen?'

Devon laughed. He tilted his head and gave the alpaca his 'shy girl' look, batting his lashes. Sam reached over to pet it but he seemed to be aiming for its eyes.

'I don't think it likes that,' I said.

The alpaca moved its head and made a low gurgle.

'I'm not surprised,' Uncle Pike said. 'I don't think many creatures like having their eyeballs fondled.'

Sam kept petting its face. The alpaca's tail stood up and it stomped its back leg.

'Stop touching its eyes,' I said.

'Why? Are you going to arrest me?' Sam moved his hand away from the alpaca, which bared its lower teeth. It blinked, its huge lashes batting again.

We kept moving around the animal pens, occasionally stopping to pet a sheep. The place was shady but not cool, maybe because the animals were heating it up.

The last pens had pigs. Devon pointed to a large sow with piglets. 'Honey, that's amazing.' He put his arm around Uncle Pike and rested his head on his shoulder. 'You looked so cute as a baby.'

'Squeal like a pig,' my uncle said in a strange American accent.

Sam chuckled and tried to reach into the pen. 'Squeal like a pig,' he mimicked.

'Okay,' my uncle said, 'maybe let's not say that.'

'But why?' Sam said. 'Squeal like a pig. Squeal like a pig.' The sow moved her head around, snapping at his hand.

Uncle Pike pointed outside. 'Look.' Sam stood up and squinted; I couldn't believe he'd fallen for that old trick. 'Come on,' my uncle said. 'I'm starving.'

We left the animals and circled back to the food vans, where we filled up on hot chips and hot dogs on a stick. We started to wander over to the grandstand.

'Keep a lookout for clowns,' Uncle Pike called over his shoulder. 'They're the modern-day equivalent of the butler.'

'Clowns make me sad,' Devon said.

'What's a butler?' Sam said. He had tomato sauce in his hair.

'Kind of like a maid with a penis for fancy people,' my uncle said.

Sam burst out laughing and whispered to me in a loud voice, 'He said penis.'

I giggled. But then felt instantly sad. It was nearly time for us to meet up with Dr Lisa at the grandstand. I was going to have to say goodbye to Sam. But I didn't know how to, or when I'd see him again. 'I'll catch up with you both,' I said to Uncle Pike and Devon.

Uncle Pike stuck out his hand to Sam. 'Merry Christmas, Sam. It's been a pleasure. You take care of yourself.'

Sam's mouth dropped open mid-shake. 'Hey, you look like Santa. Has anyone told you that?'

My uncle seemed shocked. 'No! Really? Do you think?'

'Bye, Uncle Pike.' I dragged Sam away.

'See you at the Browns' horse float, by the stage. Best hideout ever.' Phyllis had driven the horse box up from the farm yesterday to act as Melanie's undercover beauty queen 'trailer'. Melanie's dad had been too busy to help. He wouldn't even be here today.

'Bye, Sam,' Devon called out.

Sam gave Devon some weird salute. 'Baba ghanoush.'

'Come on,' I said. We walked to the changing rooms under the grandstand.

'Seriously, your uncle looks so much like Santa.'

I was quiet and felt prickles in my eyes. 'I really am sorry, Sam. I never meant for any of this to happen.'

He kicked at the concrete floor. 'It's not all your fault. They've been fighting for ages. But I just wish you'd talked to me before you dobbed in my dad.'

'Sorry.' I wondered if Sam knew how much his life was about to change.

He sat down on a wooden bench. 'You're one of the only people I can trust, Tippy. Especially since Bridge Boy's still asleep in hospital.' He looked up at me. 'Just don't do it again.'

I laughed, but he was serious. 'Of course,' I said. I gave him an awkward hug. 'Make sure you answer your phone more.'

'When I get a new one.' Sam stood up. 'Anyway, I'm going on holiday, not dying. We'll see each other soon.' He nudged my shoulder. 'Just don't go getting anyone else arrested.'

'I promise.' I nudged him back and sighed. 'I wish you hadn't dared Todd to climb that stupid bridge.'

'What? I never did that.' Sam frowned. 'No way. But of course he'd have said yes if I had.'

Dr Lisa came in and put her arm around his shoulders. 'Thanks, Tippy.'

I nodded and my eyes started to blur. I wasn't ready. I didn't want Sam to go. I gave him another quick hug. 'See you soon.'

'See you never,' he said.

I ran out before he could see me cry.

'Don't get shit on your frock,' Uncle Pike said.

'Bet you've heard that before.' Melanie wore one of the Browns' beige bedsheets over her like a cape, hiding her outfit. She hiked up her dress underneath and carefully stepped into the Browns' horse float while Mrs Brown set up guard outside.

'Let me look at you.' Uncle Pike frowned. 'Anyone would think you're hungover.'

She glanced at me. I shook my head slightly and stuffed my hands in my pockets. I asked if she wanted any water.

She groaned. 'No more, Chan. I feel like the bottom of a rabbit cage.'

Uncle Pike pulled out an energy drink. 'For emergencies. Now get this down you quickly. Try not to throw up. There's another one after this.'

She sculled back the can in a couple of goes then grimaced and belched.

'Charming.' My uncle opened his makeup kit and took out a brush and some powder, which he gently swept across her face. He leaned in for a closer look then got the lip pencil out. 'Pull back.'

Melanie opened her mouth and stretched her lips over her teeth.

'Now tell me again why you want to win this,' he said, lightly outlining her mouth again. He stood back and she wiggled her lips together.

She touched her fake eyelashes with the back of her finger. 'Told you, it's all bullshit. And vodka and cigarettes.'

'Smells like horseshit.' He clicked his fingers. 'I like vodka and cigarettes just as much as the next girl, but you were already in this competition.'

'Did you just click your fingers at me?'

'I need you to focus. Think. Why did you *really* sign up for this?

This is a quantum leap for an anti-princess with no interest in personal hygiene.'

She checked outside the door. Mrs Brown was putting up a sun umbrella. 'Okay, fine.' Melanie lit a cigarette.

I looked at the hay covering the floor.

'Grandad treats Phyllis like shit.' Melanie took a drag, then blew the smoke away from me outside. 'Do you know this was how they met? When she was Show Queen?'

Uncle Pike shook his head.

'He was nearly thirty years older. When Phyllis asked me if I would enter, she was so excited. I hadn't seen her like that for a long, long time.' She took another drag and held it in. 'Me, I couldn't think of anything worse.' She blew smoke out her nose like a dragon. 'You know how she comes across all happy, but I see her...' Melanie flicked ash on the floor. Her voice became quiet. 'It sounds stupid, but I thought maybe, I don't know, doing this might help her remember herself?'

The horse float was silent except for the muffled sounds from the show outside.

Uncle Pike cleared his throat. 'Trust me, that's the sanest thing I've heard about any of this. The judges and the audience sense what's real. Hold on to your reason and you'll blow those other pricks out of the water. Tippy, edit out the word "pricks", please.'

Devon slapped him on the arm.

'What? I'm being an equal opportunist with my swearing.' Uncle Pike held up a jar of Vaseline. Melanie put her cigarette in the empty can and passed it to me; I handed over her second energy drink. 'You've got this,' my uncle said. 'Remember: smile, big eyes, and a loud, clear, pleasant voice.'

She nodded and downed the second can. When she finished, she burped the alphabet up to D. She smiled and rubbed Vaseline over her teeth then opened her mouth; Devon sprayed in some breath freshener. She crushed her can and gave it to him.

'You're the most beautiful girl I've ever seen,' I said.

She smiled at me – not a Vaseline smile, but a kind, happy smile. She squeezed my hand. 'Right back at you, Chan.'

'Sorry about the water,' I said.

'I'm not,' she said. 'Don't worry, the energy drink is kicking in.'

Devon opened the horse-float door and peered out. 'Coast is clear.'

'Right, Claire Bates,' Melanie said in a clear, pleasant voice. 'It's showtime, you bullshit volunteering fuck.' She stepped down from the horse float, with the three of us behind her, and Mrs Brown gave her a hug. Without turning around Melanie dropped the sheet and joined the other girls lined up at the stairs, ready to go on stage. In her beautiful, sparkling yellow dress she was unmissable; it was light and effortless and seemed to float around her. She looked like the Christmas fairy at a Hollywood party. All the others wore dark shades with lots in black, except for one in a weird white dress.

'That white one obviously couldn't decide between being the bride or the wedding gazebo,' Uncle Pike said.

As Melanie climbed the stairs, I heard snatches of conversation from the crowd: 'Who's that girl?' 'Is she a celebrity?' 'Where's she from?' 'She's from that movie.' I tried to look away from Melanie, but every time my eyes would find their way back to her. I had never seen her so smiley. And also, thanks to Uncle Pike and Devon, she glowed like the sun, easily outshining all the other contestants

'Looks like Riverstone has a new princess,' Devon said. 'Sorry, Pike.'

Mrs Brown put down her camera. 'So proud.' She dabbed her eyes with the beige bedsheet.

'Oh, honey.' Devon waved her over and gave her a quick one-armed hug. 'You should be so proud of yourself. She's killing it thanks to you.'

Mrs Brown let out a small laugh and shook her head. She lifted her camera back up.

I turned to my uncle. 'It's incredible.'

He smiled at me. 'Have you worked out the inspiration yet? It's a modern interpretation...'

As Melanie walked on stage, beautiful and strong, it hit me. 'Of course!' Sixteen, blonde and glamourous, the same as Nancy Drew in the early versions we both loved. Fearless, independent and confident, something Melanie and Nancy shared.

Uncle Pike hugged me. 'She was living next door in Riverstone the whole time.'

I nodded and hugged him back. Despite everything with Sam and Todd and Mr Campbell, I couldn't stop grinning. The crowd loved Melanie, and she was loving them. A big roar would come from a section whenever she waved in their direction.

Claire Bates, on the other hand, didn't seem quite as happy as in her photo. She was squashed into a little black dress so tight under her armpits it must've hurt. She moved closer to Melanie, maybe to try to steal some of the attention she was getting.

'Amateur!' Uncle Pike yelled at her. He turned to us. 'She's just made herself look ten times worse.'

Mrs Brown nodded, smiling.

Poor Claire. I felt a bit sorry for her. She did seem a little less perfect than her *Bully* photo. As proud as I was of our Nancy-next-door my heart was breaking. I wiped the sweat off my neck and thought of my teacher. A chill running through me while I sweated. On stage Claire Bates did a twirl and nearly fell over. If it wasn't Mr Campbell, Horn-blower, Duncan Nunn, or Sally, who was it? And like Nancy-next-door, had the murderer been in front of us all this time?

CHAPTER TWENTY-FIVE
L.B.D.

The mayor introduced Ashley James. By my count there was only her, Claire Bates and Melanie left to speak. Ashley came to the microphone and stood there. She blinked a lot and made strange noises as she tried to talk. I felt sorry for her; even though she choked, I still thought it was really brave to stand in front of all those people. She finished up after only a minute, although it seemed a lot longer than that. The crowd gave her a big clap as she sat back down.

'I think they all got the same speech off the internet,' my uncle said. 'Except for that poor girl – she clearly had trouble connecting.'

'Hmmm,' I said and rubbed my chest.

My uncle squinted at me. 'What's going on with you?'

'Sam's gone.' It hurt and I didn't want to talk about it.

The mayor got up. 'Thank you all for your patience. We are nearly there. Ladies and gentlemen, girls and boys, I would like to introduce Claire Bates.'

There was a smattering of claps and one loud whoop from the crowd.

Claire stepped up to the microphone with a smug look on her face. 'How about a big hand for Ashley?' She frowned like a clown and nodded. I waited for her to pretend to rub her eyes. 'At least she tried, am I right?' Some confused claps came from the crowd.

Ashley's face and neck flushed again, and she tried to smile but it looked strange. I hated Claire for doing that to Ashley, especially when Claire's own black dress was so tight and bunched up that she looked like a burst sausage. It wasn't like she didn't have a beautiful body. Weirdo.

Claire turned back to the crowd and spread open her arms. 'Some people are worth melting for.' She paused, and her head bobbed as she made eye contact with the crowd and those up in the grandstand. 'This is a quote from my fav—'

High-pitched feedback made the judges cover their ears.

She stepped back and gave the crowd a fake smile. She tapped the microphone. 'Let's start again.'

Uncle Pike groaned. 'Please, let's not.' He put his hands on his lower back and arched backwards.

The crowd murmured. An escaped red balloon floated up towards the clouds. Two more balloons followed, with kids laughing, except for one who screamed, probably missing a balloon.

Devon put a hot hand on my shoulder. 'What's going on with her dress?'

Claire laughed loudly. 'How's this heat? Thanks for waiting. Some people are worth melting for.'

'You're not,' my uncle said, wiping sweat out of his eyes.

She continued. 'This is a quote from my favourite old movie, *Frozen*. If I win today, I promise to spread my love.'

'TMI,' Devon said.

'STI,' my uncle said.

I wasn't sure why she was saying this or what it had to do with *Frozen*. She kissed the palm of her hand and in a practised slow-motion move blew a kiss to the audience.

I moved Devon's hand off my shoulder. Something niggled at me, like it had that night at the old hospital. I felt I had missed something. Again.

'Through my volunteering...'

'Bullshit,' Mrs Brown said in a loud cough.

Claire glanced over at her. I was pretty sure she couldn't see me beside the horse float, but I moved back further just in case.

'...I meet all kinds of old people.' She pointed at Mrs Brown and smiled. 'They are so old and so wise. I applaud you.' She clapped and the crowd joined her.

'What the fuck was the point of that speech?' Uncle Pike said.

I shrugged. 'At least it's over.' I peered out again. Something about Claire's black dress was bugging me, besides it not fitting her.

On stage Horn-blower yawned, not bothering to cover his mouth, and Duncan Nunn stared at Melanie with creepy eyes. The mayor stood up.

'Also...' Claire waved to stop the clapping. There were scattered groans, and the mayor sat down. 'Also, I believe in mentoring young girls. If I win, I will be a mentor.'

'Why does she have to win to be a mentor?' Devon said.

Uncle Pike banged his head against the horse-float wall. 'Is there a time limit?'

Mrs Brown turned around. 'Five minutes.'

He groaned again. His red face looked like it was melting.

Devon did some lunges, as Claire droned on. Finally, her annoying voice stopped and there was some light clapping from the crowd.

'That was more like fifteen minutes,' Mrs Brown said. 'What a disgrace! She should be disqualified. We'd never have gotten away with that in my day.'

Uncle Pike pulled down on his cheeks, making a face. 'Closest I've been to bursting my own eardrums.'

The mayor stood up. 'Last, but certainly not least, Melanie Brown!'

The crowd cheered, and we all crowded back around the opening of the float.

Melanie walked up to the microphone, beaming and waving to the crowd with both hands, which made them cheer more.

'Cute move,' Devon said.

'Hello, South Otago!' The crowd grew even louder. She smiled and pointed to someone in the distance, gave them a little wave, then stood and waited until it quietened down. 'I'm going to be brief.' There were hollers of approval. 'First off, how about a big round of applause for our speakers today?' She turned and clapped the other girls. There were wolf-whistles and hollers from the crowd. Claire gave Melanie a sour look.

'Vagi is going to get a bonus,' Uncle Pike said. 'This is flawless.'

Mrs Brown stood up and grinned at us with tears in her eyes. Devon made a heart shape with his hands.

'Beautiful people, judges.' Melanie nodded towards them. Hornblower sat up straight and smiled, and Duncan stared while the mayor gave Melanie a nod. 'When I first entered this competition, I thought it was boring and pointless. I thought it was for people who weren't like me. People who only cared about their looks and what other people thought of them.' She smiled at Claire. 'And arse-clowns.' Melanie turned back to the crowd. 'And I was right.'

A couple of people laughed, but the rest of the crowd muttered. I couldn't believe she'd just called Claire that – Todd would be so proud. I resisted the urge to clap.

On stage Claire shot Melanie daggers while complaining to another contestant. Some of the girls who hadn't managed to keep up their smiles also gave Melanie dirty looks.

'For fuck's sake,' Uncle Pike said beside me.

'At least her voice is nice and clear,' I said.

He gave her a cut-throat signal. Melanie gave him an angelic smile. 'But what I didn't expect, through this competition, was to get to know the most amazing people, like Ashley.'

Ashley wriggled in her seat and beamed at the stage floor.

'It is a privilege to be here today, speaking to you, competing in the A&P Show Queen.'

There were a few claps.

'No, literally a privilege. A white privilege. A cisgender, able-bodied, straight, socio-economic privilege. I am so privileged that I've literally been given a platform to speak on.'

The crowd was silent. In the background came the music from the fairground rides and laughing from behind the grandstand.

'But as a community we are diverse. Women from different cultures, of different ages, in all different shapes and sizes.' Melanie turned to the mayor. 'Different sexualities.'

Uncle Pike groaned.

Melanie paused and gave a cheesy smile. 'Not that you'd know it with all us cis, non-disabled, white, straight faces on stage.'

The crowd was silent.

'Except for you, Mayor Jones,' Melanie said.

The mayor nodded, and Uncle Pike slapped his forehead. 'She is beyond script.'

Horn-blower leaned forward in his seat, grinning like the Cheshire cat. Duncan's mouth was open; it looked like he was drooling.

'But there is one privilege we don't have.' Melanie paused and scanned the crowd. 'Male privilege.'

I could hear men muttering.

'I entered this for my grandma, Phyllis Brown.' Melanie pointed to Mrs Brown, who waved at the crowd like she was the queen. 'She's my hero. But, like many women here, she is taken for granted. In our household it's assumed all she wants to do is the cooking and cleaning while my grandad pays the bills.'

Mrs Brown was standing rigid with her back to us.

Melanie pulled the mic off its stand and walked along the front of the stage. 'That she is somehow desperate to do grocery shopping and ironing. And I know she's not the only one – you only need to spend one second in the Riverstone Bowling Club to get that.'

'There goes the grey vote,' Uncle Pike said.

'To that I say, "Get real and step it up, Riverstone!"' Melanie said, in a clear, loud voice.

The audience was silent except for a couple of 'yes!' shouts and some loud claps from a few women.

Uncle Pike banged his head against the horse-float wall again. 'What is she doing?'

'I think it's brilliant,' Devon said.

'When Mum died, Phyllis Brown not only stepped in, but she also stepped up. Grandma, I love you.' Melanie blew her a kiss, which got 'awws' from the crowd.

Mrs Brown's cheeks were wet. She blew Melanie kisses with both hands. The applause grew louder and louder.

As the noise started to die down, Melanie spoke again. 'If I win A&P Show Queen, besides releasing a calendar...'

Loud hollers came from males in the crowd, and Duncan Nunn crouched over.

'I knew they would love that,' Mrs Brown said over her shoulder.

Melanie smiled and nodded to the crowd. '...I'd like to spend my reign with my fellow contestants, meeting and encouraging women from all backgrounds to enter next year. Let's celebrate this awesome community and region we live in, this great town, and its amazing women.'

The crowd was silent – and then the clapping erupted into a standing ovation. It took several minutes for people to quieten down. The judges huddled, then the mayor spoke. 'It is a unanimous decision. This year's A&P Show Queen is ... drum roll, please ... Melanie Brown!'

Melanie put her hands to her mouth in surprise, and the crowd went wild. We were screaming and jumping around.

The mayor put a sash over Melanie. Then last year's winner, Nicky White, placed a crown on her head. Melanie waved for Mrs Brown to come on stage. They hugged, and Melanie raised her grandma's arm. 'Ladies and gentlemen, Phyllis Brown, A&P Show Queen 1969.' They bowed then hugged and the crowed loved it. Melanie continued: 'There are some people I'd also like to thank, because none of this would've been possible without my team: Betty Brown-Eye, Lucy Loose-Unit and Tippy Chan.'

We ran up on stage. The crowd cheered as Melanie hugged me and Devon, and finally Uncle Pike, who hopped on one crutch.

'So proud,' he said.

Mrs Brown winked at Devon and we took a bow.

As the mayor wrapped it up, Claire Bates stormed off stage, nearly bowling me over. I had to grab her arm to steady myself, and that was when I noticed small, black lace roses around the neckline of her dress.

'Get out of my way!' she said, shaking me off.

Horn-blower headed over. 'Possibly one of the worst speeches I've ever heard.'

'Thanks,' Melanie said. 'I meant every word.'

'Exactly,' he said.

'What about that Claire Bates?' Uncle Pike said.

'Who?' Horn-blower tipped an imaginary hat to my uncle. 'Well done.' He started down the stairs.

'Hey, H.B.,' my uncle called out. 'Thanks. And sorry. For ... you know.'

Horn-blower ducked his head, and I thought I saw him smile. Then he saw me and made a crucifix with his fingers. 'Put a muzzle on that kid,' he said and continued down the stairs.

'Dick,' Devon muttered.

Duncan was lurking about. 'Just wanted to say well done, Melanie. Really looking forward to that calendar.'

'Thanks.' She turned to Uncle Pike. 'Betty, how do you say douche in Australian?'

'I think it starts with a C,' he said.

Mayor Jones stepped in and shooed Duncan away. 'Melanie Brown,' she said. 'A dark horse if ever there was one. You know, I'm going to hold you to every word you said up there.'

Melanie smiled.

'Very well done.' The mayor started to leave then turned back. 'By the way, your speech...' Uh-oh. I was ready for the mayor to tell her off for bagging the competition. 'You're not responsible for other people's happiness,' Mayor Jones said. 'Remember that.' She headed over to the other girls.

Mrs Brown snorted. 'What a load of horseshit.'

'Grandma!'

The crowd was dissolving back into the showgrounds. Claire burst out of the portaloos and stomped past the stage with her fists clenched.

I gasped. My skin prickled as I remembered where I'd seen that black lace before. I pulled off my backpack and scrabbled inside for the tablet.

'Tippy?' my uncle said. 'What's wrong?'

I pulled up the Facebook picture of Sally and Ms Everson from the night of the argument. The black rose lace matched.

'The dress,' I said, suddenly feeling cold. 'I think I know why it doesn't fit her...'

Claire caught me staring and stopped, glaring at me.

'Are you okay? You've gone pale,' Uncle Pike said.

I felt breathless and held on to his arm.

Claire gave me the rude finger. 'What are you looking at? Starer.' She barged past an old couple.

When I could speak again, my voice was shaky. 'I think Claire Bates is wearing Ms Everson's dress. From the night she was killed.'

CHAPTER TWENTY-SIX
Odeulc

'Hey, Bates, wait for us,' Uncle Pike yelled.

Claire kept moving through the crowd, heading towards the carpark.

'Shit,' I said. 'We can't lose her.' I glanced down at my uncle's crutches.

He nodded. 'Devon, run ahead with Tippy. I'll catch up.'

We took off down the stairs, Devon racing ahead. Claire looked back and frowned. She started to jog but her dress was so tight it was more like a fast walk.

'Why are we running?' Devon yelled over his shoulder.

'It's not her dress,' I managed to shout between breaths.

He stuck his arm in the air and gave a thumbs-up.

We caught up with Claire just past the grandstand, among the farm machinery. She spun around and put her hands on her hips. 'Stop following me, you freaks.'

'Just want to ask a question,' I said, puffing. A bright glare half blinded me as a man opened a tractor door behind her. I shielded my eyes and turned to face Claire side on. In the distance, Uncle Pike was hopping closer.

'Sorry you didn't win,' Devon said. He wasn't out of breath at all.

I put my hands on my head, dragging in lungsful of air.

'Well, actually that's not true,' he added. 'I didn't want you to win. But I'm sorry you didn't get runner-up. Or Miss Friendship, though that would have been a stretch.'

Claire screwed up her face. 'What?'

Devon leaned in and pointed to the sides of her dress. 'Speaking of stretch – see here, Tippy, how the seams are puckering, especially around the hips? That's called seam slippage. It happens because the fabric is so stretched. This wasn't made for her.'

Claire's face had turned a dangerous shade of red. 'Shut up,' she said. 'Of course it wasn't made for me. It's designer, stupid!'

I frowned. 'That doesn't really make any se—'

'We love vintage,' Uncle Pike panted, joining us.

Devon slapped him on the butt. 'I really do.'

'Whatever,' Claire said. 'Nobody cares.'

'Where'd you get your dress?' I asked her.

Her lip curled. 'Not everyone can afford their own celebrity stylist, you know.' She stabbed her finger at Uncle Pike. 'That's right, I know who you are.'

I tapped Devon on the arm. 'Couldn't there be lots of these dresses? Like, sold at different shops?'

He snorted until he saw me and Uncle Pike weren't laughing. 'Oh, you're being serious? No, this is handcrafted. Hours of work.' He went to touch the fabric.

Claire flinched. 'Don't touch me!'

Devon raised his hands. 'It's okay.' He turned to me. 'See? This is silk crepe de Chine. It requires a skilled machinist to sew it. And this' – he pointed to the fine black lace around Claire's neckline – 'this is handmade, definitely not mass-produced.'

She batted at his hands, like Bunny Whiskers with a piece of string, and backed up a couple of steps. 'You're all cheats. I'm going to report you and get my crown back.' She waved at a policeman in the crowd. 'Help! Over here!'

'Is that Barry?' my uncle said, squinting.

Claire Bates might have been a liar, but she wasn't acting like Ms Everson's monster.

'She doesn't know,' I said.

'Know what?' she snapped at me.

'This is *the* dress Jill Everson was murdered in,' I said.

'The murder dress?' Devon said.

Claire's head shot back and her mouth dropped open.

I quickly pulled the tablet from my backpack. I showed Devon the photo of Sally and Ms Everson.

'Good day for it,' Barry said, joining us.

Devon held up the tablet, and Uncle Pike peered over his shoulder. Claire was staring at them with wide eyes.

'Yep, that looks like it, all right,' Devon said. 'I would definitely say that's the same dress.' He pointed to a part of the lace. 'See, notice this here—'

Claire's screams must have been heard all over town. For a couple of seconds they drowned out all other noise at the show. She jumped up and down like she was covered in spiders, shaking her hands. 'Get it off me!' People all around stopped and stared.

Uncle Pike gave Barry a quick update, then the officer led the screaming Claire away.

'I don't think it's her,' I said, watching them leave.

'Perhaps we could've handled that slightly differently,' Uncle Pike said.

'Interviewing is definitely an area for feedback,' said Devon. Uncle Pike lifted a crutch and pointed towards the carpark. We shuffled along at his pace.

'It was kind of the doc to lend her that dress.' Devon frowned. 'Even though it *is* the murder dress...'

'What are you talking about?' me and my uncle said together.

'Poor thing. I bet Lisa will freak out too,' Devon said. 'Especially after wearing it to Jill's funeral. Trust me, Lisa wore it best.' He shook his head. 'This place really needs to get some more shops.'

I felt like I was off balance – Dr Lisa wearing Jill Everson's dress? I remembered her standing on the church stairs like a Greek goddess.

'How did Dr Lisa get that dress?' I asked Devon. I squeezed my thumbs in my fists to stop my hands from shaking. It couldn't be the same dress. It had to be a copy, no matter what Devon says.

He shrugged. 'I didn't ask her.'

'We need to find out,' Uncle Pike said. 'Now.'

We made our way through the showgrounds carpark. Dr Lisa's car wasn't there. They had already gone. I called her phone; it rang but then hung up. I frowned. Maybe she was driving? I called back but this time it went straight to voicemail. I rubbed my palm on my shorts. 'She's switched off her phone.'

I left Sam a message to call me and sent a text as well, just in case Dr Lisa had got him a backup phone after his dad had drowned his other one. I thought of what she'd said in the grandstand about leaving. 'She could be saying goodbye to Mum,' I said.

We piled into the car and drove the short two blocks to Mum's work. Main Street was semi-deserted; everyone was at the showgrounds. I leapt out of the car, not waiting for Devon and Uncle Pike. Inside the medical centre, the waiting area was empty. Becky was on reception again and I gave her a half-wave. She pointed to her headset and made a talking-hand sign.

'Is Dr Lisa here?' I whispered to her.

Becky shook her head. I waited while she finished the call. 'Man, that woman can talk. Hi, Tippy. Sorry, she's not here. You want to go see Mum? I think she's on her break.'

I nodded as Uncle Pike and Devon walked in.

'Your touch team. Hi again.' Becky waved in a circle, I led us through to the staffroom, but it was empty.

A large photo from the Santa Parade was pinned to the noticeboard: Becky, Mum, Dr Lisa and the rest of the medical centre team stood in a semicircle in their reindeer costumes. Nine of them, all, carrying their reindeer heads under their arms. A man with Rudolph's head lifted a wine bottle in a salute to the camera.

'Great pic,' Devon said.

My chest tingled. I ducked my head out the door; the coast was clear. 'Remember Suzie Pratt's picture?' I said.

They nodded.

'Hey,' Devon said, pointing to the reindeer. 'That's the demon.'

Uncle Pike studied the staff photo again. He stepped back on his moon boot and nearly fell. He slammed down on his crutches. 'Ow!' He stared at it again and shook his head. 'Fuck. No, no, no.'

'What? What is it?' Devon peered at the photo.

Mum strolled in, swinging a coffee mug. She jumped when she saw us. 'Shit, you gave me a fright.' She frowned. 'Tippy, what's happened? Are you okay?'

'I'm fine.' I gave her a hug.

'How did Melanie go?'

'She won!' I said.

'Of course,' Uncle Pike said.

'What? Really? That's fantastic.' Mum shook her head. 'And so surreal...'

'Is Dr Lisa here?' I asked.

'Why? Are you okay?' Mum went to put a hand on my forehead, which I dodged.

'I'm fine. Just wanted to ask a random question.' And check on Sam, I thought.

'This better not be any more Nancy Drew business.'

I kept my poker face. Did she know about Mr Campbell? She seemed relaxed, while my palms were sweaty. I needed Mum to focus. 'So, you haven't seen her?'

'Not today.' She put her coffee mug on the kitchen bench. 'What's the question? I might be able to help. Nurses do know things as well.'

'Why did she give Claire Bates her dress to wear for Show Queen?' I said.

'What?' she said. 'I thought you had a medical question.'

'It's a fashion thing,' Devon said.

Mum sighed. 'There's no way Lisa would lend her, or anyone,

one of her dresses. She's not a sharer. Besides, Claire is completely the wrong size. And anyway, she was sponsored by the medical centre. It was Lisa's idea. So Claire would've had the cash to buy her own dress. A complete waste of money if you ask me.' Mum picked up a jar of instant coffee and unscrewed it. 'Do you guys want a coffee?'

'Definitely not, and stop calling it coffee,' Uncle Pike said. 'Are you hiding my espresso machine on purpose?'

'Really have no idea what you're talking about,' she said.

'Mum, you know those origami lilies?' I avoided eye contact with Uncle Pike and Devon. I didn't want to tell her anything unless I was right this time.

'Nope.' She'd clearly lost interest as she spooned some coffee into a mug. 'There's tea as well, if you like?'

'The paper flowers? You know, the red one me and my class made?' I tried hard to keep my voice normal and not scream at her. 'Does Dr Lisa ever make them?'

'Ugh, all the time now. It must've been some mindfulness thing she picked up while I was away.' Mum filled her mug with boiling water. 'She even has her own stash of special white paper. It's so annoying, like those people who chew gum when they quit smoking.'

My mouth flooded with spit. The mailbox. She had left one on my bed. After the old hospital ... I hugged myself. She had been in our house.

Mum frowned. 'Why are you asking?'

I gulped and shrugged, trying not to look shit-scared. 'No reason. We have to head back.' I smiled, more like a grimace. 'Melanie's waiting for us.'

Devon shot me a surprised look, which I ignored.

Mum stared at me for a moment, making a 'hmmm' noise before she kissed me on the head. 'I've got to get back to it anyway. Stay out of trouble. I mean it. I'll be home later to celebrate with the neighbours.'

Uncle Pike patted her on the head. She threw a teaspoon at him with a growl, as he tried to escape on one crutch.

Back at reception I went up to Becky. 'Quick question before we go. It's kind of weird.'

She giggled and leaned forward. 'I love weird. What is it?'

'You know the reindeer costumes?' I said.

'Ummm...'

I tried to keep my voice calm. 'For the parade. You know, Rudolph?'

'Got you,' she said. 'Santa's helpers.' Becky giggled. 'That's not weird.'

I glanced at Uncle Pike; he looked worried.

'Sorry, but do you know if any of the costumes went missing?'

'Now *that's* weird.' She rubbed her temple. 'I don't think so. We would've known. They're all in the storeroom. We can check, if you like?'

We all nodded at once.

She got up and took us to the storeroom, which was locked. She tried several keys from a large bunch.

'Was Dr Lisa in at all today?' I asked.

'What's with all the Dr Lisa questions? Have you got a crush, Tippy?' Becky teased.

I crossed my arms. 'What? No.'

'She really does,' my uncle whispered.

'I do not.' I swatted his arm. My neck and cheeks started to heat up, and Ashley James's flushed face popped into my head.

Becky smiled. 'The doctor ran in and dropped off the dress for the show. Don't ask me why we sponsored Claire Bates.'

'I know, right?' Devon said.

'"The doctor"?' Uncle Pike said quietly. 'That's pretty formal.'

Becky unlocked and pushed open the door. 'That's the way she likes it with us plebs. Except for your mum, Tippy. And don't get me started on the doctor's boring dress-code rules...' The storeroom was small, more like a wardrobe with shelves. Inside she pulled out some green bags containing the reindeer costumes and sat on the floor. She started counting them. 'Dasher, Dancer, Prancer, Donner, Blitzen, Vixen, Cupid – and, don't tell me. Something. I can never remember.'

'Comet,' I said.

'That's it.'

Devon felt the fabric. 'Furry.'

Becky giggled. 'Aren't they amazing?' She rubbed one on her face, then asked me, 'Any reason you thought one was missing?'

Uncle Pike watched me.

I shrugged. One of the reindeer heads had a very shiny nose; she had counted Rudolph as one of the eight reindeer. 'There should be nine – eight Santa's helper reindeer plus Rudolph.' One costume was missing.

'Oh, right,' Becky said. 'I always forget to *add* Rudolph.' Something caught her eye, and she reached under the shelves and dragged out a black plastic bag. 'That's weird.'

'What is it?' I said.

She opened the bag and pulled out a shiny dark-green dress.

'Yuck,' Devon said, moving away from it.

It still had the shop tag. On it was a white sticker label with *C.B. Show Finale* written in black marker.

Becky's eyebrows squished together. 'This isn't the bag Dr Lisa brought in ... but this is Claire Bates's dress ... for today?'

'Ah,' Devon said. 'That makes so much more sense.'

'Bye, Becky.' I ran outside, with Devon and Uncle Pike following. There had to be an explanation for all this; we had got it wrong before. But my heart was sinking. Worst case: if we found out that Dr Lisa was the monster, it still didn't mean we had to tell the police. I had made Sam a promise.

'Do you think she might've gone home?' I said, out on the street. 'Sam could be there. We need to ask her about the dress.' I was babbling.

Devon fished around in his pockets then in his man bag for the car keys.

I told them about my meeting in the grandstand with Dr Lisa. The car beeped as it unlocked. 'If it is her, and I so hope it's not, we need to save Sam.'

We got into the car. My mind was racing. How could it be Dr Lisa? I loved her.

'Tippy?' Uncle Pike shook my leg. 'Tippy, listen: it might not be the doc.'

'But…?' I said.

Devon started the car. 'How about we try to prove it wasn't her?'

'Genius!' Uncle Pike leaned over and kissed him on the cheek. 'I love you.'

Devon switched off the car. 'What?'

My uncle shrank back in his seat. 'What?'

'What did you say?' Devon said.

'Genius?' Uncle Pike said.

Grown-ups were weird. Devon was right, though: if it wasn't Dr Lisa then that would mean Sam was safe.

'Like reverse *Cluedo*,' I said.

'Odeulc?' Devon said.

'Sure,' Uncle Pike said. 'But let's start with opportunity rather than means. A local doctor with access to a surgical saw may be a little hard to disprove right now.'

Devon ruffled my uncle's hair. 'Odeulc, you said you loved me.'

'My name isn't Odeulc,' my uncle said.

Devon turned around to me. 'You heard him, right?'

I nodded. 'Sure did.' I couldn't help but smile.

He whooped and started the car. We took off up Main Street towards the Campbells'.

'Don't worry.' Uncle Pike half turned in his seat to face me. 'We'll find Sam. One thing for sure is the doc's a great mum. She brought him in to say goodbye to you.' My uncle waggled his fingers at me. 'Now pass me your phone, please, Tippy. I'll get Lorraine to meet us there and bring the photos from the funeral … Also for backup.'

'We have to be right this time.' I leaned between the front seats and handed my phone over. 'Tell her to bring the security-cam footage as well. If Dr Lisa didn't take Mr Campbell's car, then that could also mean she didn't do it.' I kicked under my seat. Unless she'd hired, borrowed or stolen a black car.

As Uncle Pike spoke to Lorraine, I got out the tablet and pulled up the last photo of Devon's window, the one with all our clues written on it.

'She's on her way.' Uncle Pike passed my phone back. 'Right, opportunity: what time did the doc finish work on Saturday night?'

I clicked into *Cluedo* mode. 'Sunday morning at 2.07 a.m.'

'How did you remember that?' He wound down his window. 'So, she had the opportunity to do the unthinkable. How about Sunday?'

I thought of the security-cam footage for that Sunday morning. Mr Campbell was the only one who'd come into work. 'She wasn't working.'

Devon and Uncle Pike looked at each other. So far, reverse *Cluedo* was doing the opposite of proving Dr Lisa innocent.

'Devon, pull over for a minute,' my uncle said.

We stopped across from the turn-off to Old Hospital Road. Just over the street was the ditch where I had hidden that night.

'Okay,' he said. 'So far we have possible opportunity and means. Not a great start.'

Maybe I needed to start thinking of Dr Lisa as one of Nancy Drew's villains and not my best friend's mum. A fictional character was so much easier to deal with than reality.

'But did she have time to drive to the old hospital, pick up the body and the blood bags?' Uncle Pike said.

Devon was staring out his window. 'Maybe she already had the head in the...'

I reached over and rubbed his shoulder. 'On the way to the traffic lights she drops the scalp off at Sally's,' I said. 'Then stages the crime scene and is seen by Suzie at 10.40 a.m.'

'That seems like a busy morning,' Uncle Pike said. 'Did she have time?'

I remembered my trip timings; all of them had been pretty short. 'I think so.' I held up the Nancys scrapbook. 'I can double-check.'

Devon leaned over Uncle Pike and opened the glove box. 'But why dress as a reindeer?' He rummaged around with one hand.

'So no one would recognise her?' I said.

'And she did have the costume,' my uncle said. 'What are you looking for?'

'A pen,' Devon said. 'Or, even better, a pastel crayon.'

'No way.' Uncle Pike smacked his hand away. 'You're not drawing on the windscreen.'

'But I'm a visu—'

'No means no.' My uncle shut the glove box.

I dug my nails into the seat. 'What if we're wrong?'

'What if we're not?' Devon took off, spraying gravel behind us, and sped up the hill.

CHAPTER TWENTY-SEVEN
A Black Bag

Mr Campbell opened the door, naked except for a tea towel he held over his bits. His eyes were bloodshot, and he stank of whisky and old sweat. My heart thumped and I clenched my fists to stop my hands shaking.

'Tippy?' He seemed confused and annoyed. 'What are you doing here?'

My lips stuck to my teeth, and I tried licking them with my thick tongue. 'I wanted to say sorry.'

'Sorry?' He peered over my head. 'Does your mum know where you are?'

Behind him broken glass from the smashed family portrait still lay on the hallway floor.

I cleared my throat. 'Yes, we told her we were coming to see you.'

'We?' He opened the door wider. Devon and Uncle Pike waved. 'Hey, fellas. Not really a good time.' He tried to close the door.

Devon stuck out his foot, jamming it. 'Oh my God, you're not wearing any pants!'

'Easy now!' Mr Campbell said. 'Fine, just let me put some on.' He shut the door.

Pushing me out of the way, Devon and Uncle Pike cupped their hands and peered through the frosted glass.

'Why is he naked?' I asked.

'Sometimes grown-ups like doing that,' my uncle said, muffled against the door.

'Do you think he's coming back?' I said.

The door opened and Devon stumbled in, falling into Mr Campbell's arms. Wearing nothing but a pair of black tracksuit pants, he wrapped his arms around Devon and laughed, kind of giving him a weird long hug.

'Whoa, hold on there, Russell,' Uncle Pike said.

Mr Campbell stepped back and ran his hand through his hair. 'Drink?' He didn't wait for an answer, heading off to the living room.

'Coffee,' my uncle yelled after him, taking in the hallway mess. 'A lot of it.'

'Do you know where Sam is?' I called out.

Mr Campbell was banging around in the kitchen.

'Remember the plan,' I said to Devon. 'We keep him busy while you check the rooms again for Sam and Dr Lisa.'

Devon nodded, and Uncle Pike kissed him on the lips. 'Be careful.'

We avoided the broken glass in the hallway and entered the big room. It took me a second to realise the large white Christmas tree was gone. A trail of fake white pine needles, broken pearl strands and the odd red bauble led to one of the glass panel doors. Through the windows I saw the tree lying mangled and half propped against a pepper bush at the edge of the garden.

Mr Campbell stared at us, his glass full of whisky.

'Do you know where Sam and Dr Lisa are?' I said.

'You tell me.' Mr Campbell threw back his drink and screwed up his face. 'You know everything.'

'We think your son's in danger,' Uncle Pike said.

His head jerked back. 'What? Why? What have you done?' His knuckles had turned white around the glass.

My uncle put up his hands. 'Nothing. Nothing, Russell. Relax. We just need to know where he is. To make sure he's safe.'

'He's with that craz—' Mr Campbell shook his head. 'Trust me, no one fucks with my wife.'

'And where is she?' I asked.

He lurched towards me, and I hid behind Uncle Pike.

'Steady on there, Russell,' my uncle growled.

Mr Campbell stopped and took a deep breath. 'I told you, I don't know.'

'Nice toilet,' Devon said. 'Now for that drink, Russell?'

Mr Campbell huffed. 'Of course, buddy.' He padded back to the kitchen.

Devon glanced over at us and shook his head.

'How about the black dress she wore to the funeral?' I said. 'Do you know where that is?' I took a deep breath through my nose – we *had* to prove Dr Lisa didn't do it. If the dress was different, then Sam's mum wouldn't be a murderer. He would be safe.

'Tippy...' my uncle said.

Devon put his arm around me, moving between me and Mr Campbell.

'What did you say?' Mr Campbell said, handing Devon a glass of whisky.

'Thanks,' Devon said. 'You know, that beautiful black dress Lisa wore. I'd love to see it. As a design professional.'

Mr Campbell gestured to the garden, spilling his own drink.

Uncle Pike and Devon exchanged a glance. I walked to the large windows but couldn't see any clothes out in the garden or on the lawn.

'Russell, I think you need to put that down.' My uncle waved his own glass. 'There's something you need to hear.'

Uncle Pike placed his hand on Mr Campbell's shoulder, steadying him. In a gentle, but firm voice he told him everything Dr Lisa had said to me under the grandstand, about her leaving and taking Sam.

Mr Campbell stood there, gripping the kitchen bench and shaking his head. 'No. She wouldn't...'

'She has,' I said. 'This afternoon.'

'Do you know where they could've gone?' Uncle Pike asked. 'Russell, Sam's life could be in danger. Do you understand?'

'Fuck!' Mr Campbell threw his glass at the kitchen wall, smashing it and cracking a white tile. I jumped, and Devon gripped me tighter.

Mr Campbell put his hands on his head. 'She promised me Sam was off limits. He'd stay in town.' There was a banging at the front door, and Mr Campbell rubbed his face. 'The shit I know about her...' He shuffled off to answer it. 'Shouldn't surprise me. She sent round movers without even telling me.' He yelled down the hallway to us. 'Anyway, I grabbed some of her shit. When I told her that, she lost her mind – I thought she was going to kill me.' He laughed and opened the door.

Lorraine barged in. 'You stink.'

'What are you doing here?'

'Put a shirt on.' She stomped down the hallway, leaving him at the door and crunching over the broken glass. She joined us in the big room. 'Chan.' She tilted her chin at Devon. 'Nimrod.'

'What's with showing Tippy that video of her friend?' my uncle asked.

Lorraine ran her tongue over her teeth.

'I'm serious,' Uncle Pike said.

'Really?' She waved her laptop at him. 'What did I miss?'

Devon and I crowded around her as she opened her computer and flipped through the funeral photos. The first couple were crowd shots. Dr Lisa was in them, but too far away to make out any details. Next was a photo of her with Ms Everson's parents, closer this time but still too far away for us to make out the details. I bit my lip. The last picture had been taken from the previous photo, except it was a blown-up version of just Dr Lisa. The dress looked exactly the same as Jill Everson's and Claire Bates's.

Devon looked at us. 'It's the same.'

'That's what you wanted, right?' Lorraine said.

Uncle Pike frowned and pulled at his beard.

Mr Campbell appeared from behind Lorraine. 'Drink?' He held up a new bottle of whisky.

'Surprise me,' she said, watching him stumble around the kitchen.

'I haven't finished with you,' Uncle Pike said to her.

She snorted and sat on the couch. 'Actually, make mine a coffee. Black.'

'Hold on, Russell.' My uncle poured Mr Campbell a water. 'You need a chaser.'

I wiped my hands on my shorts and pulled out the tablet. I showed Lorraine the photo of Jill Everson in the black dress. Her eyebrows squished together. She glanced up at us, then at Mr Campbell sculling water in the kitchen.

Uncle Pike refilled his water and asked him, 'Can you show us Lisa's dress now?'

'What?' Mr Campbell poured a whisky and handed it to Lorraine. She frowned at my uncle and put it on the floor.

'Sam,' I said. 'Dr Lisa is taking him away, remember?' I needed to know for sure if Sam was safe, or if we had left him in more danger.

'Just show us, Campbell,' Lorraine said. 'Then we can all relax and have a proper drink.'

'Now you're talking.' He headed over to the window wall and tugged on a handle, sliding open a large glass panel. He stepped out into the garden.

'The dress is out here?' Uncle Pike followed him, squinting in the sun. We joined them on the lawn.

Mr Campbell blinked and squeezed his eyes shut. 'I need my sunglasses.'

Lorraine groaned. 'Great, a sober drunk. Think we can move this along?'

'Here,' Devon said, pulling out his orange sunnies. 'Take mine.'

Mr Campbell smirked as he put them on.

'Lisa's dress?' Uncle Pike said.

'Right...' Mr Campbell stumbled over the Christmas tree then disappeared into the bush at the back of the garden.

Lorraine stomped on the tree; its branches bent then sprung back. 'Wish I could do that to mine.' After a couple of minutes, she snapped. 'What the hell? Is he taking a piss?'

'Maybe he's trying to run away?' Devon said. 'I love you too, by the way,' he said to Uncle Pike, and grabbed his hand. 'Just in case you didn't realise.' He kissed my uncle, who kissed him back.

'Yay!' I clapped, a warm glow in my tummy.

'What is *wrong* with you people?' Lorraine glared at me. 'And this better not be another Chan goose chase. What do you have against the Campbells anyway?'

I rubbed my forehead with my rude finger. I knew it was wrong, but she deserved it.

There was a crash and the sound of branches breaking. Mr Campbell came out dragging a large black plastic rubbish bag. 'She'll be back, and when she does she'll want her stuff.'

We all looked at each other. My eyes felt like they'd pop out of my head.

He untied the knot and pushed the bag towards us. 'I know Lisa.'

Devon helped me tip the contents onto the lawn. As I spread the colourful clothes out with my foot, the good news was there was no kissing-dolphins necklace. I turned the clothes over, hoping to find the black dress she wore to the funeral. Searching for evidence that Dr Lisa had not been in possession of Ms Everson's dress from that night. That Sam's mum had not worn a murder victim's clothes. But as I searched I knew there was no other black dress. Devon was telling the truth: it was a one-off. And Dr Lisa had given Ms Everson's murder dress to Claire Bates to wear in front of the whole town. I kicked a floral dress and gasped. That sealed it. My chest tightened as I stared down at the brown fur of a reindeer suit.

Uncle Pike came over and put his arm around me.

I finger-combed my hair. What if I was wrong? Mum would kill me. It couldn't be Dr Lisa. And if it was? Either way I didn't want to lose Sam; he'd hate me forever.

'That's the disguise Suzie Pratt saw,' I said, my voice cracking. 'She meant "sleigh", as in Santa.'

My uncle nodded and Devon's mouth dropped, his face turning pale.

There was a strange silence, like time had slowed right down. I thought about poor Suzie – what if Dr Lisa had seen her? I clenched my fists. If anything happened to Sam it would be my fault. There was only one choice: Dr Lisa had to be stopped. Even if it meant Sam would never talk to me again. I couldn't risk his life.

'Call the police,' I said to Lorraine.

Mr Campbell lurched towards me. 'What you listening to that kid for?'

Uncle Pike stepped in front of me. 'Because she's a Nancy,' he said. 'And because she's right.'

'You're not arresting me again.' Mr Campbell ran inside but missed the opening, hitting the glass wall and knocking himself to the ground.

'Shit!' my uncle said.

Devon raced over and helped Mr Campbell up, then took him back inside and stuck him on the couch. 'He's pretty out of it.' Devon grabbed a tea towel and wet it in the sink.

Lorraine lifted up her laptop. 'You still want this, Chan?'

I nodded. 'The medical-centre footage you showed me. Sunday morning.'

She set it up on the kitchen bench. 'What are we looking for?'

'Not sure yet,' I said, tapping the mouse pad. 'He doesn't leave by the front door until 11.37 a.m. but keep an eye on the car.'

Uncle Pike and Lorraine watched as I fast-forwarded to 9.45 a.m. when Mr Campbell's black car pulled into the carpark outside the medical centre. When I pressed play, he entered carrying a gym bag. I hit fast-forward again. Part of me prayed the car wouldn't move.

Mr Campbell groaned as Devon put the damp tea towel on his forehead.

I gasped. In the corner of the screen at 10.07 a.m. Mr Campbell's black car drove away. My eyes prickled. Maybe it would come back in a couple of minutes – Dr Lisa was just using it for the shopping or something. But at 11.21 a.m. the car pulled into the same carpark.

11.37 a.m. Mr Campbell left work through the front entrance to the carpark. It was not him, but it was someone who had keys to his car.

I replayed it a couple of times, trying to get a glimpse of the driver, anyone getting in or out of the car, but the camera angle was all wrong.

Lorraine hit pause, and Uncle Pike put his hand on my shoulder. I kept staring at the screen in silence. My shoulders slumped. Dr Lisa had done it. She had used her husband's car to dispose of the body. There was no reverse *Cluedo*. She had killed Jill Everson.

Devon broke the silence. 'I think we need to call a doctor too.'

A nasty egg-sized red lump had grown on Mr Campbell's forehead.

'Call my wife.' He chuckled.

Uncle Pike stiffened. 'The house call ... that's when she planted the evidence at Sally's. Shit, I called her about the murder weapon.'

My blood went cold. She'd known all that time we were investigating? I thought about how friendly she'd been at her house the next day – the day she was wearing the dress.

Lorraine dialled the police. 'Your wife killed Jill Everson,' she said to Mr Campbell. 'Do you understand?'

'No, no.' Mr Campbell waved his hand and dropped it on his thigh. 'She'll be back.'

'How long have you been drinking?' my uncle said. 'Days?'

Lorraine wandered into the garden, talking to the police. Mr Campbell winced as he reached down to pick up her whisky.

Uncle Pike snatched it off him. 'You've had enough. I'm getting you more water.'

Lorraine came back inside. 'They're on their way.'

Devon returned with an icepack and tried to get Mr Campbell to hold it against his head. 'When did she move out?'

'After the service. She took Sam. I had no idea.' He pushed Devon's hand away. 'Sam and I were buzzing. Best day ... and there she was...'

Devon laid the icepack on Mr Campbell's lap, but he didn't seem to notice. 'All because that little pervert took those photos and sent them to my son.'

'Of you screwing someone else, in your wife's bed, in her sheets,' Lorraine said. 'And don't forget the video.'

Mr Campbell ignored her. 'When she saw those...' He touched his head-bump and groaned. 'She blamed me. Made me go to the bridge to wipe that little shit's phone.'

Had Dr Lisa set up Todd, hoping he'd fall? How long had she pretended to be Sam? I thought about the old hospital and wondered what would've happened if I'd texted Sam back that night in the ditch and told him where I was. Or if she'd caught me.

Mr Campbell tried to find a comfortable spot on the sofa and leaned back, sliding down. Lorraine stood over him, her notepad out. 'You knew she did it, didn't you? That's why you hid the clothes – insurance so she wouldn't kill you too.'

Mr Campbell rubbed the back of his neck and shook his head viciously. 'I wish I'd never bought Jill that fucking dress.' He sounded sorry for himself. Judging by Lorraine's expression, I thought she might kick him.

'You must've known,' I said, 'when Dr Lisa wore Ms Everson's dress to the funeral.'

'Oh God.' He ignored me, staring straight ahead. 'I told Jill to do her hair the same way...' He started crying. 'Sam. Help me find Sam.'

CHAPTER TWENTY-EIGHT
To The Nancys!

Sally Homer's place was still a dump. Papers and clothes covered her floor, but missing were the dirty plates and cups, food scraps and empty bottles. She had been released yesterday, after they arrested Mr Campbell at his house for accessory to murder.

Sally looked really healthy, like gaol had been good for her. She and Uncle Pike sat around her little round table like last time, while I perched on her stinky sofa – except this time I didn't have to fight for space with used tissues, green undies or damp towels. Devon had run off to the shops to find champagne, after realising on Sally's steps they needed some bubbles to celebrate.

The police still hadn't found Dr Lisa or Sam. And I'd heard nothing from them since yesterday at the show. It all seemed unreal, and at the same time it didn't feel like we had finished our investigation. I kept checking my phone, hoping Sam was okay. I just wanted to hear his voice.

Uncle Pike chatted to Sally about prison and her lawyers. She thanked him again, and he glanced over at me flipping my phone open and shut.

'He'll be okay, Tippy. I promise,' he said. 'She won't hurt him.'

I squeezed my phone hard and nodded. He was right; he had to be.

Sally got up to fetch some glasses. 'Tippy, did you know your uncle, Mike Horn-blower and I always talked about leaving town together, the three of us running off to Sydney?'

The change in subject was okay with me, plus I always wanted to hear more about when Uncle Pike and Mum were young. 'And?' I asked.

'We've bored Tippy enough with our ancient history,' my uncle said.

Sally handed me a glass that looked like a fingerprint exhibit. 'Your uncle did run off.' Three cloudy wineglasses chimed as she put them in the middle of the table. 'He just forgot to tell his best friend, or his boyfriend.' She sat down opposite my uncle.

'It was a long time ago, Sally, and he wasn't my boyfriend.'

I remembered what Mrs Brown had said about Horn-blower's broken heart.

Uncle Pike concentrated on scratching a spot on the table. He sighed. 'I didn't ... I couldn't tell him I was going. And if I'd told you then I'd have had to tell him.'

'He was in love with you, Pike,' Sally said. 'You knew that.'

My uncle was silent for a long time. 'I guess it was pretty shitty.'

'I didn't even have your phone number. I wasn't going to ask your sister for it. At least not in those days – she was scary. Sorry, Tippy, but she was.'

I still couldn't picture Mum as a teenager; Melanie kept popping into my head.

Uncle Pike stared at his wineglass, twisting it around with his finger and thumb.

Sally continued, 'This was before social media, Tippy.'

I nodded. It was probably before computers.

'Anyway,' Sally said, 'a couple of years later, at uni, I got to know Helen and she'd tell me what you were up to.' She gave a small smile. 'It was actually meeting Jill that helped me start to understand what it must've been like for you back then.'

My uncle sighed. 'Shit, Sally. I'm so sorry.'

The door opened and Devon came in holding up a bottle.

'Champagne!' His smile dropped when he saw the mess. 'What did I miss?'

'Everything,' Sally said.

'Nothing,' my uncle said. 'Champagne!'

'And bubbles for Tippy too.' Devon waded across the room and handed me a small bottle of orange fizzy. He kissed my uncle on the head and sat down, giving Sally the bottle. 'Congratulations,' he said. 'Is that the right word?'

'It will do.' She thanked him and passed it over to my uncle to open.

I sat back on the sofa.

Uncle Pike popped the cork and it sailed across the room, hitting the green curtains and landing in a pile of scrunched-up newspaper.

Devon grimaced. 'What did you rub on the walls to get it this colour? Didn't the Pratts have this? It must've been on trend around here.'

'Seriously?' Sally said. 'I've been locked up and that's what you want to ask me?'

'It's a start, Sally,' my uncle said. 'And a pretty valid question.' He poured the bubbles into the dirty wineglasses. I stuffed my glass under a cushion on the other side of the sofa and put my bottle down. I didn't think I'd ever be able to drink orange fizzy again without thinking about the crime scene, and there was no way I could celebrate until I knew Sam was safe.

'A toast,' my uncle said. 'Come on, Tippy.'

I sprang up and stood near them.

'To freedom,' he said.

Sally raised her glass. 'Amen to that.'

I clinked my bottle with their glasses and turned to sit back down.

'Hold on, Tippy,' Sally said. 'One more toast.'

Uncle Pike refilled their glasses.

She stood up and raised hers. 'To The Nancys!' I must've looked shocked, as she laughed. 'Don't worry, your uncle told me all about it on the phone.'

We clinked again and they drank.

'Thank you for bringing me home,' Sally said.

Devon spluttered. 'We're not responsible for this mess. Is your home on drugs?'

'Speaking of pills,' Uncle Pike said to Sally. He put his hands under his chin like he was praying.

'No way. I chucked them out,' she said. 'Anything with that fucking woman's name on it is probably poison.'

'Still ... it was good poison.' My uncle drained his glass and poured another round.

'No more for me,' Devon said. 'We've got a long drive to the airport.'

I wasn't ready for them to go. I pretended it wasn't happening and played with my phone.

'You know,' Sally said, 'she always thought she was the smartest person in the room.'

'Maybe she was,' I said, thinking that if the only people in the room were Dr Lisa and Sally that would definitely be true. 'No one at the funeral noticed Dr Lisa was wearing Ms Everson's dress – the one she was murdered in.'

Sally's lip trembled.

'And,' I continued, 'she got Claire Bates to wear it on stage in front of the whole town, and no one noticed then either.'

Sally stared at me like she might cry. I pulled on a loose thread on the couch. *Shit.*

'Her last "fuck you" to the town,' Uncle Pike said. 'But not so smart. She bet on the wrong horse. She must've thought Bates would win and be front page in that dress.'

Sally gave a weird laugh and cleared her throat. 'And she didn't bet on The Nancys. Thank God you guys did notice.'

Suddenly there was a loud bang on the lounge window. I jumped in my seat.

Sally whimpered. 'Is she here?'

Devon rushed over and pulled back the curtain. I saw him relax. 'I thought birds only flew into clean windows.'

I sniggered.

She let out a huge breath and shook her head.

With a grimace, Devon wiped the hand that had touched the curtain on his pants as he returned to his seat.

Sally topped up her glass, then Uncle Pike's. 'I just wished I had something of hers. Of our time together.' She glanced at the dolphin poster. 'Did they find our necklace?'

We all shook our heads. White frothy bubbles shrank back down in her glass. 'But what I don't get is, why did she pick me?' she asked.

'Really?' It slipped out before I could stop it.

Uncle Pike glanced over at me and frowned.

'I'm with Tippy,' Devon said, leaning back. 'You were perfect – she saw you threaten to kill Jill in public. Plus your girlfriend was sleeping with her husband.'

Sally's head jerked back. 'What?'

'Shit, you didn't know?' Uncle Pike said. He turned to Devon, who gave them both a clenched-teeth smile.

'Russell Campbell?' Sally said, her voice getting louder. 'That was her boyfriend? Russell fucking Campbell?'

'At least she wasn't pregnant,' I said.

Sally's mouth dropped open, and she glanced around like she didn't know which one of us to look at.

'Also, after what you and Ms Everson did to Sam?' I said. 'I don't think Dr Lisa ever forgave you for that.' I thought I'd forgiven Sally but it all came back, along with my anger at how unfair it was. Maybe none of this would've happened and Sam would still be here. Part of me knew that didn't make any sense, but I couldn't help thinking it.

Sally placed her hands on the table and took a deep breath. She shook her head. 'Sam? Sam who?'

I rolled my eyes. Worst. Teacher. Ever.

Uncle Pike gave me a warning headshake. 'Sam Campbell,' he said to Sally. 'Lisa's son.'

She looked confused.

'Tippy?' my uncle said.

I concentrated on a worn spot in the sofa near my knee and picked at it, avoiding Sally's gaze. 'You accused Sam of stealing money out of your bag.'

'Oh my God, I totally forgot about that. Beginning of the year, right?' Sally refilled her glass.

I glanced up. She had forgotten about it? They were all watching me. Uncle Pike gave me a nod, and I said, 'Ms Everson told us about it in class. She called Sam a thief and a liar and said he couldn't be trusted.' I remembered him pale and shaking, promising it wasn't him.

I had picked a big hole in the sofa. Yellow pieces of foam lay beside me. I brushed them into a cushion crease to hide them from Sally.

A chair scraped back on the floor. 'That blew up, didn't it?' Sally said. 'I thought Jill and Lisa were going to have a punch-up.'

'He was new, and for ages didn't have any friends. Ms Everson would keep bringing it up.' I ripped a foam piece in two. 'Dr Lisa talked to me about it at Mum's work. About you and Ms Everson. She was so angry. It's the only time I've seen her lose it, and it was scary.' Funny thing was, after Dr Lisa had calmed down, she'd given me her number and asked me to be Sam's friend, and that's when we'd started hanging out, and then with Todd. Shortly after that, Dad had died.

Devon stared at my uncle. 'Imagine when she found out about the affair.'

Uncle Pike gave a nod and sculled back his drink.

I leaned my shoulder against the sofa and brushed the foam-crumbs with my hand. Suddenly I felt very tired. It was such a big deal for Sam, and Sally had forgotten it.

She finished her drink. 'Jill could've handled that better.'

'Understatement of the year,' my uncle said.

'She did have a good side. I wish you could've met her – she was fun. It's why I loved her.'

'After that, Mr Campbell always picked Sam up,' I said.

'I guess that's when Russell got to know Jill,' Uncle Pike said.

Sally rubbed at her temples. 'Shit. If I'd known...' The room was still except for the low hum and ticking of the fridge.

Uncle Pike leaned over and rubbed her back. Sally looked up at him with a sad smile. I believed her but it was all too late, and it sucked.

CHAPTER TWENTY-NINE
Red Tail-Lights

Later that afternoon I stood in our driveway, using my hand as a makeshift sun visor. 'Can't you stay for Christmas?' I asked Uncle Pike again. 'Please? It's only nine more days.'

'Sorry, honey. You know we would if we could. Clients are relying on us and we can't let them down.' He was heading to the car. 'We'll call you as soon as we're in Sydney. I promise.'

'We love you, Tippy Chan,' Devon said.

My uncle came over and we group-hugged, then they held my hands again, like they had in the airport and at the funeral. That all seemed like months ago now.

'Ms Drew ... hell, Carson Drew, would be so proud of you, Tippy,' my uncle said.

'Proud of us,' I said.

Devon winked at me. 'We just provided the accessories.'

'Hardly,' I said. 'We did it together. Thanks for all the no-school time. But I'm still waiting on that gun.'

'That's right,' Devon said.

'Gun? What gun?' My uncle frowned. 'I must've missed that one. Maybe next holidays?'

I handed Devon the tablet. 'We need a pic of The Nancys.'

'Of course!' He held it up to take a selfie, and we leaned in together, me in the middle.

'Beautiful,' my uncle said.

Mum came out carrying some snacks for their trip and stopped in her tracks. 'Pike, are you crying?'

He swiped at his eyes. 'Of course not, you whore.'

'Pike! Not in front of Tippy!'

He gave me a big smile. 'We'll see you very soon, Tippy.' He turned to Mum. 'She's one amazing person.'

Devon blew me a kiss.

'But wait, there's more.' Uncle Pike opened the car door. 'I have a present for you, Lennie.' He leaned into the back seat and pulled out some white towels. 'I thought these might come in handy.'

'Did you steal them from the monkey motel?' I said. 'You can't do that.'

Mum ignored me. 'Thanks, I do need some new cleaning rags.'

'And they need some new towels,' my uncle said, handing them over. 'These are a disgrace – what do visitors think?'

'So you're doing this for the town?' she said.

'Indeed I am.'

'Well, well, Pike.' She gave him a shove. 'You really are a local.'

'Let's not get carried away. It's still a shithole.'

'But it's *your* shithole.'

'Eew, Mum!' I couldn't believe she was okay with stolen goods.

They laughed, then Mrs Brown materialised out of nowhere, wearing what looked like a tan, suede, tasselled cowgirl top. She handed Devon a Glory Box shopping bag.

He opened it and squealed. 'Oh, you are too much.' He gave her a big hug.

'What is it?' Uncle Pike asked.

'Fabric paint and plain T-shirts. Only the best present ever.' Devon waved the tears from his eyes like he'd shown Melanie to do. 'Please tell your granddaughter to keep using the moisturiser and lip balm.'

Mrs Brown nodded and blew her nose on her handkerchief.

'Tell her yourself.' Melanie popped up behind Devon and punched him on the arm.

'Ow! Keep using the moisturiser and lip balm.'

'Duh, of course.' She came over and stood beside me.

'Like the bell says, Anal-Lease,' my uncle said, '"accept your faults".'

Melanie grabbed her throat and made a gurgling, choking noise.

'Are you choking on your own vomit?' he asked. 'I'm impressed.'

'Thanks, Betty, you can use that for free.'

Devon held Mrs Brown's hand and swung it. 'I love your top. It's so witty.'

'I love yours,' she said, admiring Uncle Pike.

'Stop!' Devon shook his head and mouthed, 'Don't stop.'

Uncle Pike snorted. 'That's disturbing.'

'Right?' Melanie said. 'Who knew Grandma was such a fag hag?'

'Where's the big fella?' Devon said.

'In the toilet,' Mrs Brown said. 'He'll be in there for hours.'

'Sounds like someone we know back in Sydney.' My uncle smiled, and Mum elbowed him in the ribs.

Mrs Brown sighed. 'It's all right. He won't die. Literally, he will not die.' And then she put on a bright smile.

'And you call *me* creepy,' Uncle Pike said to Melanie.

Bunny Whiskers walked over and sniffed the car's back tyre, her tail twitching. Devon chased after the cat, who trotted ahead, then stopped to give herself a lick and trotted away again. 'I couldn't leave without saying goodbye to you, my muse.'

'Come on, honey, we've got to go,' Uncle Pike yelled.

And then they were gone.

Mrs Brown and Melanie walked off, and Mum headed inside. The sun went behind a cloud, and suddenly everything was quiet and still, like I was in an enormous vacuum.

A white ute drove up and a man hopped out. 'Delivery for Helen Chan,' he said. When I nodded, he lifted a brown cardboard box from the back. I pointed to the garage, out of the sun. He put it on the floor and left. On the box's label was *Espresso Coffee Machine and Refills*. I smiled – so that was espresso.

I started to amble back inside when my phone vibrated. Dr Lisa was calling.

My heart was pounding. I flipped it open, took a deep breath and pushed accept.

'Tippy...'

'Sam? Are you okay? Where are you?'

'They've arrested Mum. We'd just gone in to see Todd. The police.'

Todd. My scalp prickled. The white origami flower beside his bed.

'I was getting her a coffee,' Sam said.

Bile rose in my throat. *Shit, shit, shit.*

Sam continued. 'She was in his room fixing his machine, and—'

'Sam?' I swallowed hard, trying not to vomit. I didn't know how else to say it. 'Is Todd okay?'

'What? Todd's fine.' Sam sniffed. 'Are you fucking deaf? I just told you my mum's been arrested and you're asking about *him*?'

I sagged with relief. Todd was alive. Sam was alive.

Sam started sobbing, and my throat tightened. He sounded so hurt. I didn't know what to say. 'Sam, I'm so sorry.' I dragged the side of my sandal along a crack in the garage floor.

He sniffed. 'No, you're not.'

'What? Of course I am. Where are you? I can get Mum—'

'You dobbed in my parents. Twice. My family's munted because of you.'

'I'm sorry, I—'

'How could you? Mum loved you. You're supposed to be my best mate, but you chose your Nanny Drew bullshit over me.'

'I *am* your best mate.'

Sam gave a bitter laugh. 'Hate to be your enemy.'

'Sam, I'm sorry!'

'Stop fucking saying you're sorry, you liar!'

I jerked the phone away from my ear. As I put it close again, his hard breathing sounded distorted, like storm gusts.

'Sad thing is,' he said, 'you're so shit at it. It's a joke you don't even know the truth about your dad.'

I gasped.

'You're dead to me.' He hung up.

My heart raced. I called back and paced up and down the concrete crack, rubbing the back of my neck. It rang out, no voicemail. My hand shook as I called again. I lost track of how many times. With each call I pressed the phone harder against my ear. I needed Sam to answer, but he never did.

I knew the truth; I'd just never talked to Sam about it. Or, actually, anyone about it. The last time I saw Dad had been right here, in the garage.

Mum had been working night shift, and Dad had been out with his mates. As usual I pretended to be asleep when he snuck into my room and over to Piggy-Cat. He took it with him; sometimes he did that when he was putting in coins so as not to wake me. It was getting so heavy – I only needed another forty-seven dollars for my smartphone. I lay there thinking of all the apps I'd download. A couple of minutes passed before he snuck in and put Piggy-Cat back.

As soon as he shut my door, I threw off my duvet and switched on the light. I rushed over to Piggy-Cat, using two hands to lift it, but it didn't feel right. I shook it but there was no noise. Sitting on my bed I opened its bottom. It was empty. I relaxed and felt a big grin as I realised Dad must be going to buy the phone for me. I had to go and thank him, but more importantly make sure he knew exactly which one I wanted.

I peeked out of my door; all the lights were off. I smiled. Mum wasn't cool about the whole smartphone thing and I didn't want to wake her if she was back. I crept down the hallway and opened the garage door. Out on the street, Dad's car started up. The concrete floor was cold on my bare feet.

I cringed now, remembering how I had stood there, grinning and waving. 'Hey,' I called out, holding my broken, empty Piggy-Cat.

Dad wound down his passenger window. He stared at me; the bags under his eyes had got worse.

With my other hand I made a phone sign. 'Thank you,' I said into it.

His eyes widened and his mouth fell open. The car revved. In that instant I knew he wasn't going to spend my money on a smartphone. His head dropped and he said something – I think it might have been 'sorry'.

Dad never looked at me again. He gunned the engine and peeled off as I ran out onto the street.

'Dad?' I screamed at his red tail-lights. I hurled the cat after him. It shattered on the road. But he was gone. Maybe if I hadn't got up, if I hadn't upset him, then he'd have been more careful, and he wouldn't have crashed. He would still be alive.

I should've just told him he could have the money.

'Chan?' Melanie was standing in the brightness outside. I had no idea how long she'd been watching me.

Suddenly I couldn't do this anymore. Pretend everything was okay. I sat down hard on the cold floor and hid my face in my arms. Uncle Pike's sad chimp at the zoo popped into my head, and I buried myself, pulling my arms in tighter. I hoped that monkey had never felt like this.

'Hey, hey.' Melanie's gumboots came into view. 'What is it?'

My lungs felt heavy. 'It's all my fault.'

'What?' She tapped on my head. 'What's your fault?'

I lifted my head slightly. She crouched down, resting her elbows on her thighs.

'Everything,' I said.

'Bullshit.' She waved a small rectangular present in my face. I wondered if it was a book. 'Come on, take it. My Merry Fuck-mess present for you. I'm off to the farm.'

I took it. 'Thanks,' I said, my voice tiny.

'Open it.' She sat beside me as I unwrapped it. 'You're not alone, Chan. Literally.'

I pulled out a silver photo frame. Inside was a photo of me, Dad and Mum on the balcony. We were laughing at something. It looked like it was taken from the Browns' dining room – using a long lens, like the paparazzi.

'Grandma's such a creeper,' Melanie said, nudging me.

I giggled and wiped my nose. I hadn't seen his beautiful face for so long. I'd forgotten how he put his head back when he laughed. 'Thank you.'

'Anytime.' She leaned back on her hands. 'I was so jealous of you and your dad. Still am.'

'Really? Why?'

She pointed to the photo. 'I've never had that. You guys may as well have been twins – always hanging out, having fun. I'm lucky to see Dad for an hour and even then he's on the phone or doing farm shit.'

My heart broke all over again. 'I think I killed him.'

Melanie sat beside me quietly as I told her my story.

When I finished, I couldn't look at her. 'So maybe if I hadn't—'

'Nothing you did caused this. If anything, we should've stopped Grandad encouraging him with his fucking racing tips. I'm truly sorry for that.'

I rubbed my feet back and forth in my sandals.

'Your dad was a gambling addict,' Melanie said. 'He had an illness. Do you get that?'

My chest tightened and I wrapped my arms around my knees.

'Look at me, Chan.'

I turned. Her eyes narrowed. 'Don't you let that define him. Don't you fucking dare.' She pointed to Dad in the picture. '*This* is your dad. This man right here. Got it?'

I gulped and nodded. She was still scary.

'Good. You know, there are secrets everywhere but it's only the really brave who reveal the truth. That's you, Tippy Chan. Thank you for telling me.' Melanie got to her feet. 'Now stand up.'

I stood as she brushed the back of her jeans.

'I'll deny this ever happened.' Melanie Brown gave me a hug.

CHAPTER THIRTY
Christmas

At least setting the table for Christmas lunch was easy this year. It was just me and Mum. We'd had a quiet morning, opening our presents. She gave me my very own tablet, and a new Santa hat to replace the 'lost' one. And from Santa (aka Mum), I got lots of sugar and a book voucher. I gave her a book voucher as well, and a picture frame I'd made at school. Inside I had put the selfie Devon had taken of The Nancys.

Twice that morning I'd tried calling Uncle Pike and Devon in Sydney, and each time it went to voicemail. It had only been a week and a half since they'd left, but it felt like a year.

Lorraine had kept me up to date on Dr Lisa. Mr Campbell hadn't dobbed on her yet, but the evidence was piling up against her. She'd been wearing the kissing-dolphins necklace when she was arrested at Dunedin Hospital. Forensics had confirmed traces of Ms Everson's blood and DNA in the boot of Mr Campbell's car, as well as on the reindeer suit we'd found in their garden. The Case of the Missing Necklace was finally closed. I hoped Sally would get the necklace back – bring it home to be with all her other dolphins. To have something to remind her of someone she loved. I understood that all right.

I still hadn't heard back from Sam. Mum reckoned he was with his grandparents in the North Island. I missed him almost as much as Dad. Sometimes, like today, I wished I'd just left it alone.

I wondered what kind of Christmas Todd's parents were having at the hospital. Mum told me I had to be prepared that Todd might not be the same boy when he woke up. I refused to believe her. He was tough – if anyone would fight their way back, it would be him.

'Last but not least.' Mum handed me a bundled mess of tape and inside-out Christmas paper. It reminded me of Dad's terrible wrapping skills.

Inside was a blue, plastic snail Sellotape dispenser. My vision blurred and my chest tightened.

Mum rested her head against mine. 'Let's face it. Your father wasn't the most creative gift giver, but he was consistent.'

I snuggled into her, letting my tears fall as I stroked the blue plastic snail.

She put her arm around me and gave me a squeeze. 'He'd be so proud of you, Tippy. So very, very proud.' She kissed me on the cheek, my wet face hot. 'You're a lot like him, you know? Brave, kind, and shit at choosing presents.'

I pulled back. 'What?'

'Oh my God, kid, I'm just joking. I love your presents. You clearly get that gift from me. Gift – get it?'

I nudged her. 'Not funny.'

'Speaking of not funny, guess who came to see me at work yesterday?'

For some weird reason, Ms Everson flashed into my mind. I wondered how her family were doing today.

Mum continued. 'Lorraine Ashton. Did you do that?'

I tried not to look surprised. I didn't know what Mum was talking about.

'She said sorry. For all that crap she put me and your dad through.'

I raised my eyebrows. Lorraine had kept that quiet.

'I asked myself whether Joe would've accepted her apology, and I realised that I should. We're not at brushing-each-other's-hair stage, but it does feel good to have one less fuckwit in the world.'

'That's great, Mum.' I gave her a kiss.

'It might take me a while to stop calling her Cunt-Hooks every time I see her in the paper, though. Just saying.'

I shrugged. 'It's probably a common nickname for Lorraine anyway.' I took a deep breath; I needed to try one more time. 'Mum, I have one more present.'

She sat back and slapped her thighs. 'Well, all right then.'

'Wait there.' I hoped she wouldn't crack it. I ran to my room and reached under my bed. When I came back into the living room, I held it behind my back. 'Close your eyes.'

She frowned. 'Okay, but I hate surprises.' She closed them.

I rolled my eyes.

'I saw that,' she said.

I handed her my present. I didn't know what I'd do if she didn't like it. 'You can open them.'

She sat there with Melanie's framed photo of our family on her lap. She froze. Her face went pale, but I couldn't tell what she was thinking. Slowly she picked it up.

Fuck. 'I just thought...' I said.

'Sorry,' Mum said. She reached out her hand to me. I held it and sat beside her. 'I am so, so sorry,' she said. 'I didn't mean to...'

She put the picture up on the side table, beside the Nancys photo frame, and then it was my turn to hold her. She made my ear and neck wet with her tears, but I didn't care. I held her, staring at the picture of us all happy and laughing on the deck.

Eventually she pulled back and wiped her eyes. 'Told you I hated surprises,' she said and laughed.

I thought of Sam's last words about Dad and dug my fingernails into my palm. 'What really happened to Dad?' My voice was a croaky whisper.

Mum sniffed and put her arm around me. 'Why are you asking?'

I shrugged but couldn't look at her.

She sighed. 'Truth is, we don't know. None of us were there that morning.' She shifted on the couch to face me, lifting up my chin. 'But no matter what, I need you to remember him as you always have, as your dad.' She searched my face. 'Promise me.'

I bit my tongue and nodded. That's what Melanie had said as well. Months of grieving had hollowed me out. Sometimes I couldn't feel anything inside, not even a heartbeat.

I gave Mum the best smile I could and pulled down on the sleeves of my grey tracksuit. 'I'm sorry about your best friend.'

She sat back. 'Hey, you did the right thing, all of you. What Lisa did was terrible.' She wrapped me up in her arms and rocked me, like she had when I was little. 'I'm proud of you.'

After tidying up I video-called NaiNai in China. She asked in a loud voice if Mum was feeding me, and I showed her all the food. I spoke to NaiNai for ages; I knew she understood without having to say anything. I really missed her. Near the end I told her it was a bad connection and switched off the video so she wouldn't see me crying.

Mum, meanwhile, had cooked a huge feast, blaming it on Christmas. I wasn't hungry and had no idea how we were going to finish it. Even the Browns, who usually ate all our food, were away.

Mrs Brown had come over in the morning. She seemed years younger with a cool spiky haircut, and she had on a stunning silver jumpsuit. It took me a second to realise she wasn't wearing brown. She looked amazing, just like a movie star. 'A present from Devon,' she said and twirled. 'And from your uncle.' She patted her hair. 'Before they left.' She winked at Mum. The Browns gave me a tin of Brazil nuts, which felt like a random regift. I supposed it was the thought that counted. Then they'd left for the farm to spend the day with Melanie and her dad.

I sighed and set down the last knife. I didn't see the point in today.

'If I see another fuckwit wearing tinsel in their hair.' Uncle Pike climbed the balcony with one crutch; he was dressed as Santa from hat to boot. 'Ho, ho! You didn't think we were going to miss out on Christmas, did you?'

Devon slapped him on the butt. 'After all, it is her busiest day of the year.'

I squealed, ran out and hugged them.

Devon had on a tight, metallic-gold T-shirt with a picture of a leopard licking its bits and the word *Licky* spray-painted across it. His white culottes and sandals topped it off.

'Does that make you Nana Claus?' Mum asked.

'I'm Santa's bitch,' Devon said.

'Language in front of Tippy!' Uncle Pike said.

'*Now* you worry about language?' Mum said. 'I know she heard worse from you two when I was away.'

'That's true,' I said.

We laughed. She gave my uncle a hug. 'Thank you.'

'No, thank you,' he said, squeezing her. Then he frowned and pulled at my tracksuit. 'I thought we threw all these awful things out? Unacceptable, Tippy Chan. Change immediately and bring these back for burning.'

I giggled.

'I'm serious. Fifteen seconds.' He clapped his hands then looked at his white Santa gloves. 'Do you think he wears these for breaking and entering?'

Mum squinted at the table and leaned down. 'Hang on. What are all these dents?'

My uncle froze. 'What?' he said to someone in the next room. 'What? Now?' He tried to run out of the room on one crutch as Mum threw a wooden salad fork at him.

I ran past him and got changed into my purple shorts and a red T-shirt for Christmas.

When I came back into the kitchen, Devon was unpacking duty-free bags of alcohol on the table. 'One more thing in the car. And no, Helen, it's not your brother's douche.'

'Eeew,' Mum said, as Devon skipped off.

Uncle Pike poked his head out from the hallway. 'I told you we had lots of sex in your bed.'

Mum made a gagging sound.

'You need to relax your throat,' he said.

'Pike!' She threw the other salad fork.

He ducked but it hit him on the shoulder. 'Ow!'

'Serves you right,' she yelled.

I giggled. 'Hey, Uncle Pike?'

'Hey, Tippy.' He shuffled back in, rubbing his injury.

'What happened to the chimp?' I said.

'What?' He frowned.

'From the zoo, in your story.'

'Ah.' He leaned against the kitchen bench beside me. 'What do you think?'

I shrugged.

'For a long time, I hoped it ran away.' He nudged me. 'But now I'm pretty sure it found some other chimps. And they solve mysteries.'

I leaned into him and smiled. 'I'm glad it did.'

'Same here.'

Devon rushed in. 'Tippy Chan.' He and my uncle looked serious, and I wondered what I'd done. 'For being the best detective partner we have ever worked with, for being awesome—'

'And also because it's fucking Christmas,' Uncle Pike said.

'Merry Christmas, Tippy,' they said together.

Devon handed me a beautifully wrapped red box with a shiny gold bow on it.

'Did you wrap it?' I asked him. He nodded, his eyes shiny.

I pulled off the bow and ripped it open. 'What?'

They stood there grinning. Mum smiled. 'Go ahead.'

I must've looked like that little girl at the airport when she saw Santa. Inside was the latest smartphone. 'Thank you!' I gave them a huge hug.

'I preloaded all our social media, including alerts,' Devon said. 'Accidental fashion is trending, BTW.'

Uncle Pike raised an eyebrow.

'What?' Devon said. 'Okay, I may have used the tablet once or twice – the soap wasn't enough.'

My uncle kissed him. 'But it made your ear smell nice. And remember, Tippy...'

'No tit pics,' the three of us said in unison.

Mum frowned.

Bunny Whiskers meowed outside the door.

Devon squealed and clapped. 'Hello, puss! Merry Christmas!' He chased after the cat, who bounded away from him into the garden.

Uncle Pike handed Mum a red envelope. 'Merry Christmas.'

She punched his arm. 'But you already got me towels.' She opened it and pulled out a Christmas card. A folded piece of paper fell from it.

'You didn't want it. This is to help out Joe.'

Mum frowned and picked it up.

My uncle grabbed a bottle of tequila. 'Good to know this town's lack of privacy is finally useful for something.'

Mum went white under her tan. Her hand shot to her mouth and I thought she was going to puke.

Shit. 'Mum?' I ran over to her. 'You all right?'

She was dazed and her hands trembled. 'I can't accept this.'

I read the letter; it was from the bank. We were debt free. I hugged her tight. Mum wouldn't have to work so hard.

'Not yours to accept. Like I said, this is between me and Joe. Trust me, Lennie, I know you don't need rescuing.' Uncle Pike poured us all a drink – lemonade for me and tequila for the adults. 'I call this session of ganbei-masters to order.'

'But Pike...' Mum said.

Devon came back in with a freaked-out Bunny Whiskers pinned to his chest.

'Here she is.' Uncle Pike handed Devon a shot. 'Come on, Lennie, keep up.'

Mum held her shot glass with both hands.

Uncle Pike raised his glass. 'Here's to Weifang. An amazing husband, a great brother-in-law, and a wonderful father.'

'Wait!' I said. The adults all stopped and looked at me. I ran over, grabbed our family picture and propped it up against the tequila bottle in the middle. I raised my glass. 'To Dad.'

My uncle smiled. 'Merry Christmas, Joe.'

We all sculled and showed each other our empty glasses.

'Ganbei-masters,' my uncle roared.

Mum hugged him. 'Thank you.'

'Let's get this party started.' He cranked up the stereo.

'You okay?' Devon asked me.

I was never going to be okay again. But I realised, with Kylie's 'Better the Devil You Know' blaring, Mum and Uncle Pike dancing, that this was my life now. The old everyday-normal was gone.

I smiled and handed Devon my Christmas present. He stuck it under his chin and lowered Bunny Whiskers to the floor, robot style. The cat bolted for the Christmas tree and got tangled up in the lights, nearly pulling it over, then shot out the door. 'Wow ... Clumsiest. Cat. Ever.' Devon put my present to his ear and shook it. 'Thanks, Tippy.' He unwrapped it carefully. 'I don't want to rip the paper. Great colour blocking, by the way.'

'For fuck's sake, just open it,' Uncle Pike said, refilling the glasses.

Devon pulled out a book and smiled at me. It was my copy of *The Secret of the Old Clock*. He opened the cover. '"This book belongs to Pike, Tippy"...' He started to cry and hugged me.

I'd written: *and also Devon. Merry Xmas. Love, your little sister, Tippy xxoxx.*

ACKNOWLEDGEMENTS

Huge thanks to my brilliant agent, Craig Sisterson, you are a living legend. Thank you for making this writer's dream come true; you are one in a million. Thank you to Karen Sullivan and the team at Orenda Books for welcoming Tippy, Uncle Pike and Devon, and their secret amateur detective club from the small Kiwi town that fashion forgot, into the Orenda Books story, and huge thanks to West Camel for his insightful, excellent editing advice (sorry about the horse float!).

As always, to my children, Ali and Grier, you are my full stops. Thank you for sharing our life with Tippy and the gang and for being so patient and clever when I needed to write and run lines by you.

Grace Heifetz, what can I say but I love you and thank you from the bottom of my heart.

Jane Palfreyman, thank you for believing in *The Nancys* and seeing the story for what it is, what it could be, and for basically everything.

Rebecca Kaiser and the team at Allen & Unwin, thank you. You are first class.

Ronnie Scott and Kate Goldsworthy, thank you both for your brilliant, in-depth, insightful and compassionate editing.

My wonderful, supportive writing group, Melbourne Faber Academy Class of 2016. Thank you for being there every step of the way with *The Nancys*, not only in workshopping but also in friendship and encouragement. Katherine Kovacic, Renee Singleton, Nada Kirkwood, Narelle Hill, Jean Ross, Sherryn Hind, Shay Ffewkes, Sarina Holmlund, Ella Lamb and Annie Drum. And you too, Tom Latham and Odette Kelada!

Paddy O'Reilly and Toni Jordan, besides being the best teachers a writer could wish for, thank you for your tremendous support, belief and kindness. Because of you both I am able to write this acknowledgement sentence in my first book.

Faber Academy, thank you for giving me the structure and tools to call myself a writer.

To the judges from the 2017 Victorian Unpublished Manuscript Awards. Thank you for highly commending *The Nancys*. You made me cry. I remember sitting on the plane in Singapore and thinking, *These people who I've never met before got my story*. It is in great part because of you that The Nancys are now loose in the world.

Sally Bird and Felicity Blunt, thank you both for your generous feedback. I would also like to thank Jennifer Fisher for her excellent Nancy Drew research and website: www.nancydrewsleuth.com.

And all those who read early drafts: Duane, Debs, Vicci, Jenni, Jane, Roz, Karen, Rachel, Shaun and Carley. Thank you.

My glorious Rainbow family made up of strong, brilliant women – Annie, Katie and Gill – and of course Ali, Grier, Hugo and Baby Will. Thank you for all your support and generosity. And to your families, thank you for your kindness.

My family for being my family, I love you. Dad and Jenny, thank you for being there, no matter what.

My sister, Jude, you are the most gifted educator I have ever met and I can't wait to see more of your paintings. Pete, thank you for your friendship, and Caitlyn, Rueben and Olivia – I am so very proud of each of you.

My bro Lachlan, thank you for being the patron saint of writers (and artists – Jude, take note) and for believing in my writing – not giving up, but pushing me to do it all these years. Thank you.

And my brother Donald, thank you for being you.

And to my *other* family – my friends – thank you, thank you, thank you. I am the luckiest person I know to have you all in my life. As I was saying to Abe, Cetrece, DanDan, Fionn, Gregory and Mel (thank you for babysitting while I was writing *The Nancys*) I wish I had the word count to name all of you right here – the next book I promise I will.

Finally, to all those people who have been kind enough to ask how my writing is going – and my international education friends

– Deakin University (thanks Greg) and CQUniversity Australia friends – thank you all for your interest and your support.

Mum, thank you for the love of reading and writing. I will always love you.

P.S. Murphy and Elaina, you are both awesome.